D1649058

Cambridge Street

A Novel

Steven Decker

Cambridge Street
A Novel

Copyright © 2019 by Steven Decker

All rights reserved. No part of this book may be reproduced or transmitted in any form or by any means without written permission of the author.

ISBN 978-0-692-97847-4

Dedication

Cambridge Street is dedicated to my Sicilian immigrant grandparents, Leonardo Tomasello and Vincenza Sacco, for their bravery in coming to this country. I look back now with a sense of awe and wonder at how they managed to survive from their early years in Chicago's Little Sicily in the 1920's and beyond. But they did it.

My book is also dedicated to my wonderful aunts and uncles Mae, Lil, Ida, Mary, Joseph and Martino and especially to my mother, Katerina. Because of you me, my sister, brother and our many cousins grew up immersed in love and family.

All gone now but never to be forgotten.

Author's Note

Late one night in May of 2015 I sat with my mother, who lay quietly sleeping. At age 93, she was nearing the end of her long, beautiful life.

Thinking about the terrible and wonderful things that happened to her, her siblings and parents in the Roaring Twenties in Chicago, I began making notes.

It seemed appropriate that while the last of her generation would soon be gone that I should make a record of their story. I did not plan to write a book but even though Cambridge Street began as random jottings, it became much more over the next two years.

I created a fictional Italian family and, through their experiences, I tried to capture the heartbreak, bravery and struggle of the millions of people who came here to become Americans a century ago.

Those immigrants were not wanted or welcome. Jobs were scarce, there were virtually no social services available to them and mobsters and crooked cops ran the streets. Life was tough; they had to be tougher. Some returned to their homelands but the majority stayed and persevered through sheer grit and determination.

Sadly now, with the passing of years, the determination and sacrifice of the millions of immigrants from that era is being forgotten.

My hope is that *Cambridge Street* will help preserve the memory of what those amazing people did for us.

Chapter One

Most of all, the young woman loved seeing things grow.

The afternoon Mediterranean sun warmed her back as she knelt in her garden and worked the soil by hand. The touch and feel of the moist, soft earth pleased her, and she loved the smell of it.

The scent of the full, green leaves of *basilico* especially delighted her. As she leaned into one of her favorite plants, she inhaled its fragrance and plucked enough for tonight's sauce.

Her garden consisted of rows of healthy, growing fruits and vegetables. She had ten tomato plants next to three rows of tall bean plants. Along one side, she nurtured six eggplants and six pepper plants. In the row closest to the farmhouse were twelve garlic plants, and a dozen artichokes thrived close by. Lettuce and cabbage grew bigger and, on the far end, she kept an eye on cantaloupe and watermelons happily growing on their vines. Several rows of red, yellow, pink, and smiling purple flowers blossomed around the garden. Some were opened in partial bloom; others spread their petals wide and reached for the sun.

The young woman nurtured each plant as if it was special because every growing thing was, in fact, precious to her. She hummed, lost in thought, while she worked, and stopping for a moment, looked around at the farm she loved.

The roomy farmhouse, with its wide, oak plank porch, sat fifty yards from the garden. The barn, made of river rocks fitted together by her husband's great grandfather a century before, was fifty yards from the house. In the distance, she saw the family's lemon orchard set amid the rolling, green hills she loved to walk.

She closed her eyes and listened to birds chirping and insects buzzing. She felt good inside.

"Gianna! Gianna! Come to the house! Gia! Where are you?" Katerina was anxious to get her daughter-in-law back to the kitchen. She needed help. There was a meal to prepare, a table to set, and a hungry family to feed.

Serving dinner wasn't the only thing on the mind of *La Signora* Tomaso. Tonight, after the evening meal, she and her husband Tomas would have a hard talk, an impossible talk, a-once-in-a-lifetime talk, with their family. At the thought of what was to come, *Signora* Tomaso dabbed tears from the corners of her eyes with a handkerchief she carried in a pocket of her apron.

"Kids, go get your Mama. Hurry!" With that, the children ran out of the kitchen, heading to the garden. The screen door slammed behind them and they crossed the porch.

"Luca, wait for your sister," said *Nonna*.

Luca stopped in his tracks, turned, held out his open hand and waited for his younger sibling. "Come on, Isabella," he coached.

Gianna left the garden with a straw basket full of tomatoes, basil, spinach, and red and green peppers hooked on her hip. Her eyes lit up and she smiled when she saw her two little ones running toward her, hand in hand. She dropped to her knees, put the basket on the ground, and scooped her two *bambini* in her arms. The forward momentum of the kids forced Gia off balance and backward. The three rolled onto the ground, laughing.

Gia wore a full-length, long sleeve floral patterned dress that covered her from neck to ankles. A long beige apron protected the front of her dress, both dusty after her late afternoon work in the garden. A colored scarf was loosely wrapped around her neck, and a wide brimmed straw hat sat atop her dark brown hair. Her big brown eyes and full red lips highlighted her radiant smile. Something about the attitude, look, and touch of this young woman exuded warmth. Everyone who met her felt it.

A farm girl by birth, by nature, and now by marriage, Gianna was happiest out in the open. She loved the fresh, clean air, the smell of the farm animals, and the buzzing of insects in flight and on the ground. In fact, she and Luca captured scores of bugs large and small and kept their insect collection in jars of alcohol in the barn.

Marriage agreed with her. Raised by old fashioned parents, who were also farmers, Gia was a devoted wife and mother. She kept a clean and organized home, cooked, and looked after the health and education of their children.

As a Sicilian woman, she knew that respect was all–important to the men of her island, including her man. She tried to agree with whatever her husband, Paolo, wanted, and if she ever chose to disagree with him, she did so only when they were alone.

Gianna stopped Luca and Isabella on the porch before they could enter the farmhouse. She brushed the reddish dust off the kids and then cleaned herself. After she shook her apron, hat, and scarf, she hung them on a peg that had been on the porch wall forever. Gianna opened the screen door and the three of them walked into the delicious-smelling kitchen.

"*Ciao*," she said to her mother–in-law and to her mother.

"*Ciao*, Gia," came the reply.

She put the basket of produce on a countertop, washed, and joined in the preparation of the evening meal. The men would be home soon and hungry after a day of hard work.

The afternoon sun faded as Katerina stood on the farmhouse porch drying her hands with a red towel. She looked beyond Gia's garden toward the orchard where Tomas and two of their sons Paolo and Leonardo had spent the day working. When Kati saw them approaching, her heart fluttered a tiny flutter as it always did when she first saw her husband, even after all these years.

As they drew closer, she saw a dozen lemons topple out of the cart. One of the men tossed the escaping fruit back aboard. The old wooden cart groaned and stretched with the weight of their labor.

"Move, Sancho!" prodded Paolo. Each time the cart came to a bump in the road, the donkey would stop. After pulling the same heavy cart along the same dirt path for ten years, the animal knew the spots in the road that needed more effort, and he knew that he would get help where needed. Each time Sancho stopped, Leonardo and his father walked to the rear of the cart and pushed to help the old animal do his job. The fat, juicy lemons would be on their way to the market in Palermo in the morning.

As the three men walked in silence along the dirt road, they watched the hanging orange sun slip into the sea, as if sleepy and turning in for the night.

Leonardo, the youngest and always the romantic, said "*Buona sera, Signore Sole.*"

It would be dusk when they reached the farmhouse, and they all wondered what would be on the table that evening. When they got closer, Luca and little Isabella saw their father Paolo and ran to him. He dropped to his knees and opened his arms to them.

"Papa, Papa!" they said as they smothered him with love. He adored his two children, and hoped to have many more. Gianna agreed. She too wanted a big family.

Paolo and Gianna had met six years earlier in 1911, when he attended Mass in a small town not quite ten miles from the Tomaso farm. Paolo was instantly attracted to her—Gianna, not as much, or so Paolo thought. The truth was that at first sight, Gianna wanted to get to know this tall, handsome stranger. She noticed his broad, bright smile and white teeth. He had blue eyes, and light hair - something she hadn't seen often.

Paolo looked like a young man who worked outside with his hands, and she liked that about him. She was pleased that he lived and worked on his family's farm. Things for Gianna became more serious when she spent time with him. She loved that Paolo was intelligent, funny, hard-working and, most of all, that he treated her in a gentle and respectful way.

The first time Paolo came to call on her, and most times after that, he rode the farm's work horse, a large black gelding named Dante. Paolo wore his best riding clothes that first day: shiny black boots that ran up to his knees, black slacks, a dark red shirt and his black *coppola* hat, a style that many Sicilian farmers wore.

Tomaso, to follow proper protocol, needed permission from Gianna's father to call on his daughter. His palms sweating, Tomaso knocked on the door. Gianna's father, *Signore* Cassio, came to the door and said "*Buon giorno*. Can I help you with something?"

Gianna hadn't told Paolo that her father was sick, and he was surprised by his condition. The older man suffered from untreated diabetes and was nearly blind. He shuffled when he walked and the twenty foot distance to the door seemed to have exhausted him.

"*Buon giorno, Signore* Cassio. I'm Paolo Tomaso, and I'm here to call on your daughter Gianna, with your permission, of course, sir."

Now Cassio was surprised. Gianna had not told her father about this young man. "You present yourself to call on my daughter? I had no idea. Come in."

Paolo entered and was offered a chair and a glass of wine. He accepted both. Gianna's father asked, "What do you have in mind?"

"Sir," began Paolo. "I want to get to know your daughter. She is a fine young woman, virtuous to be sure, and I assure you that I will respect her in every way."

Signore Cassio said, "Did you say your name is Tomaso? Are you one of the sons of Tomas and Katerina Tomaso?"

"Yes, sir. I am the oldest."

"Yes, yes. I know your parents. They are fine people."

"Thank you, sir."

Earlier, when Gianna saw Paolo ride up to the house, she ran to her bedroom to wait. That this young man was interested in her made her excited and happy. She had never felt this way before.

Stella Cassio entered the room. Her husband introduced the two.

"Stella, this is Paolo Tomaso. He's here to call on Gianna. Paolo, this is Gianna's mother, *La Signora* Cassio." She smiled at the handsome young caller and now understood why her daughter spoke of him in such glowing terms.

After two hours of conversation, questions and answers, *Signore* Cassio felt that he had fulfilled his obligation as a father.

With a serious expression and with Paolo sitting across from him, Cassio asked his wife "Well, what do you think of him?"

Stella Cassio smiled at Paolo knowing her husband's sense of humor and that he could have no possible objection to him calling on Gia.

She smiled and played along. "It's up to you, Papa."

The old man tried to appear gruff but soon relaxed and granted permission for the two young people to spend time together - but only in and around the farmhouse. Gianna's mother got her daughter.

When Gia entered the room, Paolo's heart pounded.

He smiled and said, "*Ciao*, Gianna."

A smile peeked out at him when she said, "*Ciao*, Paolo."

"*Ciao*, Gianna," he said again.

Gianna asked, "Can I ride your horse?"

For the many visits that followed, Gia insisted on riding Dante. Paolo would give her a boost into the saddle, and she would ride away and leave Paolo to talk, sometimes for an hour or more, with her serious father. Whether the abandonments were intentional or not, her father got to know Paolo. He soon knew that if asked, he would enthusiastically support a marriage between the young farmer and his daughter.

As Tomas, Paolo, and Leonardo drew closer to the farmhouse, the fresh scent of the lemons blended with the delicious smell of cooked food. In the kitchen, Katerina and Gianna seasoned and roasted three fat chickens in the open fireplace. To top the evening's *pasta*, the women created *pomodoro* from garden tomatoes, garlic, salt, pepper, a dash of sugar and plenty of basil. Hot baked bread, olive oil, grated cheese, and butter. A jug of water and another of *vino nero* were already on the table.

The three dirty and sweaty men crossed the porch and entered the kitchen. Tomas smiled at his wife and said, "Katerina, you look good today."

He walked toward her. She put both hands in the air and said, "You...the three of you... stink. You know better. Get out! Go wash!"

The three obeyed, but before he went to the well, Paolo reached for Gianna and kissed his young wife quickly. He said, *"Ciao, Tesoro."* The young woman blushed but allowed the affection.

For as far back as anyone could remember, the Tomaso families had farmed the land. Work days were twelve hours long for all family members. It was a hard life, but it was their life.

Tomas and Katerina were the heads of one of a half dozen Tomaso families in the area.

While farm days were long and money was usually scarce, cooking skills were plentiful. The family's recipes and cooking techniques were handed down from great grandparents to grandparents to parents and outward to their children and dozens of cousins, nieces and nephews.

All of Tomas's brothers and sisters were married and all had children of their own. Their sons, Paolo, Renzo, and Leonardo had thirty first cousins and more on the way. The entire family attended Mass every Sunday. They confessed their sins regularly and observed the many religious holidays. They never ate meat on Fridays or during Lent. The Tomasos believed strongly in their faith and worshipped with conviction and passion. Gianna would not have married Paolo if he were not a devout Catholic.

The Tomasos were known by their peers as hardworking, accomplished farmers and good citizens. They were respected and valued. Each member of the extended family, regardless of age or family rank, felt responsible for the other. They cared for and loved each other. At home and at gatherings, the many children of the clan, like kids everywhere, were active, mischievous and sometimes a handful.

Scoldings, sit-down breaks, and even an occasional slap on the bottom of a misbehaving child were administered by an adult family member. There was no need for an aunt or uncle to consult with the parent first: bad behavior was bad behavior.

Gentle discipline was given with regularity; so was love and tenderness, and there was always plenty to go around. Each child knew that he or she was a cherished member of the clan.

Family disagreements and arguments didn't last long. When they ended, they were completely finished. Through the worst disputes, the extended family stayed close, shared their problems, and helped each other.

The members of the Tomaso family—brothers, sisters, aunts, uncles, cousins, nieces, and nephews—stood strong and together. They survived. They outlasted droughts, survived insect infestations, struggled through epidemics, endured tragedies, lived through crimes, and outlasted acts of vengeance and retaliation. They suffered government malfeasance and malpractice in silence. They had no choice but to accept excessive and unfair taxation, land seizures, and the lack of adequate police protection. Somehow, unlike most of the local farmers, the Tomasos managed to avoid Mafia entanglements.

The one problem Tomas and Katerina could not solve was that their family had outgrown their farm production. It had become impossible to grow enough lemons, melons, garlic, and livestock to feed the family, pay their taxes, and doctor and educate the children. With two more sons nearing marrying age, there would soon be more mouths to feed, and that would be impossible.

After months of talking, praying, and consulting, Tomas and Katerina had come to a painful realization and had made a decision. Tonight, after supper, they would tell the family what must happen.

It would be a hard talk, a heartbreaking day.

Chapter Two

On the outskirts of Palermo, beside an ancient cobblestone road, sat an abandoned 200-year-old barn. The entry was over-grown with ten-foot-high bushes and three-foot-high weeds making the stable nearly invisible from the road. A dozen lanterns hung in various locations illuminated the old structure. Light and fresh air flowed in from large and small windows.

The structure had not been used for animals in many years and was now a hang-out for petty thieves, pickpockets, thugs, and other *teppesti* from the city and nearby towns and farms.

Young men gathered there to smoke and drink and to learn from the older men how to rob tourists, steal, extort money, and avoid being caught. The young guys talked about who had bro-ken down a girl's defenses and bedded her, and who had paid a prostitute. The older men explained what the younger men should expect from women.

Several young men sat at a small wooden table, smoked, and planned their next burglary. Two others threw knives at a support beam, betting who could stick the blade the most times. Several smoked and talked about their real or imagined exploits and their plans to make money.

These young men didn't fit the mold or the plan given to them by tradition or by upbringing. They refused to work the fields, get jobs, or follow the path laid down for them by their families and society. Family was not their concern, and these young men didn't think or care much about the future. The recruits were being schooled by older men who already turned the corner to a life of crime and hustling.

Renzo Tomaso was one of these young men.

The middle Tomaso brother was different than his brothers, Paolo and Leonardo. He wanted to be a hustler and a thief. Renzo wanted to learn the ways of street life, how to steal, extort, drink, whore and enjoy life as he saw it. He was a fast-talker, a petty con-artist, and a sneak. His lifestyle was embarrassing and hurtful to his family, especially to his hardworking, straight-laced father.

Renzo often disappeared from the farm to walk to town or jump on the back of a cart headed that way when his father turned his back. When he got to the city, he went to the old barn or hung out with other street hustlers in the tourist areas. There he could lift a wallet or meet a foreign woman traveling alone. If possible, he would sleep with her, and then steal her jewelry or money from her purse.

Over the past few years, Renzo developed his skills and now made his living hustling tourists. His appearance was that of a typical hustler of the day. He dressed like a city man. His dark brown hair was always slicked back, and he wore a thin mustache. He always smelled good. Renzo had grown into a tall, lanky, and handsome young man. He realized that he loved the ladies a little too much, and they loved him back.

While he was usually selective in his choice of partner, he was at the same time ruthless and careless. He wanted and felt entitled to bed any woman he chose. The status or the age of the female of his moment's interest didn't matter to him. He courted and did his best to seduce married or engaged women, as well as uncommitted ladies. What's worse, Renzo's sexual greed did not stop at the women of his friends and partners in crime. He used his soft voice and his good looks to sleep with those women whenever one would fall for his charm.

Just after his twenty second birthday, Renzo met *La Signora* Adriana Lazzori, the wife of Carlo Lazzori.

Lazzori was an old friend and now one of the bosses of the local Mafia. Renzo and Carlo had met years before in the old barn. For a while, although Carlo was ten years his senior, the two hustled and stole together. The problem with Carlo was his love of violence. Renzo had seen Carlo kill more than once; he also saw him inflict unnecessary pain on his victims.

During one robbery, Carlo pistol-whipped an older man, even though the man had promptly given up his wallet and jewelry. He then belted the victim's wife when she went to the aid of her injured husband.

Late one night, having robbed a tourist and scored big, the two were drinking in a seedy, out-of-the-way tavern near the boat docks in Palermo. At the far end of the bar sat a thick, muscular Armenian sailor whose cargo ship docked recently and was now off-loading. He took a few hours to go ashore to find a whore and a bar.

Carlo, drunk and aggressive, sat drinking *grappa* and getting drunker. "Hey you, sailor!" he said "You!"

The Armenian looked at Carlo, and then back down at his glass of vodka.

"You got some big fucking arms on you, man!"

The sailor ignored him.

Carlo said, "I got some big fucking arms, too! Let's see who's stronger!"

The man replied, "No, *Signore*. I want to finish my drink and leave."

Carlo said, "Sailor, give me the chance to see if I can beat you. We arm wrestle. Three rounds." Lazzori put a pile of bills on the bar. "If you beat me, you take this money. If I beat you, I keep it. Costs you nothing... no risk to you. What do you say?"

The Armenian looked at the bills and at Carlo, who smiled at him.

Carlo said, "Come on, let's have a little fun."

The sailor lifted his glass. Before he could reply, Carlo said, "Don't be a chicken-shit, man. Let's do it!"

Irritated from Carlo's prodding, the man belted down the vodka, banged the glass onto the bar, and agreed. He was suddenly anxious to begin. He intended to shut the mouth of the Sicilian, take the money, and get back to his ship.

Most of the men in the dimly-lit bar were drunk. They placed bets and gathered around the table to watch the competition. Carlo and the big sailor sat across from each other at a small wooden table. They were like two rams scraping and snorting the dirt, each ready to smash the head of his opponent.

The men looked like opposites. Carlo wore a casual blue shirt and pleated tan slacks with blue suspenders. His black hair was slicked back and he was clean shaven. The sailor wore dungarees and a heavy blue ship's sweater cut high around his neck. A bushy black beard covered the lower half of his face and his neck. When the sailor grinned across the table, Carlo noticed that one of his front teeth was missing. Both men were thick and strong, swarthy, hard, and experienced. Both intended to dominate the other.

Carlo and the sailor gripped clenched hands and looked into the other's eyes. Carlo smirked; the sailor glared. They put their elbows on the table, nearly touching. The little bald man who ran the bar stepped up to referee the match. He stood not five feet tall and spectacles clung to the tip of his nose.

He said, "Bring the coals."

Two red-hot coals from the fireplace were put on each side of the table. The back of the hand of whichever man lost the round would be seared from the small, hot bricks. Carlo looked nervous when he saw the screaming embers. They didn't appear to bother the confident Armenian who smiled at Carlo as if to say, *Do you have a problem with that, tough guy?*

Others in the bar, including Renzo, gathered closer around the table to watch the battle.

The judge tied the two men's hands together with a foot-long strip of dirty cloth. He cupped his hand over the top of their locked grip. He looked at both men and said, "Ready...One...Two... GO!"

The contest began. Neither man could budge the arm of the other, and they stayed locked in silent battle. The eyes of the sailor showed no sign of strain or pressure and never left those of Carlo. He smiled and was calm. Carlo's eyes darted from the face of the sailor to the table to the red coals, and back and forth again.

The two men stayed in their starting position for a quarter of an hour; then a half. After forty-five minutes, the forearm of the sailor moved forward a millimeter, and then another. Soon, he gained an inch, then two. Both men were soaked with sweat. Spittle crept from the corner of Carlo's mouth and ran down his chin. He quickly wiped the drool with a swipe of his free hand.

The Sicilian's arm appeared to bend backward as he struggled with all his strength to stop the advance of the sailor. Lazzori held off the loss for another fifteen minutes before the downward pressure on his hand, wrist, arm, and shoulder became too much.

The bearded sailor ground Carlo's hand against the burning coal and held it there. Carlo grimaced but could not allow himself to show pain or defeat. He lifted his hand off the ember and removed it from the rag that still held their two mitts together. He brushed off the residue from the hot brick.

The men in the bar waited in silence to see if Carlo would cede to the stronger man. He did not—could not. It had now become a matter of respect. Carlo smiled. Only Renzo, who knew his friend well, could see through the façade.

"We go again, Turk!"

The Armenian slammed his palm onto the table. "I am not a Turk! Put your arm up. I'll beat you all night!"

The hands of the two men were again tied together and their elbows matched up. Fresh hot coals were brought from the fireplace. The referee held his hand atop the two clenched and locked fists. He said, "Ready...one...two..."

Before the little man could say the word GO! Carlo slammed the back of the hand of the Armenian to the table, jumped out of his seat with their hands still fastened together, and yelled, "I beat you! I fucking beat you!"

It was now the back of the sailor's hand that was seared and he who refused to show pain or to concede.

He said, "You stinking Sicilians are all alike. You cheat. You steal. You'd steal a *lire* from your own mother. Fuck you, cheater. *Imbroglio!*"

Every voice in the bar went silent at the insult hurled by the foreigner. Carlo sat, as if stunned, his right hand still tied to the muscular paw of the other. Without hesitation, he pulled the sailor's hand toward him.

Palming a short piece of lead pipe he always carried in his pocket, Lazzori threw a straight left hand punch. The assault landed square on the other man's nose, smashing it and driving shards of cartilage into his cheeks. The force of the attack knocked the sailor backward off the chair and pulled Carlo down over the shattered table on top of him. The Armenian was barely conscious. Carlo disengaged himself from the rag that tied him to his opponent.

Renzo, knowing his friend's capacity for wanton violence, said, "Carlo, let's go!"

Carlo stood and turned to leave but then, turned back and kicked the sailor in his abdomen, quick and hard. The man groaned.

Renzo said again, "Let's go, Carlo!" He waited for his friend.

Lazzori turned his back to the sailor and took a few steps toward the door.

In a flash, the sailor got to his feet and pulled a long, razor-sharp knife from his boot. He ran at Carlo. Renzo saw the sailor raise the knife and yelled, "Carlo!"

As he yelled, he threw himself head-first at the seaman and knocked him to the floor.

Carlo was on top of the sailor in a split second and pinned the sailor's arms under his knees. He grabbed the man's right hand, in which he held his knife, and turned the blade toward the Armenian's throat. The sailor pushed back with all the strength in his arms, shoulders, and chest but the intense downward pressure from Carlo was too much. The seaman tried but failed to throw Lazzori off of him by driving his hips up and from side to side. With Lazzori's face inches from the sailor's, the long knife entered the man's neck just below his chin.

The sailor continued to push back against Carlo's force, but the blade slowly continued to cut into him. Carlo grinned. The long blade was one inch into the flesh, and then two, when the sailor realized that Lazzori was going to kill him. Sweat dripped from the tip of Carlo's nose and fell onto the sailor's face.

Tears dripped out of both sides of the man's bulging eyes. Snot and bright red blood drizzled out of his shattered nose and into his beard. He bucked upward in a final attempt to throw Carlo to the side. His upward movement only helped the knife go further into his neck. The blade continued its slow plunge upward into the neck of the sailor. Finally, the exhausted seaman could no longer push back.

The sailor managed a word that sounded like "mercy."

Carlo ignored it.

The pointed steel entered the back of the man's mouth and cut its way through his tongue. It split the soft tissue of his upper mouth. When Carlo realized the man was near death, he paused. His victim, now helpless, choked and gagged in his own blood and coughed the warm, red ooze into Carlo's face.

Carlo said, "Who's stronger now, asshole?"

With one final push, the tip of the knife passed through the nasal cavity of the sailor and up into his brain. The big Armenian struggled and gasped for air one last time. Then, he died, his eyes wide open in terror and his mouth stretched into in a hideous, bloody, gaping grin. Carlo stood. His eyes were wild and his face was red with blood. He left the knife in the man's neck.

Lazzori yelled to the room, "You all saw it. He attacked me! You all saw it!"

As he spoke, Renzo pulled him by the arm. He said, "Let's go!"

Carlo again yelled, "None of you know me! Understand? None of you know who I am!"

Renzo said, "Carlo!" The two of them darted from the bar.

Once outside, Carlo, his face, neck, and shirt red with the Armenian's blood, said to Renzo, "You saved my life, man. You saved my fucking life! I owe you! I really owe you, man!"

Renzo said, "Carlo, it's okay. It's okay. You shouldn't have killed that guy! Why did you get so nuts? Let's just get outta here before the police show up."

After the killing, the relationship between Renzo and Carlo would never be the same. The incident was not a part of the life Renzo wanted. Soon after yet another violent incident, he ended his association with Carlo Lazzori.

Carlo and Sal Niello, a good friend of Renzo's, got into a fight over an argument about a soccer match. Sal yielded quickly to the stronger and more aggressive man, but Carlo continued to punch and kick him until Renzo and two others pulled him off. Niello suffered a broken jaw and a concussion, all after he yielded. It was brutal, unnecessary punishment inflicted by Carlo because he enjoyed hurting people. After the beating of Sal, Renzo avoided Lazzori and chose to spend time with men who were more compatible with his way of thinking.

Renzo had no contact with Carlo for several years. Lazzori climbed the ranks of the local Mafia. He gained the respect and trust of his superiors by committing murder and violence and by inflicting *la vendetta* as ordered. The rise of Carlo Lazzori advanced and, in a few short years, he attained the rank of Lieutenant.

In a scheme to further advance himself, Carlo convinced his bosses that people in his way were stealing money from them and could not be trusted. His offer to eliminate them was accepted, and he was promoted to fill the void. Two years later, the local *Capo* died mysteriously in his bed and Carlo Lazzori assumed the role of Mafia boss.

Now, through sheer coincidence, Renzo saw Carlo's wife, whose name he knew was Adriana, across the restaurant from where he sat with his lecturing father. He had heard she was a beauty, but he had no idea how stunning she was. He didn't care that she was married, even if it was to his old friend Carlo. Regardless of the violence of which Carlo was capable, Renzo had to know this woman.

Having run the streets with Lazzori and having seen him with more than one woman, he knew that Adriana had to be starved for attention and affection. He knew she was probably being physically abused as well.

Renzo had to know this woman. Maybe it was because of the sick thrill in the risk of violence or maybe this was the only way that he could be superior to Carlo. Whatever the reason, Renzo decided to test his chances.

To get close to her, Renzo positioned himself in a location in the *piazza* that he knew *La Signora* Lazzori would pass. When he saw her approaching, he turned his back to her and walked ahead, giving her time to catch up. When she reached him, he feigned surprise, smiled at her, and walked a few steps, chatting with her.

Renzo, the perpetual con man, evaluated Adriana's reactions, and they seemed favorable. *Maybe I have a chance*, he thought.

What Tomaso didn't know was that wherever *La Signora* went, she was followed by two of the jealous Lazzori's men.

While planned, it seemed unintentional when Renzo ran into Adriana a week later. After receiving a glorious smile from her, he decided to go to the next level and made sure that there would be a third encounter.

When he saw her next, he said simply, "You have a lovely smile." She smiled at him and laughed.

The shadows saw it all.

The two encountered each other again in the *Piazza* Pretoria where he knew she often went for a walk. Adriana saw him from a distance and walked to where he sat.

"Hello," she said and looked into his eyes.

Renzo stood and said, *"Buon giorno, Signora.* Would you care to join me?"

She smiled and sat at his table. The two had a glass of wine together in the beautiful piazza. They were together twenty minutes.

When she stood, thanked him, and walked away, he said to her back, "I'll be here in exactly one week."

She didn't look back at him, reply or acknowledge his comment in any way. Renzo feared that she wouldn't return to meet him. In his confused state, he wondered if she would be just another conquest. He thought that this may be something much deeper. *What was love?* he wondered. *Would she return?*

One week—to the minute—later, Adriana came back to the *piazza*. She was radiant in light pastel colors with a fashionable wide-brimmed hat pinned to her thick brown hair. *So beautiful*, he thought, *and living with that animal Carlo. Well, if she was happy, she wouldn't be here right now.*

As the summer passed, the two met for wine in the *piazza* every week at the same time. Each time, Adriana stayed a little longer. They ate together and laughed at nothing. Tomaso stopped seeing other women to allow himself to focus all his thoughts and attention on this one special woman, Adriana.

The two goons reported every move and every gesture between Renzo and Adriana to their boss. Lazzori sat in silence and said, "Not a word of this to anyone. Not a word!"

Near the end of a sweltering August, the time came for their weekly rendezvous. Adriana went to their table, but Renzo was not there. Instead, he had left her a piece of paper folded into an envelope with the initials A.L. on the front. The note said, "*Via 149 Corso di Mare*. Room 7. Waiting for you."

The message took Adriana's breath away. She wanted this day to come but didn't expect it now. *La Signora* Lazzori knew where *Corso di Mare* was, and she walked toward it, her two tails in secret pursuit. She tapped on the door of the hotel room. Renzo opened it. He said, "I wasn't sure you'd come."

Adriana stepped through the doorway, touched his lips and said, "Don't speak."

Renzo felt as if shock waves of electricity were passing through his body. They embraced and kissed. Both were timid at first but soon became bold and intense with passion.

Adriana pulled back and said, "Renzo, before anything else happens here, know what you're doing. If Carlo finds out, he'll kill us both."

Renzo said, "I'd rather die than not be with you. I've never felt like this; I can't sleep; I can't eat. Sometimes, I can barely breathe thinking of you. I want you more than anything, even more than life itself."

She smiled and said, "And you will have me, Renzo."

Adrianna stepped into Renzo's arms. He embraced her, kissed her. She was not like any woman he had ever been with, and she felt right in his heart and in his soul.

When he kissed her, it was as if tiny shock waves were passing through her body. She felt herself breathing hard and joined Renzo on the bed. They helped each other out of their clothes.

Their lovemaking was slow and passionate. Afterwards, the two lay there, content.

He said, "I will never leave you."

Adriana said, "You better not. I love you too much to be without you."

They kissed, bathing in the love they felt for each other and then slept for a while. She dressed at the end of their time together, repaired her hair, and re-pinned her hat.

As Adriana stood by the door, Renzo said, "Next week?"

She smiled and nodded her consent. "See you then."

Adriana walked home alone.

They followed.

Chapter Three

"Father Edo! Father Edo! We need you!! Hurry, we need you! It's my grandmother! She's dying!" The terrified voice was that of Georgio DeSalvo, a twenty-year-old immigrant parishioner. His family came to Chicago from Naples three years before, and *Our Lady of Divine Mercy* was a big part of their lives.

"Come in, Georgio. Wait here," Father Farrucio said when he opened the door in his night clothes. The priest threw his clothes on, grabbed his precious purple stole, his crucifix, and a small bottle of holy water. It was 2:45 AM.

The priest and the young man darted from the rectory and ran the three blocks to the building where the DeSalvos lived. They rushed up the four flights of stairs, taking two at a time before running into the apartment. Farrucio was out of breath.

"Thank you for coming so quickly," said the dying woman's husband, *Signore* Salvatore DeSalvo. "The doctor left. He said he can do nothing for her. He said it is a matter of time now."

Farrucio said, "Of course, of course. Please, let me see *La Signora*."

"Come right this way, Father."

DeSalvo led the priest to the bedroom where his wife of sixty-one years lay in bed, her arms atop her blanket. A rosary lay on her hands. The old woman's breaths were far apart and shallow. She was barely conscious. A dozen flickering candles lit the room. One candle, smaller than the others, illuminated a framed photograph of a much younger Theresa DeSalvo. A silver crucifix leaned against the picture frame.

The priest kissed his silk stole and placed it around his neck, the two ends trailing to his mid thighs. A cross was embroidered on either end with off-white colored thread. He placed the vial of holy water on the small table next to the bed.

Father Farrucio sat on the side of the bed. He spoke to Theresa in a soft, comforting voice, knowing that he was to her at that moment the right hand of God.

"I am here, Theresa. Do not be afraid. Your family is here. Jesus has his arms around you. Feel his love."

The priest began to perform Last Rites. As he prayed and absolved the woman of all sin, he wet his fingers with the holy water and made the sign of the cross several times on her forehead.

The woman woke and looked with clear eyes at the gentle face of the priest. She smiled at him and died. The priest leaned forward and kissed her on her forehead.

Father Edo looked at Salvatore, her sons, her daughter, and her grandchildren, who had all come into the room. He said, "She is with God. No more pain."

The daughter began to cry.

Father Farrucio said, "Now she will watch and love you from above. She is at peace. Please, everyone, step close and say goodbye."

As a parish priest, Father Farrucio regularly visited his sick and dying parishioners. He prepared them for their transition from the physical life to the spiritual existence that he knew waited for them. He prayed with them, blessed them, and held their hands at their moments of passing. He often cried with the families when their loved ones left this world.

"Come in, sister," Father Farrucio said to the gentle rapping on his door. As she did every morning at 4:30, Sister George entered the priest's bedroom carrying a tray holding coffee, milk, and sugar. The smell of the hot, brewed coffee filled the room.

"Good morning, Father," said the younger nun. "It's another beautiful day."

Farrucio stretched, rolled his legs out from under the blankets, and put his feet on the carpeted floor. As the senior priest of *Our Lady of Divine Mercy Catholic Church* in this devout Catholic neighborhood, Farrucio had a lot to do every day and always got an early start.

"Thank you, Gretchen," Farrucio said. The German nun, whose name before taking her vows was Gretchen Weiss, was beautiful, and Edo always admired an attractive woman.

She smiled and said, "You're welcome, Edo."

He knew she would return with his breakfast soon.

The priest spent the first hour of his day in his personal rooms at the rectory. He ate a small breakfast, showered, dressed, and listened to the news of the day on his large, brown Motorola radio. The news from Europe that day was bad. It looked like the United States would soon enter the war that was raging in France.

Farrucio was a thoughtful man whose parents had brought him to America in 1880 when he was a year old. He spoke English without an accent, was fluent in Italian, pretty good in French, and passable in German and Spanish. He needed all his language skills in this large, diverse parish.

Every day, after his morning ritual, the priest made his way to a small, private chapel adjoining the large main church. There, from 6:00 until 7:30 AM, he knelt, prayed and communicated with his God. The daily morning intention of the priest was to conduct the 8:00 AM Mass, and he did so regularly. There were days, however, when he was so immersed in prayer and contemplation that he didn't emerge from his chapel until it was too late. On those days, a junior priest conducted the service.

Sometimes, lost in prayer in his private chapel, he had to be interrupted for lunch or to attend to church matters. Priests and the nuns at the church admired Farrucio's ability to concentrate so intently on prayer, but Father Edo never gave it a second thought. It was his nature and his passion, and he knew that it was a big part of the fiber that made him who he was: A man of God, a man of peace.

Nearly as much as he loved his Lord, he adored and cared for his flock. Most of his parishioners were the families who lived in the tenements in the low-income area of Chicago known as Little Sicily, which was referred to in the Chicago newspapers as Little Hell.

On most days, Father Farrucio walked the streets of the neighborhood to be with the children and keep a watchful eye out for problems. He often stopped to kick a soccer ball or hit a baseball with the boys or to jump rope with the girls. Father Farrucio liked to chat with the kids, especially with the older boys who might be tempted to touch the girls where they shouldn't or to do even worse, God forbid.

As he walked the street one morning, he saw a large group of neighborhood kids making a circle. He knew a fight between two or more of the young men had started, and he hurried to break it up. The priest pushed his way through the circle of kids and saw two boys who were squaring off. He said, "That's enough, fellas. There will be no fight here today."

The larger and more powerful-looking of the two combatants, apparently the aggressor, who was not from the neighborhood, said, "Mind your own business, priest. This ain't your concern."

"Son," said the priest, "this *is* my business. Now you walk away. Don't come back, and we'll forget this ever happened."

The muscular young man turned and looked in the opposite direction.

He said, "I don't want no trouble," and then he turned back, bent at the waist, and rushed the holy man. Father Farrucio stepped aside and let the charging young bull rush past him, like a matador. The attacker stopped, turned and swung a gnarled-up fist at the priest. The punch landed solidly on Farrucio's jaw whose head snapped back from the impact.

Farrucio said nothing but took off his jacket.

He sidestepped the next haymaker and landed one of his own squarely in the center of the young man's face. He grabbed the youth's arm and twisted it behind his back. He pushed the attacker's arm forward until the momentum drove the youth to the sidewalk. Farrucio put his knee in the center of the boy's back and pushed.

"I said, this is done! Do you get that?" demanded the priest.

When there was no reply, Edo pressed his knee harder into the back of the aggressive youth. Then harder.

The young stranger said, "Okay, okay. It's over. I'm beat."

The priest stood. The young man sat up and looked around. Edo extended his hand and helped his conquered opponent to his feet.

The priest dusted off the kid's shirt and said, "You okay?"

All watched to see his next move, but there was none. The aggressor was beaten. He pushed his way through the crowd and walked away. The crowd of kids who watched the battle clapped for the priest. He smiled, put his jacket on and went back to walking the neighborhood.

Later that same day, Farrucio was stopped by a small boy he knew from Catechism class.

"Fodder," the boy said. "I stole candy from the corner store, and I'm sorry."

The priest looked down at the boy and said, "Oh, that's not good, Tony. Take the candy back and tell the store clerk what you did. And come to church to confess your sin."

"But Fodder, I already ate it all."

"Oh, I see. Well, that means you have to confess your sin, then mop the floors at the church to get the money to pay the store."

"Okay, Fodder, okay. I'm sorry." The small boy's eyes brimmed with tears.

Edo dropped to his knees. "I know you're sorry, Tony. But make it official this Saturday."

The priest knew he was well-loved, and he cherished these young people and their parents. He felt honored to be a part of their lives and loved being the pastor, the confessor, and the protector of his poor, immigrant flock. Father Farrucio was a neighborhood priest, and he had no desire to be anything else. He made himself responsible for the safety and physical health of his people, as well as their spiritual health.

When necessary, he visited and spoke with employers whose workers had to labor in unsafe conditions. He often took parishioners to the doctor or dentist and acted as their translator when needed. When needed, Farrucio met with city officials about everything from garbage removal to inadequate water pressure to the lack of health care facilities and services.

When a rat gnawed through a bedroom wall and bit a three-year-old girl, Farrucio went to city hall. He requested and got a face-to-face meeting with Chicago Mayor William Thompson.

Big Bill Thompson was a larger-than-life figure who the priest had only read about in the papers. After waiting in the outer office for two hours, Farrucio was escorted to the inner-sanctum of the mayor's office by a skinny, white-haired woman of seventy-some years.

"Mr. Mayor, respectfully, I must demand that you do something more for my parish. We have little police protection, and when they do show up, they assault innocent people. My boys are afraid of the police."

The Mayor replied, "Well, isn't that as it should be? Fear of the police is a good thing, isn't it?"

Edo replied, "It's good for criminals to fear the police, not for innocent people, and especially not children. I'm not here only about the police. Our alleys and basements are crawling with rats and roaches. We need traps and poison."

The mayor looked over the top of his glasses at Farrucio as he considered the best way to deal with him.

"Mrs. Carmichael," he called to his secretary. "Come here. Bring your note pad."

Sadie Carmichael rushed into the room, carrying a steno pad and a pen.

"Yes, sir?"

The mayor said, "Send a memo to O'Reilly at Streets and San that there's a rat problem over on Cambridge near *Divine Mercy*." He looked at the priest and, with a slight smile, said, "Tell him I said to get double traps and poison over there - and I mean now."

The woman jotted notes on her pad. "Will there be anything else, sir?"

"Yes, there is. Have the police commissioner in my office in one hour," Mayor Thompson said with another small smile and a nod toward Farrucio, as if to say, *Don't worry. We'll take care of this police problem right away.*

"Yes, sir," said Sadie.

The priest stood and extended his hand to the mayor. "Thank you for your help. These are good people."

"I know they are," said the mayor. "Yes, they are."

Mayor Thompson escorted Farrucio back to the outer office where Mrs. Carmichael again sat behind her well-organized desk.

"Thank you for coming by today, Father."

"And thank you again for your help." They shook hands. The priest left and closed the door behind him.

Mayor Thompson turned to his secretary. "Sadie, shit-can those two orders. Cambridge Street is nothing but a bunch of dagoes. They can go back where they came from if they don't like it here. Hell, they don't even vote."

"Yes, sir," was the reply.

The one exception to Farrucio's life of devotion to his parish was his military service in World War One where he served as a battlefield chaplain in France. When the United States entered the war on April 6, 1917, the 38-year-old priest enlisted in the Army.

Father Edo Farrucio knew the soldiers would need God over there.

Chapter Four

A month after they met in church, and nearly every Sunday after that, Paolo would saddle up Dante and ride the ten miles to the Cassio farm to spend time with Gia. Her parents were always glad to see the handsome young farmer riding up and welcomed him warmly.

Emilio and Stella Cassio had met and married later in life than most; they were both forty years old at the time of their wedding. Within a few months, Stella was pregnant, a welcome surprise to both of the expectant parents. Gianna came along later that year and was the joy of her parents' lives. Now, their little girl was a grown woman and a man was calling on her. As he watched the young couple together, Emilio wondered, *Where did the years go?*

After several months of courtship, Paolo had become a part of the family and was expected for Sunday dinner. After those meals, the two women would clean up the dining room and the kitchen while the men sat outside and smoked. The four would then have coffee and *dolce* on the patio.

Paolo was in love with Gianna and he was certain that she loved him too. He finally summoned enough courage to ask *Signore*

Cassio for his daughter's hand in marriage. He made a special trip
to the Cassio's farm to speak to her father.

La Signora Cassio greeted the young man. "Paolo, *Signore*
Cassio is too sick to leave his bed today. Come with me," she said,
as she urged and escorted the young man through the small
house to the bedroom. She suspected the purpose of the visit
and wanted it to happen sooner rather than later, knowing that
her husband's health was getting much worse. She was painfully
aware, in fact, that he was approaching the end of his life.

Stella Cassio said, "If you have something to say to him, Paolo,
now is the time. Do you understand?"

"Yes, I understand," he said.

Paolo entered the Cassio's bedroom and pulled a chair to the
side of the bed to speak to the dying man. The two greeted each
other warmly. Red-faced, Paolo, who was usually calm and in
control, sat up straight, cleared his throat nervously and said,
"Sir, I am a responsible, religious man. I work hard and save my
money. People like me and they trust me. My family is well-known,
and we can see our ancestors back two centuries."

Cassio put his hand up and said in a voice just above a whisper,
"Paolo, young man, don't speak. I know why you're here."

"Yes, sir."

"I know you love my daughter and she loves you too, more
than you realize." The old man paused and gathered his thoughts
and his breath. "I'll be gone soon," he said, as he put his hand in
the air again to silence Paolo, "and I need to know I can rely on
you to care for Gianna properly after I pass."

"Yes, sir. Yes, sir," replied Paolo. "I want my life with her."

The older man said, "That's good, son. She wants the same."
Cassio went on. "I worry about my wife. About her life after I die.
La Signora will need her daughter—soon possibly your wife—to
care for her."

Paolo just looked at Emilio Cassio, not understanding how the man could think that his and Gianna's life could *not* include her mother.

Paolo said, "*Signore* Cassio, it couldn't be any other way. Never. Gianna's mother will be my mother too. I promise you that she will always have a warm home with us, no matter what. I will care for her as if she gave me life, naturally."

The older man's eyes filled with tears. He said, "*Gracie*, Paolo. You've relieved me of a terrible worry." Emilio Cassio straightened himself and used both arms to sit upright on his bed. He summoned all the breath in his body and said, "Paolo, yes, of course, I give my permission and I will bless your marriage to my daughter. Absolutely."

Paolo smiled and said, "Thank you, *Signore*. Thank you, thank you."

"Did you ask Gianna?"

"I wanted to ask you first, but I guess I better ask her too," said Paolo.

A week later, just after sunset, and after Emilio and Stella went to bed, Paolo, on foot, led Dante up the road to the Cassio home. Emilio heard the clip-clops of the animal and went to his bedroom window to look out.

Stella said, "Who is it?"

Emilio said, "It's Paolo! What's he doing here at this hour?"

At that moment, the front door opened and closed without making a sound. Emilio, from the darkness of his bedroom, saw his daughter, carrying a blanket, run to join Paolo, who helped her onto Dante's broad back.

"What the hell?" Cassio said. "She just got on Paolo's horse. They're leaving."

Stella Cassio said, "Come to bed, *caro*."

He said, "This isn't proper. I have to go stop them."

"Emilio, *basta*! Just come to bed. Did you forget what it's like to be young? Leave them alone. Paolo is honorable. Come to bed. Please my darling - come to bed."

The old man listened to his wife and got back in bed with her.

She said, "Emilio, you know you can trust Gianna...and Paolo, too. Go to sleep, my love."

Paolo jumped onto Dante's back, sitting behind Gianna and feeling the warmth of her young body and smelling the freshness of her skin and hair. The night was brightly moon-lit and the two rode into the countryside until they came to a certain spot.

Paolo slid off the horse and helped Gianna down. She spread the blanket on the tall grass. He removed the saddle and bridle and let Dante munch grass and sleep. He knew the animal would stay close. He lit a fire with dried leaves and twigs. After it got going, he added thicker branches to bring it to a blaze before it settled into a warm, flickering glow.

Gianna, sitting on the blanket, slowly untied her hair and let it fall. Paolo watched her by moonlight and by firelight. She was the most beautiful woman he had ever seen, and he would savor those moments forever. He was so in love with her and so nervous that he could barely speak, even though he rehearsed what he wanted to say to Dante not an hour before.

"Gia. I...I... I..." was the best he could do.

She laughed a little and touched Paolo's face. He looked like a little boy, and he seemed helpless. Gia, seeing his serious expression, became concerned that something was wrong,

She said in almost a whisper, "Paolo. What's the matter? Do you want to say something? It's all right."

Paolo remained silent.

She said, "Paolo, it's all right. Just tell me what you want to say, my love. They are just words. Tell me the words."

His heart was pounding. *The words?* he thought. That brought him out of his fog. *Yes, they were only words.*

Paolo took a deep breath and said, "The words are that I think about you all day, every day. I cannot do my work because I daydream of you. I love you, and I want my life with you. There will never be another for me."

Gia smiled. "Oh, I see." She touched his cheek with the back of her fingers on one hand.

Paolo said, "I want to marry you, Gianna. I ask you for your hand. Marry me, Gia. Come and live with me. Be my wife. I spoke to your father and he gave his permission and his blessings."

Gia smiled again and took his face into her two hands. Without hesitation, she said, "Paolo, yes, I will marry you. Yes, I will come and live with you. Yes, I will have your babies. Yes, I will always love you."

Paolo, overcome with happiness and emotion, kissed his bride-to-be for the first time. It was her first kiss, as well. They kissed shyly; tenderly, again and again. As their bodies pressed against each other, they both became more and more aroused. When she gently pushed him away, he respected her wishes.

The young man fed the fire and they sat, warm and happy, talking about their future together for several hours. Eventually, they lay on the blanket, her head on his shoulder, and slept until just before dawn. They had to get Gianna home before her parents started their day.

Paolo saddled Dante and boosted Gia up. They rode back to her home where he helped her dismount. Gianna kissed his fingertips and pressed them to her lips.

"*Ti amo,*" she whispered. She smiled, put the rolled-up blanket under her arm, turned, and ran into the house, hoping her parents were still asleep.

Because of the rapidly failing health of her father, their wedding was scheduled for two weeks later.

The day of the ceremony was clear and mild, with a beautiful blue sky highlighted by scattered white, round, puffs of clouds. *Signore* Cassio was already too sick to travel, even to the church in town, and so the priest came to their home to perform the ceremony. Two dozen Tomasos attended, as did the Cassio relatives and a few friends from the area. Tomas and Katerina Tomaso sat with Emilio and Stella Cassio.

The two younger Tomaso brothers, Renzo and Leonardo, had erected a tall archway and decorated it with hundreds of flowers of all sizes and colors. At two o'clock in the afternoon, Leonardo led the large and gentle Dante through the flowered archway. The horse was decorated with red, yellow, white and pink flowers in his braided mane and tail and on his bridle. The big animal seemed to know this was a special occasion and he behaved perfectly. Sitting side-saddle atop the large horse was the beautiful bride, Gianna.

The guests and participants of the wedding all looked toward her. *Signore* Cassio rose from his seat and, with the help of Tomas Tomaso, walked to stand in front of the altar with Paolo at his side. Tomas then joined his wife and Stella Cassio.

Quietly, almost solemnly, Leonardo led Dante near to where Emilio Cassio stood waiting. The only sounds were a mandolin playing an old Sicilian love song and the sniffling of a few in the audience. Seeing Dante adorned with flowers reminded Katerina of the first time she had seen Tomas sitting proudly atop his racehorse, which had been decorated with streaming long red ribbons and flowers.

The priest in his vestments stood at the makeshift altar. Paolo stood facing him, rubbing his hands together.

Renzo and Leonardo helped the radiant Gianna down from the horse. She walked, smiling, to her father. She did not take her eyes off him. Emilio Cassio looked at his daughter and knew that the love and goodness into which he and his wife had immersed their daughter would carry forward to their grandchildren and beyond. The sick old man loved that thought, even knowing that he would never see Gianna and Paolo's children.

The Catholic marriage ceremony was concluded, and the two were married in the front yard of the Cassio family home on October 1, 1912.

That night, Paolo paced the candle-lit bedroom in his nightshirt waiting for his bride. Gia came into the room dressed in a cotton nightgown. She got in bed still in her sleepwear and pulled the blanket up to her chin. She lay flat on her back.

Paolo followed her lead and climbed in bed in his nightshirt. He kissed her and could feel that she was uncomfortable. He lay back. After a long pause, Gianna sat up on the bed. In silence, she turned sideways facing her new husband. A large window allowed moonlight into the room and it exactly framed her from behind and presented her in a perfect silhouette. As Paolo studied the outline of her face, her breasts, her hair and shoulders, he was in awe of her beauty.

"Paolo," she said. "Kiss me again."

The kiss was warm and contained hints of unreleased passion that were slowly rising to the surface. Paolo kissed her neck. Gia responded by tilting her head to the side. She untied the ribbon holding her top together and moved her shoulders enough to cause the garment to drop to her waist. She took his hand and placed it on her breast.

They made love slowly, shyly, and tenderly and afterwards, slept in each other's arms. They made love again in the morning, with sunlight beaming into the room, under the covers and both still wearing their night clothes.

They would never spend another night apart.

Chapter Five

"What ya got there, honey? What ya got there?"

The voice was like gravel being ground into a sheet of coarse sandpaper. The boney old man sat like a decrepit entry guard and was propped up against a building at the opening to a dark, narrow alley deep in the bowels of Naples.

The lice-infested, grayish-black beard and hair of the ancient vagrant were long, twisted and matted. Fleas crawled over his body and bite marks littered his face and hands. He stunk of body odor and urine. The old man had lost his left eye years before to an infection after a severe beating by several street toughs. The doctor at the clinic removed the crushed eyeball and sewed the eyelid closed. It was not covered.

A shabbily dressed young woman staggered toward the entrance to the alley. The scabby old man could see that she was carrying something. When he reached out to grab her, she swerved to avoid his grasp, almost falling. The used-up prostitute stumbled past the man and into the stinking alley, leaning and feeling her way with one hand on a wall.

The young woman was holding a new-born baby in the fold of her free arm. She was filthy. Her clothes reeked of body odor and afterbirth and were caked with both dry and fresh, bright red blood.

Like most of the alleys in 1890, especially in this part of the city, the passageway stunk of human waste and was a dumping ground for rotting food. It was a haven for rats and roaches.

Maria Salvino was 29 years old but looked 49. She was a common street whore who sold herself to men who had battered and badgered her since she was fourteen years old. The young woman's hopes and dreams were long ago forgotten, like the hundreds of men who paid to use her body.

The prostitute was beaten and scarred from life and now her earthly journey was drawing to a close. Syphilis had been eating her brain and body for several years. She knew she was dying.

That she got pregnant from a client was just more bad luck. Salvino needed to eat and so she worked her street corner up until the day she went into labor. Some customers liked a big, pregnant belly.

She was six months along when some sick bastard beat her and kicked her hard in the abdomen before he staggered away.

When the baby was coming and she couldn't stand the pain any longer, Maria walked to an abandoned horse stable not far from her corner. She bunched up hay, laid back, and waited. She endured the rise and fall of increasing labor pains as the time drew near. With a final push and yell, she squatted out a baby boy.

The newborn infant lay in the dirty hay, motionless. Maria lay there, too, semi-conscious and bleeding. She cried while she rubbed the baby's back until he gasped in his first breath. She cut the cord and tied it off, wrapped the minutes-old infant in her shawl, packed her crotch with old rags she found on the dirt floor, and staggered from the barn.

The sick prostitute thought *I should just leave him to die*, but she didn't. She couldn't. She carried the infant from the stable, not knowing where to go or what to do. It was still dark with just a peek of the morning light yet to come. She saw an alley not far ahead and walked, stumbling, toward it.

The bleeding woman walked around the human gargoyle at the alley's entrance. Halfway down the putrid passageway, she dropped the tiny infant onto a short stack of empty fruit crates littered with maggots and cockroaches. Maria fell to her knees, weak and delirious, then slowly got up and staggered away without a look back.

The dead body of Maria Salvino - daughter, whore, and mother - was found a couple of hours later, curled in a fetal position at the base of the *Fontana del Carciofo* in the heart of the wealth of Naples. She lay across the street from the art gallery *Umberto*, near the *Basilica Chiesa del Gesu'* and just a short walk from the luxurious *Pallazo del' Uomo*.

A city employee noticed the crumbled shape of the dead woman on the ground. He stepped up to have a closer look and bent over Maria's body thinking he would wake up yet another homeless woman and send her on her way before the *piazza* got busy. The workman shook her shoulder and said, "Let's go, you. It's time to move on."

When she didn't move, he looked closer at her and noticed the bloody clothing, her pale face and her eyes half open, half closed. He reported it to his boss.

Not long after, a horse drawn cart entered the *piazza* and stopped at the fountain. Maria Salvino was lifted by two city workers and thrown onto a cart on top of a half dozen more dead bodies from the night before. The unidentified corpses would be dumped in a mass grave on the outskirts of the city.

The sun rose and bathed *Napoli* in its sweet, delicious warmth.

People filled the *piazza* as on any other day.

Just after sunrise that same day, a bent-over old woman limped and shuffled her way into the same alley that Maria had left not an hour before. She was there to pick through last night's garbage for her next meal, maybe two if she got lucky. More than a few times, the old lady found scraps here and came to this particular passageway often.

The octogenarian carried a six-foot-long stick to scare off rats. She kept a canvas bag strapped over her shoulder for her findings.

Ever mindful of the nasty rodents who lived in these alleys by the thousands, the woman poked each can of garbage, every pile and box with her long stick. When she jammed the stick into a short stack of boxes, a large rat ran out. Green and yellow puss-oozing sores covered its back. The rodent sat back on his haunches and hissed at her. She swung her stick at the big ugly thing and said, "Get the hell out of here." The rat scurried away.

The woman began to pilfer through the empty fruit boxes when she heard a muffled, tiny whisper of a sound. She looked hard at the top box, straining her weak, old eyes to see. There, wrapped in an old shawl, covered in dried blood and crying loudly, she saw a newborn baby boy. The woman picked the infant up from the crusty boxes and wiped his face with her thumb.

She said, "How did you get here, eh?" She put the newborn infant into her canvas bag and continued her food hunt. She stuffed a half-eaten loaf of bread in her bag along with the baby and shuffled her way out of the alley with the baby, the bread, and her six-foot-long rat stick.

As she emerged from the passageway, the ragged alley guard that reached out for Maria a short while earlier yelled to her, "What's in the bag? What's in the bag?"

The filthy vagrant lunged toward the woman and grabbed the bag carrying the baby with both hands. The lady pulled the bag away from the man, took a step back, and swung her stick at the man's head. The staff caught him on top of his skull, thudding with a loud *crack!* The man fell to his side, stunned, his hand grasping the top of his head. He said, "Goddamn it! You didn't have to do that! Why did you do that?"

The woman took the infant home to her one-room, cold-water living space where she rinsed and washed him. She put his thumb in his mouth to quiet him. She resolved to keep the baby alive until she could sell him, but he had to eat.

There was a newborn infant across the lane and down a few houses. She carried the baby boy to the home across the way. The old woman knocked, and an obese young woman answered. The crone held the baby, looked at the huge breasts of the younger woman and said, "He's hungry."

The younger woman looked at the older and, without a question, motioned them inside. The woman sat, exposed one enormous breast and held her arms out to take the infant. She put his tiny mouth to her huge nipple. The baby nursed until he fell asleep. The infant was given back with a small nod.

The old lady said, *"Grazie,"* and walked back to her hut. She laid the infant in her bed. For the next month, this feeding procedure was repeated several times a day, until the old woman took the baby across the lane one morning and the house was empty.

The woman begged cups of milk from a nearby man who owned and milked a cow every day. She fed the creamy liquid to the baby, who slurped it with joy. She decided to keep the infant, at least for a while, because she had been alone for many years and enjoyed a human life in her dreary existence, even one so small. Another month, then two, and three went by. She fed the boy and kept him in a large box padded with one of her two blankets on the other side of the room.

The old woman did not have the strength or the desire to hold the baby or to rock him. On her daily searches for food scraps, she picked up rags to use as diapers. She rinsed them in the cold water of a running stream where the local women did their wash. After a few more months, she smashed *pasta* on her plate and fed it to him with her fingers. The baby grew stronger.

The woman never named the boy. She simply called him *ragazzo*. As time went by, the reference was somehow shortened to Gazzo.

As the toddler grew and his features became more defined, it was obvious that he looked different than other children. His nose was wide and flat. His eyes were set back deep in their sockets and his forehead overgrew his eyes.

When Gazzo was three years old, the two would search the alleyways together. She would beg for a few *lire*, and he would watch. The old woman didn't pay him much attention and never felt motherly toward him. She was there. He was there, too, following and emulating her.

The woman once had a husband and children of her own, but that was long, long ago. She hadn't heard her name spoken in many years and sometimes wondered if that other life had all been a dream.

Her name was Amalia.

Life went on for her and Gazzo.

The old woman aged.

The boy grew.

Chapter Six

"Hey, friend. This is a nice girl. Show her some respect."

Paolo and Renzo were there to enjoy the *festa* that evening. They saw their cousin Roberto step up to protect a young woman who was being pestered by a young thug. The brothers stayed close-by.

Roberto Tomaso was a nineteen-year-old college student. He was what the women called *pretty* with a wide smile, straight white teeth, and a large dimple curved around the left corner of his mouth. He had blue eyes, a Tomaso trait that was rare on the island, and wavy blond-brown hair. The young man was quick to laugh and slow to anger. A hard worker and a good student at the University of Palermo, he had been raised to believe that girls and women are to be respected and protected.

It followed, naturally, that he rose to the defense of Graziella Tamborini, a pretty seventeen year old, who was being bothered by a young punk trying to impress his friends.

The young punk was Lurio Scarletto, one of a gang of street thugs who were being groomed to be brought into the Mafia.

The low-life walked over to the smiling Roberto. He stood with feet planted, ready to strike. He said, "I'm not your friend."

Scarletto's friends gathered around to watch.

Roberto put his hands in front of him in the air; palms turned toward the hostile drunk, and said, "Forget it, man. Just leave the girl alone. Please."

Scarletto turned as if to leave, and then spun back toward Roberto and hit him, hard enough to stagger the young man back a few steps. Roberto had spent his life working on the farm and was much stronger than he looked. He had learned wrestling and fighting skills from his cousins and other farm workers and was not intimidated by Scarletto.

Roberto charged Lurio, tackled him, and within a few seconds had the face of his opponent pushed to the hard surface, his strong right arm wrapped tightly around his challenger's neck. Tomaso knew he had beaten his foe and released his grip. He stood, smiled, and offered his hand to help his opponent to his feet. The gesture was slapped away; Roberto turned and walked away.

That should have been the end of the fight, but the older thugs were jeering at their younger counterpart for having been beaten so easily by a farm boy.

Scarletto got to his knees. Then he stood, looked at his friends, and pulled a knife from his belt. He ran at the back of Roberto.

Paolo saw the knife pulled from its hiding place and yelled, trying to warn his younger cousin, "ROBERTO!"

His warning was too late and Scarletto rammed the knife blade deep into Roberto's rib cage. Roberto cried out in pain and fell to his knees.

Paolo and Renzo ran to Roberto, but before they could reach him, Scarletto slashed the throat of their young cousin from behind. He then turned and ran, bloody knife in hand. It had all happened so fast and was so unexpected that the brothers couldn't react in enough time to help Roberto.

The young Tomaso toppled face-down to the cobblestone pavement and grabbed at the gaping wound in his neck. His breaths were choked with blood, and he was racked with fear as he saw his own blood—his life, squirting from his throat.

Paolo tried to stop the pulsating gusher of blood with his jacket. It was no use; the cut was too deep and far too severe. They were powerless to save their young cousin, and their calls for a doctor were answered too late. It wouldn't have mattered anyway. Roberto Tomaso took his last breath while the two Tomaso brothers knelt at his side, holding his hands, weeping, praying, and comforting him.

The entire Tomaso clan and most of the people from the surrounding villages and farms attended Roberto's funeral.

The mourners had to swallow this terrible outrage—this horrific injustice—yet again. All knew that through their tears they had no choice but to still their anger, suffer their grief, and continue with their lives as usual: raising their children and finding joy where and when they could.

The mourners didn't dare to look at the crime leaders at the funeral for fear of even more violence. There were other children to protect from these heathens, and they could not invite retribution. Those grieving the loss of another fine young man knew that the police would do nothing out of fear and bribery. They knew, too, that the judges and magistrates were all bought and paid for. There would be no legal justice.

The dark cloud over Sicily was the organized, violent, and greedy Mafia that ruled much of the island. Their power was absolute. A single misspoken word had gotten men both young and old beaten, shot-gunned, garroted, or knifed.

To add to the seething rage felt by so many at the funeral, they had to accept that the known murderer, Lurio Scarletto, disappeared into hiding while his Mafia bosses attended the funeral. Roberto's mother walked slowly, arm in arm with Tomas and Katerina.

When she saw her son in the casket, she cried, "My boy! My boy!" and fell to her knees.

Days after the funeral, while they were alone and washing up after a day of farm work under the hot sun, Paolo said to Renzo, "We cannot let this go, brother. We have to avenge Roberto. You know that."

"I know," replied Renzo. "Let's find that son of a bitch and do to him what he did to Roberto."

"I have inquiries out," Paolo said. "Leave Papa out of this. Not a word to him."

A week passed when the Tomaso brothers received word from a friend that Scarletto was holed up in the mountains in a town called Cibuono, where he drank himself drunk every night in a small tavern. Their simple plan was agreed to: They would ride on horseback to the village, find Scarletto, neutralize any associates, and put a bullet in his head.

Leonardo overheard his brothers talking, and he felt duty-bound to help with *la vendetta*. Leo also knew that Paolo and Renzo would leave him out, knowing that he did not possess the personality to kill someone, even as revenge.

Leo sat with Renzo on the front porch of the farmhouse. He said, "I want to come along with you when you go for Scarletto."

Renzo looked at his younger brother for a long moment. He replied, "It's not for you, Nardo. It's dirty, dark business."

Leonardo answered, "Roberto was my cousin, too. I loved him just as much as you and Paolo. I'm going with you."

Renzo thought for another long moment and said, "I'll speak to Paolo. Don't talk to anyone about this."

Renzo approached Paolo about Leo's involvement and was surprised with his brother's quick reply when he said, "Yes, he should be with us."

The matter was settled. A few days later, the three brothers talked as they sharpened their knives and cleaned and oiled their three pistols and two shotguns. They defined their goal and assigned duties. It was agreed that Renzo and Leonardo would secure whoever was with Scarletto, and Paolo would kill him.

Gianna was cleaning the kitchen when she overheard the three men talking on the porch. She was horrified that her gentle husband, the man she loved, could be capable of such violence. In bed that night, she summoned up the courage to confront Paolo.

"*Caro*," she began. "I heard what you're planning, and I don't like it. It isn't right. Another dead man can only bring more suffering and revenge."

Paolo's tone of voice was stern, and Gianna knew she was seeing another side of him for the first time. He replied calmly, "Roberto was my uncle's son. My first cousin. He was just a boy and did nothing to deserve what happened. My aunt weeps and we will all grieve forever. His murder cannot go unavenged. Forget what you heard."

She replied, "Paolo, this is not you, not the man I married."

Paolo shot back, "Yes, I am the man you married! Roberto was murdered. Murdered! The police will do nothing. Revenge is the only justice we have on this island, the one way we have to protect our family. Now, enough. Please... go to sleep!"

Gianna tried again, "But, Paolo..."

He cut her off in a tone of voice that frightened her. "Gia, listen to me! These animals have to know that if they use a knife or a *lupara* on a Tomaso, they will pay with their life."

"Paolo..."

"Enough!" he said, as he put his hand in the air, palm toward his wife. "Not another word." Paolo had never spoken to her in this way; he had never before silenced her.

Gianna was a Sicilian woman and was aware of the way things were done in her homeland but never expected this treatment from her gentle, soft-spoken husband. Gia knew this was serious, ugly business, and she knew, too, that her husband would not be deterred. She accepted what was to be.

A month after Roberto Tomaso's funeral, Paolo, Renzo, and Leonardo began their long horseback ride up into the mountains. Four hours later, they arrived at the small, centuries-old village of Cibuono. It was just before dusk, and the three brothers stayed outside the town for a few hours to feed, water, and rest their horses and themselves.

That night, they walked their horses into the village. The only sound was the clip-clops from the hooves of the three animals. The sole bar in the village presided over the *piazza*. A pock-marked grey and white statue paying tribute to St. Jude sat in an empty cement pool in the center of the cobblestone square. The brothers hitched their horses and silently approached the tavern on foot, carrying their weapons.

All of the men inside the bar had walked there, and so the Tomasos knew their escape would be effective because they likely would not be followed. Paolo looked through the window and saw Lurio Scarletto sitting by himself at the bar. He looked drunk.

Paolo nodded to Renzo and Leo. There were a dozen men inside. Renzo and Leonardo loaded their shotguns, and each tucked a loaded pistol his belt. Paolo held a large revolver in his right hand.

Paolo said, "Renzo, you go in the back door and keep everyone sitting. No one leaves until we're done. You give the orders."

Renzo said, "Got it."

"Leo, you come in the front with me."

"OK," Leo said.

Paolo ordered, "No names. Got it? No names."

The brothers pulled grey canvas hoods with large openings for their eyes over their heads. Paolo and Leo burst into the bar through the front door; Renzo entered through the back door.

Renzo, according to the plan, took control. He stood in a corner opposite Leo, who was on the other side of the room. They leveled their shotguns at the room but kept them tilted toward the floor.

Renzo yelled, "Stay seated! No one move!"

It quickly became apparent that none of the men planned to move. In fact, they glanced at the bar to where Scarletto was sitting as if to say, *He's right there. Take him.* The men fell silent. Most kept drinking and watched the drama unfold. One older man lit up his pipe and turned his chair toward the bar.

Paolo walked to Scarletto, poked him with his pistol and said, "On your feet."

Scarletto looked around the room for help. He saw that he was on his own. Scarletto said, loud enough for all the hear, "Help me! My boss will give you money. Help me—stop this guy! I didn't do anything!"

No one spoke or moved. Paolo grabbed Scarletto by the collar and said, "Get up!"

The terrified Scarletto looked for an avenue of escape. There was none. Again, he refused to stand. He said, to Paolo, "Leave while you can. My bosses will kill you and your family!"

Paolo struck Scarletto on the side of his head with his pistol. Scarletto went for a knife in his boot, but Paolo got there first. He took the knife and tucked it into his belt. He then grabbed Scarletto around the neck with his arm. Paolo pulled the man backwards off the bar stool while Scarletto tried in vain to cling to the bar. Paolo banged the man's fingers with his heavy pistol.

Paolo said, "You're coming with me, you son of a bitch!"

Again, Scarletto begged for help. "Someone help me. Please. I'll give you money! I'll give you anything—just help me!"

No one replied.

Renzo and Leonardo kept the shotguns alert, just in case. Renzo looked at Leonardo's hooded face. The young brother's hands were shaking as he held tight onto his shotgun. Renzo said, "Steady, you!" Nardo steadied his grip, but his hands were wet with sweat.

Lurio Scarletto's bloody and broken fingers slipped from the bar. He fell backwards onto the floor with Paolo still holding him by the collar of his jacket. The bar stool crashed to the floor. Tomaso dragged the now whimpering thug across the floor. He banged the door open with his foot and pulled his prey, kicking and screaming, outside.

It had become eerily quiet in the tavern. The plan was for Renzo and Leo to keep the men in the bar until Paolo's pistol shot was heard. They waited in silence.

Paolo pulled the struggling Scarletto across the dirt street that ran alongside the bar and into the *piazza*. He said, "On your knees, shithead!"

Scarletto looked at Paolo. "Please, don't kill me! Please! I'm sorry...so sorry! I didn't mean to do it!"

Paolo banged Scarletto on the side of his head with his pistol. "I SAID, KNEEL, SHITHEAD!"

He struck Scarletto on the side of his head three more times with his pistol. Scarletto knelt, his head now spilling blood over his ears and into his eyes. Tomaso took Lurio's knife, the same blade that had killed Roberto, from his belt. He pulled the canvas sack from his head and grabbed a handful of the man's hair. He forced Scarletto to look at him.

He said, "Remember Roberto Tomaso, you piece of shit." Tomaso plunged the blade into Scarletto's heart. He released his hold on the punk who fell, gasping and choking, to the ground. Paolo stood next to the dying man and watched the blood pump from his chest, just as he had watched the life force drain from Roberto's dying body.

He drew his pistol and shot Scarletto once in the head. He left the knife in his chest, replaced his canvas hood, and walked away.

When the shot from the pistol was heard in the tavern, Renzo said loudly, "It's done. If any of you come out that door in the next five minutes, you will be shot."

The words didn't matter. No one cared enough about the young thug to follow, and they all knew this was *la vendetta*. They continued to drink their wine and beer. Several lit up cigars.

Their bloody work done, Paolo, Renzo and Leonardo, still carrying their weapons at the ready, left the bar. Renzo walked backwards, his shotgun at his hip.

When they got to their horses, Leonardo pulled the hood off his head and said, "Wait, wait." He bent over and vomited.

Paolo said, "Leo, get on your horse."

They mounted, rode out of town, and headed home. No one followed. A mile out of Cibuono, the brothers tossed their canvas head covers to the side of the road. They rode side-by-side in silence for an hour until Paolo said, "You did well, Nardo." No other words were spoken on the ride home.

The brothers were asleep in their beds before sunrise.

When Paolo awoke later that morning, Gianna heard him stirring on their bed. She came in from the kitchen and handed him a cup of hot, strong coffee.

She left the room without speaking.

Chapter Seven

Tomas Fernando Tomaso was born in 1862 in the family farm-house. The Tomasos had lived in this area, had their babies and raised their families here for more than two hundred years.

Tomas was the oldest of seven children of Angelo and Vicenza Tomaso. He was smarter than most his age and loved to work the farm at his father's side. Angelo Tomaso was a strong man and a hard worker who adored his family and loved working with his son Tomas.

Every morning, Angelo and Tomas would feed and water the animals before the boy would head off to school. Angelo would tend to the fruit trees, the vegetable garden, and the garlic field. It was a full day of hard work.

Some days after school or on a weekend, father and son would climb onto the wide back of their draft horse and ride into the country to hunt or fish. Other times, they'd take the cart into town to buy whatever provisions were needed. It was a well-oiled routine, physically demanding, but satisfying. The father taught his son life-lessons handed down to him from the generations that went before.

One hot summer day, Angelo and Tomas were picking oranges. The air was thick and humid and the long canvas bags grew heavier with every orange as the day went by. Suddenly, and without a word, Angelo vomited, grabbed his chest and fell to his knees, gasping for air. Tomas heard the thud as his father hit the ground and ran to him.

Angelo barely got the words out, "Tomas, run! Go get Mama!"

The boy stood looking down at his father for a terrible moment, stunned, and then flew as fast as his feet would carry him. He returned with his mother.

The forty-nine-year-old Angelo Tomaso lay dead, clutching his chest, eyes wide open, white foam and vomit on his purple lips. The twelve-year-old Tomas dropped to his knees, collapsed atop the dead body of his father, and wept. All he could say was, "Papa! Papa!"

Vicenza Tomaso, between sobs of grief, pulled her son off his father's body and held him close. They wept together. Three days later, Angelo Tomaso was buried in the family section of the graveyard next to the Catholic church in town.

After Angelo's death, there was no choice but for Tomas to stop attending school and to take over, as best as he could, the role of farm manager. Under his mother's direction and with the help of an uncle, Tomas learned how to run the farm. His mother's focus had to be on her other six children, two of whom were still in diapers.

La Signora Tomaso focused primarily on her younger children, two of whom were still in diapers. No matter how busy or tired she was, the mother always found time to continue her young son's education in mathematics, literature, politics, and history at home. Tomas loved to read and would do so for hours at night by the light from a lantern.

Mother and son proved to be a good team. Every day at sunrise, Tomas fed the chickens and ducks, gathered eggs, and milked and fed the cow and work horse. He fed his personal horse oats and hay, watered the animals, and mucked out their stalls. After the livestock was cared for, Tomas would clean and prepare whatever farm equipment would be needed for the day's work. He learned to run the farm from planting and harvesting, to the sale of the lemons, oranges and garlic they grew.

Fate handed Tomas much responsibility at a young age, and he grew into the role of head of the family. He thrived on the responsibilities.

Breakfast was always a happy event for the family. Afterwards, Tomas would get back to the business of running the farm. The young man worked tirelessly, took on every task, and no matter how difficult the chore, he never wavered in his dedication to his family.

When he was eighteen years old, Tomas had grown to his full height. He was 5'8" and a muscular young man, made so by his daily backbreaking work. He wore a handlebar moustache and his thick dark brown hair was always brushed straight back.

Tomas's three sisters adored him and felt safe with him as head of the household. His three brothers loved him as well and respected him. His mother was grateful to him: She knew that she would have lost everything when Angelo died if not for Tomas.

Under the skilled management of mother and son, the farm thrived. The produce taken to market was some of the best in the region, and soon, the people in the surrounding area noticed the success of the enterprise.

As he aged, Tomas Tomaso became a well-respected member of the community. He grew to be a methodical thinker, wise beyond his years, and many often sought his advice. When asked for his opinion, he took his time, weighed all the pertinent information, and asked the right questions before he came to a decision. It came to be that his words carried great weight.

These were skills that would stay with Tomas forever. By the time he was twenty-five years old, he was known in the area as a reliable and sensible neutral voice to whom local farmers and townspeople could bring their disputes. Tomas would consider both sides and offer his objective decision, which was almost always accepted.

At a community festival one summer day, Tomas entered his grey-speckled mare, Spirito, in a race with himself as the rider. He had competed in this race for the past three years but never won. There were eighteen horses entered in the event and the objective was to be the first rider to complete the five-kilometer cross-country obstacle course. At the last kilometer of the course, the riders would gallop at full speed for the finish line.

The big race was the culminating event of the annual *festa* and a large crowd had gathered to watch. An enthusiastic band played the three songs they knew. All the riders and horses were decorated with strands of colored ribbons. Tomas was adorned by his three sisters with red streamers tied around his arms and legs and a two-foot-long red scarf tied around his head, the back of which would flow behind him as he rode. The riders gathered on the starting line. The women and girls in the crowd eyed the boys and young men who would soon be challenging the course.

Many of the young ladies noticed Tomas, who cut a dashing figure, as he calmed the nervous Spirito who reared back as they approached the starting line. The women and girls talked and giggled about each of the riders, especially those men who were not married.

One young lady was quieter than the others and kept her eyes on Tomas. Katerina Balsamo had heard about this smart young man from her brother, who once went to Tomas for advice. Tomaso noticed her too and smiled at her from high atop his excited mare.

With a blast from a pistol, the eighteen horses and riders roared off the starting line. They raced through the town and into the country where they would negotiate the obstacles. At the halfway point, the race was close with a half dozen horses remaining. Spirito was one of the six.

Exhaustion forced three of the six finalists to drop out two kilometers from the end. The three remaining animals and riders approached the final kilometer of the race at a furious pace. One of the three horses injured his hoof and was pulled up by his rider. It was then a two-way competition between Tomas and another young man who rode a beautiful, slender black stallion by the name of Stiletto.

The two horses ran neck and neck and nose and nose for the rest of the race. The ribbons Tomas's sisters tied to him streamed bright red. Both Tomas and his opponent became as one with their mounts. The spectators cheered for their favorite, and the animals crossed the finish line at the same moment. The race was called a dead heat by the judges and both riders were given large, colorful victory bouquets.

Carrying the cluster of flowers, the dirty and sweaty Tomas steered the white-sweated Spirito across the cobblestone street to where Katerina stood with her friends. He looked only at her, and directly into her eyes. She looked at him and smiled.

Tomas said, *"Buon giorno, Signorina,"* and handed her the winner's bouquet. Tomas didn't know it, but at that moment, but he was also handing her his heart.

Katerina Balsamo

Katerina Domenica Balsamo was a Sicilian woman through and through. She loved the people, the food, the religion, and even the many superstitions of her land. Most of all, Katerina loved her family, which consisted of her parents, one brother, one sister, several aunts and uncles, and many cousins.

Katerina's father, Luigi, was a butcher in the town of Cannita in western Sicily. Katerina was a good student and a loyal and pure daughter. She was a slender and beautiful young lady who had a few young women who were her best friends.

Like many young girls, Katerina often dreamed about the path her life would take. She wondered if she would marry and have children, or if she would have a career instead. When Katerina completed her education, she took a job at the local hotel and helped her parents around the butcher shop by wrapping meats and taking money from the store customers.

Katerina, like many young people, was bored and wanted to taste adventure or, at least, begin to experience life as an adult woman.

Her wise parents encouraged Katerina to keep all her options open and to take her time with important decisions. They also counseled her that if marriage was meant to be, the right man would appear when she least expected him and not when she sought him out. She knew that was wise advice and her life changed one day, in a flash.

Katerina and a few friends meandered through the attractions at the All Saint's Festival in her home village. At the time of the annual horse race, the girls walked to the starting line to look at the horses and the decorated riders.

The first time she saw him, sitting atop his excited, speckled mare, Katerina thought that Tomas Tomaso was a handsome and exciting man, not to mention incredibly dashing with his handlebar mustache and broad smile.

The horse was giving Tomas trouble lining up for the race, but he managed to calm the animal and get her in position. Just before the starting gun, her eyes met Tomas's. She smiled. The starting gun exploded, and the race was on.

Spirito leapt forward, and Tomas, who was looking back at Katerina, was nearly thrown to the ground. He righted himself in the saddle and joined in the race.

Katerina and her girlfriends watched and cheered the riders on. One-by-one, contestants dropped out until the race was between Tomas and another rider on a black stallion.

The crowd of spectators, many of them bettors, cheered their approval as the sweaty animals and riders roared past the finish line. After the race, Tomas, still seated atop Spirito, guided the animal toward Katerina. He reached down and handed her the winner's bouquet. Her heart was pounding in her chest with pride and joy, having been selected by this handsome young man to receive this honor.

For years after, Katerina told the story of how Tomas won the horse race by the tiniest of margins. The truth was that she knew the race was a draw. She also knew that she fell in love with Tomas that day.

Two years after the race, in 1888, and after a proper courtship, during which all Sicilian protocols were properly observed, Tomas Fernando Tomaso married Katerina Domenica Balsamo. They moved into the farmhouse in which Tomas had been born a quarter century earlier, along with his mother Vicenza. Several of the Tomaso children were still living at home, although they were young adults now and would be on their own soon enough.

Ten years later, upon the death of his mother, Tomas and Katerina inherited the farm. There were no objections from his siblings; they all knew that Tomas sacrificed greatly to keep them safe, well-fed, and educated, and they all wished him and Katerina well. By the time of his mother's death, Tomas and Katerina had brought three fine sons into the world.

Chapter Eight

"Pa, men with guns! Pa! Pa!" Gianna yelled as she lifted Isabella to her hip and grabbed Luca. She was on the porch watering her hanging plants. When she saw the armed men riding toward the farmhouse, she grabbed the kids and rushed them inside.

She shouted again, "Pa! *PA!* Men are coming with guns!"

Tomas and Katerina hurried into the kitchen from the adjoining room.

"Where? Who are they?"

Gianna said, "They're coming closer, now. Look!"

One week to the day after the killing of Lurio Scarletto, a Model T Ford escorted by six armed men on horseback drove and rode along the dusty country road to the Tomaso farm. As the entourage advanced, plumes of reddish dust formed around them and streamed a mile behind like a low-hanging cloud that announced their approach.

Each of the six horsemen held a shotgun, pointed upwards with the butts of the weapons on their hips as they rode. The riders formed a circle around the automobile. Each stayed within twenty feet of the vehicle. The car pulled up to the front of the farmhouse, stopped, and the engine turned off. The automobile shook, backfired, and belched a cloud of grey exhaust.

The six armed riders stayed mounted and spread out in a semicircle facing the house, their shotguns still on their hips. Two white-haired men, one slender and one heavy, got out of the Ford and walked to the shaded porch. Both wore dark wool suits and a dark colored fedora hat

One of the men knocked on the door. Katerina politely greeted the men when she opened it.

"Marco Raposo! I haven't seen you in years!"

Katerina was concerned, but she had known this man since childhood and so felt that Tomas would not be harmed, even though she knew that her old school mate had become a Mafia chieftain.

She did not know the other man, and no introduction was offered.

Tomas Tomaso opened the front door and stepped onto the porch. He knew at once why this visit was being made; the murderer of his nephew was dead. He saw the six bodyguards and noticed their shotguns, especially the way they were positioned.

He said, "If you want to speak to me, they must go."

The thinner of the two old men gave a signal to the horsemen, and as if preplanned—which it was—the six bodyguards lowered their weapons and rode a half kilometer back. There, they grouped close together and watched the farmhouse, waiting for a gesture from either of the *Capi* that they were needed.

Tomaso and his two visitors sat at the round, wooden table on the porch. Gianna, with little Luca and tottering Isabella following, came out from the house. She carried a tray with a bottle of wine, glasses, and a pitcher of water, which she placed on the table. Her hands were shaking.

"Thank you, Gianna," said Tomas.

He took her hand to calm her and said to the other men at the table, "Gentlemen, this is the wife of my son Paolo, Gianna Tomaso. These are my grandchildren, Luca and Isabella."

"*Molto piacere,*" said the two men in unison.

The heavier of the two men smiled at the children, extended his hand, and ran his fingers over Isabella's tender baby cheeks.

"*Bellisima. Bellisima*," he said.

Gianna looked down and never made eye contact with the men. She knew they were Mafia bosses and was afraid of men who wielded such power and used it for evil.

"*Piacere,*" said Gianna as she and the kids went back into the house.

She got Luca and Isabella busy playing with *Nonna* and stayed close to the door so she could hear what was said. She wanted this meeting to be over quickly and for the two men and their armed entourage to leave.

The older of the two visitors began, "*Signore* Tomaso, you know why we're here. An employee of mine, a young man by the name of Lurio Scarletto, was pulled by his neck out of a quiet bar in the mountains. He was stabbed and shot."

Tomaso sipped his wine, "I'm sorry to hear that, Don Raposo. It is indeed a tragedy. How does this affect my family?"

The man said, "We both know this killing was *la vendetta*. Scarletto was the young man who fought and killed your nephew Roberto, for which I am sorry and sad. But we cannot tolerate a murder like this."

Tomas Tomaso was thoughtful, as was his way, and sat quietly for a few long moments. He then began, "My brother, Roberto's father, died years ago. My nephew was a smart and industrious young man. He stepped forward, as he should have, to defend the honor of a virtuous young girl who was being bothered by this valued employee of yours, this Lurio Scarletto."

Gianna could feel the old man bristle. "Yes, true. But Scarletto had value to me, and he was mine to punish."

Tomaso ignored this semi-veiled demand for a payoff and put his hand in the air to stop the man from talking, "Please," he said. "With all respect, Don Raposo, my dead brother's son did nothing but defend the honor of a young girl. Your man was disrespecting a Sicilian maiden and, as I'm sure you agree, that is the worst sin a man can commit."

Raposo said, "Yes, I agree. That is a terrible thing, and he was wrong. But again, he was mine to punish." He looked directly into Tomas's eyes. "*Mine.*"

Tomaso continued, "My nephew stood to protect her. They fought. It was a fair fight. Your boy was beaten and pulled a knife. He attacked my nephew from behind, as a coward. He murdered the boy."

The Don spoke: "Tomaso, we know all this. We know what happened."

Tomas said, "He brought shame to your family. He is dead and I am sorry that happened. I do not know who killed him. Was it my sons? Maybe, but I hope not."

The man was not accustomed to being disagreed with and was now angry. "It was Paolo, Renzo, and your youngest, Leonardo. There is no doubt, and you and I know it. I demand retribution!"

It was then that Tomaso bristled. "Retribution? Never! And so, you come to my home—*to my home*—with guns. You scare the women and children and want to scare me, too. I do not scare so easily, Don Raposo!"

The three sat in silence for a moment or two. Raposo said, "Tomaso, we came here to find a reasonable solution to this—"

"No! You came here to intimidate me! This cannot stand. NEVER, Don Raposo, *Never*!"

The two men sat and contemplated their next words, knowing that the conversation was on the brink of collapse and beginning to go in a direction that none wanted. No one stood.

In the silence, Tomas refilled the three wine glasses. He took three cigars out of a case and cut off the ends. He handed a cigar to the older man, and then gave one to the second man. He stood, struck a match, and held it to the older man's cigar. Tomas looked over the match into the man's eyes. He struck a second match and held it to the other man's smoke. Again, he looked into his visitor's eyes. He sat, struck a third match, and lit his cigar.

His actions of respect and humility diffused the tense situation. The three smoked their cigars and drank more wine before anyone spoke.

Raposo said, "Tomas, you have a nice breeze on this porch. *Mi piace.*"

"I like it, too," said, Tomas. He continued "I think we should drink this wine, smoke these cigars, and stop this revenge here and now. It was an eye for an eye. Two young men are gone; two families are suffering in their grief and despair, and all for no good reason."

The visitors did not speak but listened attentively.

Tomaso continued, "My nephew is dead. Your man is dead. Why? For nothing. Ego. Revenge. No good reason. Will we never learn?"

As he spoke, Luca walked onto the porch from inside the house and went to his grandfather. Tomas lifted the boy onto his lap. He kissed the top of his head.

"Let's agree that this stops here. Two boys are dead. Let them rest in peace."

The heavier of the two men, who hadn't spoken during the exchange between Tomaso and Raposo, was transfixed by little

Luca. He seemed lost in his thoughts and memories. After a long silence, he said, "You are right, Tomas. Let us stop this here."

Raposo stood and walked to the end of the porch. He looked at the garden and toward the orchard. Finally, he turned and said, "My friend is right. You are right. More pain will not help anyone."

With that, the two men shook hands with Tomas and walked to their car. The driver started the machine, the horsemen formed a circle around the vehicle, and the entourage drove back along the dusty road that had brought them to the farm.

Gianna came out of the house to retrieve Luca. "I'm so sorry, Papa. He wanted to be by you."

She looked at her father-in-law and was comforted by his smile. It was as if he was saying to her, *Our boys are safe; they are out of danger.*

At that moment, Isabella cried from inside the house. Gianna lifted Luca from Tomas's lap and went back inside.

She had heard it all and was terrified at the thought that life, which she believed was a gift from God, could be negotiated, and given or taken so easily.

Most of all, Gianna gained a deeper respect and an appreciation for the intelligence and the calm ability to reason of her father-in-law.

Chapter Nine

The cart full of lemons sat next to the barn where it would stay until moved to the market at dawn the next morning. Sancho, having been cooled and watered, munched happily on a pile of hay in front of him in the small corral that was his home.

Tomas, Paolo, and Leonardo came into the kitchen after washing up at the well as the middle brother, Renzo, came to the table. As usual, Renzo was not willing to help the workers, and his father tired of trying to motivate him.

Katerina, Gianna, and *Signora* Cassio had already set the table and positioned large serving dishes and bowls where they could be easily accessed and passed. The family took their usual seats. Tomas sat at the head of the table with his wife on his left. The parents ate their meals without talking; they knew what they had to do.

The rest of the family ate and joked as usual; they could not know that a terrible disruption to their lives was coming.

After they finished eating, Tomas cleared his throat and began. "Your mother and I need to have an important talk with you all." No one at the table had ever seen Tomas so serious and so sad, excepting his wife.

Tomas Tomaso continued, "Your mother and I have come to a difficult decision. We at this table have a problem: We can no longer grow enough produce to feed, educate, and care for all of us, and our family continues to grow as it should and must."

That the ever-so-serious patriarch would talk this way commanded the complete attention of all present. His three sons and his daughter-in-law could see on his face and hear in his voice that this was a vital matter.

Katerina sat there just looking down at her hands.

"To be clear," Tomas continued, "Our farmland is maxed out, and still, we do not and cannot grow enough to both eat and sell."

He had the complete attention of everyone now. "There are other problems. This island has become a hard and a dangerous place to live, and it's not just violence and crime. Government corruption is out of control. Taxes are increased every year. Poverty is worsening."

The sons were looking quizzically at each other, and at their mother. Gianna now looked only at Paolo, but all he could see was that she had tears in her eyes.

"Papa, what are you getting at?" asked Leonardo.

From a young age, this man, their father, the leader they all respected, had been a thinker and a reader. He was smart, knowledgeable, an arbiter of disputes, and now, he had something important, something life-changing, to say.

Because he was who he was, the family knew that he had thought it through; that he believed that what he was about to say was the right thing for the family. Tomas sipped his wine and took a deep breath.

He continued, "Well, here it is everyone: Your mother and I have decided that we have no choice but to split the family."

He paused and waited for those words to sink in.

"What are you talking about, Pa?" asked Paolo.

Tomas said, "Some of us must go to live in America," he paused, then looked around the table and again waited for the shock to subside.

Gianna's heart skipped a beat, and she looked at Paolo.

The three brothers went silent. Paolo looked across the table at Gianna. They all sat, stunned, speechless.

Tomaso went on, "Mama and I sold the farm. After taxes are paid, there will enough money to get you three boys, Gianna, *Nonna*, and the kids settled in America, but just barely enough. Momma and I will have to stay here. We'll move to town with your grandparents; they are too old to go anywhere, and we cannot leave them."

When the reality of the words spoken by her father-in-law set in, Gianna felt a silent explosion in her chest. *America?* She couldn't move or speak and was only able to look across the table at her husband. *He'll refuse*, she thought. *He won't move us. He wouldn't do that to us. Never.*

Renzo spoke first. "I won't go. No, no, no! This is crazy talk. I'll get by. I won't go."

Tomas said to his middle son, "Boy, you have no skills. You sleep late every day. You hardly help around the farm, and you have no job. How would you live? America will be a new beginning for you. An opportunity."

Renzo raised his voice, "I will not go to America or any-where else!"

Paolo, Gianna, and Leonardo sat still, unconvinced.

The older Tomaso said, "Listen to me, everyone: Your mother and I have talked and prayed about this for months. We've con-sulted with experts. We believe there is no other way. If we all stay here, we will always be hungry. If some of us go, we will all thrive. Here, your children will live the same life our people have lived for two hundred years. We want more than that for our grandchildren."

"Papa," said Leonardo. "Papa, no."

Tomas glanced at his youngest son and then at his other boys. "There is not enough food. Understand? Soon, there will be no money for medicine or education. There is no future on this island! We lose young men every day to shotgun blasts and knifings."

"But, Papa..."

"The police do nothing. It's only a matter of time until it strikes our family again. Your mother and I want all of you to have families of your own—children, lots of children—but you cannot bring babies into this country."

They all sat silent for a moment.

Paolo asked, "When do you plan for this to happen?"

Gianna fixed her gaze on her husband. *No, no, no. This wasn't happening. Paolo, no!*

The elder Tomaso hung his head and said, "You're leaving at the end of the year."

"I AM NOT GOING!" said Renzo.

Tomas, irritated with his second son, raised his voice for the first time and said, "Renzo, be quiet! Use your head. Think for a change. Yes, it will be difficult and heartbreaking, but here we cannot grow; we cannot thrive."

"I am not going!"

Tomas stood and banged the table with his fist, voice raised, "I broke my back for forty years and have nearly nothing to show for it, and it's because of this damn government, taxes, and crime."

Gianna felt her cheeks wet with tears. Paolo looked at her without completely understanding her feelings.

Renzo said, "You have nothing because you're a fool. That's your fault, Papa. You're a fool."

Katerina raised her voice for the first time, "Renzo! That's enough! This man worked to put food in your lazy mouth, and now you disrespect him like that?"

Tomas touched his wife's arm. He went on. "Listen to me everyone. In the New World, you can all have great lives, families, money, real futures. Do you get that? Opportunities that you will not have here."

No one spoke as the words of the head of the family soaked in. Katerina patted her husband's arm and motioned him to sit back down.

"Boys," a now calm Katerina said. "Boys, your father and I have talked about this for months. We met with Father Fiori, and he respects our conclusion. We don't want to divide you from each other or from us, but there is no other way. We want a better life for you and your children."

Renzo stood and started to leave the room.

Tomas said, "Renzo, I'm not done!"

Renzo replied, "You're done, and I'm not going to America. I'm staying right here where I was born and where I will die." Renzo remained standing but did not leave the room.

Tomas said, "I will explain this to you one last time; maybe you'll get it. Taxes consume us. Our government is our enemy. We are controlled by the Mafia. People—our friends and relatives—will not and cannot stand up to them. Can't you see that?"

Renzo said, "Are you done yet?"

Leonardo didn't speak. He sat quietly with his head down.

Paolo jumped in, "Renzo, listen to what Pa has to say. He may be right."

Gianna begged Paolo with her eyes. *No, Paolo, no.*

Renzo said, "I don't care what he says."

Tomas said, "No. You will hear me out. Sit down."

Renzo said, "I'll stand."

Tomas proceeded calmly. "Young men are being slaughtered on this island every day. How long will it be before one of you is caught up in this violence like Roberto? Your mother and I cannot bear the thought of losing one of you."

Renzo said, "I'm not going to be slaughtered. I know how to survive."

Tomas said, "Renzo, listen to me. Hundreds and hundreds of our good young men have died. Whole towns have no men, all killed by *vendetta* and their—"

Renzo interrupted "Not me."

Tomas continued "—women and children are left to go hungry."

Renzo said, "Not me."

Tomas stood and slammed his open hand down on the table. "HEAR ME, RENZO! You are NOT special."

Katerina lightly touched her husband's arm. "Tomas, calm down.'"

Renzo said, "Okay, so you don't think that I'm special. Well, here it is from me: If I die, I die. At least it will be here, in my homeland."

Tomas replied, "That's just it, son. Our homeland is the problem. Our government is the problem. *Omerta* is the problem. Our only law is *la vendetta.* Murderers, thieves, and rapists go free, even though their identities are known. We live in fear. Who to tell of a crime? The police? That's a joke. The army? For what?"

Paolo said, "He makes sense, brother."

Gianna screamed a silent scream deep in her chest. *No, no. This can't be happening.*

Nonna Cassio, who was sitting next to her daughter, did not say a word. She simply put her hand on Gianna's arm to calm her, to encourage her to still herself and to respect the men of the family. Gianna knew she had to get control of her emotions; this was the way of Sicilian women, the way they had survived for centuries. It is the way she had learned from her mother.

Gia would have to ignore the explosion in her heart and do what she must to please her husband and more importantly, to protect her children.

Paolo got up from the table and went to the window above the sink. He stood for several long moments, looking out, lost in thought. Gia remained seated but never took her eyes off her husband.

After a long silence, Paolo turned and said, "I agree. You are right, Pa. In America our kids will have better lives, but here, they'll only be poor dirt farmers, breaking their backs for years, like you said. Just to pay the government and die young."

Gianna felt sick to her stomach.

Paolo continued, "Why should they live like that when we can give them opportunity in America? Think of it! We can open a whole new world for them and give them better lives. Isn't that what we're supposed to do?"

Gianna sat still, her heart pounding so loudly she thought everyone in the room could hear it. Her face was red, and she felt the veins in her neck pound.

Tomas said, "That's right. In America, you'll have opportunity... the chance at a good life. Here, not so."

Renzo replied, "Are you done talking yet, Pa?"

Tomas said, quietly, "Yes, I'm done."

Everyone was silent again.

Finally, Tomas said, "Paolo, Leo, you are grown men. Your mother and I will respect your decisions. I am telling you what I—what both your mother and I—see and what we think is the best course of action for the future of this family. These are impossible decisions in impossible times."

No one spoke until Tomas went on. "Renzo has made his decision. Paolo, what will you do?"

"We'll go to America," said Paolo.

A stunned Gianna in a rare display of confrontation said, "Paolo! I won't leave my mother. Leave the farm? Leave our home? I can't. I won't!"

"Gia," Paolo said calmly. "My father is right. This is a dying place. Do you want Luca and Isabella to have this life? I don't, not when we can do so much better for them. In America, they will have futures."

Gianna was speechless.

Paolo took his wife's hands in his. "They will have opportunity. And we both want more children. We must leave. It's the only thing we can do for the future of our family."

Gianna didn't speak. It was not in her heart or in her nature to defy her husband further at that moment. She sat with her hands in her lap. Her head pounded with controlled chaos, and she struggled to quiet her emotions. It was as if her world had suddenly caved in. Her inner voice was quietly screaming, *No. Please, God, no.*

Katerina said, "Nardo, *caro*, will you stay with Renzo or go with Paolo?"

Leo stared at his lap and replied in a voice so soft that Tomas could barely hear, "I will stay in Sicily and join the seminary. I want to be a priest."

Tomas said, "That's it then. Paolo, Gia, the kids and *Nonna* go to America. Leo to the seminary, and Renzo...I don't know what you'll do, son."

Tomas stood, looked at his three sons and his wife, rapped the table twice with his knuckles, and said, "It is decided."

He walked through the doorway onto the wooden plank porch, leaned against an upright beam, and breathed deeply of the fresh, cool evening air.

Tomas Tomaso prayed for strength.

Chapter Ten

"Let's go, *cara*. I want to get there early."

Renzo and Adriana were headed to the seaside resort of San Vito Lo Capo, about two hours west of Palermo. Renzo rented a motor car for the day, and they started out early. The two lovers looked forward to a long day together.

Renzo wanted their time to be special because he planned to tell her that he was going to confront Carlo and tell him everything. He would tell Lazzori that he wanted Adriana for his wife. *After all*, he thought, *Carlo owes me. I saved his life.*

This, Renzo knew, would be a perfect time to have this long day and long talk with Adriana because Carlo would be in Rome on a business trip all week. Although he felt badly that he was betraying an old friend, it never started out this way. It was supposed to be a secret love affair, allowed to run its course and end. He didn't plan it, but he fell hopelessly, madly in love with this woman. He wanted his life with her.

Both Adriana and Renzo were hungry and when they got to San Vito, they enjoyed a long, slow breakfast. Afterwards they went to their room and sprawled out on the biggest and softest bed either had ever seen. They made love slowly and fell asleep together.

An hour later, Renzo woke to the soft crying of Adriana. "What's the matter?" he asked.

She said, "I've never known love before, never felt his thing I always wondered about."

Renzo agreed. She had perfectly put his feelings into words. He felt his own warm tears as well as hers. Adriana dried his eyes and said, "Don't cry, my love. You've made me happier than I ever thought I could be."

Later that day, the two walked barefoot along the beach with the glimmering Mediterranean Sea at their sides. Families ate basket lunches on the beach; children played in the warm surf.

Renzo rented horses, and they rode through the surf at the water's edge. Three miles from the hotel, they tied their horses to hitching posts and stopped for lunch. They ate clams and oysters pulled from the sea just an hour before. They ate *pasta con vongole*, tender grilled *polpo*, fried *rapini,* and drank a bottle of chilled *vino bianco.*

As the sun was setting, the tired lovers rode back at a leisurely pace. They returned the horses and walked, hand in hand, to their hotel.

Renzo now saw Adriana in the soft and fading light of dusk and thought that she was the most perfect woman he had ever met. He was certain that he wanted to grow old with her. She was the one woman for him.

Both Renzo and Adri wanted to make love again and sleep for a while before returning to Palermo, but they dozed off almost as soon as their heads touched the pillows.

As the two lay together, Renzo was snapped awake by loud voices in the hallway, just outside. The door burst open with a hard kick from a strong, heavy man. The two goons who followed them from the beginning of their meetings came into the room, followed by Carlo Lazzori.

Carlo was dressed in a light tan suit, with a pure-white silk tie. His cufflinks were made of gold and each sported a large diamond. His fingernails were polished, and he wore a thin, trimmed moustache.

Lazzori grabbed his naked wife by the arm, pulled her from the bed, and threw her across the room. "Dress yourself, *putana!*" he ordered.

Adriana put on her clothes and ran from the room in terror, carrying her hat.

One goon held a knife to Renzo's throat and said, "Ah, ah, ah... Stay right there. Don't move."

The other thug tied Renzo by his neck and hands to the bars at the head of the bed. The man stuffed a rag into Renzo's mouth, who realized that struggling would be pointless and would only make it worse.

Carlo sat on the edge of the bed. He didn't look at Renzo as he removed a long, thin cigar from a solid gold case. He lit the smoke and began speaking, calmly and softly. "What the fuck, Renzo? You were my friend. We came up together. We robbed together. We even killed together. How could you do this to me?"

The bound and gagged Renzo couldn't respond.

"What should I do to you now that you have shown me such disrespect?"

Renzo stared at his former friend, eyes bulging.

"Stay calm," Carlo said. "You know who I am now, and you know I can't just let you walk away. Word spreads around here like the wind, and I cannot afford to be a cuckold. Respect is everything on this island. You know that. If I decide to kill you, please understand that it's not personal. I don't care much about the girl. She's just another piece of ass to me, and I have a stable of them. I won't hurt her. I'll just send her back to the farm where I found her."

Lazzori paused to look at Renzo.

"But hear this good, Renzo because the life of that little whore depends on it. If I decide to spare your life—and that's a big if— you must never try to see her again. If you ever try to contact her, I will sell her to a whorehouse in Istanbul. You know I will, my old friend, so if you care about her, YOU WILL NEVER SEE HER AGAIN. Understand?"

Renzo made a muffled sound.

"It's you, Renzo, who is the problem here. *You.* I am a *Capo.* You know that. I can't afford to be disgraced, that's all. *Capice?*"

Renzo nodded as best he could and tried to speak.

"No, Renzo. Don't try to defend yourself. Your actions have spoken for you, and now, there is nothing you can do." Lazzori moved closer to Renzo and held his face just a few inches from his captive.

Then, for the first time, Lazzori raised his voice and no longer controlled his anger. "You fucked my wife, man! My wife!" Lazzori stood and slapped Renzo hard across the face. "My wife!"

Lazzori left Renzo tied to the bed for the next two days. Goons came and went a few times a day to ensure that he stayed secured to the bed. The hotel staff was paid to stay away from the room and to remain silent.

Carlo wanted Renzo to pay the price for his betrayal; he wanted him to piss his pants, to shit himself, and to tremble in fear and anticipation of his fate. Lazzori didn't want to kill his old friend; after all, it was just over a woman. Plus, he knew he owed his former friend his life: he had no doubt that he would have been killed by that sailor in the waterfront bar a few years before if not for Renzo. But Carlo's elevated Mafia status demanded retribution.

Friend or not, life saver or not, Tomaso must pay dearly for what he did.

Chapter Eleven

"Gazzo! Gazzo! Bring me water," the old woman commanded from her cot.

Over the past few days, her coughing had become a terrible hacking, and the yellow-green phlegm she had been spitting out turned into a reddish slime.

The five-year-old boy was terrified.

The next day, and every day after, was worse than the one before as the woman became sicker. Her breathing was strained and labored. Eventually, she gasped for each breath as she lay motionless.

On the sixth day, a famished Gazzo, who ate and fed the woman every morsel of food in the room, shook her with no response. He shook her harder and poked her. She didn't move. He yelled in her ear, "Hey! Hey!" but got no response. The old woman had completed her earthly journey: she was dead and cold.

Gazzo went to the street corner where he and the old woman had often begged together. The ragged, filthy boy held his hands out to strangers. A workman gave him a half a loaf of stale bread, edged with dark green mold. He devoured it. A streetwalker gave him a few *lire*. A fat, bald old man handed him a half-eaten apple. Gazzo found a scrap of old meat in the alley.

He survived.

A few days later, after smelling the stench of decaying flesh, the old woman's neighbors summoned authorities. When Gazzo saw the *polizioti*, he climbed out the back window. The young lad hid in a doorway across the narrow cobblestone street and watched as the covered corpse was carried out.

The landlord locked the door behind the last of the officers. Later, try as he might, Gazzo could not get into the room. That day, the five-year-old boy began his life on the street. He ate from garbage cans, stole food, and begged scraps from vendors. Gazzo slept in alleyways, parks and empty horse carriages or wherever he could safely close his eyes.

Life on the street was hard for everyone, and more so for so young a child. Older homeless boys helped him survive. They taught him to steal and, as always, he begged for scraps. Occasionally, an adult would toss him leftover food or a few coins. Sometimes, Gazzo would hide in alleys and wait for fresh garbage to be dumped so he could get his next meal.

Summers turned into winters and back again as the years rolled by.

Gazzo learned to steal from tourists during the season and where to grab warm clothes when cooler weather returned. When he grew bigger and stronger, Gazzo would sometimes get an offer from a local merchant or housewife to work for room and board. These arrangements lasted a few weeks or months. Invariably, Gazzo would steal something from his benefactors and be put back out on the street.

Soon after this eleventh birthday, Gazzo was hired by a goat farmer named Lorenzo Tedesco and his wife, Carmella. The two sold goat's milk, cheese, and meat to the local townspeople. His job was to clean the pens, feed the animals, spread their droppings in the vegetable garden, and tend to the planted rows. The boy was content with the work and had enough to eat, a rare treat for him.

Tedesco was a fat man of forty-five years whose personal hygiene was as atrocious as his work ethic. He had realized years before the sad definition of his life: He was a goat farmer—always would be—and he hated it. Any ambitions to be something more than what he had become were long gone. Carmella had seen any initiative and drive drain from the eyes and mind of her husband over the years. She now found him unattractive and knew that he had become mean. She would leave him but had nowhere to go.

The goat farmer spent most of his days in a sagged-out easy chair under a shade tree drinking wine or beer. He was too lazy to work, bathe, or shave. His most strenuous activity was arguing with his corpulent wife, who always had plenty to complain about.

The farmer didn't like his wife. He found her to be unattractive and undesirable, and he hadn't touched her affectionately in years. Carmella couldn't stand the sight of him, either. She saw him to be the dirty, lazy, and repulsive man that he was.

The truth is, the goat farmer preferred young boys. Tedesco had molested every boy who had worked at the farm. His wife knew what he was doing to them in the shed, and while disgusted, she looked the other way.

One hot day, the goat man was drunker than usual as he sat in his chair watching Gazzo tend to his chores. He stood and waddled toward the nearby tool shed. As he walked, he called out, "Gazzo, come here, boy." The man's wife saw what was happening and went into the house.

When Gazzo entered the shed, the pedophile grabbed him by the hair and pulled him close. He smashed his thick, slimy lips to the boy's mouth. Gazzo swung wildly at the man and yelled for help. Tedesco clenched him around the neck with his fat, hairy paws and squeezed until Gazzo went unconscious. The goat man then turned him around and ripped the boy's pants down.

Gazzo came to and struggled to free himself, but the man held him in an unbreakable grip. Tedesco raped the boy who screamed in pain. No one heard him. After he finished, the fat farmer released his grip on the boy and let him fall to the dirt floor. He left the shed. Gazzo lay there, bleeding, whimpering, and crying.

The boy left the goat farm that night and slept, however poorly, in an open field on the edge of town. The next day, Gazzo used his few earned *lire* to buy a long, thin knife from a man on the street. He kept the blade in his boot where he could grab it quickly. He returned to work on the goat farm where he knew he could fill his belly.

The boy could have left the farm at any moment, but he wanted revenge. Just like the older guys on the street said, life was about respect. Gazzo couldn't let his rape go; he had to pay back the pain and humiliation.

A week later, as Gazzo was feeding the goats, the fat man said, "Boy, come in here!" Gazzo walked to the shed terrified but determined. The farmer grabbed the lad by his hair and turned him around. A terrified Gazzo pulled the long blade from his boot and drove the razor-sharp stiletto deep into the overstuffed thigh of his attacker. The pedophile roared in pain and punched Gazzo hard and full in the head. The blow lit a rage somewhere deep in the boy, and he pulled away from the farmer.

Gazzo turned and stood defiantly, holding the knife in a defensive position. He did not think of running. The rapist reached out to grab the boy, but Gazzo began to slash the air left to right and back and forth with his arm fully extended. He sliced the man across his hands and arms four, five, six times. His eyes closed. He was crying, yelling, and cutting the goat man. As blood spurted from the wounds on the fat, dirty man, Gazzo ran out the door, his hands, arms, face, and hair covered in the bright red blood of his attacker.

The man ran after Gazzo, limping and screaming in pain and rage, but he couldn't catch him. As the boy ran past the farmhouse, the man's wife came out. Carmella Tedesco saw the fleeing, blood-covered boy and then looked towards her hated spouse. She made no attempt to catch the boy or to aide her husband. She went back inside.

Gazzo would never again trust another person.

At dusk, the boy stood across the street from several prostitutes who were on parade for the night. One of the women waved him over. He cautiously approached her.

Eleven-year-old Gazzo was filthy and bloody, his clothes were in tatters, and he was hungry. He stared at the women from a distance until he was coached out of his safe spot. An older hooker said, "Hey, boy. Come and eat." She placed a bowl of *pasta ala putanesca,* which the street walkers prepared nightly for their clients, on the street.

Gazzo approached without taking his eyes off the women. He didn't say a word and as he gobbled the hot *pasta,* he continued to watch the whores like the scared, wild animal he was. Gazzo put the empty bowl on the sidewalk, turned, and ran away.

Frequently after that night, as the street walkers stood outside hawking their goods, the large, homely boy appeared. The women felt sorry for him and gave him food. Gazzo usually ate and disappeared without a word.

Gazzo became accustomed to life on the streets and spent the next half dozen years living hand to mouth, begging for scraps, and stealing what he could. As he matured, his features developed. His nose grew wider and flatter. His close-set eyes were deep and set under a more pronounced forehead, giving him a Neanderthal look. He became thick, tall, and muscular.

The young man learned that he liked to kill living things. He felt that it gave him a sense of power and control. He had started by crushing ants and other insects with his thumb. He caught crickets, spiders, and even scorpions. He held them down while he plucked their legs off and took their bodies apart.

Gazzo advanced to the killing of mice, rats, and birds when he could catch them. He eventually worked his way up to cats and dogs, which he would club, slit, stomp, or otherwise destroy.

There was no reason for his sadistic conduct; he just needed to hurt and to kill, and he did. Killing gave him the same satisfaction as when he slashed the stinking goat farmer.

Like most street people, Gazzo had a regular route, sleeping places, and spots where he could steal a meal or find a smaller, weaker person to beat and rob. He felt comfortable on the street and was fine with the violence that sometimes touched him. The young man learned along the way that to survive, he had to give more pain than he got. And he learned to be merciless.

Gazzo, now more a thug than anything else, often hung out with the prostitutes, who paid him for running errands. Soon, the street walkers paid the powerful and hulking young man for protection from potentially violent encounters with drunken sailors and well-dressed gentlemen who liked to hurt women.

Gazzo grew into a brutish young man. The top half of his left ear had been bitten off by a Russian marine during a violent encounter. The man from Petrograd was left lying in the street unconscious from a half-dozen boot-stomps delivered by Gazzo. Gazzo's missing half-ear made his thick, ugly, and crude appearance even more foreboding. He became a feared young street brute with a reputation for violence and cruelty. Years of street life, abuse, stealing, and brutal encounters had made the young man violent and anti-social.

His first killing of a human – at age fifteen - came in a fight with a drunken Corsican seaman ten years older than him who attacked one of the women. The gruesome battle was fought with fists, teeth, boots, knives, and clubs. It finally ended with Gazzo on the back of his opponent, choking off his rival's air supply. When the body of the man went limp, Gazzo released him, not knowing that the man was dead.

When he later learned that he murdered the sailor, he felt nothing. After that killing, violence and death seemed to follow Gazzo wherever he went. The prostitutes noticed that he became even more withdrawn, and that he seemed to want—to need— aggression and violence in his life.

One whore told her friends, "Gazzo's eyes are dead. The devil took his soul." She may have been right. The streets and his life had made Gazzo a hardened criminal and a murderer. And it was true; his eyes were dead.

Over the years, Gazzo had become a sociopath who lacked the ability to feel love, remorse, guilt, or empathy. His world was one of kill-or-be-killed, and he thrived.

Late one night, a well-dressed young son of a highly-placed Roman magistrate held a knife to the throat of one of the hookers. Gazzo approached the man from behind. When the man waved the knife in the air, Gazzo grabbed it with one hand, put his strong left arm around the man's neck, and dragged him to an alley. The offender was beaten and kicked until he was near death.

When he heard of the beating, the magistrate in Rome put intense pressure on the Naples' cops to find and arrest the thug who had savaged his son. As the police swept the area, Gazzo reasoned correctly that he would probably be the prime candidate in the beating.

He walked away from his filthy slum room with only the clothes on his back, not knowing where he would go.

Before Gazzo could flee, he needed to resolve a problem. A month before the beating of the Roman, he grabbed a thirteen-year-old girl off the street. He kept a cloth tied around her mouth and left her chained in his apartment. He fed the girl scraps and raped her at will. He left her a bucket of water to wash, and she could make it, although barely, to the bathroom. If she resisted him at all, he beat her.

When Gazzo took flight, he left the girl chained to the wall and walked out the door. He went a few steps and then stopped when he thought better of the problem. He went back into his apartment.

The two of them looked at each other. The young girl was terrified and wet herself uncontrollably. Gazzo silently walked across the room. The girl scrambled to the farthest corner, her chain rattling, and squatted there whimpering, crying and trembling. Gazzo walked to her, grabbed her by her head and lifted her off the floor.

While looking straight into her eyes, he snapped her neck and dropped her dead body to the floor. He quietly closed the door behind him and left the building.

Gazzo walked to the boat docks.

Chapter Twelve

"Soldier, I'm here. I'm right here with you," said Father Edo kneeling by the critically injured young man.

"God, it hurts. It burns so bad."

"I know it does. What's your name, son?"

It was just after daybreak when the priest saw the boy lying there, half buried in mud. The air smelled of sulfur and death. American soldiers carrying pistols walked the battlefield to kill any wounded German troops who were injured but still alive.

"Norman," the soldier gasped. "My name is Norman Lane. Stay with me, Chaplain, Please stay. It's bad."

Every minute or so, the silence was interrupted by the sharp *crack!* from a pistol round being fired.

The priest neither confirmed nor denied the gravity of the wounds to the young man, but he could see they were horrific.

"I'm here with you, Norman. I won't leave you."

Norman whispered, "Thank you, Father."

The young soldier from Boise, Idaho had taken shrapnel to the back of his head and neck. A three-inch piece of his skull had been blown off, and his brain was exposed. The revealed brain and surrounding bone did not bleed; however, blood was pulsating out of a wound in the neck of the nineteen-year-old with every heartbeat.

The priest said again "I won't leave you, Norman. I'm right here."

The young soldier was aware of his surroundings during what he knew would be his last minutes on earth. Norman looked up at the priest without hope. So softly that the priest could barely hear, the young soldier said, "Letter home," as he patted his chest. "Letter home."

Farrucio knew that many of the boys carried letters to be sent home in the event of their deaths. Edo reached into the youth's breast pocket and removed the letter. He nodded to the young man and stuffed the envelope into his side pocket.

"Don't worry. I'll send it for you."

Norman's lips moved, "Thank you, Father. Thank you."

Father Edo anointed the youth, prayed, and made the sign of the cross several times on Norman's forehead. He prayed for life everlasting for this innocent boy-victim of war. The young soldier grew weaker in just moments and was in and out of consciousness. He began to tremble.

"I'm so cold. I'm cold," said the dying man.

The priest lay down and pulled Norman close to warm him.

Father Farrucio said, "Pray with me, Norman."

He began, "Our Father who art in Heaven..."

The soldier moved his lips, whispering "...hallowed be Thy name," before he stopped.

Private Norman Lane gasped for his last breaths. He said, in barely a whisper, "Mama, where are you? Mama, I need you. Mama? Mama?"

Lane's body shuddered and rattled then lay still, dead. Farrucio sat up, closed Norman's eyes, and folded his hands across his chest. He kissed the forehead of the dead warrior and blessed his body.

While in France during services near the front lines, Army Chaplain Captain Edo Farrucio never balked and never flinched, even when nearby explosions sent rocks and shrapnel flying just inches from his head.

The priest believed on a deep, internal level that he represented God, and that he was there, in that war, at that time, on those battlefields, with those men and at those makeshift altars to serve Him.

Father Edo Farrucio knew he could serve the soldiers best if he understood their lives on a personal level, and so he often lived with them. He ate the same cold meals and slept in the mud trenches alongside the troops where rats and roaches would crawl over him during the night.

More often than he cared to remember, Father Farrucio performed the Holy Sacrament of Last Rites on the dead or dying bodies of soldiers from whom he heard Confession just hours earlier.

The priest prayed and cried over countless young men who were gassed to agonizing deaths, blown to pieces, shot, or had their bellies split open by enemy bayonets.

Father Edo often held the hands of near-dead boys and stroked their foreheads to soothe their way to what he knew were the waiting arms of God. The priest prayed with or for them, whether Catholic, Baptist, or Jew, while they lay bleeding out or suffocating.

Farrucio would never forget those moments when he looked into the eyes of these dying young men, many not yet adults, who were often crying out for their mothers as the moment of death approached.

As the soldiers slipped from this life into the next, this good and holy man often said, "Don't be afraid. God is waiting for you. Be not afraid."

Occasionally, the priest was housed in a tent with another holy man, or with a medic. The soldiers, nearby in their hospital cots, couldn't know that the priest was racked with emotional pain as he prayed for them and tried to absolve them of both their suffering and their sins.

It was just after 3:00 AM on March 3, 1918, that six German infiltrators, armed with razor-sharp knives, crawled on their bellies to unleash a murderous attack aimed at the doctors, nurses, and patients at the mobile hospital.

When the attack began, the priest was sleeping in his cot. He never knew what woke him that morning, but he recalled being shaken, as if an invisible hand grabbed his shoulder and shook him. He heard his name being called, "Edo! Edo! Edo!" He wondered for the rest of his life who had called his name.

Farrucio sat up, listening intently. Two of the attackers were right outside his tent, just ten feet from where he lay. He saw them in silhouette and heard their whispers.

The priest rolled off his cot and lay on the dirt floor, flat on his belly. He couldn't have known that four sentries had already been stabbed to death or that the enemy soldiers were making their way to the hospital tent to wreak havoc and terror.

For a long moment, Farrucio lay on the cold ground trembling and paralyzed with terror. He wanted to crawl out the back of his tent and run for his life, but worse than the fear of dying was the thought that the men and women to whom he ministered were in mortal danger.

Father Edo Farrucio prayed as never before. He begged God to save the medical staff and wounded soldiers until he heard the first of the young doctors attempt to stop the attackers.

Minutes passed, and as Farrucio laid petrified, a young Army physician grunted when a twelve-inch knife punctured his abdomen and ripped up to his sternum. The priest heard the terrible sound the doctor made, and he heard his body land with a thud.

Edo crawled to the door of the tent and watched in the early morning light as the hunched- over Germans quietly advanced toward the hospital tent, knives drawn. Farrucio ran from his tent toward the invaders.

He yelled at them in his accented German, "In the name of God, this is a hospital—stop!"

The soldiers looked at the priest. The lead officer said a few words and gestured toward him with his head. One of his men walked toward Farrucio. The rest of the squad continued their silent advance.

Farrucio stumbled into his tent and fell forward. His out-stretched hand found the bayonet of his tent partner. Until that moment, he had never held a knife, a gun, or a weapon of any kind. After all, he was a priest, a man of peace and of God, and now he held an instrument of death.

The attacker was just twenty feet away and walking toward him with his long knife in his right hand. He was mumbling something to himself.

Farrucio turned toward the approaching enemy soldier. He kept the knife concealed behind his back, but he held it with a tight grip. He somehow got out the words, "Halt! I am a priest!"

The soldier kept advancing.

The holy man knelt on the ground, his heart pounding. He squeezed the handle of the knife.

The enemy soldier stood nearly directly above Farrucio when he raised his knife over his head to strike. When he did so, the priest lunged forward and sunk his tent-partner's knife to the hilt in the man's groin, slicing open a main artery.

The young German screamed in pain as he first pulled back and then fell forward. The attacker's troop-mates heard him yell and assumed the shout of pain came from the American.

In fear and fury and still kneeling, Farrucio stabbed and slashed at the man, striking him a dozen times across the face and throat. The honed knife blade split the attacker's carotid artery and partially severed his neck. The soldier's full body tumbled on top of the priest. As he died, his punctured artery pumped and spewed warm blood onto the priest's face, mouth, nose, down his neck, and onto his shoulders.

Farrucio struggled under the weight of the dead invader until he managed to free himself. As he lay gasping and struggling to breathe, he heard shouting and screaming as the remaining assassins killed two doctors and three young nurses.

The priest got to his knees as he reached for the knife in the hand of his attacker. When he pulled it from the dead hand of the soldier, he got to his feet. Covered with blood, with a knife in each hand, he ran to defend his flock.

Farrucio had the advantage of surprise because the remaining attackers thought he was dead. He came up behind a short, stocky German and stabbed him horizontally with both knives in and through his throat. The invader gurgled, clasped his hands around his neck, fell to his knees, and dropped face first into the semi-frozen mud.

The priest ran behind the next soldier in line, thinking how simple it was to get them from behind. He plunged both knives downward, one along each side of the man's neck. The man ran forward and collapsed against his comrade.

The stabbed man's troop-mate turned when the body fell against him, and Farrucio was on him like an attacking lion. He stabbed the man in the heart and chest a half dozen times. Covered with bright red blood, the crazed priest ferociously slashed and stabbed until two more men lay bleeding to death.

The officer who led the attack was the last invader alive, and he faced off against the priest. The blood-soaked Farrucio held a knife in each hand and crouched low as he moved toward the soldier. His face was bright red and all the German captain could see was the whites of the wide-open eyes of the priest.

Farrucio looked like a mad man but was coldly sane. He was protecting those weak and vulnerable men and souls to whom he was entrusted. He would save them or die trying. The enemy officer took a hard look at the blood-drenched man, saw the bodies of his fallen comrades, dropped his knife, turned, and ran.

Two minutes later, the priest heard a *bang! bang!* from the rifle of a sentry, followed by two more shots. He knew the final invader was dead.

Later that morning, Army Chaplain Captain Father Edo Farrucio, Catholic priest, said Mass over the dead, including the five he himself had killed. He went from corpse to corpse and said Last Rites over each, regardless of nationality.

The priest and the man within him wept, as he often did in this killing place, for the cruelty of men and for the senseless waste of life.

Chapter Thirteen

Late in the evening of the following Saturday, two thugs working for Carlo Lazzori dragged the weakened Renzo from the resort hotel in San Vito Lo Capo. His hands were tied behind his back; a rag had been stuffed into his mouth and tied in place with a thin black strip of cloth.

As they walked past the front desk, one goon said loudly to the innkeeper, "Send the bill to Carlo Lazzori!" They both laughed. The desk clerk turned his back to the three.

The two men chosen to beat Renzo were sadists and were selected by Carlo for that exact reason. Lazzori wanted Tomaso hurt, humiliated, suffering. He wanted to teach him a lesson he would never forget.

Carlo didn't care about the woman who had since been branded as a whore and banished back to her parents, but he needed to mete out a severe punishment to Renzo to save his reputation. After all, this was Sicily and for Carlo Lazzori, Mafia *Capo*, respect was all-important. All else followed.

The two low-lifes loaded the barely conscious Renzo onto a wooden donkey cart and plodded away. Their orders were to go to the edge of the city and beat Renzo severely, but not fatally, and then bring him to the *piazza* where Lazzori would be waiting.

Three kilometers out of town, they pulled the cart to the side of the dark road. One of the men lit a lantern and hung it on a low-hanging tree branch fifty feet into the woods.

The other man yanked Renzo from the wagon by his feet. Renzo's hands were tied, and he couldn't break the fall. The back of his head hit the ground hard with a loud thud. One brute grabbed each foot, and they dragged Renzo toward the lantern light.

The older of the two men, a toothless beanpole of a man, went back to the cart and got a bottle of *grappa*. He drank from the bottle and passed it to his friend. The heavier of the two men walked to Renzo and put his boot on the young man's face. He pressed down, then raised his foot and slammed it into Renzo's unprotected face.

The other man laughed. "Did you hear that? Must've been his nose."

The skinny man took a knife from his boot. He pulled the blade slowly across Renzo's forehead, just above his eyebrows and down his right temple. Renzo screamed in pain; both men laughed.

"Now, you're not so pretty," he said. Blood filled the helpless Renzo's eyes.

The two criminals beat and kicked Renzo without mercy for the next thirty minutes, pausing only to drink *grappa* and to urinate on him. They punched both of his eyes until they were bloody and swollen shut. The beanpole pulled an arm backward until Renzo screamed in agony. The men stomped his chest until they were sure some of his ribs were cracked. Renzo lay there praying for death.

"How's that feel, boy? Was she worth it?"

As he lay there bleeding and moaning, the two assaulters took a break. While they sat smoking and drinking from the bottle, Renzo tried to crawl away but collapsed.

"Let's kill him. We could just say he died."

The other laughed and said, "No, we better not. Lazzori wouldn't like that."

"What else would the boss like? Should we cut off his balls?"

"No good."

"I need to piss," said the fatter of the two men. He unbuttoned his fly and relieved himself again into Renzo's face.

"Now, what?"

"Let's crush his hand!"

With that, the fat man untied Renzo's hands, extended his arm, and forced his clenched fist open. He held Renzo's hand in place with a large boot on his wrist.

"Get that big rock and drop it on his hand."

The toothless man picked up the heavy rock and dropped it onto the back of Renzo's hand. The victim screamed in pain.

"Was she worth it?" asked the smaller man again.

Renzo whimpered through his broken mouth, "Stop... please... stop. Kill me. Kill me."

"We can't kill you, boy. The boss is waiting for you."

Lazzori had ordered the thugs to drop the bloodied and broken Renzo in front of the bar in the *piazza*. He knew that many of his peers and workers would be there drinking and would see the young Tomaso filthy, bleeding, and humiliated. He had instructed Adriana's two tails to be there. They were the only others who knew firsthand what had happened between Renzo and his wife, and he knew without knowing that they had told others.

The wooden cart rolled up at midnight and the unconscious Renzo was carried and dropped at Lazzori's feet. Renzo was bloody and swollen beyond recognition. Both eyes were shut. His right arm was twisted into a grotesque angle, and his left hand was mangled and bloody. He stunk of urine and feces.

The two assailants brought a chair over and lifted Renzo into it.

"Wake him," ordered Lazzori.

The fat man tossed a beer into Renzo's face and said, "Wake up, boy. Wake up!"

Renzo tried to open his swollen eyes.

"Can you hear me, my old friend?" asked Lazzori. "Can you hear me?"

Renzo nodded, almost imperceptibly.

Carlo then spoke to his former friend loudly enough for all to hear. "Renzo Tomaso, you have offended me, and I should kill you. However," he said, strutting and puffing himself up for all to see, "I am a big man, a loving and compassionate man, and I have decided that I will allow you to live. You will live because you once saved my life, and I always pay what I owe."

Lazzori made a grand gesture for the benefit of the observers.

"But now, *Signore* Tomaso, my debt to you has been paid. I have spared your life. There is, however, one more thing that you must do."

The Mafia boss paused to light his long, thin cigar and then continued so all could hear. "You must leave Sicily and never return."

Carlo stepped close to Renzo and spoke directly into his ear. "You must leave this island and never come back. If you defy me, you will die."

"If you so much as try to see her again, I'll sell your little *putana* to my favorite whorehouse. They would pay me well for a fresh, young whore. *Capice?*"

Renzo nodded.

"Oh, and one more thing. If you ever come back to Sicily, your family will suffer more than you can imagine. Do you understand me?"

Renzo whispered, "Yes."

Lazzori said to the torturers "Take him home," and walked away.

The two sadists loaded the beaten young man back onto the donkey cart. They smoked and drank as they transported him to the Tomaso farm.

At 3:00 AM, one hundred yards from the front porch of the Tomaso farmhouse, the fat man pulled back on the reins and stopped the cart. The skinny thug stepped down from the front of the cart and walked around to the back. He pulled Renzo, tied and gagged again, by his feet. He fell crudely to the ground. The two sadists rode away.

Tomas Tomaso woke before sunrise as he did every morning for the past forty years. When he stepped onto the wooden porch to breathe the morning air he loved, he saw a shadowy shape lying not far from the house. Tomas walked toward the shape and then ran to it when he saw his son lying there, near death.

He said, "Oh no. No, no, no. Please, God. Not my son. Not my boy!"

He ran to Renzo and yelled for his wife, "Katerina, come here quickly! Katerina, come! It's Renzo!"

Katerina, in her nightgown, rushed out onto the porch and saw Tomas kneeling over their son. She dropped the towel in her hands and ran to them.

Tomas looked to the sky and said, "Please, God, don't take my son!"

Gianna came onto the porch and saw the badly beaten young man and his parents trying to sit him up. She grabbed the porch railing to keep from fainting. She was terrified and stunned by what she saw and staggered into the house to wake Paolo.

"Paolo, Paolo, Paolo..." she gasped the only words she could manage. Paolo jumped from their bed, saw his wife, who still could not speak, pointing to the front yard. He ran from the house and saw his parents leaning over Renzo. Leonardo was right behind him.

When Paolo saw that his brother was critically injured, he yelled, "Leo, get Dante and fly to town. No time to saddle him— just fly. Go get the doctor! Go, go, go!"

Leonardo, wearing pants and no shirt or shoes, ran to the stable, led Dante out of his stall, jumped on his back, and rode him out of the barn, bareback. When Dante emerged with Leonardo on his back, he reared almost vertically. Leo pulled back on the thick mane of the horse and kicked him hard on both sides. Dante exploded into a full gallop.

Tomas said, "Paolo, go get the shotgun and pistol. Load them. Whoever did this might come back." Paolo ran to the house and returned with the loaded weapons.

Katerina had patched up her sons' and her husband's cuts and farm injuries for many years, but this terrible beating—so hostile, so malicious—shook her to her core. At the sight of her middle son so badly beaten, Katerina froze. She could not function. In her terror, she thought *What kind of monsters would do this to another human being, or even to an animal??*

She rocked back and forth on her knees and said, "He's dying! Oh my God, he's not breathing. Blood is coming out of his eyes and ears. My boy! My boy!"

Renzo lay nearly unconscious, still bleeding and moaning. Katerina couldn't help her son; she was in shock, crying and rocking.

At that moment, and for no reason she would ever understand, Gianna felt no more fear and no panic. She was instead calm and resolute. She walked to her mother-in-law's side and said, "Mother, stop. Hold Renzo's hand."

Still crying and rocking, Katerina took her son's hand in hers.

Gianna knelt next to Renzo and said, "Water."

No one moved.

Gianna looked up and shouted, "*I said, water!*"

Tomas ran to the pump and drew a bucket of water. He carried it back and placed it at Gianna's side. She ripped open Renzo's shirt and removed it along with his boots, socks, and pants. She scooped double handfuls of the cool liquid onto Renzo's wounds.

"More water," she said. "Now!"

She examined Renzo's bloody face, neck, torso, legs, arms, and hands. Both eyes were swollen shut. His shoulder was dislocated, and his arm appeared to be broken. His hand was crushed and at least two fingers and several ribs were broken. His nose was flattened against his face, and there was a long thin cut along his forehead. Gia wet cloths and squeezed more water onto Renzo's wounds, rinsing off both the dried and fresh blood.

"Paolo, tear me some bandages 'this big.'" She showed him the size with her hands.

He ran to the house, returned with a bedsheet, and tore it into the sizes his wife requested. "Tear me a strip one meter long," she ordered.

Gianna said out loud and to no one in particular, "I need tape."

Tape appeared.

The knife wound across Renzo's forehead and curving around his right temple was ten inches long, not too deep, but still bleeding. After she rinsed it, Gianna folded a cloth several times and laid the improvised bandage on top of the cut. She took the long strip of cloth from Tomas, wrapped it around Renzo's head twice, and tied it tight.

Katerina, glad to see her young daughter-in-law calmly and efficiently in command, patted her son's hand and soothed him. "You're home now, Renzo. You're safe. You'll be fine."

Gianna worked on Renzo's injuries for an hour, and before she stopped to take a break, she pulled two broken fingers on his right hand straight and taped them to makeshift splints.

"Blankets," ordered Gia, without looking up. No one moved and Paolo stood looking at her. She looked at him and said, "Paolo! Get me blankets!" Her husband ran to the house.

"We'll leave him here until the doctor arrives," she said.

The four of them—Gianna, Katerina, Tomas, and Paolo, who again held the shotgun—stopped all activity. In the early morning light, just as the sun was appearing, they knelt around Renzo and prayed. Paolo never stopped looking in all directions for danger.

The doctor arrived in his Model T Ford with the shirtless Leonardo atop the galloping Dante leading the way. The physician supervised the carrying of Renzo into the house where he went to work immediately. He dressed the ugly cut on Renzo's forehead, cast the broken arm, reset the smashed fingers, and wrapped his ribcage. He instructed the family as to his care.

The doctor looked at Katerina and said, "You did well."

Katerina said, "She did it all," and nodded toward her daughter-in-law. "Gianna."

"Well," he said. "Gianna, you did a fine job."

When the doctor left and Renzo was asleep in his bed, the family sat at the large table in the kitchen.

The exhausted Katerina began, "He will recover. Thank God."

Paolo said, "The bastards that did this to him will pay!"

Gianna looked at her husband. She stood and spoke in a voice none of them had ever heard before. She said, "There will be no *vendetta*. No revenge at all. If there is," she continued, looking directly at Paolo, "...If there is, I will not go to America. Your children will not go. This, I promise you."

Paolo said, "So we should let it go like nothing happened? That's my brother lying in there, beaten half to death. Someone has to pay for this."

Gia replied, "I have asked you for nothing over the years, but this I demand," she said, surprised at her show of strength. "If you value me, if you value your family, there will be no revenge."

Paolo, Leonardo, and Tomas sat quietly, stunned by this new voice of Gianna. Katerina stood next to her daughter-in-law and said, "Gianna is right. There can be no *vendetta*. This stops here, now. *Basta!*"

Gia looked at her husband and said, "Not by your hand, Paolo. Not by your hand or by any other."

The two women left the kitchen to tend to their patient.

Renzo slept for the better part of the next five days. Slowly, he showed small improvements and grew a little stronger. On the morning of the sixth day, Renzo stood without assistance and walked into the kitchen. He took his usual place at the table. His body was less swollen but clearly damaged. He wore a cast on his arm and fingers. His ribs had begun to heal, and he was breathing a little better.

Tomas came in from the barn and joined his son at the table.

Katerina brought them both coffee and turned to the stove to make breakfast.

Tomas spoke first. "So, I can only imagine that you're not going to tell us who did this to you or why."

Renzo looked at his father. He did not speak.

"As I thought," said, Tomas. "Word of what you did and who did this to you is everywhere, so let's just hope you learned an important lesson. The world does not revolve around you. You cannot just take what you want or what you think will make you feel good."

Renzo was feeling the emotional upheaval for the first time. He was shaking with both relief and from memory of the beating. He feared for Adriana and hoped she was safe.

"Papa, I fell in love with a woman for the first time in my life. Now, look at me!"

Mama said softly, "That's enough for now. Stop talking and eat."

Katerina put the food on the table. She wasn't eating but sat at the table anyway to enforce her demand that they stop bickering.

The three sat in silence.

Finally, after what seemed an hour but wasn't, Renzo, through his swollen lips and with tear-filled eyes said, "I will go to America."

He stood slowly and walked from the room.

Chapter Fourteen

The actions of Father Edo Farrucio the night of the attack at the hospital compound saved the lives of twenty-one hospitalized soldiers, one physician, and three nurses. For his heroic actions, the priest received the French Croix de Guerre and the United States Congressional Medal of Honor.

Two days after he defended the field hospital, Father Edo Farrucio, the humble priest to every man, again stood at a make-shift altar in the middle of a battlefield. As he made the sign of the cross over the men who sat and kneeled in front of him, he led them in prayer.

Farrucio and some in his audience said together, "In the name of the Father and the Son and of the Holy Spirit."

The memories of the terrible sights, the stench of death, the carnage, and the pain and suffering the priest witnessed in France affected him deeply and would shape much of his spirit and his thinking for the rest of his life.

The priest felt he now better understood evil, fear, suffering, and death. In November of 1918, a few days after the Armistice to end the Great War was signed, Father Edo made his way on foot and by train to Paris.

Hungry to experience normal life again, Edo spent the next two weeks walking the avenues and boulevards of the beautiful city. It was difficult for Farrucio to understand how such violence and devastation could happen in such a beautiful country, or anywhere, for that matter.

The priest stopped at a different outdoor café every day and talked to locals in the little French he knew or in his native Italian. The locals thanked him for helping save their country.

Edo made it a point to visit the *Cathedral of Notre Dame*. The beauty of the enormous and finely detailed building stood in absolute contrast to the battlefields he had been on just a week before. The basilica was beyond anything he could have imagined. The priest visited the Stations of the Cross and said a prayer at each.

Farrucio took a seat in a middle row to better see the look of the cathedral and the altar as a parishioner would. He prayed the rosary and thanked God for letting him live and putting him in a position where he could serve soldiers and save lives.

Edo missed the prayer and contemplation he had enjoyed every morning in his private chapel at *Our Lady of Divine Mercy*. He missed home.

For the next week, from morning until night, the priest walked the narrow streets and the big, beautiful boulevards of Paris. Life had changed for him; he had killed men and he now had doubts about his calling to the priesthood. He was searching for answers.

The priest entered every small or large Catholic Church he encountered. He always dipped the tips of his fingers in the font of holy water as he entered, then selected an aisle, and crossed himself before entering the row. He attended dozens of Masses and prayed long and hard, pleading for his God to embrace him.

In the streets and parks of Paris, Farrucio saw children of all ages playing every sort of game. As he watched them play, run, and kick soccer balls, he realized more than ever that he was homesick for his street, his kids, and his church.

In every cathedral, basilica, and church he visited, Farrucio lit a candle for each of the lives he took that early morning at the field hospital. He didn't pray for the soldiers killed in battle because he knew they were in Paradise.

Instead, the priest prayed and wept for the parents of the dead warriors, whether German, French, American, or British. From his experiences as a priest, he knew that the mothers and the fathers of the dead boys cried for years through their broken hearts, and he prayed that God would ease their grief and suffering.

Even though the enemy invaders were there to kill him and others—and there was no choice but to act—the faces of the men he killed haunted him and kept him from sleep too many nights.

Before he began his voyage home, the priest wanted to see the Vatican and attend Mass in the *Basilica of Saint Peter*. He left Paris and headed for Rome by train. Soldiers, all happy to be going home, filled the train.

Upon Farrucio's arrival at Vatican City, the soft-spoken manager of the visitor's residence greeted him warmly. Soon, he unpacked his few belongings in a small, private room overlooking the majestic Papal Gardens. Beginning that evening, Farrucio spent hours in the cathedral deep in prayer and lost in thought.

A few days after his arrival, as he sat in a center pew in *St. Peter's*, he heard a rustling of robes and heard men's voices approaching from the entrance to the Basilica. He turned and saw the entourage of His Holy Eminence Pope Benedict XV, followed by his staff of five priests of varying ages and two secretaries.

The Pope stopped and sat beside Farrucio. "Your Eminence," said Farrucio. He kissed the papal ring on the extended hand. "It is an honor to meet you, Your Eminence."

The Pope addressed the much younger priest. "Father, I've seen you here for days. I've watched you in prayer. Is there anything you'd like to speak to me about? What troubles you this way?"

Farrucio thought for a moment and said, "I'm a neighborhood priest from America. I serve the sick and the poor. Your Eminence, I joined the American army to help soldiers spiritually. But I had to decide who would live and who would die. Was I right to do so? Shouldn't life and death be in the hands of God?"

Pope Benedict replied, "My son, God put you there in His wisdom. Maybe that was why."

"I killed five men, Your Eminence."

The Pope, ignoring Edo's statement said, "Father, do you doubt your faith?"

"No, I don't doubt at all, not at all. I only wonder if I am still fit to be a priest. I question only my actions. I do not doubt my faith."

The Pope placed his fingertips on Edo's cheek and brought their eyes into direct contact. His Holiness Pope Benedict made the sign of the cross on Father Farrucio's forehead. He said, "*Ego te absolvo a peccatis tuis.* I absolve you of all sins."

A chubby, bald priest from the group cleared his throat and said, "Your Eminence, the Ambassador is waiting."

"Yes, of course," said the Pope. He stood, smiled at Farrucio and said, "Your flock needs you, Father." Pope Benedict walked away, his entourage fussing close behind him.

Father Edo Farrucio slept that night as he had not slept in a long time. He felt that that he was in a safe, warm place for the first time in too long. He felt restored both physically and spiritually.

A week later, Edo began his journey home. A boat from Rome brought him to the French port city of Marseilles where he boarded a troop carrier for the journey across the Atlantic. Ten days later, he got on a train headed from Baltimore to Chicago.

Farrucio first went to his quarters in the rectory of *Our Lady of Divine Mercy*. While he was gone, his staff had only dusted the rooms and had not moved or changed anything.

He renewed friendships, attended Mass, ate home cooking and slept for the better part of the next two days. On the third day, he received a phone call. "Father Farrucio, hold the line for the Archbishop, please."

The high-ranking priest came to the phone. "Edo, my boy! Welcome home!"

"Thank you, Father," said Edo.

"I'm glad you're back, safe and sound. Come to the Residence for lunch today. We have some things to discuss."

Edo arrived at the Residence and was greeted warmly by the Archbishop. The two priests embraced. Lunch was served to them, and they talked extensively about the war and about Farrucio's encounter with Pope Benedict.

"Edo, you're famous for what you did over there. The Church is proud of you. So am I. What was it like?"

Farrucio said, "Your Eminence, I'd rather not talk about it. I served the soldiers. I did what I had to do. I survived. I came home."

"Very well, Edo. If you ever need to talk or to confess, I'll always be here for you."

"Thank you, Father. I'm just glad to be home and want to get back to my work at *Our Lady*."

The Archbishop stood and said, "Come to the window, Edo. The church has a welcome home gift for you."

Edo stood and walked to the window. He said, "A gift for me, Your Eminence? I don't need anything."

Farrucio looked out of the second-floor window and saw a new 1918 Pierce–Arrow automobile parked below.

The Pierce-Arrow sported long running boards on either side. The body of the car was a highly polished medium green with a black roof. The passenger compartment was high and square. The large vehicle could easily fit six or eight people. A spare tire was mounted on the car, just in front of the passenger's side door. Another spare was attached to the rear of the car. The spokes on the wheels and spares were a matching green color.

Farrucio turned to the Archbishop and said, "I can't accept this, Your Eminence! It's too expensive. I'm just a neighborhood priest."

"You're a neighborhood priest who is known around the world, now. You're a hero, Edo, and a hero of the Church."

"It's not right," said Edo. "We can use the money to feed the hungry or get them to doctors and dentists. Please, Your Eminence, no."

"Edo, we feel that in the long run, the people in your parish will be better off to respect the wealth of the church. Wealth says power, you know, and our parishioners need to know that the church has both."

Farrucio said, "Father, please. I cannot accept this."

"Edo, listen to me. This is not a request. You will accept the gift. You will keep it clean. You will not sell it."

Father Farrucio stood silently.

The Archbishop added, "You will use it to do God's work as you see fit."

"I understand, Your Eminence."

The Archbishop said, "A reporter and a photographer are downstairs waiting for you to accept the gift. So, let's go."

A few minutes later, the two priests stood in front of the shiny new car. They shook hands and smiled for the camera. The caption under the photo in the newspaper said, "Hero Priest Gets Welcome Home Gift."

Chapter Fifteen

"Leo, you ride Sancho. We're riding Dante," ordered Paolo. Leo didn't like the idea of having to ride the donkey, but he loved going on one last overnight hunting trip with his brothers.

Leonardo walked to the small corral, entered, and placed the halter on Sancho, who didn't object. The animal had been a part of this family for many years and he was always agreeable.

With Dante and Sancho hitched to the rail in front of the farmhouse, Leonardo and Renzo got their shotguns and shells. Paolo got his powerful pistol, tucked it in his belt, and joined his brothers. They were going out for rabbits and maybe some birds. They were camping overnight, but he brought the pistol for some target shooting and for protection—just in case.

"Let's go to the pond and set up camp," said Renzo. They had camped at this secluded spot many times over the years. It was the perfect place: secluded, quiet, and with plenty of game in the surrounding forest.

The day before, Leonardo had gone to visit Father Fiori in the rectory for some badly needed advice. Nardo sat in the waiting room of the priest's office, anxious to meet with the red faced, white-haired priest.

The room smelled of old, well-used furniture, musty books, and cleaning soap. Sister Maria, an ancient nun, sat behind a desk. She had known Leo and his brothers since their birth. After she greeted Leo, she stood, walked into an adjoining room, and told Father Fiori of his arrival. The nun returned, smiled at Leo, sat back down, and continued to sort and file papers.

She said, "He'll be right out, Leonardo."

How can she sit in this heat in those heavy black clothes? Nardo thought. "Thank you," he said.

The nun asked, "Leonardo, have you been honoring our Savior?"

"Yes, Sister," he replied.

The priest burst into the room, as enthusiastic as ever.

"Leonardo! How are you, my boy? Glad to see you!"

Father Fiori knew the young man well. He had baptized him, heard all his confessions, given him his First Communion, and confirmed him in the Catholic faith. The two relocated into the priest's office and took seats next to each other in front of the cleric's desk. Fiori turned his chair to face Leonardo.

He said, "Tell me what's on your mind, Nardo."

"Father, you know I want to attend the seminary. I want to become a priest. Now, my parents want me to go to America with my brothers."

The priest replied, "Yes, I know. They talked to me about it over many months. This separating of your family...is impossible for them, too. They don't want to do it."

Leo just looked at the priest.

"You know that your father is a thoughtful man, one who considers all the possibilities. He thinks there is no future here. Your mother agrees. I agree."

"But everything will change," the seventeen-year-old said. "Our family will end..."

The priest put his hand in the air and interrupted Leo. "Your family will not end, Leonardo. It is separating so that it can grow bigger and stronger, not ending. There's a big difference."

"Okay, but things will never be the same. I don't think I want to go. I want to stay here, stick to my plan."

Father Fiori said, "It's a dilemma for you, I know. You can stay here, attend seminary, and become a priest. Or you can follow your parent's wishes for your future. Go to America. Work and go to school there. They need priests in the New World too, you know."

Leo replied, "So, here we are. Paolo and his family are going, and so is Renzo, now—you know what happened, right?"

Fiori nodded.

"My parents are moving to town with my grandparents. And then there's me. I want to be with my brothers, and I want to be with my parents. And I want to go to school. I don't know what to do, Father. What would you do in my shoes?"

The priest replied, "I can't tell you what you should or shouldn't do, Leo. Pray on it, think about it. You'll do the right thing. If you stay here, you'll have distance between you and your brothers, but they will always be your brothers."

"I know, Father, I know. I just don't want the split."

"It has to be, Leonardo. As hard as it is, the separation has to happen."

"I know you're right, Father, but I hate it."

"Leo, I have to get back to work. Confessions, you know," smiled Fiori.

With that, the priest etched the sign of the cross onto the young man's forehead with his thumb and looked hard at this boy he had known since birth.

"Leo, pray for guidance. Pray for a sign. It will come. I promise."

The brother's ride into the woods took two hours, but they enjoyed the trip. They set up camp next to the pond and watered and fed the animals before they walked into the deep woods to hunt for their supper. The three walked along in a line with twenty feet between each of them. They were quiet knowing that their voices would scare prey away.

An hour into the deep forest, with not a shot fired, the brothers stopped cold in their tracks when they heard sounds coming from a large patch of heavy growth fifty feet ahead. The sound was the snorting of a massive boar. The brothers had seen the animal on several occasions over the years but always managed to avoid contact.

The boar raised his head and sniffed the air. Focusing on the source of the strange odor, he spotted the three men squatting behind bushes, trying to stay hidden. There would be no avoiding the monster this day: The boar was about to attack.

The massive animal had survived in these woods for a dozen years, and he had the scars from fighting off challengers to prove that he was the dominate male. His tusks were a foot long and easily sharp enough to maim or kill.

The beast emerged from the brush and stood motionless for a moment or two, then scraped billows of dirt into the air with his hoof and snorted. He had made up his mind to charge. It was too late for the brothers to run. They had no choice: They would have to kill the animal to protect themselves.

The boar broke fast and charged the brother closest to him: Leonardo.

Paolo, armed only with his pistol, commanded the shotgun-wielding Renzo. "Shoot it, Renz! Shoot it!!"

Renzo fired both barrels of his shotgun into the boar, but the blast only forced the animal to stumble and pause for a moment.

The pellets glanced off the thick hide of the animal spraying a pink mist into the air.

Injured and incensed, the boar shook his head and resumed his attack on Leo. Renzo was fumbling for another shell to stuff into his shotgun. Leo stood with his shotgun ready but froze.

"Shoot the damn thing. Leo!" ordered Paolo.

Leo didn't move.

"Leo! Shoot it! Shoot it, now!!"

Leo stood frozen in place.

Paolo, pistol drawn and in hand, ran to stand in front of Leonardo to shield him and receive the full charge of the boar to protect his brother.

The older Tomaso brother aimed his large pistol at the charging beast and fired. The slug exploded from the barrel of the gun with a loud BANG! and struck the dirt in front of the raging animal. Paolo fired again, twice. The bullets seared from his pistol and flew past the boar, missing his head by a few centimeters.

The crazed animal, squealing and snorting, continued to charge directly at Paolo who stood motionless, protecting Leonardo. This attack was happening in slow motion, and Paolo knew he would only have time to fire one more round before the boar ripped him apart.

Paolo took careful aim. He squeezed the trigger. The shot split the day, and the large bullet scorched through the air. It struck the charging wild pig in the center of his forehead. The strike scattered flesh, hide, teeth, and fragments of tusk into the air.

At the instant of impact, the enormous animal squealed and dropped to the ground, his head ripped half off his shoulders. The momentum of the beast propelled him forward, and he slid the last ten feet, his front legs splayed wide, stopping at Paolo's feet, dead.

Paolo turned to his young brother.

"Leo, are you okay?"

Leo was shaking.

"Oh my God, Paolo. I couldn't pull the trigger. I couldn't do it. Thank you. You saved me. He could have killed you—but you protected me!"

Paolo mussed his brother's hair. "Just as long as you're all right, Nardo. I'll always protect you."

He turned to the boar, drew his sharp hunting knife from his boot, and began to field dress the animal. Renzo took hold of the rear feet of the beast. Leonardo watched. The three brothers knew they had narrowly averted a tragedy.

It was Renzo who broke the silence. He said simply, "He's a big one."

Two hours later, as the sun was nearly set for the night, Leo built a fire. The men roasted rabbits they had shot after the episode with the boar, which was dressed and hung by its rear hooves from a nearby tree branch.

The brothers ate the fire-grilled rabbit with chunks of cheese and bread dipped in olive oil. They drank strong red wine. The three were lost in their own thoughts and sat quietly for a long while.

It was Renzo who spoke first. "Hey, little brother. Why do you want to be a priest? You should come with us to America. Start a new life in a new world. Make money. Have fun. Like Pa says, *a better life*. You know?"

The vicious beating Renzo suffered had faded to only a bad memory. The one remaining physical mark was the long, thin scar across his forehead. Despite an occasional nightmare, Renzo was finally learning to smile again. He had accepted that he had lost Adriana forever and that he was leaving Sicily. In some ways, he looked forward to a new life.

Paolo added, "He's right, Leo. We should stay together, like always."

Renzo said, "It'll be fun. You can get a woman, maybe two." Renzo knew that Leonardo had never been with a woman, and so he would tease until his brother's face blushed red.

Paolo put more dry branches on the fire. He loved the smell of the burning wood.

Renzo said, "You know, Leo, if you don't come with us, I won't have anybody to push around. You don't want to do that to me, do you? Come with us, man. You know you want to."

Leo said, "I kind of want to g,o but I think Ma and Pa will need me here."

"Is that why you're not going?"

"Mostly."

Paolo looked up and said, "Leo, they'll be fine. They have enough money to live out their days and to take care of the old folks. They want you to go with us."

Nardo said, "But I'm already signed up in the seminary. It's too late."

Renzo added, "There are seminaries in America, too. And who knows? Once you get off this island, you may meet one of those... um...what are they called again?... um...oh yeah. One of those girls."

Paolo, protecting his little brother as always said, "Enough with the girl talk, Renz."

With that Renzo dropped to his knees and said, "Leonardo, I am begging you to come with us to America. Please, Leo, please. We three have always been together. Let's keep it that way. Please."

"He's right," added Paolo.

Leo barely smiled, but that was the way he was.

"Fine," he said. "I'll go to America. I'll go to America."

Renzo leaned toward Leonardo, hugged him, and kissed him on the head. "I love you, my brother! America!"

Leonardo said, "I'll go, but I still want to be a priest."

Chapter Sixteen

"Greetings to all! Greetings to all!" Tomas Tomaso spoke from the raised platform to the one hundred or so guests who gathered at the Tomaso farm. The visitors assembled tightly around the makeshift stage to better hear the speakers.

"*Ciao! Benvenuti*! Hello! Greetings!" Tomas repeated louder to get everyone's attention. The crowd grew quiet and gathered even closer.

Tomas began, "Our friends. Our family. Katerina and I thank you for being here today. We thank you for the respect and the love you show us."

He paused to eye the crowd. When he was sure he had the full attention of everyone, he continued. "Today is a sad day and today is also a happy day. Our son Paolo, his wife Gianna—my wonderful daughter-in-law, who is like a daughter to me—and their children, Luca and Isabella, are leaving soon for America, as are our boys Renzo and Leonardo. To watch over them all, Gianna's mother *Nonna* Stella is going as well."

Someone in the crowd yelled, "We'll miss them, Tomas!"

Tomas paused and looked into the crowd. He smiled.

"We Tomasos love our homeland, but poverty, no jobs, crime, government corruption...well, you all know. We cannot grow here. We cannot thrive. Our children will not have the chance to have their own children."

"*E justo!* That is right!"

"So, do not think of this as a separation; it is a prospering and a growing of our family."

"You are right," said another in the crowd, loudly.

"And so, we must do this split, as painful as it is. We will cry tomorrow, but tonight we celebrate! So, eat and drink and dance, my friends, and say your goodbyes. Raise your voices with me to my family and to America!"

The crowd cheered together, "America! America!"

Tomas Tomaso waved his hands in the air for quiet and said, "Father Fiori, bless us!"

The celebration could not officially begin until Father Francesco Fiori blessed the food and the event. The chubby, white-haired holy man climbed onto the platform.

Fiori began, "I went to school with Katerina and Tomas, and we have been friends for life. As a newly ordained priest years ago, I had the great fortune to perform their wedding ceremony."

Tomas and Katerina stood at the side of the stage and smiled at each other.

"I have known Paolo, Renzo, and Leonardo since their births. I baptized them, helped to teach them our faith, gave them their First Holy Communions, confirmed them in the Church, and heard their confessions. These are wonderful young men, and they will be a loss to our country and to our community."

Gianna began to cry a little. Paolo put his arm around her.

"But there is no doubt that what Tomas said is true. It is time for migration to a new land, and this is the way it must be."

Tomas took Katerina's hand.

"With God's blessings, then, for safe travel and success and happiness in their new home," the priest made a large sign of the cross in the air, "I bless this celebration in the name of the Father, and of the Son and of the Holy Ghost.

The crowd watched Father Fiori and waited for his announcement.

The priest looked around the assemblage, smiled his big smile, and said, "Let's eat!"

While on some days, the adults went hungry so the kids could eat their fill, the Tomasos looked forward to special occasions with great anticipation. They stored food for weeks and left fat animals un-slaughtered to save them for those great and important events.

On those special occasions, such as weddings and Communions, the extended family gathered, feasted, danced, and celebrated together.

At the more significant events, in addition to the entire Tomaso clan, all the in-laws, the mayor, and other village officials would attend. The priests and the nuns from the local churches were invited as well.

Today's event was not just special. It was a momentous occasion and turning point for the Tomas and Katerina Tomasos. This was a going-away celebration, and a feast to end all feasts.

Twenty people cooked and served. Some of them worked over hot grills, others baked and carried *paste*. Others pried open oysters and clams, then rinsed them and arranged them on large platters atop ice brought from town for this special day. Table after table was filled with hot and cold meats, fish, and vegetables. The ladies spent days baking bread, shaping pastas, and making sauces, cookies, and pastries.

A favorite of all was the tender, juicy, breaded and baked *pollo limone* made from farm chickens and lemons grown on the Tomaso farm.

A special, six-foot-long grill that Tomas made years before was brought out from the barn and erected near the serving tables. *Polpi e calamari,* pulled from the Mediterranean that morning, were placed into buckets of marinade *of aglio, olio di oliva, limone, e sale e pepe*, where they stayed most of the day.

Hardwood, aged years for just this purpose, was ignited in the bellies of the grills and allowed the time necessary to achieve the perfect level of heat. Just at mealtime, dozens of the marinated baby *polpi e calamari* were tossed on the hot grill and allowed to sizzle to perfection. They were then transferred to yet more large platters and placed on the many tables to be enjoyed by the hungry guests.

There were platters of *carciofi ripieni*, red-sauced *braciole*, gigantic bowls of *pasta pomodoro* and more of *pasta con piselli*. To accompany all were a dozen large bowls of *caponata*. Large, thick rectangles of *pizze* were baked in an outdoor oven and served in squares to the many guests.

The dozens of kids in attendance drank milk or lemonade. The adults drank homemade red wine, *grappa* or *limoncello* made from the finest lemons from the Tomaso orchard. People came from miles around, and each brought still more prepared food, wine, or fresh fish.

In addition to *La Famiglia* Tomaso, townspeople of all positions and rank happily attended the event knowing they were going to eat wonderful food, drink perfect wine, and spend hours renewing friendships.

After eating and drinking for several hours, and just before the evening turned into night, torches, large bonfires and lanterns were lit. The band played; dancing began.

It was customary that the first dance would be the priest and the matriarch of the family, Katerina. Tonight would be no exception. Father Francesco, his rotund face now redder than usual from *vino*, his mound of snowy hair sitting on his head like a white hat, approached Katerina Tomaso.

He said to his old friend, *"Signora per favore, ballare con me.*

Katerina smiled and walked to the center of the dance area with the priest. They danced to the ballad *Mi votu e mi revotu.* Before the first dance was over, young people in the crowd began clapping and shouting, *"Tarantella! Tarantella!"*

The band broke into the faster tempo *tarantella* and, as a dozen people came to the dance floor, Father Fiori and Katerina returned to their seats.

The new dancers formed a circle in boy-girl order and began the hopping and gyrating dance that was popular throughout Italy.

The band would play on well past midnight.

Before the end of the feast, it was certain that many of the men would be arguing politics or sports, and most would be drunk. The party ended a few hours after midnight. Most of the guests left in horse or donkey-drawn carriages. A few drove home in horseless carriages. Those who drank too much slept in the field and left when the sun rose.

Guests who slept longer into the morning were served hot coffee, fresh baked rolls, and peach marmalade at an outside table before they left.

It was a celebration that would be remembered and spoken of for years to come.

Chapter Seventeen

"Tomas, are we doing the right thing?" Katerina asked without turning to look at him. "Sending them to America? Maybe we should keep them closer ...send them to *Roma* or *Napoli*?"

Tomas Tomaso sat sipping coffee at the kitchen table.

His wife stood not ten feet away, looking out the window toward the stone barn.

"Kati, we've talked this through for a year. The future is in America. Italy...who knows? With the war going on now and the rotten government in this country...crime... taxes...you know it's the right thing."

"But we may never see them again, Tomas, and I cannot stand that thought. How can you live with that?"

Tomaso stood and put his hands on his wife's shoulders. She put her hand up and touched his face. He kissed her hand.

"Listen to me. We will see them again. We will. After the old folks are gone, we'll go to America, too."

Tomas didn't entirely believe his words, even as he spoke them. He doubted that they would never have enough money to immigrate. His hope was that the three boys would send for their parents when they made their fortunes.

Katerina swung the door open, stepped onto the porch, and looked at the panorama that was their farm, now sold. *All those years...all that work...* she thought... *Our children born here...They grew here and learned here.*

Their country had failed them, and soon their sons would be moving on to new lives. She dabbed her wet eyes with the cotton handkerchief she had not put down in days.

Tomas sat quietly at the kitchen table. It was two days since the big send-off party and his head still ached from too much drink. He poured himself another coffee, enjoyed the smell of the kitchen, and the quiet of the moment.

Gianna entered the room and kissed her father-in-law on the cheek. She said, "Good morning, Papa."

Tomas smiled but didn't hear her; he was lost in thought.

Gianna wanted to sit quietly with this man she loved and respected. Katerina came back into the kitchen from the porch where she was thinking about today and breathing the cool, fresh morning air. She wore a black dress, just as she did every day.

One by one the family would come to the kitchen table. Each knew, although they never talked about it, that this would be the last meal they would share. Hearts were breaking.

Katerina had cried most of the night before. Countless times during the preceding weeks, she asked herself, *How will I live without ever seeing my grandchildren again? How can I possibly kiss them goodbye?* She couldn't bear the thought of it, but she knew all eyes would soon be on her. She knew, too, that as the equal head of the family, she must be strong.

Paolo came in from the barn and walked to the sink to wash his hands. He then sat at the table next to his wife.

Leonardo entered the kitchen from the front living room, smiling as usual. He was carrying a book, which he placed on the countertop.

"Good morning," he said.

Nardo had enjoyed the party but didn't drink much. He spent a lot of the evening watching people dancing and enjoying themselves.

Last to arrive was Renzo, still a little drunk from his private drinking of the night before and tired from not enough sleep. He sat at the table without speaking.

Nonna Cassio sat quietly at the table as well.

The long wooden table held the family of nine. As Katerina looked at them all assembled for this last breakfast together, she remembered Paolo, Renzo, and Leonardo—grown men, now— as young boys, sitting at the same table squabbling about some problem important to only them.

In her mind's eye, Katerina saw dozens of precious birthday parties and celebrations they all enjoyed together at this very table.

Now, her sons, Gianna, and her grandchildren were leaving for a foreign land. She forced herself to snap out of her private thoughts and smiled at her beautiful family. Katerina absorbed each facial detail.

Just at that moment, they all heard a rapping on the screen door as it swung open simultaneously. Father Fiori, a puffy ball of energy as always, entered the kitchen.

"Ciao, tutti, ciao, tutti." The priest said, "I thought I could get a good breakfast here this morning, and I see I'm just in time. And just in time to bless the meal."

Tomas knew the priest was there to give the family much-needed support, and both he and Katerina were grateful for his unexpected arrival. The table seemed more complete. Father Fiori started and maintained a continuous line of chatter, jokes, and stories that put a smile on all the faces, even Katerina's.

With everyone seated, Gianna and Katerina carried platters of hot and cold food leftover from the feast to the large wooden table. They brought over sliced ham, cold roasted chicken, several loaves of bread, pizzas, beans, and cold pastas. Gianna put a pitcher of fresh milk, another of cold water, and a large pot of steaming coffee on the table with cups and a bowl of sugar.

The Tomasos and the priest ate this last meal together, all aware of its significance. The family was dividing that day.

After breakfast, Katerina felt that she needed to speak to her three sons. She asked her husband to gather the boys on the front porch. Father Fiori stayed in the kitchen to help *Nonna* with the clean-up.

The oak-planked porch was sometimes big and sometimes small.

Over the years, on rainy days, the kids often played under the shelter of its roof. On many evenings, Katerina or Gianna would read to Luca and Isabella on the porch until it became too dark. Injured birds, baby bunnies, and a myriad of other creatures, including caterpillars, spiders, and scorpions, were brought to the porch by the children for further inspection or medical attention.

As years rolled by, Tomas Tomaso would often gather his sons on the porch to discuss farm business or family matters. Tomas chose the porch to sit and talk with the two Mafia bosses who came to call on him after the killing of Lurio Scarletto.

It was on this porch that Tomas wept when his mother died years before. On hot nights, Tomas and Katerina would get a cool drink and sit on the porch. He smoked while Katerina knitted or sewed. They both loved those quiet times together.

This morning, the porch would be used for a talk Katerina wanted and needed to have with her sons before they sailed for America. The decisions were made, the celebrating done, and now it was time to ensure a smart departure and a safe and proper life in the New World.

Katerina sat in one of five chairs positioned around a hand-made wooden table, her back to the wall. The first to arrive, as usual, was Paolo. He kissed his mother and sat.

Next, was Leonardo, smiling and happy as always. He kissed his mother and sat next to his oldest brother.

The last to arrive was Renzo. He was never a happy person, nor content, and this had always been of concern to his parents, neither of whom could understand why their middle son was so different, why he chose the wrong path, and why he had so often made the wrong decisions.

Tomas took the fifth chair and sat next to his wife. Gianna stood on the porch near the door to listen for her children. She wanted to hear this talk from the woman who was such an important part of her life.

Katerina sat with her hands folded in her lap and, as her family and her life assembled around her, she felt overwhelmed with love.

"We all knew this day would come," she began the talk she had played in her mind a dozen times before. "Now, it's here, and I have things to say to each of you."

"The oldest first: Paolo. You are my first child, and you have grown into a fine young man. You are blessed with a wonderful wife and two beautiful, healthy children. Now, you are leaving this island, your home, and your parents for a foreign land. You're smart and will always do what's right and take care of your family. Your father and I rely on you for that. Know that you are loved and will be in our thoughts and prayers every day. Every day, Paolo."

Paolo replied, "Yes, Ma, I love you and Pa and this family more than anything."

Now, she swung her focus to her second son, Renzo.

"Renzo, your father and I adore you, as we do your brothers. I worry most for you and that's because we have failed to bring you into the family fold. You have been wild, but I know that you will find your way. Carry our love for you in your heart, son. Know that you are loved and will be deeply missed by your father and me until the day we die."

Renzo didn't speak. He just looked at this mother.

"The feel-good, shortcut way is not the true man's path. In fact, it is the harder path to follow. Don't forget that you were nearly beaten to death because of your ways. Take this advice with you: Marry a good woman and start a family. Keep them close to you. Work for your money. There is no other good way."

Renzo did not speak.

"Leonardo," she smiled at her youngest. "My Nardo."

Leo looked at his mother and smiled. "Yes, Mama."

"Leonardo, you will not be happy in your life unless you are learning and creating. Make sure you get a job in America where you can use your brain more than your back."

"Yes, Mama."

"You know how you are loved."

"Yes, Mama, I do," Nardo's eyes were getting misty.

Katerina continued to all three of her sons. "You are a part of a family that can look back for centuries. Where you are going, no one will care about your history. You will get jobs and work hard. That's what you must do. Do not be tempted to break any laws," she continued looking mostly at Renzo. "Earn your way. In the days ahead, you will have only each other. No one else will care about you. Stay together. Take care of each other. Do you all hear me?"

"Yes, Mama," she heard from Paolo and Leonardo.

"Renzo, did you hear me? Gianna?"

"Yes, I heard you."

Katerina went on. "I expect you to honor our traditions to keep us alive in your hearts." She looked over at Gianna. "That is for you, too, daughter. Honor and respect each other, your friends, and your employers."

She continued, "Above all—hear this well—is family." She looked into the eyes of each of her three sons. "First and always, family."

"Yes, Mama."

"Next to God, family is the most powerful force on Earth. Do you all hear me? Our family can be strained and broken but will always heal. This family will go on long after death comes for each of us."

Tears wet Gianna's cheeks thinking of how much she would miss this woman and her father-in-law, this farm, and this life.

Katerina stood. "Now, you boys are men and you need to be strong. Go do what you must. Lead good lives. It's almost time to leave for the ship."

Chapter Eighteen

Isabella was wide-eyed as trunks and suitcases were carried from the rooms of the farmhouse and piled up on the porch.

"Where are we going, Mama?" asked four-year-old Luca.

"We're going to America today, my darling,'" was the faux-cheerful reply.

The boy ran out of the farmhouse to watch the loading of the cart.

The thought of the long journey that lay ahead was intimidating to Gianna, but she couldn't show that doubt and worry to her children.

She had never left the area surrounding the two farms, and now she was traveling halfway around the world. Gianna had never imagined that a life-changing event like this would happen to her family. She was happy on the farm, even with the problems, and didn't want to leave. She understood the reasoning behind the move in her head but not in her heart.

When the young mother finished brushing and braiding Isabella's hair, she turned to see her mother-in-law watching her and her little daughter. At her age and with an ocean between them, the grandmother knew that she would likely never see her precious Isabella and Luca again. Just the thought of it was breaking her heart.

Katerina said, "Luca, come to *Nonna*."

The young boy, dressed in a suit, his hair slicked back, was ready for the trip. He walked to his grandmother. Katerina cupped his face in her two hands and looked into the big brown eyes she loved. She wanted one last private moment to imbed the face of her grandson in her mind forever, not that she could ever forget anything about him.

"Look at how nice you look!" she said.

Luca said, "I don't want to leave you, *Nonna*. Don't make me go."

"It's OK, my darling, it's OK. You'll be with Mama and Papa and Isabella. And *Nonna* Cassio." She hugged the boy so he wouldn't see her tears.

He said, "But I won't ever see you again, *Nonna*."

Katerina said, "Luca, Luca, you can see me every day! Just close your eyes and think of me, and you'll see me smiling at you. You'll see our farm, *Nonno*, even Dante and Sancho."

"Are you sure, *Nonna*?"

She said, "Certainly! And you need to take care of your sister, right? And Mama and Papa need you."

He said, "OK, *Nonna*."

She kissed the boy on both cheeks. "You'll be back to Sicily one day, Luca. You'll be back."

"Really, *Nonna*? Really?"

"Yes, definitely. Now give me a big hug and go say goodbye to Sancho—but stay clean."

The boy put his arms around his grandmother and hugged her tight. The grandmother closed her eyes and felt the love from this small boy. She thought, *Is there a better feeling in the world than a hug from a child?*

Luca ran from the room to go see Sancho.

"Isabella, come to *Nonna*," The little girl walked to her grandmother. Katerina, on her knees, hugged the young girl and breathed deeply of her scent, of her soft skin and clean hair. She held her close and kissed her chubby cheeks.

"*Nonna* adores you, baby."

The little girl fussed, and *Nonna* released her to go outside and play.

Gianna said to the back of her running daughter, "Stay clean, Isabella!"

For a long moment, the older and younger woman were lost in their own thoughts until Katerina said, "Come here, child."

The farm girl daughter-in-law and the matriarch of the family embraced. The older woman placed her hands on the younger women's face and looked into her eyes.

The older woman began, "Gianna, you are like my own daughter and my heart breaks that you're leaving."

Gianna stood and listened. She did not try to hold back her tears. She loved this woman. Katerina went on. "Now, that the time is here, I need to say a few things to you. Important things. I want to share with you some of the knowledge I've gained as a wife and mother for these past forty years."

"Yes, Mama. I want to hear."

"You will be the center of your family and the head of it. Yes, I know Paolo will make decisions, love, and feed the family. Yes, he's a good man. But it is you who will keep everyone in harmony. As a mother, everyone knows that you keep them healthy and clean. As a wife, you support Paolo. Keep him at the center of your life. Make for him the home he wants, and it will come back to you a thousand times over. Cherish him—he loves you more than anything."

"Yes, Mama."

"I cannot imagine your thoughts about leaving your home. I know you want to stay. A part of me wants that, too, but the world is changing, and it's the right thing to do. It's the only thing to do."

"But, Mama, I may never see you again...and the babies...your sons...America is so far."

"Gianna, now, you need to be strong. You will set the example for the family. You are a loving and kind girl, and I love that about you. But you have strength in you too, we have seen that, and you'll be fine in America."

"Yes, Mama."

"The shelter of this home will no longer embrace you. Now, you will make your own home. You will care for your family and keep them safe. I know you can do that."

"Yes, I can."

"I know you can and will, child."

"Live your faith, Gianna. Pray. Pray for guidance, pray for health, pray for wisdom. Pray to the Holy Virgin. Pray every day."

The older woman removed a rosary from her pocket. The well-worn prayer beads were red many years ago; now they were pink from decades of use. The crucifix was made of silver.

"This rosary was given to my grandmother at her first Communion, a century ago. She gave it to my mother and her to me. Now, I give it to you." Katerina placed the beads in Gianna's hand and closed her hand around them. She held Gianna's closed hand in her two.

"This rosary has helped me to live. Pray it every day, daughter."

"I will, Mama."

"In times of tragedy, and God only knows, there will be those times," Katerina now looked directly into Gianna's eyes. "Hear me, daughter: There will be tragedy. It is part of life. Pray the rosary."

Gianna was quiet and somewhat tearful.

"There will be times when you will be tested more than you know. Understand that suffering is the price we all pay for full lives. You will worry; at times you will be afraid, maybe terrified. But listen to me: You are a strong and a smart woman. You can manage anything that will come your way. There is no doubt in my mind."

"Thank you, Mama. I hope so."

After a thoughtful pause, Katerina said, "The babies, oh, the babies!"

Katerina broke for a moment at the thought of them leaving.

"Save every piece of them in your heart...every scrape and cut and every bug in a jar. Hold onto the memory of every tooth that comes out, and every little problem that means the world to them. Carry those moments of their lives with you forever."

Gianna could not speak.

Katerina went on. "*Figlia mia*, we women are stronger than you may realize. It is us who holds our families together during the worst of times. It is women who push forward when our men want to quit. It is women who hold them back when they want to fight or even to kill. When life is at its darkest, it is women who light the darkness."

"Yes, Mama."

"I will love you and pray for you every day, for as long as I live."

Gianna sat, quietly absorbing everything her mother–in-law had said.

"Thank you, Mama. You know how much I love you and this family. I will miss you and Papa, this farm and this life every day. I would stay here forever and never leave. You and Pa, the little ones. Everything...the animals, our garden, even the way the kitchen smells," she said.

The two women had cooked many meals here together and had always enjoyed the labor of love.

"Never forget our life here."

"Never," said, Gia, crying again. "Never."

"One more thing, daughter."

Gia looked up, dabbing her tears.

"There is no such thing as *half love*. There is only *full love*. So ,love hard. Love with your heart and soul; love with your mind and your body. Love completely. It's the only way."

Gia, wide-eyed, just looked at Katerina.

"And know I love you, Gia. I cannot imagine my life without you in it. You brightened our home from the day you arrived. Now it's time to go. They're waiting for us."

There were now just tears for both women; each understood the life-changing event that was happening that day. There were no words left to say.

The two embraced one last time, then held both hands, looked at each other, and smiled.

"Are you ready?"

They walked out onto the porch, arm in arm. A horse drawn wagon in front of the farmhouse was being loaded with suitcases.

"Catch this one!" commanded the smiling Paolo as he tossed a carpetbag up to Leonardo.

The yard was full of well-wishers who came to escort the Tomasos to the shipyard. There were a dozen carts, buggies, and wagons waiting to form a procession. Clouds of dust pre-announced that more horse and donkey-pulled carts and wagons were arriving. Red, white, and blue streamers were tied to each cart and buggy for the procession to the boat docks.

The drivers and passengers, including many children, were excited about the adventure that was soon to begin. Father Fiori was busily blessing the carriage, the carts, the animals, and even the luggage.

A large, brightly decorated coach pulled up in front of the house. It would carry the travelers. A flag of Sicily was fixed on one side, an American flag on the other. The two large horses that would be pulling the wagon were also colorfully decorated with streamers and ribbons tied to their manes and braided tails.

Finally, the moment the family dreaded arrived: They were leaving the farm.

The woman and children had already boarded the coach along with Tomas, Katerina, and *Nonna*. The three brothers walked around the farmhouse together one last time. None spoke. They climbed into the large coach that would carry them from their home.

The older Tomaso did not say a word as the wagon plodded ahead. He knew that most of his family would board a ship in Palermo for the voyage across the Atlantic Ocean. Tomas was confronting the idea that he would likely never see his sons or grandchildren again. The old man was lost in his thoughts and memories; his heart was breaking.

Signora Tomaso was crying softly as the coach moved them along the rough road in silence. She cried for the grandchildren she would never hold and never kiss again, and for those not yet born who she would never see.

Two dozen cousins and friends formed a line of decorated buggies, horses, and donkeys behind the decorated wagon. The procession began.

Upon their arrival at the docks two hours later, the entire entourage assembled to walk the group to the ship that would carry them to their new land. They formed a tight group as they approached the pier, all holding hands or walking arm in arm. No one spoke.

At the boarding area, each cousin and friend stepped forward, one by one, hugged and kissed the group, and wished them all *buona fortuna.* Some laughed with them; some cried. These good-byes took longer than an hour.

Father Fiori stepped forward. His tears fell as he hugged and solemnly blessed the children, then the women. He made the sign of the cross on the foreheads of these brothers he knew since their births. He blessed the ship as well.

Gia and her mother took Luca and Isabella to their grandparents for one last goodbye. Tomas dropped to his knees and scooped little Isabella up.

"Goodbye, my little angel," he said. "Don't forget me."

He then embraced his grandson.

"Luca..." He could say no more than "*Nonno* loves you."

Katerina bent to hug the children. She said to both, "I'll think of you every day, forever."

Both kids cried at seeing their grandparents' tears.

Gia and her mother took the two children by their hands and walked toward the gangplank to leave the parents and sons together for one last private moment.

Renzo first embraced his mother and then his father. His mother whispered words to him that only he could hear.

Tomas said to his son, "Renzo, I have always loved you and been proud to be your father."

"I love you, too, Papa," he said.

He hugged his father again, hard, then turned and walked away to join the others.

Leonardo walked to his parents. His mother embraced him first.

She said, "God bless you every day, son. You are good for this world, and you will do good things wherever you go. Know how deeply you are loved."

"I love you both," he said. "I'll be back to see you again."

She smiled and said, "That will be good, Nardo. Good."

Leo stood in front of his father. They looked at each other. No words were spoken; none were needed. They embraced. Leonardo turned and walked away.

The ship continued boarding as Paolo came close to his parents. Katerina was crying openly now, as she hugged and kissed her first-born son.

She said, "Paolo. Paolo. I'm so proud of you, son. America is lucky to get you." She could not say more. She touched his face with both of her hands and kissed him.

Tomas was standing on the pathway that Paolo would walk to board the ship. He stood there, looking at his beloved son. He almost broke and nearly said, *No, Paolo, this is crazy! A mistake! You're all coming home with us, where you belong. You can't leave.* But he didn't, he couldn't say that.

Steadying himself against the emotional storm that raged in his gut, the father stood looking at the son he adored. Paolo walked up to his father and stood close, so that no one else could hear their words.

Tomas put both of his hands on Paolo's cheeks. He held his son's face in his hands and studied it for a long moment. Paolo felt his father's calloused and gnarled fingers against his skin.

"Paolo," said, Tomas. "Paolo, your mother said it right: The key to life is family. Please don't ever forget that. Family first, before all things."

"Yes, Pa."

The Tomaso patriarch continued, "You're the oldest. Your brothers are under your care and they will make mistakes. Do not expect them to be perfect."

"I won't."

"Let Leonardo be free to choose. Let him find his own path—it will lead him to a beautiful life. He is gentle and kind and he will share that with the people around him."

"Yes, Pa."

"As for Renzo. Your mother and I brought you three boys up the same and I'll never understand why he went the way he went. I can only say what I remember my grandfather used to say. *Every Angel has a past. Every Devil has a future.* Just love him."

Tomas put his hands on his son's shoulders. "We are putting heavy weight on you, Paolo. Heavy weight. You will be the head of the family. If you fail in your guidance of them, our family will have failed. The centuries of work, all the burdens we have shouldered, will have been for nothing. Do you understand what is expected of you?"

Paolo nodded and said, "I understand."

Tomas pulled his son close and hugged him. He kissed his cheek and Paolo could see tears on his father's rugged face. He had never seen his father cry before.

"I love you, son."

"I love you, Papa." Paolo turned and walked to the ship.

Tomas watched his son walk away. After a long moment, he said gently to his wife, "Come, Katie. It's time for us to go."

With those soft-spoken words, Katerina and Tomas turned and walked arm in arm to join the well-wishers. The parents, the priest, cousins, and friends waved, shouted, and cried from the dock at the group who was aboard the ship, now and stood at the railing waving, shouting, and crying.

The American branch of the Tomaso clan began the journey to their new lives.

Chapter Nineteen

"Atten-chun!" ordered the watch supervisor as Chicago Police Sergeant Michael Johnson strode into the room.

All the men in the meeting room jumped to their feet and stood erect, eyes forward. Michael Johnson, the overweight, red-faced, fifty-year-old watch supervisor sauntered his way into the meeting room. As usual, he chewed on a fat, black cigar and trailed a long line of stinking fumes behind him.

"Sit down and listen the fuck up!!" the sergeant ordered, his Irish brogue evident in every word. The rookies dropped into their chairs. The young men were the city's freshly trained police recruits, anxious to do their jobs of protecting the people and the businesses of the city. They were all male, all white, and mostly Irish.

"Smoke 'em, if you got 'em," said, Johnson.

Most of the thirty rookies reached for cigarette packs; some pulled cigars out of their jacket pockets. The room filled with blue-gray tobacco smoke.

Johnson continued, "I'm Sergeant Johnson and I am the watch supervisor here at the Maxwell Street Police Station. I'm here to welcome you raw recruits to the Chicago Police Department. I am not your friend or your counselor. I am your boss. Address me only as Sir or Sergeant Johnson."

He looked around the room.

Johnson continued, "You boys have a lot to learn and your education begins today."

Sitting in the center of the group of young men listening to the scarlet cheeked Johnson was newly hired Patrolman Jimmy O'Shea. O'Shea was a little older than the rest of the recruits. He wanted to be a cop like his father and grandfather before him and maybe someday a detective. Jimmy was the only man in the room taking notes.

Before he applied to join the force, Jimmy, like so many others in the room, enlisted and served his country fighting in France in the Great War. As an infantryman, O'Shea made it through gas attacks, artillery bombardments, and hand-to-hand combat. He killed and he survived. Now, he was back home in Chicago.

The sergeant went on, "I don't know what you think you know, and I don't give a shit. I'll give you the layout of our fine city and you go get with your trainin' partners. You already know who they are and, hopefully, they'll keep you from getting your arses shot off until you learn what to do on your own."

"Yes, sir," someone said, from the back of the room.

Johnson looked in the direction of the voice and said, "Did you not hear me say *listen the fuck up*?"

Silence filled the room.

"Most of you boys know the layout of the city. You got your Jews up north, coloreds on the south side, dagoes west and near north. On the east, well that's Lake Michigan. Your pollocks, krauts, and micks, are northwest and southwest. Downtown, you got a lot of rich stiffs, hotels, and the like. Questions?"

Johnson paused and looked around the room. There were no questions.

"Now, listen good to me here: There are people dyin' in the streets that shouldn't be dyin'. There's shootin's, stabbin's, beatin's, and you name it. Some killin' is gang on gang, which I personally do not give a shit about, but a lot of it is just from drunks fightin' too hard and punks who are robbin' good folks. You name it."

The police sergeant looked around the room as he puffed on his fat stogy.

"I'm going to talk about our street punks and gangs. It don't matter to you where they operate, but I'll show you anyway. When they kill each other, it's one less animal you have to deal with so don't worry about it."

Johnson took a few steps to a large black chalkboard mounted on the wall behind the rostrum. An outline of the city, split by the Chicago River, was drawn on the board. The city outline was labeled with the name of the prominent gang in each neighborhood.

The sergeant said, "Here's your gang territories: Near north you got Dion O'Bannion—a real crazy bastard—and Bugsy Moran's bunch. You got the Touhy gang, also up north. Just west of the Chicago River, you got the Maddox Circus gang of low-lifes."

He outlined their area on the chalkboard.

"South and some west, you got Joe Torrio's outfit. Torrio most likely bumped off Big Jim Collisimo a few years ago, and then took over his organization. He runs more than 200 whorehouses, gamblin' joints, and numbers."

Johnson drew an outline around the Torrio area.

"You got the Malo Tancredi Gang on the near west side, along Taylor Street, up and down Halsted, Cambridge, and west to Damen. That's Little Italy and they stick to the dago areas. The Tancredi boys are six brothers from Sicily or some other Goddamn place. These guys are all nuttier than squirrel shit, and any one of 'em would sooner shoot you dead than say, 'Good morning, Officer.'"

Johnson used chalk and outlined the Tancredi turf to the listeners. "Anything to do with the Tancredi gang, you bring straight to me, and no one else."

He once again chewed on the end of his cigar and blew stinking fumes into the air. As he spoke, rookie Patrolman Jimmy O'Shea copied and labeled the diagram.

Johnson continued, "And then you got your smaller players. Small—but watch yourselves with any of them. Out west you got the Klondike O'Donnell crew and the Druggan and Lake Gang." He drew a circle around their area.

"Along the river you got the Aiello's, the Murrays, and the Ralph Sheldon Gang."

He drew another circle.

"Further south and west you got the Saltis Gang and south of them you have the Spike O'Donnell crew."

Two more circles on the board.

"Questions?"

There were none.

"There's more bad guys, lots more, and they're always changin'. You're all Chicago boys and I ain't telling you nothin' you don't already know. Just stick close to your bosses: We don't need any dead heroes. Out on the street, make your deals, protect and help where you can, clean up the stiffs, and keep your heads down. Do your best."

He looked around the room, making sure he owned everyone's attention.

"One more thing: Boys, when you see someone wavin' a gun around, don't ask no questions: blast 'em. I don't want to go to no more cop funerals. Just be sure it's a gun they're flashin' and not a Goddamn flashlight or something."

Again, he paused. He puffed as he looked from recruit to recruit.

"I'm gonna say that again, cause it just might save your lives: If you see someone—anyone—holdin' a gun... I don't care if it's a black or a brown spic or a dago, kraut or shit—anyone—shoot the Goddamn bastard and ask questions later."

Johnson once again looked around the room.

"Got it?"

There was no reply.

"I asked you a question. Got it?!"

The young cops answered in unison, "Yes, sir!"

Sergeant Michael Johnson picked up his papers, looked at the group, stuffed the end of his cigar back in his mouth, and left the room.

These were hard times in America, and every immigrant knew it well. Work was difficult to find, and if a person was from another country, especially Italy, or worse, Sicily, making a living was frequently denied for no other reason.

Every day of the week, the sidewalks of Chicago's Little Italy were crowded with hundreds of housewives and their children. Street vendors and shop owners were selling their goods, and delivery men were guiding their trucks or their mule and horse-drawn wagons along the busy thoroughfare.

On what was a normal afternoon, a short man with a pale complexion and freckles who wore a dark three-piece suit and brown fedora hat, walked to the corner of a busy intersection. He stepped behind a thick wooden telephone pole and drew a revolver from under his suitcoat. The freckled man took careful aim at a similarly dressed, much taller man across the street.

Disregarding the mothers and children, the vendors and the shop owners, he fired three shots from his pistol. A puff of smoke, yielding his hiding place, went up as the man ducked back behind the wooden pole.

The man across the street, the target of the freckle faced man, felt the bullets whizz by his head, missing by just a few inches. He heard the large plate glass store window behind him crash into a thousand pieces, but he stood firm, glaring across the street.

Gianna, Luca, Isabella, and *Nonna* Cassio, on their way home with groceries, were crossing the street when the shooting began. The slugs of hot lead screamed directly over their heads.

Gianna shouted to her children and to her mother, "Get down! Lie down flat! Lie down flat!"

The two terrified women dropped their grocery bags, and each grabbed a child to the pavement. They shielded the little ones from gunfire with their bodies, as oranges, tomatoes, and eggs fell to the street.

The people in the immediate area scrambled for cover, even though they didn't know exactly what had happened. They had heard the shots fired and the crash of the glass.

The targeted man saw the puff of gun smoke from across the street. He stood without cover and drew his long-barreled pistol from a shoulder holster he carried under his coat. Holding his gun with two hands to enable a more accurate aim, the man fired four shots in rapid succession at his would-be assassin.

Smoke from the barrel of the tall man's revolver filled the air around his head as the shots rang out. BANG! BANG! BANG! BANG! Each bullet struck the telephone pole at the exact height of his assailant's head but did no harm to the freckle-faced man. The tall man then lowered the pistol to his side and walked a few steps to get a better shot at his attacker.

Gianna prayed, "Please, God, protect us. Please, God, protect us," as bullets flew just a few feet above the four who were trapped in a crossfire. Again, bullets whizzed over the heads of the terrified innocents as they lay in the street, praying.

The pale man dropped to one knee and peered around the side of the telephone pole. He fired two more shots, then turned his back to his opponent and ran down the street.

When the tall man saw his opponent run, he holstered his weapon and continued walking in his original direction, as if the event never occurred.

When the shooting stopped, a shaking, crying Gianna reached for her two children and hugged them hard. "Are you okay? Are you Okay?" was all she could say.

Gia, *Nonna*, Luca, and Isabella bundled their groceries up, and quickly resumed their walk home. Gianna, through anger and fear and trembling at what might have happened, muttered to herself, "Animals. Animals. Animals."

On the sidewalk, a hundred yards behind the Tomasos, a fourteen-year-old Lithuanian girl lay dead. Most her neck had been blown out by a bullet from the exchange of gunfire.

The next morning, an editorial in the Chicago Post read, "That a young girl is gunned down while walking home from school is not acceptable and will not be tolerated. This is too much! All decent citizens demand that the mayor and our police force rid the city of this scum once and for all."

The two shooters were long-standing enemies from rival gangs. The tall man was in the Dion O'Bannion gang and the freckled-faced man worked for Malo Tancredi, the Don of Little Italy. That the two thugs jeopardized the lives of innocent women and children and killed one girl was unforgivable.

Punishment was swift.

The man who worked for O'Bannion was beaten so severely that he was hospitalized for a week. He lost an eye and three fingers as a warning and a reminder to any of the men in the gang who put the life of an innocent person in danger.

The pale, freckled gangster who fired the shot that killed the girl was himself murdered on the orders of Malo Tancredi. He was shot in the head and his dead body was dumped on the sidewalk in front of the Maxwell Street Police Station.

The first police officer to come out of the station house and see the dead body was Officer Jimmy O'Shea. He rolled the corpse onto its back and shook his head.

Chapter Twenty

"Hello, Tomasos! Hello, Tomasos! Welcome to Chicago!" shouted LaDonna Mazzone.

She and her husband, the almost always quiet Emilio, were at Union Station to meet the train that carried the family they knew from back home in Sicily. It was Christmas Day, 1917.

LaDonna Mazzone was Paolo's and Renzo's first school teacher. She was a mainstay of their youth and they loved her. The day she and Emilio left for America with their family, the Tomaso boys skipped school to say goodbye to them.

The Mazzones and the Tomasos were good friends since childhood, especially LaDonna and Katerina who were close since they attended school together as children. It was heartbreaking for the women to separate after so many years together watching their children grow and living life's events together, but six years before, separate they did. The Mazzones were the reason the younger Tomasos were now in Chicago.

La Signora Mazzone wore the physical characteristics of many Sicilian women: She was short and thin when young but after having five children and adding thirty years, she was now stout and matronly.

Her husband, Emilio, on the other hand, had not changed over their three decades together. He was tall and thin and towered twelve inches above his wife. Emilio gave up on talking much some time during their first few years of marriage when he realized his wife was always louder, quicker, and more expressive.

Emilio Mazzone was an undertaker. Solemn, soft spoken, and empathetic, as fit his role, his business had grown steadily since their arrival. As an undertaker in Sicily, he did well, but the opportunity for the futures of his children was limited as it was for so many.

In Chicago, Mazzone opened a small funeral parlor on the near west side of the city. He had financial help from the local mob boss who asked for nothing financial in return, just for help when needed.

As the Mazzone children came of age, each started their own family. They all lived within walking distance of their parent's home.

LaDonna was so excited to see the Tomasos that she couldn't stop talking.

"I'm so happy you're here! Merry Christmas!! How's your mother? How about your father? Do they still have that big horse... what was his name? Dante, right? Ha Ha Ha, and the little donkey Sancho, Right? Right? Right? Ha Ha Ha! I love that little guy!"

The Tomasos, *Nonna* Cassio, and the Mazzones, along with eight suitcases, two trunks, and two carpetbags rode the streetcar to their new home.

On the way, Paolo exclaimed, "Will you look at how tall that building is? I heard about buildings like that, but I didn't believe it."

"That's what we call a skyscraper here in America," laughed LaDonna.

Paolo said, "They look like mountains made by men!"

LaDonna said, "We're going to our part of the city. It's called Little Sicily, but it doesn't look anything like home, that's for sure. I've been cooking all day, so I hope you're all hungry!"

The Mazzones took the Tomaso family to their fourth-floor apartment in a large brown tenement building on Cambridge Street. The building was one in rows of dozens of nearly identical buildings stretching for blocks in all directions and housing thousands of immigrant families. The Tomasos would be living across the hall from the Mazzones in an identical three-bedroom apartment.

The new arrivals joined LaDonna and Emilio around a large kitchen table. They all ate their fill of hot *pasta* with sardines, freshly baked bread, sautéed eggplant, stuffed artichokes, and homemade red wine. Even Luca had a few drops of wine stirred into his water.

While they ate, Paolo and Gianna filled Emilio and LaDonna in on politics, deaths and marriages back home. Renzo didn't say too much, but threw in a line here or there. Leonardo added a bit to the update as well, but was mostly his usual quiet self.

Gianna was curious about their new hometown and asked LaDonna "How is it here? I mean, for immigrants?"

LaDonna and Emilio looked at Gia. LaDonna said, "What do you mean?"

Gia said, "Well, are the people friendly?"

LaDonna said, "We stick to our own. The people who got here before us are not too friendly. Stick to your own."

"Is it safe here?"

"It's safe enough. There are *teppesti* here, just like home. Don't count on the police for anything. They don't help us too much."

"Is it always this cold?" she asked.

"This is not cold yet. Wait a month, and you'll see what cold really is," laughed LaDonna. She looked at her husband and said, "Right, Emilio?"

He said, "Yes."

Nonna Cassio and Gia helped LaDonna clean up after the meal. The whole time they laughed and reminisced about friends and family back home. The Tomasos were just glad and thankful to have a safe end to their journey.

After dinner, the Mazzones escorted the Tomasos across the hall to see their new home. The apartment was already furnished and stocked with food by Emilio and LaDonna with money sent to them by Tomas and Katerina. LaDonna had even made their beds.

The family, exhausted from the journey, slept soundly that night and late into the next morning. After a large breakfast, the new arrivals went for a walk to see more of their new hometown. Everything they saw looked, felt, and even smelled foreign to them. They were strangers in a strange land.

The stark reality of big city America struck Gianna as they walked along Cambridge: There were no mountains, nothing green, no animals, no garden, and no friendly faces. The air she breathed stunk of fine coal dust and fuel oil exhaust. She spent much of the first day sick to her stomach and holding a scented handkerchief to her nose

Instead of the many vivid shades of green and gold she knew all her life, she saw only gray, black, and brown. There were no trees along the rows of tenements in this enormous city. The street, the sidewalks, and the buildings were concrete, brick, and asphalt. It was all grey and cold. Chimneys pushed grey smoke from the tops of their stacks on both sides of the street. Kids, lots of kids, were playing in both the street and on the sidewalks.

This city could not possibly have been more the opposite of their home. They walked a block and came upon *Bepi's Taverna*, where they looked in the front windows. The owners waved at them and smiled.

Another block and they stood in front of *Our Lady of Divine Mercy Catholic Church*. Gianna said, "Let's have a look inside." The family entered the church. Each dipped their fingertips in the basin of holy water near the front doors and crossed themselves. The church was large, with a high arched ceiling and gorgeous, colorful stained-glass windows on two sides.

They walked slowly around the perimeter of the basilica stopping at each station of the cross. Gianna found the statue of the Virgin Mary where she knelt and asked for her guidance and her blessing. The Tomasos couldn't know then how important *Our Lady*, and its senior priest, Father Edo Farrucio, would be in their lives.

The newcomers walked the city most of the day, stopping to look in store windows and observing the ways and habits of these people with whom they now lived. They stopped and ate lunch in an Italian *trattoria* on Taylor Street. The food was good, and the family was happy together.

The next morning, Paolo had a job interview with Gaetano Bellavia, another fellow Sicilian.

Bellavia owned and operated a successful meat distribution business on Fulton Street. He was pleased to meet Paolo and greeted him warmly. "*Ciao*, Paolo. Come in, come in."

Gaetano was a short, stout man of fifty-five years. He was bald with a fringe of short black hair and a thick moustache. He had a big chest and a big belly to match. His voice boomed out, commanding attention from anyone within earshot.

In the ten years since he left his homeland, Gaetano built *Bellavia Meats* into a successful business providing fresh beef, pork, lamb, and chicken to restaurants and stores on the west side of the city.

To his receptionist, he said, "Laura, bring us coffee, please."

"Paolo, I received a letter from your father, and that went a long way with me. He and I were boys and young men together in the Old Country. Your Papa saved me a lot of problems with his knowledge and sound advice. A smart man."

"Thank you," said, Paolo.

"I have a job lined up for you, but first let's talk a little about America, okay?"

"Yes, of course," said, Paolo.

"Many people come here because they think things are so different here. We all come here because the streets are paved with gold, right?"

"Maybe just the chance to work…"

"Well, the streets here are *not* paved with gold, my young friend. They are not."

Paolo sat and listened.

"Why do you think the bosses in Washington decided to open the gates for us? Because they like us? HA!"

Paolo didn't know if he was expected to answer Bellavia or sit and listen. He listened.

"They let us in because they need strong backs to dig their ditches and their tunnels…shovel their shit…haul their garbage… gut their animals to fill their bellies."

Paolo just looked at Bellavia.

"Don't be surprised. I'm telling you like it is. Did you think you'd be welcomed into society here with open arms? You are entering the lower class, Paolo. You are now the lowest of the low."

Paolo just looked at the older man.

"But that's a good thing, my young friend. A good thing."

Paolo replied, "I only want to work, that's all, and I want nothing given to me. Just a job, no more than that."

"Good, good. Let me tell you why being here as a laborer can be a good or maybe even a great thing."

"Why, then?"

"First of all, you got here. You made it to The United States of America, man! You have your wife and kids with you. Yes, you'll work like a farm mule, but while you're putting bread on the table and paying rent, these kids of yours will be in school learning to speak the language, learning numbers and letters, learning to think American, learning to be American."

Laura carried the coffee tray into the room and set it on the table nearby.

"Understand? While you're breaking your ass for that low pay, those kids of yours will be growing into the next generation. And here's why this is all GOOD: Your children will be accepted. Your sons will get good jobs, maybe your girls will, too. Maybe you'll start your own business, like I did. Maybe one of your kids will be a lawyer or a doctor."

Paolo said, "God willing."

Bellavia continued, "Then you'll have grandchildren, and they will be *American* grandchildren! My God, man. Just think of what this country will be for them and all because you and your wife gave up your home, and had the courage—*and I am saying the courage*—to come to this country and shovel shit."

"That's why we did it, sir. For our children."

Bellavia stood, walked to the coffee table, poured them both a cup and returned, handing Paolo his drink.

The older man continued, "I have arranged a job for you. As I said, your Pa helped me solve a problem back home, and now I have the privilege to repay the favor and help his son."

"Thank you."

Belavia went on, "You're just beginning here, and it's important that you know your place. You will work harder than you ever imagined and for lower pay than is fair. That's how it is. Our people either do their dirty work or they rob and steal—and I know your family better than that."

"*Grazie*, *Signore* Bellavia, thank you," said Paolo. "Will I be working on the loading dock or driving a truck for you?"

"No, no, you won't be working here. I am full with family and friends. You'll be working at the slaughterhouse on Halsted Street. It's hard work and long hours, but you got to start someplace."

"I'll do good work. You won't regret this. And thank you again."

The two men drank their *espresso* and talked about Italy, Sicily, and people they knew in common. It was clear that Bellavia was enjoying the talk, but soon it was time to go.

"One last thing, Paolo", said Bellavia.

Paolo said, "Yes, sir?"

"You are now a WOP. A dago. A Guinea. And if those aren't enough, here in America, the land of opportunity, you are also a grease ball. You'll be called all of those names and more."

Paolo just listened.

"People here think you're stupid. Uneducated. Dirty. Lazy. Violent. That you can see your ancestors back two centuries, that you come from a fine and an educated family doesn't matter here at all. Here, you are a peasant."

Paolo looked solemn. "Is it that bad?"

"It's worse. The police will not treat you fairly, so avoid them no matter what. You'll have practically no medical services. Your own people will steal from you. Be prepared to be treated without respect and always to do the dirtiest and hardest work."

Paolo just looked at the older man.

"I just want you to understand what you're in for."

"Thank you," Tomaso replied and headed for the door. The two men shook hands, and Paolo turned to leave.

When Paolo's hand was on the doorknob, Bellavia yelled, "Hey! Wop!"

Paolo turned to see a small smile on the slightly cracked, aging face. "Good luck!"

At six the next morning, Paolo reported to the slaughterhouse as instructed. His new boss, Helmut Schmidt, was just called "Boss" by his twenty-man crew. Schmidt had come to Chicago from Germany twenty years before as a young man of nineteen years. He met his wife at a White Sox game, and they were married within a month. Ten kids and fifty pounds later, Helmut Schmidt had climbed the ladder of success at the Halsted Street meat processing plant.

Schmidt got right to the point with Paolo: "I only have one other dago on my shift, and I hope you work harder than him. I got stuck with both you guineas and can't do nothing about it—but lemme tell you, I'll be watching you."

"I understand, sir. What do I do?"

Schmidt hollered "Hansen! Come here!"

A husky, red-faced, red-haired man of about thirty years came to the German's side.

Schmidt said, "Take the dago here to the gut shed, get him suited up, and show him what to do."

Hansen grunted and walked away. Tomaso followed.

Paolo soon learned that his job was to shovel animal entrails and urine-soaked feces into large tubs on wheels. When the tubs were full, he then had to push the three-hundred-pound loads of slimy, stinking contents along a set of tracks to a dump. He was then to push the tub over, spill the guts and their contents out, and go back to do it all over again.

Paolo's new job was stinking, miserable, utterly exhausting work that he was hired to do for twelve hours a day, six days a week.

Paolo learned quickly that Gaetano Bellavia was correct: He had no stature in the New World. He worked harder than anyone in the plant for less pay because he was the new immigrant. And because he was Sicilian.

Tomaso accepted the way things were because he knew he had to earn the respect of his immigrant and American coworkers and his bosses every day. He was the first worker on his shift to get to work every day and the last to leave.

Even though he had the worst job there, and he hated every minute of it, he had mouths to feed and was determined to succeed. Paolo remembered his talk with Bellavia. He understood that it was both the plight and the opportunity of the immigrant to take to lowest form of work and to use that labor to prove his or her worth.

In September, after a long, hot week of work, he climbed the stairs to their apartment and was greeted at the door by Gianna.

"*Ciao*, Paolo," she said.

"*Ciao, cara.*"

He sat and put his head down on the kitchen table, exhausted. "I'm so tired," he said.

She said, "I know you are, Paolo. I know how hard you work."

"Sometimes, I wish we stayed in the old country," said Paolo.

"Paolo, stop it! The money you make there, everything you do, is for the family. That's why we came here, remember? No handouts. We came for a better life and to have a safe place to raise Luca and Isabella.

"You're right, Gia. You are right. I'm just tired."

He felt the rebuke but didn't lift his head.

"There is one more thing," her voice trailed off.

"What is it?" he asked.

Gianna sat next to him at the kitchen table. She took his hand in hers, looked in his eyes, and smiled. "We're going to have another baby. In May." She waited for his reply.

Paolo sat up straight. Shocked, he sat for a moment or two without saying a word, and then his face relaxed. He smiled.

"Gia, oh my God! Thank you! That makes me so happy! I love you. Another baby! Oh, my God!"

From that day on, Paolo worked harder than ever, never looked back, and never complained about being tired again.

He had left Italy with plenty of dreams and hopes in his mind and his heart. He had no real idea of what to expect in this new country and new city. Now, just a short time later, his life blossomed. Despite the filthy and degrading work, he was happy. His children were healthy and doing well. His family was growing.

Paolo and Gianna felt blessed in their new lives.

Chapter Twenty-One

"My God, Gia, look at all the kids!" said Paolo, looking down at the street from their fourth-floor kitchen window. The January day was unusually sunny, and it was warm enough for hundreds of tenement kids to be outside. Gia joined him to see the street below.

"So many children! I've never seen so many at one time, even in our schools at home. Pretty soon, Luca and Isabella will be old enough to play with them."

To Gianna and Paolo, the street below appeared to be engulfed in a tornado of random activity, but it was far from it. Much like the swarming of bees on their hives, what appeared to be disorder was actually organized chaos. The simultaneous and exhausting activities of hundreds of kids were segmented by age, by gender, and oftentimes by nationality.

There was a multitude of young people on the sidewalks, in the streets, and even in the alleys, playing dozens of games of soccer, baseball, hopscotching, jumping rope, flirting, and puppy loving. There were boys chasing girls, girls chasing boys, and small enemies squaring off. There was fighting and fleeing, respect and shame, victory in games and in combat, and there was defeat.

As in every gathering of human beings since time began, drama played out daily, even hourly on the streets. The throngs of kids were steeped in competition; there were heroes, losers, love, hate, greed, and jealousy.

For the boys, the street became alternately their battlefield and their stadium. It often served as a baseball diamond where a base could be a tin can, a post or square drawn on the pavement with chalk or coal.

The girl's games were more social events than competitions as they developed friendships that might last a lifetime. They liked that the boys showed off for them.

On Cambridge Street, like hundreds of other streets and avenues in Chicago and in the other big cities in America, row upon row of four-story apartment buildings each housed hundreds of people. Most, but not all, were married adults of varying ages and nationalities and their offspring. They didn't know that they were poor.

Many of the couples living in the tall, brown tenement buildings seemed to have a half a dozen kids or more. Every first-generation American spoke English or was learning to speak it in school and in the street. They spoke their parent's language of Italian, Polish, German, or whichever at home.

The apartments were poorly maintained by the landlords, who were getting wealthy from the labors of their residents. As if the buildings didn't each hold enough people, the owners added basement apartments and filled them with newly-arrived families, as well.

The immigrants stayed close to each other and to the traditions and the culture they knew and brought from the countries of their births. As importantly, each spoke their own language at home, right down to the dialect. Each cooked their traditional food from their own region, town, and table.

It fell upon the children of immigrants to learn the ways of this country and this city apart from their parents, aunts, uncles, and grandparents. Much of the learning happened in school, but even more happened on the streets where some days were more special than others.

Every Tuesday morning, the Fruit Man rolled his large, heavy pushcart down the street. Every so often, he would draw in a deep breath and yell to the housewives in the apartments above "Strawberrrrries! Strawberrrrries!"

An Italian immigrant, the produce man did his best to offer his wares in English and other languages in the multicultural neighborhood. His product announcements were heavily accented but transcended all the languages in his marketplace. Bananas became "BANANNNIES," apples were "APPPLIES" and onions were announced as "OHNIOHNES." The peddler would lapse into various languages at what seemed to be random intervals but was actually aimed at certain of his customers. "TOMATOES," became "POMODORI!" then TOMATEN!" and then "TOMATES!"

Windows throughout the building, some as high as four flights, would open. Women would shout instructions to the vendor below such as, "One pound" or "Two baskets." A minute or two later, doors would burst open and sons or daughters would run to the cart with coins, retrieve the various packages as ordered, and take the fresh produce back into their own buildings and into their respective apartments.

Behind the tenement buildings were miles of dirty alleys. These passageways had a life of their own, and it was as interesting, as challenging, and as much fun for children as the activities on the other side of the building.

Some of the business conducted in the alleys was the delivery of fuel oil, coal, and the removal of the garbage and the trash discards of the thousands of residents in the brick and mortar habitats.

Although usually filthy, the alley, strangely enough, was a fun place for kids who were bored with, or exiled from, the street. The same games were played in the alley as were played on the street with the added attraction of the garbage truck, and the coal and oil trucks coming through every week.

The kids loved to watch the beefy garbage men at work. To scare off rats, they raised the lids of the metal fifty-five-gallon garbage drums, held them up like shields, and kicked the large cans with their heavy boots. They often heard scratching and scampering as the rats in the can jumped out and ran to another dark hiding place. Then, with two men on one can, they lifted and dumped the large drums of fresh garbage into the back of their truck.

When the can was empty, one of the men would yell, "Yo!" to the driver or hit the side of the truck. The driver would shift the truck into gear. The heavily laden vehicle would then fart out pressure from the brake with a PSSSSH! and groan its way forward in twenty-foot increments.

Junk Day was the best alley day of the week. Every Thursday afternoon, an old white horse pulled a large wooden junk wagon along the alley. The cart creaked and moaned with every clip-clop of the animal, as if it were protesting having to work yet another day.

The horse wore canvas blinders and was strapped to the yolk of the wagon with heavy, dark, well-worn leather bindings. The animal was gigantic, and the many young people would look up at his large head and face with awe and wonder. The ancient junk man called him *Cavallo.*

Gianna always made it a point to be in the alley on Thursdays to see *Cavallo.* Most days, she brought him an apron full of carrot stubs and apple cores. On certain days, when the flowers in their apartment were blooming, Gia would bring a handful of red, white, and yellow blossoms to the alley. She would tie them to the horse's bridle and decorate his straggly mane with color.

Gia would hold the horse by its bridle and pull his face down to her level. She would kiss and rub her face against the soft nose of the animal. When she was so close, she closed her eyes and breathed deeply. The smell of *Cavallo* reminded her of Dante and her life on the farm.

She would say, "How's my big boy doing today? Are you working hard?"

When Gianna was having her moments with *Cavallo*, the junk man would sit, puff on his pipe, and wait for her to have her time with the horse, even though he was ready to move along.

When she looked up, smiled at the old man, and stepped back, he would make a clucking sound, and the animal would continue his job of pulling the wagon down the alley. When he saw a possible selection for his wagon, he would say, *"Cavallo! Aspeta!"* The animal would stop, stand, and wait as commanded. There was no need to tie back the reins; after all these years, he knew that the old horse wouldn't move.

The junk man would set his pipe aside, climb down from his lofty perch, and examine the piece of potentially profitable garbage. If he saw value in it, he would hurl the item, often with a grunt, onto the wagon. By the end of most days, he had collected a full load of steel scraps, lead bars, and dozens of empty bottles and tin cans. Even rags and old clothes were tossed aboard.

Cavallo didn't object as he trudged down alley after alley, day after day, pulling his ever- increasing load behind him. Finally, at day's end, the old, white animal pulled the wagon full of salvage to the scrap yard where the junk man sold his load.

In the Little Italy neighborhood, those children whose parents could afford it, attended school at *Our Lady of Divine Mercy*. By far, more children attended public schools than parochial.

Most of the thousands of tenement kids throughout the city went to school in faded clothes and well-worn shoes, anxious to learn the ways of America outside of their national enclave.

There was only one language spoken by the teachers and the schoolbooks were printed in one language: English. The young students, regardless of the age at which they started their education in America, learned their new language quickly.

After school and on weekends, regardless of weather, hundreds of tenement kids were sent out looking for odd jobs to pick up a few cents. They swept sidewalks, shoveled snow, scraped car windows of ice in the nice neighborhoods, delivered packages, and did any odd jobs they could find for a few pennies, a nickel, or even an occasional dime.

When the tenement kids completed their odd jobs, they ran home before any of the many street punks could rob them of their hard-earned coins. Each girl and boy proudly and solemnly handed over the change they earned to their mothers: three cents for sweeping out old saw dust from *Bepi's Taverna*, a nickel for emptying spittoons, ten cents for delivering packages around the city, or a clear nickel profit per stolen apple sold.

Whatever the amount, Mama would smile and put the coins in her sacred change purse. The money was added to whatever Papa earned that week and brought home after visiting the neighborhood tavern on Friday.

Immigrant kids grew up smart. Most traveled first on ships to America, and then by train to New York, Boston, New Orleans, Chicago, or any of many other cities. The kids learned the ways of the city quickly.

On most days, amazing aromas of hot food would drift down from thousands of windows in an endless row of brown, brick buildings. Pastas and their sauces, stews, *wiener schnitzel,* and *sauerbraten* teased and delighted the senses as did a dozen more aromas from a dozen countries.

For centuries, Italian mothers taught each daughter and son their cooking secrets and techniques, and the food prepared by these humble arrivals was amazing. The simplest ingredients were skillfully transformed into delicious pots and plates of incredible food. Various shaped pastas were created simply from eggs, flour, and water. Sauces were formed from tomatoes, garlic, olive oil, and spices and were cooked to perfection.

There was somehow always enough food to go around for the growing Tomaso family, for hungry neighbors, and new arrivals, even in bad times. The important thing was that every belly was satisfied, and that there was always room at the table for one more. Maybe no one was ever turned away because these humble immigrants understood hunger.

After dinner, it was homework, then clean-up and bed for the kids. Papa would likely go for a walk and a smoke in good weather. During summer vacation, the kids were allowed to go outside to play until the streetlamps were lit.

Baths were a weekly event, and the boys bathed together, as did the girls. The water in the tub was used several times, as hot water was added from a large pot heated on the stove. When each child stepped from the tub, his or her mother would wrap them in a clean or maybe slightly used towel, dry them, and send them to kiss Papa goodnight and then go straight to bed.

In these immigrant families and buildings, few went hungry for food or, more importantly, for love. Each adult and each child understood deeply and internally that they were a part of something greater, something infinite, unbreakable and irreplaceable: family.

Chapter Twenty-Two

Gazzo walked the long line of piers at the Bay of Naples, past steamships and freighters large and small from all countries of origin. He had never been outside of Naples, but he realized then how easy it would be for him to disappear to anywhere in the world.

Along the docks, hundreds of longshoremen were hauling boxes of cargo by hand and by truck. Winches were lowering nets loaded with goods from the ends of the earth. Horse-drawn carts and motorized freight trucks were lined up, waiting to receive the cargo, which they would then deliver to warehouses around the city.

As he walked the docks with his sack of personal items over his shoulder, Gazzo saw a long wooden table with ten or so men standing in a line, waiting to advance.

He asked one of the men, "What's going on?"

The man replied, "This is the table to sign up to work on that ship." He pointed to a freighter who showed her age in rust and barnacles.

The old ship had been hauling freight from one side of the Atlantic to the other and back again for forty years. Painted in three-foot-tall red letters on her bow was the name, *SS Stigman*, and in smaller letters beneath, was the word *Bahamas*. Gazzo was in a hurry to leave Italy on the first ship going anywhere, so he joined the line.

Seated in the center of the long side of the rectangular table where he could best see the men walking the pier sat a skinny, heavily tattooed man of fifty plus years. He was at the table to sign up able-bodied men to serve aboard the *Stigman*.

Gazzo waited his turn and got to the head of the line. The tattooed man pointed at the muscular young man and said in heavily accented Italian, "You. Step up here and talk to Bruno."

The man's darkish brown face was creased from years of hard work at sea. Half of his teeth were absent, but that did not discourage him from smiling broadly. He had nearly no visible lips and his eagle's beak of a nose, having been broken more than once, was bent and crooked. Bruno was completely bald, and his braided snow-white moustache ran down to his chin and another twelve inches.

The upper half of the shirtless and sweaty man was splattered with tattoos. The top of his head was nearly covered, as if by a hat, with a large blue and black octopus. The legs of the sea creature ran down in eight directions. Bruno's forehead and his cheeks down to his chin were covered with tattoos of small and large fish, all swimming in different directions in a complete jumble.

Around his neck, like an ink necklace, he wore two inter-twined snakes locked in coitus. On his left shoulder, was displayed a naked woman bending backward that went partway down his arm. Her large round breasts were on display, as were her long legs and bushy crotch. His right shoulder was adorned with another naked woman. Her face and body were on the top of his shoulder, showing her large, round buttocks as she looked over her shoulder and smiled at the observer.

Down both Bruno's left and his right arms were pictures of rope knots, insects, a sea turtle, an orca, whiskey, rum bottles, demons, angels, two dogs from his childhood, and a likeness of his lost-at-sea brother.

A sea battle between two men of war was raging across his chest, cannon blasting away, and dead men flying through the air. The sea was stained blood red. Sharks circled in the water, feeding on jettisoned sailors. On the deck of each ship stood a captain, each waving a large sword above his head.

Gazzo stepped up, pointed to the *Stigman,* and asked her destination. He didn't particularly care where the ship was headed, but it seemed to be the right question. Bruno replied, "Marseilles. Azores. America. Print your name here and sign it. The job pays a strong back one dollar per day, food, and a bunk."

Gazzo, who couldn't read or write a word, just looked at Bruno. The recruiter asked him, "What's your name?"

"Gazzo," was the reply.

Bruno printed the name Gazzo and then asked, "What's your last name, *Signore* Gazzo?"

"Only Gazzo,'" he said.

"You need two names to sign on," Bruno said. He asked, "Where are you from?"

"Napoli" answered Gazzo.

Bruno added the word *D'Napoli,* and pointing to a spot on the sign-up log said, "Put your mark here, friend."

Gazzo put a large X next to his name: Gazzo D'Napoli.

The tattooed man pointed to the gangplank at the rear of the vessel. "Go up there."

Gazzo boarded the *Stigman.* There was another Italian on board who confirmed to Gazzo that the ship would drop off and pick up freight in Marseilles and in the Azores. They would then cross the Atlantic, dock, and off load in New York City, in America. They put to sea.

By the time the *Stigman* left the Azores, having offloaded crates of oranges, lemons, and limes, Gazzo had his fill of threatening stares from an oversized seaman named Oik who was the ship's tough guy.

"Why the fuck are you looking at me every day?" Gazzo demanded of the enormous man.

Gazzo didn't question why violence was always a part of his life. He just accepted, a long time ago, that it was.

The muscular, tattooed Oik rose to his feet without taking his eyes off Gazzo. He had wanted to fight the ugly new arrival since he first saw him. He loved to fight, to feel his fist cracking jaw and rib bones, to make opponents double over and to club them unconscious. He even somehow liked to be hit, even kicked.

Gazzo looked like a worthy opponent, but Oik felt certain he could beat him and maybe make some money while at it.

The first mate stepped in and told the men to cool down, saying that he would talk to the captain about making it a real ship-board fight with betting.

The captain, being a man who liked to watch others beat the hell out of each other, happily agreed and the fight was on. The captain and his two officers placed bets along with the rest of the crew.

The afternoon of the fight, the two hulking men stood across from each other. Oik was red faced, hopping from foot to foot and punching the air. He glared and growled, and a large vein on his neck throbbed.

D'Napoli watched him. He didn't care what the other man did. His heart rate did not increase, and he did not warm-up. Gazzo simply waited to release his violent rage and power against his excited opponent who stood a few feet away from him. The man could not know that Gazzo, who had grown into a strong, fearless and Godless sociopath, had fought dozens of brutal matches and had killed several of his opponents with his bare hands.

The ship's cook was doubling as the referee and he began, "This is a winner takes all prizefight. You men have pooled your money and put up $43 dollars in cash, one pouch of tobacco, and one slightly rusty skinning knife." He held the tobacco and the knife over his head.

"The rules are: One, you cannot use weapons or tools of any kind on each other and two, when one says "enough" the other stops, and three, you can't kill each other because we need all hands to work the ship. That's it."

The crew formed a circle around the combatants.

Oik removed his shirt and flexed his muscles for all to see. When Gazzo pulled his garment over his head and dropped it to the deck, most of the crew shook their heads in amazement.

D'Napoli wore his scars like medals. He had been stabbed and slashed several times, and severely bitten by an opponent and by a wild dog. He had been shot while escaping from a burglary and had been whipped by a brutal kidnapper when he was in his teens. Most of his chest and back were covered with tattoos depicting mayhem, rape, devils, and blood. After Gazzo removed his shirt, bets were switched from Oik to Gazzo, and some were doubled in his favor.

The cook-referee held his hand up and looked at each of the men to see that they were ready to fight. When he received a nod from both, he dropped his hand and said loudly, "Fight!"

The two men approached and circled each other cautiously, fists balled and raised. Each was looking for an opening or a weakness in the other.

With lightning speed, Gazzo kicked Oik hard in the liver. He went down, moaning in pain. The crew members who bet on Oik went silent. The others cheered. The Italian could have finished Oik at that moment, but he chose to let him get to his feet so the fight could continue.

Oik stood, looked at Gazzo, and grinned when he realized that he faced the first opponent in years that would be a threat. The two men faced off again and each stood his ground. They exchanged punches to the face that would render lesser men unconscious or whimpering. A granite fist thrown by Oik banged into the cheekbone of Gazzo. He was unmoved and responded with a rocket-powered left jab backed up with a right roundhouse. The tandem punches staggered his giant-sized opponent.

Fifteen minutes into the battle, Gazzo was stunned when a rock-hard fist crashed into his chin, staggering him backward. Oik seized the moment to pounce on Gazzo and take him down. Gazzo landed with the full weight of the enormous man on top of him. From his back, Gazzo elbowed Oik hard in the face three times, shattering his nose.

In his rage, Oik sunk his teeth hard into the upper left bicep of the Italian. This time, Gazzo roared in pain. He turned his body hard and slammed his open palm into the side of Oik's head. The tooth-grip of Oik ended with a front tooth broken off and remaining stuck in Gazzo's arm, who punched, kicked, and stomped until the big man was no longer conscious.

The referee yelled, "It's over! End of fight! Done!"

Even after the call to stop fighting, Gazzo kept brutalizing the other man. Two men stepped in to pull him off. One caught a powerful elbow square in his face. The other was punched away. Two other men tackled D'Napoli around his shoulders, and two more stepped in. The four men together were finally able to subdue Gazzo and end the fight.

The cook threw a bucket of water into Oik's bloody face. He came around slowly. Another bucket was tossed into Gazzo's red face, who gradually calmed down. From that moment on, every man on the ship gave the Italian a wide birth. He went where he wanted and did what he wanted.

A week later, the *Stigman* docked in the port of New York City. Gazzo tossed his bag onto his shoulder, stuffed a wad of cash from the ship's paymaster into his pocket, and walked down the gangplank. It had been an easy voyage for him. He had food and a bed and if he had to swab a deck, clean a toilet, or shovel coal for it, that was fine for the time being.

At the end of the gangplank, as Gazzo stepped onto the wooden pier, he stopped, closed his eyes, and took a deep breath of diesel-smelling ocean water and New York City air. The new arrival had no destination and no plans. He walked the city streets and marveled at the crowds of people, at the noises and at the smells of his first American city.

Gazzo D'Napoli had no way to know that it was his twentieth birthday.

He walked for hours until, late in the day, he found himself on Mulberry Street. It smelled of garlic and lemon, of fish, freshly baked bread, and *pomodoro*; much like home.

D'Napoli found a restaurant and was glad and relieved when his waiter addressed him in Italian. He devoured the first good meal that he had eaten in weeks. That night, having walked the city streets for several more hours, Gazzo slept in a cheap hotel on the lower east side in a bed that didn't roll like the ocean.

The young man wanted a woman and found a prostitute willing to come back to his room. For two hours, he beat and sodomized her, eventually dozing off just long enough for her to creep out the door and run for her life.

Gazzo roamed the city from top to bottom for the next several days. In Central Park one afternoon, he heard two young men speaking Italian. Santo and Lupara looked like rough guys, and they became friends quickly. The three of them hopped a freight train out of New York. It carried boxes of goods destined for Midwest markets. The next morning, they jumped off the train in the Chicago railyard.

Chapter Twenty-Three

"Here's the thing, Nardo," Renzo said, using his mother's pet name for his brother. "You cannot just meet her yourself and expect to get past the first hello. No proper woman, especially one from a good Italian family, would accept that unless she was a bad girl, and you don't want to meet a bad girl, do you?"

"No, no," stammered Nardo. "I don't."

"Exactly," said, Renzo. "And so, you have to go through the proper steps. You must be formally introduced by a respected person. It must be a priest, a lawyer, or a doctor; a man who is trusted and respected."

"Maybe Father Farrucio," said, Leo.

"Yes, maybe Father Farrucio," confirmed Renzo. "Where is she from?"

"Ferrara."

"Does she go to school?"

"I don't know."

"How old is she?

"I don't know."

"Nardo, what do you actually know about this girl?" asked Renzo.

Nardo blushed even to talk about Francesca. "I know her name: Francesca Bianchi. I know she's the most beautiful creature on Earth, a work of art with the soul of an angel. And she's nice. Really nice."

Renzo couldn't help but laugh at his red-faced sibling. "Do me a favor, little brother. Forget about Francesca Bianchi. In fact, forget women all together. Go be a priest."

"I'm not sure I can forget her, Renz."

Renzo knew from the look on his brother's face that the young man was serious, and that he was confused and lost. And probably in love.

He said, "Okay, okay, Nardo, I don't know how, but I'll help you."

At some point, after the move to America, Leonardo gave up on the idea of joining the priesthood. He still loved the Catholic faith and was at home in *Our Lady of Divine Mercy*, but he wanted more to pursue a career in another direction.

Leo always loved the museums in Palermo. Now, he was a regular at the great museums in Chicago and spent many hours in them. He particularly loved the Art Institute, and he longed to be a part of it. Because of its location, Leo applied for and was hired as a bus boy and dishwasher at a café on Michigan Avenue, across the street from the Institute. He was able to visit the museum either before or after work and enrolled in art history and art restoration classes.

While his restaurant hours were long, the work was easy, even pleasant. Leo made friends, which was never easy for him, and he began to socialize after work. The awkward, shy young man liked that new part of his life.

Leonardo soon learned that he loved Americans. He found them to be friendly, smiling, open, and generous. The more he learned to speak the language, the more he learned that they liked to joke and laugh. Now, he was becoming an American.

Nardo went from being a student at the Institute to being a part-time employee when he completed his education in art restoration. He now spent his days cleaning and restoring paintings from all over the world. It was important work, and he loved it.

People came from different countries to visit the Institute and the nearby Symphony Hall. Nardo marveled at modern fashions worn by both men and women.

The men often wore carefully tailored, three-piece suits and stylish hats of varying types. Many of them carried long, thin canes and some wore gloves to enhance the elegant look. Their suits varied from the darker tones of browns and greys to the lighter colors of blue, off-white, pale yellow, or green. Their shoes were elegant as well, he noticed—light in color, thin leather shoes, and spats buttoned up to their ankles.

Leonardo noticed that the men he saw wore one of three kinds of hats. Most often, he saw the wide-brimmed fedora. Many wore a short, stocky bowler hat and just as many, particularly the younger, wore the popular straw hat. Often, he noticed, the stylish men wore well-groomed goatees and moustaches as they completed their portrayal of the modern urban gentleman.

Nardo loved to watch the women, too, and especially their new styles. A sense of freedom and a new energy had come to American women along with the right to vote. The new attitude affected clothing styles.

The bunched-up shoulders of just a few years before were gone. Dresses and skirts crept up from the ankles to the knees and additional frills, laces, and bows were gone. The heavy dresses were replaced by light weight, form-fitting skirts, tops, and dresses in light pastel colors.

It was a more streamlined look for a modern woman in a new age. The era of the covered, buttoned-up look for women was over, and women seemed to be somehow freer and lighter. The artistic flair of the designs and the colors of women's styles sang to Leonardo's eyes and his mind.

Many of the women wore the popular round *cloche* hats, covering their short, bobbed hair and their ear tops. Others wore peekaboos, covering their forehead down to their eyebrows. The smaller hats replaced the large brimmed, feathered hats worn by women not long before.

Oddly, Nardo thought, *women seemed to smile more. Or maybe they were smiling more at him.*

Even after he became an employee at the Institute and made a fair wage, he continued to work at the café. He liked the people there and put any extra money in the bank.

One warm, early spring day in 1927, Leonardo couldn't help but notice a young woman sitting at a small, outdoor table of the restaurant. She was a dark-haired beauty with smooth, olive-tinted skin, and she was quick with a radiant smile.

Leonardo was completely taken with the young woman. Every time he went near her table, his heartbeat quickened, and his face turned red. He was far too shy to approach her, other than to take her order and deliver her food.

Over the next few weeks, he noticed her more and more. The shy young man liked to look at her from a distance and to watch her talk with friends, her waiter, or the people at the next table. Unlike most other women Leonardo saw in the café and in the museum, Francesca did not wear the popular round felt hat. She wore her hair simply pinned back.

The young woman became a regular, and Leonardo always looked forward to seeing her. On a day Leo would never forget, he was taking orders and serving food when he saw the hostess seating her. While the young lady was reviewing the menu, she noticed Leonardo looking at her from the waiter's workstation. She smiled at him; he turned his head away.

She sat up straight and removed the bobby pins that were holding her hair in place. With a shake of her head, her hair tumbled down like a waterfall of long, soft curl after long, soft curl of what Nardo knew was sure to be luscious, sweet, clean-smelling, delicious, long, brown hair.

Leonardo was breathless.

He loved the confidant way she presented herself, and it was as if she brought sunshine with her. On the days when she didn't show, he was disappointed.

One afternoon, while the outside section of the restaurant was particularly busy, Leonardo was taking an order. As he turned, he found himself standing face-to-face with the young woman. She smiled and said, "Hello."

The bashful Nardo turned red and couldn't identify the strange feeling in his stomach. He blurted out, "Yes, yes, hello," as he bowed his head and walked quickly back to the kitchen.

For days after the encounter, she was all he could think about. Her fresh, clean smell and her smile dominated his memory. He had never felt this way before and didn't know what to do. The girl frequently returned to the café and seemed to be in his immediate area more often. She always made a point of greeting Leonardo and of smiling in his direction. Leo always blushed, usually mumbled something incoherent to her, and walked away.

One warm summer day, she arrived with a handsome young man. She smiled and greeted Leonardo as always, but this time Leo felt something different. He didn't know or understand the emotion called jealousy, and he felt as if a wall had fallen on him.

Later, after the two young people left, Leonardo went to clean up the table. He lifted her dish and under it saw a small piece of paper folded in half. Leo opened the paper and read "My name is Francesca. Yours?"

Again, Leonardo did not understand the emotion he felt and had more questions than answers. *Was this what joy felt like? Why did he look forward to work every day? Was it because he might see her again?*

The next day, he printed on a piece of paper, "I am Leonardo Tomaso." He folded it over and placed it inside of a menu that he would be sure to give only to her, to Francesca. To the amazing and beautiful Francesca.

She arrived by herself later that day for lunch and was seated at an outside table. Leonardo reached for the menu with the note in it, but it wasn't there. The menu intended for Francesca was taken by a coworker and was, at that very moment, being handed with a smile to a chubby older woman from Germany.

Too late to retrieve the note, Leo walked to Francesca's table, put a glass of cold water on the table, and handed her a normal menu. Leonardo was able to say, in a voice barely above a whisper, "I am Leonardo Tomaso." His heart was beating so hard he was sure she could hear it. His face was red. He felt faint and couldn't look down. He put his fingers on the back of a chair to steady himself.

Francesca put out her hand to shake his and said, "I am happy to meet you, Leonardo." He looked into her eyes, shook her hand, and said, *"Piacere."* Leo walked away smiling.

The German tourist who received the menu with the note in it smiled from across the restaurant at the young waiter who gave it to her.

As May turned into June, Francesca and Leonardo would see each other at the restaurant nearly every day. In fact, they looked for the other at lunch time. Each would smile and greet the other warmly.

Leo liked to say her name as he would say, "Hello, Francesca."

She would in turn reply, *"Ciao*, Leonardo" or *"Buon giorno, Signore* Tomaso," as she flashed that gorgeous smile at him. Each time she spoke his name, his heart felt as if it would erupt in his chest.

When Leonardo had a slow moment or two, he would find a chore in the area of Francesca's table just so he could be near her and maybe speak a little.

This was new emotional territory for both young people. Clearly, they liked each other and shared a mutual physical attraction. The problem was where to go from there because in their inexperience and in their restrictive Italian culture, neither knew the next step.

Leonardo decided that he needed advice from Renzo, who knew all about women. Renzo had girlfriends, and usually more than one. Leo knew his brother would tease him, but it would be worth it.

Renzo and Leonardo, the two look-alike brothers, sat on the front porch of the building on Cambridge Street. They discussed and planned the most serious issue of proper Sicilian courtship.

Chapter Twenty-Four

At the midway point between the Tomaso's building and *Our Lady of Divine Mercy Catholic Church* sat *Bepi's Taverna,* an Old-World style bar and restaurant. Lit by electric lamps on the ceiling and walls and with clouds of blueish-grey smoke always filling the air, *Bepi's* could have been on a small side street in Palermo or Napoli.

Bepi's had been there for many years and, as the most convenient eating, drinking and gathering place in the neighborhood, business was always good. On any day after work, a hungry working man could get a bowl of hot *pasta con sugo* for twenty cents and add meatballs for five cents each. Bread was always *gratis.* A cold beer cost a dime, a shot of whiskey was twenty-five cents, and wine cost twenty cents a glass.

Bepi's Taverna was owned and operated by Franco and Alessa Zignano, two Italian immigrants in their mid-fifties. They named the business after Alessa's childhood cat *Bepi.*

Franco had left Sardinia and wandered the United States for two years before ending up in Chicago. He was short and squat with a dark complexion and a bald head. *Signore* Zignano wore a handlebar moustache, his only tip of the hat to fashion.

After midnight six days a week, and after Alessa had locked the doors to the bar for the night, Franco cleaned the tables, the bar, washed all the glasses and swept the floor. He spread new sawdust for the next day's clients and restocked the beer, wine, and hard stuff.

Zignano never had a problem keeping his larders full of alcohol, even during Prohibition. After all, this was Chicago.

Alessa, his wife of thirty-five years, came to America with her parents and three siblings as a young girl from Puglia.

Like her husband, Alessa was short and squat and dark in complexion. Her tied-down, coal black hair did not have a single grey strand in it. She always dressed as an Italian grandmother. Her daily attire was a simple black homemade dress, stockings, and black, no-nonsense shoes.

Franco Zignano and Alessa Mora met in 1882 on a bright, warm April day in Lincoln Park, not far from where they opened *Bepi's Taverna* a few years later. The two fell quickly in love, married a month later, and had their first son, Lorenzo, exactly nine months to the day after their wedding. They managed to raise five kids to independence, all of whom were well on their way to success in America.

Their first born, Franco Junior, was now a practicing lawyer. Two daughters, Gina and Georgetta, who followed in birth order, opened and ran a successful restaurant in the LaSalle Street financial district with the help and business guidance of their parents. Giulio was their fourth child, a son. He was also a college graduate, held a good job with the Italian Embassy, and planned to become a diplomat for the United States. The youngest, Ernesto, a fine young man with a bright and promising future, was a senior at the University of Chicago studying physics.

Franco and Alessa Zignano thanked their God every day that they made their way to this country, that they met and married, and that their five children were successful Americans.

Chapter Twenty-Five

"Morning, sweetheart," said, Jimmy's mother. "How do you want your eggs today?"

"You decide, Ma."

"Okay, honey."

A minute later, she filled a hot skillet with thick-cut bacon strips, placed side by side. The bacon sizzled and popped until it was done just the way Jimmy liked it. Ma then cracked three eggs into the hot bacon grease. She basted the eggs with the hot liquid until they were done.

Mrs. O'Shea placed the eggs and bacon in front of her son, along with a thick slice of homemade bread from the day before, coffee, and freshly squeezed orange juice.

"Apple butter, Jimmy?" She placed the butter on the table before he could answer.

"Sure, Ma."

Mrs. O'Shea sat next to him and took small sips from a cup of steaming coffee while he ate. "I have an odd feeling today, Jimmy," she said, "Be extra careful."

"I always am, Ma. Don't worry."

"I can't help but worry; you know that. Just be sure to take Polly along with you today. Your father always carried her, and she saved his life more than once."

"I take Polly with me every day, Ma. Never used her yet, but I always carry her loaded and ready, just in case."

He finished his breakfast and stood.

"Gotta go, Ma."

Jimmy leaned over and kissed his mother on the cheek. He said, "See you tonight."

"Okay, sweetheart. See you tonight."

Jimmy walked to the front door, strapped on his shoulder holster with his service revolver, and covered the leather strap and pistol with his suit coat. He clipped a second holster that held Polly to his belt.

Jimmy's father, James William O'Shea Junior, always carried two guns on his patrols: his police-issued sidearm and a Smith and Wesson that he nicknamed Polly after his first girlfriend, although he never told his wife that detail.

James William O'Shea III, known by all as Jimmy, was born in1896 and lived his entire life (except for his years of military service) in a first-floor apartment in a building just west of Kedzie Boulevard on Palmer Avenue in the Logan Square neighborhood of Chicago.

His two older sisters had moved out years before, but he still lived with his mother. She needed him, and so he stayed with her.

When he was twelve years old, Jimmy came home from school and found his father sitting at the kitchen table with a cold, burned down cigarette between his two fingers and a glass of warm whiskey in front of him. The cigarette was out; his fingers were burned; Jimmy's father was dead.

Young O'Shea became the man of the house that day. Jimmy finished high school in 1914 and enlisted in the Army the next day. After basic training, he served in the Military Police at Fort Dix, New Jersey before he shipped out to join an infantry company and fight in the Great War in France. He was discharged in 1919.

Jimmy always wanted to be a cop, like his father and grandfather before him. The day after he arrived home from the war, he applied to the Chicago Police Department and was immediately accepted.

O'Shea worked hard and did whatever his superiors asked of him, no matter how difficult or repulsive the task. In 1925 his intelligence, family history, and dedication paid off, and he was promoted to detective second grade. He was assigned to the police station in the 900 block of west Maxwell Street.

He was assigned mostly homicides and nearly always worked in Little Italy. It was ugly work, and he saw more than his share of murdered and mutilated bodies. Now, in 1927, at 31 years of age, O'Shea had been on the force for eight years.

Jimmy would have liked to have a wife or at least a girlfriend, but he felt that he didn't have enough time for such a commitment. His mother was getting older now and she, too, wanted a woman in his life to care for him. She encouraged him to at least try to meet someone.

O'Shea was paid $120 per month and was provided an unmarked police car, a1922 black Buick. He worked fifty or more hours each week and was on call around the clock. Detective O'Shea owned three wool suits; one grey, one blue, and one brown. Jimmy always wore a suit when he worked.

Mrs. O'Shea kept her son's suits and ties clean and his white shirts laundered and ironed. She shined his shoes and made sure he always had a hot meal ready for him no matter what time he got home.

An hour after breakfast, Jimmy was sitting at his desk cleaning up some old paperwork when his lieutenant barked at him from the front of the squad room. "O'Shea!"

"Right here, Lieutenant" Jimmy said. "Whatcha got?"

"There's a bank stick-up happening right now. Get over to First National on Ogden, quick. We're closest so you might catch 'em leaving. Take Ellis with you."

"Got it," replied O'Shea. He stood, put on his suit coat, and grabbed his hat. "On the way."

"There's two cars heading there now. Wait for them."

Detective Jimmy O'Shea hurried out of the squad room, putting on his hat as he walked.

"Let's go, Ellis," he said. "Come on, real quick-like." Ellis jumped from his chair and followed Jimmy out the door. It would be Ellis's second case since he earned his detective's shield.

Detectives O'Shea and Ellis sped west on Ogden to the First National Bank. When they arrived, the two detectives jumped from the car and ran toward the bank, guns drawn. The squad cars had not arrived yet.

When they were fifty feet from the bank, they heard gun shots. The doors burst open and three armed men rushed out. Loud alarms were screaming from the roof of the bank building.

O'Shea yelled at the robbers, "Police! That's enough! Halt!" He drew his two pistols. "That's enough!"

The three men kept advancing, pistols in hand.

Jimmy said, "Last chance! Chicago police. Lay your guns down!"

One of the shooters took aim at Detective Ellis who was thirty feet from O'Shea with his pistol drawn. The bullet struck the young cop squarely in the center of his forehead. He fell as if pulled backward by a giant invisible hand.

Jimmy saw Ellis go down and faced the three shooters alone. He squeezed the handle of Polly with his right hand and his service revolver in his left hand. The two pistols were all that stood between him and death.

The leader of the gang said, "Listen, cop. You can leave now, or you can die now. It's your choice."

The bank robber's guns were pointed at O'Shea, but Jimmy didn't flinch or move. He commanded, "That's enough. Put 'em down! Now!"

When the cop killer started to raise his gun, Jimmy fired his two pistols, one to the left and one to the right at the same time as if he had two sets of eyes. The robbers fired their weapons at O'Shea, and for that instant, the street in front of the bank sounded and smelled like a battlefield.

Two of the bank robbers were struck at almost the same instant.

The one on Jimmy's left was shot in the center of his neck. The impact of the slug fired from such a short distance made the man turn a back flip in the air. He came down on his face, crumpled in a ball with blood gushing from his nearly severed neck and arteries.

The thief on Jimmy's right was shot twice in the center of his chest. The force of the impact of the bullets was as if he was jerked up and backward by the same invisible hand and pulled Ellis down.

Jimmy turned both guns on the man who had killed young, Detective Ellis. The man immediately threw his gun onto the pavement. He said, "I give up! Don't kill me! I give up!" He stood motionless, petrified.

"That's enough," said, Jimmy quietly. "That's enough now. Get down on your knees and lock your fingers behind your head." The man obeyed, his hands shaking in fear.

Jimmy holstered Polly and reloaded his service revolver. He took two steps toward the man who killed Ellis. He said blandly and without anger, "You killed a cop, you dumb shit."

O'Shea pointed his pistol at the man's chest and squeezed the trigger twice. The cop-killer jerked and spasmed as the force of the impact of the bullets pushed him back ten feet. Blood spurted from the entry hole in his chest and from the gaping wound in his back as his heart pumped its last few beats. The crimson ooze pooled up around the man's body.

Jimmy holstered his service revolver. At that moment, two police cruisers pulled up and four uniformed officers ran from their cars into the scene. They carried their pistols and two shotguns.

"Holy shit, Jimmy! They shot Ellis! You killed all three! You okay?"

The only sign that O'Shea was in a gun fight were four burn marks on his suit coat where bullets passed through the fabric. "I'm okay," said, Jimmy. "Go call it in."

Jimmy leaned back on his car, tipped his fedora back on his head, and lit up a Lucky. He sucked in a double lung full of smoke and waited for the ambulances to arrive.

"Damn it," he said when he noticed the bullet holes in his suitcoat.

Later that night, after all the reports were completed and all the questions answered, Jimmy drove home. He left his suit coat at the station.

"Hi, Ma. How ya doing tonight?" Jimmy asked his mother when he walked through the doorway.

Even though it was after midnight, he knew she would be sitting in her easy chair listening to the radio and waiting up for him.

"I'm fine, James, fine. How was your day? Where's your coat? You're late tonight."

Jimmy kissed his mother and said, "Had to work a little late today, Ma, that's all. I forgot the coat at the station. Long day. I'm beat."

O'Shea hung his holster and gun on the hook near the front door. He would take the suit jacket to a tailor tomorrow and have the bullet holes mended. Jimmy set the leather case holding Polly on the table near the door.

"I made meatloaf today, James. I know it's your favorite."

"Thanks, Ma."

Jimmy sat at the table in the kitchen and began to eat. His mother took a beer from the ice box, opened it, and placed it in front of her son on the table.

Some days after work, Detective James O'Shea III preferred to not talk.

Chapter Twenty-Six

"Jesus Christ! Look at the buildings!" said Santo as he, Lupo, and Gazzo jumped off the train in the massive Chicago train terminal next to Lake Michigan. They crossed twenty sets of tracks and walked into the city, not knowing where they were going.

Most of their money, including the $43 Gazzo won in the shipboard fight, was gone. Two hours later, the hungry and cold men found themselves on a street lined with tall, brown tenement buildings. The aromas of cooking food drifted from the many windows and teased and antagonized the three young men.

"Hey, look! There's a food cart up ahead. *Mangiamo*," said a hungry Lupo.

A half block ahead, a crowd of men stood in a line in front of a food vendor's cart. Gazzo, Lupara and Santo pooled their cash and got in the queue. Other Italians waiting to eat welcomed the new arrivals to Little Italy.

A loud, aggressive young man pushed his way forward from behind the three. No one dared challenge the big, obnoxious brute. He was a violent brawler, and all the men in the food line, except Gazzo, gave way to him.

Soon, the man stood behind Gazzo and said in accented English "Move aside, or I'll crack your head open for you."

D'Napoli did not understand what the man said but knew the tone of voice. Many street fights back home began because of a few careless words spoken in that tone.

The intruder said, "Move out of my way, wop!"

Gazzo didn't move.

The man said, "Get the fuck out of my way, now! Can't you understand me? Move, you fuckin' dago!"

Several jabs in his back, each harder than the one before, made Gazzo turn to look at the bully. He was fine with fighting for his meal and for the respect of the others in line. D'Napoli turned his eyes forward. Before another word could be spoken, Gazzo drove his elbow upward into the man's solar plexus, causing the bully to double over and gasp for air.

The Italian turned and landed a concrete fist squarely on the offender's chin. The force of the contact lifted the hulking bully off his feet. He fell backwards and landed with a thud. The fight was over quickly, and the unconscious aggressor lay with all fours splayed out flat on the sidewalk.

Mafia *Capo* Don Malo Tancredi liked to stroll along the sidewalks in Little Italy. This day, he walked side by side with Renato, one of his five brothers. As always, the Don liked to dress for the occasion when going out in public. He was famous and he knew it; he was famous, and he loved it.

Tancredi chose colorful suits created for him by Italian tailors and made from the finest pastel colored fabrics. Today, he wore a light green, three-piece suit, spats, and a white fedora. He wore gold cufflinks in the shape of a letter T and a shiny diamond pinky ring. He smoked a long, thick cigar.

As the *Capo* walked on these outings, he waved and smiled to onlookers. Most who saw him stopped to get a good look at the Chicago crime boss. Some of those observers came from out of town and went to Little Italy, hoping to get a glance of the infamous criminal.

Ever aware that he was a permanent target for rival gangs, Tancredi never ventured out without his bodyguards. Two men walked twenty feet ahead of him; two more walked twenty feet behind. Each of the four carried two concealed pistols beneath their suit coats and plenty of ammunition to reload in the event of a gunfight.

Two large, black cars crept slowly along the street not far from Tancredi. The lead car held four more bodyguards, each holding a Thompson sub machine gun. In the event of an attack, their job was to encircle their boss and kill every attacker in sight.

The second car, following the first by twenty feet, was an armored vehicle with bullet-proof glass windows and welded-on extensions that covered the tires. It was the escape vehicle for the Don, who was a thoughtful man, one who took no chances and to whom image and respect were everything.

The commotion on the sidewalk ahead caught the eye of the crime boss. With a head gesture in that direction, Malo sent one of his bodyguards to investigate.

Gazzo had been attacked more than once by a beaten opponent. He saw the beaten man on the ground at his feet as a threat, and his instinct and experience demanded that he extinguish the danger.

D'Napoli was calm as he stomped the man's face. One.... Two... Three.... times Gazzo drove his boot into the face of the bully. One well-aimed boot heel crushed the man's left eye socket; the second landed on his right eye. The third smashed his nose flat against his face. Everyone in line, including Gazzo's two friends, took several steps away.

Blood gushed from gaping punctures and cuts on the bully's face, but that still wasn't enough. Gazzo could not stop himself when the urge to maim or kill overcame him. He rolled the unconscious man over onto his belly and pulled his left arm backwards. He raised the man's arm until it was at a forty-five-degree angle and both twisted and pushed the arm toward the center of his back, dislocating his shoulder. Even though unconscious, the man moaned and cried out in pain.

Gazzo let the useless arm fall to the sidewalk and reached for the other. As he pulled the man's arm backward, the loud, firm voice of Tancredi's bodyguard yelled, "*Basta!*" Stop now! *Basta!* I said, stop now!"

Gazzo looked over his shoulder at the man who shouted at him. He turned, squatted, and prepared for an attack.

Others in the food line grabbed him and told him, "No, no, that's Tancredi's man. That's Malo Tancredi over there," one said, pointing to the group of men. "The one with the cigar. He's a boss. He runs Little Italy."

"*Come ti chiami?* What's your name, you?" asked the bodyguard.

When Gazzo didn't answer, the man said, "Are you deaf? *Come ti chiami?* What the fuck's your name?"

"Gazzo."

"Gazzo? What kind of name is Gazzo?" he asked.

"D'Napoli. Gazzo D'Napoli."

Tancredi walked up to the site of the beating. "Get him out of here," and he nodded toward the crumpled body of the beaten man who was just coming to. Two of his men dragged the bully away and dropped him in a nearby alley.

The gang boss said to Gazzo, "You! Tough guy. Where are you from?"

Gazzo glared at Tancredi, still coming down from the evil exhilaration of combat and not sure of what was happening. *Maybe he beat their man,* he thought.

Malo said, "I'm talking to you, dummy! Are you Sicilian? Answer me."

"No, not *Siciliano. Sono Napolitano*," said, Gazzo.

"Well, that's too bad, but all right. You need work? Can you do what you did here today, and more, for money when I tell you to?" asked Tancredi.

Gazzo looked at him, trying to comprehend.

He grunted, "*Si.*"

Tancredi put his head close to Gazzo and said, "You ever kill anybody?"

Gazzo said, "*Si.*"

"I have work for someone like you. You're hired."

Malo looked at Gazzo's two companions. "You men want to work?" he asked.

Santo and Lupara looked at each other and smiled. Lupo said, "Yes, boss!"

He turned his thumb to the man on his right.

"Boys, Edoardo will take it from here. You're now reporting to him, and he works for me."

Malo continued, "Edoardo, get these boys some food and some decent clothes. Put them in the apartment over on Dickens Street; you know the one. Clean 'em up. Send a few girls over later. Have them at the warehouse tomorrow morning."

Edoardo replied, "Done, Boss. Got it."

Don Malo Tancredi walked to the man behind the food cart. "It is unfortunate what happened here today," he said, as he reached into his pocket and pulled out a thick stack of folded bills. "Sometimes, boys will be boys." The Don smiled a big grin as he peeled of a dozen twenties and handed them to the cart man. "Feed them all on Don Malo Tancredi," he said, loud enough for all to hear.

Fighting, stealing, extortion, prostitution. and murder were the stuff of Gazzo's life, and he felt right at home in his new land. Within a week of his arrival in America, Gazzo D'Napoli had become a soldier in the crime gang of Don Malo Tancredi and his five brothers. The violent sociopath, criminal, and immigrant became a small but important part of a vicious and powerful crime machine.

A few months after they were hired into the gang, Edoardo said to Gazzo, "The boss wants to see you in his office in one hour."

Gazzo grunted, a sound that Edoardo had come to understand meant "I understand."

"Bring your two buddies with you." Another grunt.

An hour later, in Tancredi's office, Malo began, "Sit down, boys." They sat across from Tancredi at his massive desk.

"A piece-of-shit hood boss in New York by the name of Buonasera wants a cut of our Chicago business. I told him to go fuck himself. A friend of ours in New York told me he's sending a button man to kill me."

Santo and Lupara looked at each other; Gazzo looked only at his boss.

"The shooter's name is Manfredo LoMantia. They call him Freddie. He'll be here tonight. I want this Freddie asshole dead before he wakes up tomorrow. I want you three to handle it. *Capisci?* Do you understand?"

Gazzo grunted. The boys nodded.

Malo went on, "My source said LoMantia will get off the train tonight, just after midnight. He'll be checking into the Palmer House. Get him up in his room."

Santo said, "How will we know who he is?"

Tancredi nodded and said to Edoardo, "Bring her in."

Edoardo opened the door to a small ante room and said, "Come on." He pointed to his boss's desk and said, "Go over there."

A woman who had been waiting in the small room straightened her dress and huffed her way the twenty feet to stand at the side of Malo's desk. The redheaded woman was fortyish, had big breasts, an ample middle section, and an oversized rear end. She wore a shiny, tight-fitting red dress with matching lipstick and high heels.

"This is Cherry McCoy," Malo said to the three gorillas.

"Cherry, this is the boys."

"Hiya, boys," said, Cherry.

"Cherry here has been screwing our Freddie boy for the past year. Problem is, he beat her one time too many and now she wants him dead, ain't that right, doll?"

"Yeah, that's right. I'd kill him myself if I could," Cherry said.

"Cherry will finger Freddie when he checks into the hotel, then she'll leave and let you boys do your job. A friend of ours will be on the front desk. He'll give you a key to the room. Just make sure it's Freddie and only Freddie. We don't need no more heat. Our cop friends can only cover so much. Got it?"

A grunt and two nodding heads replied.

"One more thing. Take this piece of shit out tonight and tomorrow go to New York and knock off that other asshole, Buonasera. Here's where you'll find him and where and when to clip him." He handed Gazzo an envelope. "There's plenty of money in there, too."

Late that night, Cherry and the three hit men sat in the ornate lobby of the Palmer House Hotel on State Street in downtown Chicago. Freddie LoMantia walked to the front desk and checked in, just as they expected, at about one o'clock.

Cherry McCoy hid behind a large planter and saw Freddie when he entered the hotel lobby. "There he is! That's the asshole! That's Freddie LoMantia!" The men stayed hidden until LoMantia finished checking in and left for his room. Gazzo and Cherry walked to the registration desk.

The clerk didn't look at them but slid a key to Freddie's room across the counter and walked away. The number on the key was 704.

Cherry left the hotel. An hour later, Gazzo, Lupo, and Santo stood in the hallway outside the door to room 704. Gazzo slid a twelve-inch knife out of his belt and nodded at Santo who inserted and turned the key. He silently swung the door open.

The dim light entering the room from the hallway was enough to wake LoMantia. When he saw the three shadows in the room, he shot his hand out for his pistol on the nightstand. Santo sprung at the dark figure like a panther and grabbed his gun hand. Lupo was on Freddie a split second behind Santo. Gazzo watched from the doorway.

Out of nowhere, they heard Cherry's shrill, hysterical voice screaming from the doorway "Kill the son of a bitch! Kill him! Kill him! Kill him!"

Freddie said, "Cherry? What the fuck are you doing here??"

Gazzo turned to Cherry, grabbed her by her throat and lifted her off her feet against the wall. He slammed the door and drove the knife into her chest. Her ribs blocked the blade from penetrating deeply. Gazzo felt the resistance and turned the knife ninety degrees to allow it to slip through her ribcage. When he felt the honed blade enter her chest, he moved the handle left and right, slicing her heart in half. D'Napoli released his grip and Cherry dropped to the floor, dead.

Freddie was immobilized by Lupara and Santo. He said, "Do you know who I am?"

Santo laughed and said, "Yeah, we know who you are."

Lupara smashed LoMantia's face with a large marble ashtray off the nightstand. The ashtray cracked in half. Blood spurted from Freddie's mouth and nose. "Yeah, we know who you are."

Gazzo took the half dozen steps across the room and jammed his knife into the eye socket of Freddie LoMantia. He drove the knife to the hilt. Freddie was dead.

The three men, having completed their work, stood and walked toward the doorway.

Gazzo said, "Throw the whore on the bed." Lupara and Santo picked the dead body of Cherry McCoy up off the floor and dropped her on top of her former lover.

The next morning, the three took a cab to Union Station and boarded the first train to New York City.

Chapter Twenty-Seven

"Where is she?" Anna Moliare demanded as she burst through the door to the Tomaso apartment.

It was past midnight. Paolo showed the midwife down the hall to the bedroom where Gianna was in early labor. Mrs. Anna Moliare delivered babies for tenement families who didn't have access to doctors or hospitals. She had delivered more than three hundred babies and was well-experienced both in Italy and here. Anna was good at her job.

Ten years before, Anna Barone knew she wanted something more and decided to completely change her life and to come to the America. She immigrated to America and put her midwife skills, acquired in her home city of Rome, to work almost immediately.

Within a month of her arrival in Chicago, she delivered the first of many babies to come. Word spread about her skills, and she became the go-to person for pregnant women, from pre-natal care and advice all the way to delivery. Anna was busy year-round with the many pregnancies in the tenements of Little Italy.

A year after her arrival, Anna met and married countryman Arturo Moliare. A skilled cabinet maker ten years her senior from Florence, Arturo was successful and ready when his family came along. In addition to delivering more than three hundred infants, Anna managed to have five babies of her own, one every other year since her arrival. All boys.

Anna was in the Tomaso apartment to deliver a baby and wanted to get right at it, knowing that the infant wasn't due for eight weeks.

Mrs. Moliare entered the bedroom and said, "*Ciao* Gianna. Any problems so far?"

"No, just that this baby isn't due until April. Am I in labor for sure?"

"Yes, you are *cara mia*." Mrs. Moliare replied after a quick exam. "You sure are."

Even though he was barred from his bedroom, which was now a labor and delivery room, Paolo promptly produced whatever Mrs. Moliare needed. He preferred to not be in the room with his wife moaning in pain.

Early on a freezing morning in February 1919, Rosa Esmerelda Tomaso entered the world two months early. After the birth, Anna put the tiny baby on her mother's chest. "*Signora* Tomaso, *mi dispiace*. She's so small. Keep her warm."

Gianna cried when she held her tiny premature baby girl for the first time and realized that her just-born daughter may soon be with God. Moliare wrapped the baby tightly and carried her to her father. With tears in her eyes, Anna handed the bundled infant to Paolo.

"She's too small, Papa. I'm sorry."

Paolo accepted the infant. He thought at first that the baby was stillborn because she was so still and so tiny. As he held her, he saw her tiny mouth open a little and heard her struggling for the breath needed to stay alive.

The new father cried as he marveled at this premature baby, so small and so vulnerable, fighting for her life. He resolved to do anything in his power—anything—to protect their help-less daughter.

Gianna slept. Baby Rosa, who Paolo placed back on her mother's chest, slept too. After a short hour, the tiny baby cried. Her voice was so soft and weak that she could barely be heard.

Nonna Cassio was listening and waiting for the baby to wake up. When she heard her new granddaughter whimper, she took over care of the infant.

La Nonna hummed and sang softly the entire time she tended to Rosa. The grandmother rinsed the newborn in warm water, dried, swaddled her, and softly placed her back on Gianna's chest where she was offered a milk-engorged nipple.

Rosa was too weak to nurse, and her mouth was too small to accept the nipple. *Nonna* Cassio squeezed milk from the breasts of her daughter into a cup. She sat and held tiny Rosa in the crook of her arm. The grandmother dipped a white, clean cloth into the cup of breast milk. She then held the cloth over the baby's little mouth and squeezed the tiniest of drops into the partially opened mouth.

The little girl smacked her tiny lips at the taste of the first drop of her mother's milk. "*Mangia*, Rosa, *mangia*," said *Nonna.* She fed the baby another drop, then another and another. Soon the baby swallowed her fill and there, on her grandmother's warm chest, immersed in the love of the old woman, the three-pound baby girl slept. *Nonna* hummed and softly sang an Italian ballad.

Later that morning, Paolo held his daughter. "Look at how she fits in my hand. So small," he said. Her little legs dangled over the sides of Paolo's hand.

Renzo, Leonardo, Luca, and Isabella didn't sleep much through the early morning hours during the birthing of their niece and sister. When they emerged from their bedrooms in the morning, they were greeted by a somber looking Paolo, not by the happy father of a healthy new baby they expected.

Nonna held the tightly swaddled infant in her arm as she sat in a large chair. Each of the four came and stood close to see Rosa for the first time.

"Why is she so small?" asked Isabella.

"Because she was born early and didn't finish growing in Mama," was the reply.

"Will she grow now?"

"Yes, she'll grow. Yes."

Rosa's two uncles preferred to look at the baby and not to hold her just yet.

The day after the birth of Rosa, Gianna, her mother, Paolo, and LaDonna sat at the kitchen table. The baby was asleep in *Nonna's* arms.

LaDonna said, "Believe me; I know how these things are here. You are immigrants who do not speak English and have no money. A hospital is not possible for Rosa."

"Well, then, we'll nurse her to health right here at home," said Gianna. It seemed like an overwhelming task, and even as she spoke the words, she had no idea what to do.

Gia continued, "If our daughter is to have even a chance at life, it'll be up to us. We have to dedicate ourselves to her care around the clock," she told her husband and her friend, tears filling her eyes and spilling onto her cheeks.

Nonna rocked the baby and hummed softly.

Gianna said, "This baby is from God and I will not let her die. God gave her to us because He wants her to be here. With us. I will not let her die."

Later that same day, Gianna fed her little baby. "Here you are, *figlia mia*. Eat."

Rosa was too small and too weak to nurse. Gianna followed the path created by her mother: she collected her breast milk in a cup and then fed the precious liquid into Rosa's tiny mouth one drop at a time.

Paolo said, "She has a good appetite. That's a good sign."

Gianna smiled at him. "Yes, that's a very good sign. She's always hungry."

Paolo came home from work the next day and said, "*Cara*, use this." He handed Gia an eye dropper he had bought at the drugstore.

Gia smiled. "Good idea," she said. "I have an idea for a bed for her. Bring me a clean shoe box. Line it with cotton and maybe cover it with a soft cloth. I think she'll fit perfectly." She was right: Baby Rosa fit into a shoebox.

Gianna said to her mother, "She needs to stay warm. Set the oven on the lowest heat and open the door." *Nonna* did as requested and Gianna set the shoe box bed with Rosa in it on the opened door. The oven provided the warmth that the infant desperately needed.

Every four hours, around the clock, Gianna or her mother would lift Rosa from her tiny bed, clean her, rub oil into her skin, and feed her fresh drawn breast milk.

Because she believed that the life or death of Rosa was in the hands of God, Gianna prayed long and hard. There were nights when she knelt next to her bed and softly and tearfully prayed the rosary her mother-in-law gave her until the sun rose or until Paolo would say, "Enough, *cara*. Come to bed. You need to sleep."

A month after her birth, Rosa had grown but she not thriving as the other infants did in the beginnings of their lives. Gianna felt that she needed to present the baby girl to the Virgin Mary at their church.

When a break in the bitter cold weather happened, Gianna wrapped Rosa in a warm blanket and nestled her against her chest.

She put her coat on and wrapped a shawl around her shoulders and chest. Another woolen shawl went around her head.

Gianna left Luca and Isabella with her mother and walked with the bundled Rosa inside her coat to *Our Lady of Divine Mercy*. She hung her heavy clothing in the cloak room, walked into the church, and blessed herself and her daughter with the holy water from the basin at the front of the church.

When Gianna entered the church, she felt the warm feeling of peace that she always felt there. It comforted her to be in God's house. She could feel His presence.

In the dimly lit church, Gianna walked to the statue of the Virgin Mary. She held the small infant up, one hand under the back of the baby's head and the other holding her legs, directly in front of the statue of the Blessed Virgin Mary. She offered the infant, prayed, and begged the Holy Mother for the life of her daughter.

After a long while of whispered prayer, Gianna turned to leave. Only then did she notice that Father Farrucio had been watching her.

He walked to the mother and infant. "So small," the priest said.

The priest made the sign of the cross on the baby's forehead and then on Gianna's forehead. He prayed. Gianna had no way to know that Farrucio had recently returned from France.

"*Signora* Tomaso, we should baptize your daughter now." He looked into Gianna's eyes.

She understood the significance of his words and the importance of the Sacrament. "I want my husband here," she said.

"*Signora*, hear what I'm saying. We need to baptize her now, while you're here. You can do it again with the family later, but with your permission, please let's do this now."

She nodded. "All right, Father. I understand," she said.

"*Grazie.*"

The priest touched Gianna's elbow and gestured with his other hand. "This way," he said.

They walked past the altar to the Baptismal font. As she stepped into the Baptismal area, Gianna noticed that it was immersed in beautiful colors. She was certain those hues were not there a moment ago. The blended colors were unlike anything she had ever seen before. They were a blend of gold, pink, and red, but somehow, there were shimmers of silver and what looked like ripples of light blue. And it felt warm in the cool church. *How amazing,* she thought.

For those minutes, holding baby Rosa in her arms, immersed in those colors and feeling the presence of God, Gianna felt as if she was being held in the arms of a loving parent: warm, safe and adored.

It was completely still and quiet in the church except for the movements of the priest and the soft mewling of the tiny infant in her mother's arms.

Father Farrucio retrieved his purple stole from a small cabinet. It was the same stole he brought to the battlefields of France. He kissed it and placed it around his neck for the occasion of the Holy Sacrament.

The priest smiled at Gianna and said, "Let us begin."

Gianna stood by the Baptismal font holding tiny Rosa in her arms. Father Farrucio asked, "Gianna Tomaso, do you believe in God, the Father almighty, creator of Heaven and Earth?"

Gianna said, "I do."

The feeling of the love and the presence of God that day would stay in her heart and mind forever. Father Farrucio spoke the same sacred words for the Sacrament of Baptism that he had spoken a thousand times before, but this time was special.

When the Sacrament was completed, the priest said, "Rosa Esmerelda Tomaso, I baptize you in the name of the Father," (he poured holy water on the forehead of the sleeping infant) "and of the Son," (he poured holy water onto her forehead a second time) "and of the Holy Spirit." The priest poured holy water onto the forehead of the baby a third time.

Father Farrucio then anointed the infant on her forehead with consecrated oil in silence.

He said, "Go with God, *Signora* Tomaso."

Gianna said, "Thank you, Father. Thank you."

Gianna bundled her baby and began the walk home in the freezing sleet and snow.

Chapter Twenty-Eight

"Renz, sit with me for a minute," said Paolo.

Renzo looked at his older brother with suspicion and then took a chair across from him at the kitchen table. "Um, okay. What's up?"

"I'm worried about you, brother. You're gone for days, sometimes weeks at a time. You come home stinking like whiskey and whores. What kind of life are you living? Didn't you learn your lesson back home?"

Renzo looked at Paolo with no answer.

"Not only that: The kids miss you. They ask about you every day. Gianna and I miss you, too. So does Nardo."

Renzo still did not reply and gave his brother a look that said, *Mind your own business.*

"And what about work, Renz? You need to come back to the stockyards and see if you can get your job back."

Renzo replied a little too loudly, "I don't want that nasty job. I'm not going back. They give us the worst work for the lowest pay. They call us names. They hate us there."

Paolo said, "Right, but they pay us and then we can eat. How are you making money? What the hell are you up to?

"Renzo said, "I'm earning money with my friends. Don't worry about it."

Paolo said, "Friends? Like back home? Did you forget what your "friends" did to you back there? Do you really want to throw all your hard work in the yards away? Start over someplace?"

Renzo raised his voice. "Paolo, you clean shit out of animal guts, man! Is that what our family has accomplished? Is that why we came here? Mopping blood off the floor? Don't you get that they hate us here? We'll always be under their boot. Do you hear me, dago?"

Paolo cringed at the use of the word by his brother.

Renzo said, "I'm never going back to that shit-hole again. I'll make money the best way I know. That's the end of it! I'm going to bed."

Renzo threw a handful of bills onto the kitchen table and stormed from the room. He never liked living in America, even after ten years. From the beginning, he felt the discrimination and hatred to which he, his family, and his countrymen were subjected. He not only heard the names he was called, but he also felt them deep in his heart.

Renzo would still be in Sicily lifting wallets, hustling tourists, and seducing solo females if he could. Or had things gone differently, he would have married Adriana. Thanks to Carlo Lazzori, neither possibility existed.

Soon after Renzo arrived in Chicago, he reached out to the criminal element. He wanted to use his skills as a petty thief and street hustler, but every door that opened for him was soon closed. Not only had Lazzori forced Renzo to leave his homeland, he had also poisoned the water for him.

Before Renzo even arrived, Lazzori sent word to every Italian street gang in the city and beyond that he could influence: Do not hire this guy. He is not to be trusted.

Word spread. The request of a Mafia capo in Sicily meant a lot in the New World. That boss could have a person shunned, beaten, or even killed.

Over the course of Renzo's first few years in America, Chicago, New York, and Kansas City mobs rejected him. Even the smaller gangs in Milwaukee, Cleveland, and lowly Peoria shunned him.

The pattern was always the same. Soon after Renzo would make a friend or a contact, he would be exposed, or his name would be recognized. Wherever Renzo went, he found that he was blackballed by Carlo. Renzo, the professional petty criminal and hustler, realized that he had no choice but to get a real job. He had lived off his big brother's generosity long enough.

Tomaso worked for a few months as a warehouse laborer. As an immigrant, and especially a Sicilian, he got the dirtiest jobs in the warehouse. When the job proved to be too physically demanding, he signed on as an able-bodied seaman on a Great Lakes freighter. That lasted just a few months.

He got a job selling ice cream at Lincoln Park Zoo, got fired, and then cleaned the toilets at Cubs Park. Time rolled by and finally, after several years of part-time jobs, back-breaking labor, and earning little money, Renzo had no choice but to join his big brother and work at the slaughterhouse.

After three months there, Renzo felt that if he worked one more shift in ankle-deep, stinking, bloody animal guts, he would lose his mind. Paolo got tired of trying to get Renzo up and out the door for work in the morning. Soon, Renzo stopped showing up at the slaughterhouse and was fired.

After the break with the slaughterhouse, Renzo slept late every day and then went to the local pool hall or wandered the busy city streets. He would occasionally join a labor team and pick up a few bucks, but other than that, he had no ambition. He was lost.

One morning at the pool hall, a fight broke out. It was a simple disagreement about some minor point, but both men took it seriously. The taller of the two men held a pool stick with both hands at the thin end. He swung it wildly and tried to strike the other man with it.

The shorter man clenched a pool ball in his fist and ducked under the swinging stick. The fight ended when the shorter man was able to step in close and swing the pool ball hard. He connected the ivory ball with his opponent's forehead and split it wide open. The wound looked like a smile at first, and then filled with blood. The man fell to his knees and then onto his face.

The shorter man was Mario Ventimiglia. Back home in Turin, Ventimiglia had been a leg breaker and a collector for a petty hoodlum. During an attempt to collect a debt, Mario was shot twice in the belly and left in the gutter for dead. When he recovered from his wounds, he left Italy to start a new life in America.

Later on, the day of the fight, Tomaso and Ventimiglia shot a few games of pool and found out that they liked each other. They had a few beers and a bowl of pasta at a local bar. Renzo and Mario became friends. Tomaso thought that his own brush with death at the hands of Lazzori's thugs and the near death-by-gun of Mario somehow formed a closer bond between the two.

Mario Ventimiglia was the physical opposite of Renzo Tomaso. While Renzo was tall and slender, Mario was short, dark, and muscular. Renzo wore his hair slicked back, tight on his head. Mario had a full head of wild, curly, bushy, dark-brown hair that rarely felt a comb. Renzo was by far the more serious of the two. Mario, despite his hard life and brush with death, always had a smile on his face, a joke on his lips. He laughed a contagious, full-throated laugh often and saw humor everywhere.

Renzo and Mario spent a lot of time together. They would meet at the pool hall most days, shoot for a while, and then leave together to work the streets, just to see what they could produce.

After a few months of idling their time away, Renzo and Mario sat across from each other at a small table on Taylor Street in front of a family-run deli called Palermo's. Each had an enormous bowl of red-sauced pasta in front of them. There was a basket of freshly baked, crusty bread on the table and a bottle of red wine.

Renzo said, "We can't go on like this, Mario. We have to start making some money. I'm even thinking about working."

Mario replied, "A job?"

Renzo said, "Yes, man, a job."

Mario laughed and said, "Employment?"

"Yep, employment. A real job. I don't want to go on hustling the streets for money and running from the cops. I'm tired of it, Mario. Tired of it."

Mario replied, "Don't get crazy on me, man. I've been thinking about a way we can make plenty of money. There's an easier way than shoveling shit."

Renzo smiled and asked, "Will we end up in jail?"

Ventimiglia laughed again. "No, man, no. Here's my idea: There's thousands of families living in these apartments. Mostly Italians, all poor."

Renzo said, "Yeah, we all know that. So what?"

Mario replied, "Well, most all of them are making illegal booze in their kitchens for the Tancredi gang."

"Yeah, and so what?"

In 1927, Chicago's Little Italy was like a beehive for humans. It was sixteen square miles and lined with tenement buildings forty feet high. Every day of the week, runners from the Tancredi gang carried liquor-making supplies into countless apartments. Thousands of hungry immigrants needed the money and jumped at the chance to distill liquor at home using stills provided by the Tancredi mob.

More runners were sent to pick up the cases of illegal hootch. Cops were paid off, as usual. Policemen on patrol sometimes helped load the illegal liquor into the pickup trucks. The booze was then transported by the pick-up crews to the warehouse on Taylor Street where it was stored until sold and delivered.

It was a brilliant and massive bootlegging scheme without a main distillery, and the Tancredi Family turned thousands of dollars in cash every week. They used the profits to operate Speakeasies, brothels, and gambling joints.

A month before, Mario and Renzo had worked day labor jobs cleaning the city's gutters and streets for cash. While sweeping streets, they noticed that regular deliveries and pick-ups were being made in tenement buildings by Tancredi gang runners. They figured out the scheme.

"Here's the idea." Mario took a drink of wine and said, "My cousin Cesare works in the Tancredi warehouse at night. You, me, and him are gonna rob some booze and sell the stuff on the street."

Renzo said, "My friend, you are fucking nuts. Too dangerous. Leave me out."

Mario replied, "That's why it would work. They would never think we'd do it. Cesare will pass the cases to us when it's safe."

"No way, Mario. I love you, but you are crazy. No! No!"

"Renzino, listen to me: We borrow a truck and go to the alley behind the warehouse. My cousin cuts a hole in the back wall and passes us the booze. We fill the truck in just a few minutes. He covers the hole and we go into the bootlegging business."

Renzo asked, "You mean we're gonna steal from the bootleggers?"

"Yes."

Renzo said, "From the Tancredi brothers? You're out of your mind! Leave me out...I want nothing to do with those crazy bastards. They're Sicilian and I know what that means. They would kill you and me both for just thinking the thought of stealing from them."

Mario said, "We won't need much. We take it, we sell it, and we split the money three ways."

"No."

Mario said, "Look, man. I'm doing this with or without you. I'm telling you; we will not be caught. Trust me, just a little. Let's try it once and see how it goes."

The two sat in silence while they finished their meals and their wine.

Mario said, "Renz..."

Renzo cut him off and said, "Mario, stop. You got me. I'll do it. You happy now? I'll try it with you one time and see how it goes."

Mario jumped from his chair and kissed Renzo on the top of his head and laughed his big laugh. "This'll be good, Renz. You'll see!"

The test run went well. Cesare cut a small hole in the back wall of the warehouse and stacked two dozen cases of whiskey, gin, and vodka nearby. Mario pulled the truck up, he and Renzo got out, and they walked to the opening in the wall. Cesare passed the cases through the hole. The two loaded the truck and drove away. They had been in the alley for just ten minutes.

With their easy success, Mario and Renzo continued the theft once a week, every week, at five in the morning. Renzo and Mario secretly peddled the illegal liquor to private buyers, one case at a time. This way, they wouldn't step on Tancredi's toes.

After just a few weeks of stealing from the bootleggers, life was good again for Renzo and Mario. They always had a pocketful of money and women to help them enjoy it. Their scheme continued.

Once a week, well before sunrise and before the family began their day, Renzo Tomaso waited on the porch of the tenement building on Cambridge. A canvas-topped truck rattled down the street and stopped in front of the building. Renzo walked to the curb and got into the cab of the truck alongside his good friend Mario Ventimiglia.

Each week, the two stashed the stolen hootch in a rented garage where it sat until they sold it. Toward the end of summer, after a new load was transferred to the garage, Renzo said, "Let's get some sleep. We'll take this around and sell the whole load later."

Mario said, "Good. Listen to me for a minute, Renzo. Keep this quiet; don't even tell your girlfriend. Tell no one. I've already got most of it sold to a couple of Speakeasies around Twenty Second and Halsted."

Tomaso said, "Shit, Mario. That's Tancredi area. You told me we'd sell to just people, not to bars."

"We need to grow, man. Come on, let's get bigger."

"Mario, that's not what we said."

"Yeah, but that was then." Mario said with a short laugh. "Don't worry about it. It'll be done before anyone even knows about it."

"Shit, man," said Renzo. "I don't think we should do it. If we get caught, we're dead."

"Renzo, you once said you wanted to be bigger than two guys selling a few cases a week, right? This is how we do it. Let's peddle this load and do it again. C'mon, man."

As usual, Tomaso gave in. "Okay, Mario. Okay. Just don't get us killed."

"No worries, buddy," said Mario. "I'll take a case now and drop it off at Jackie's Tap. He'll pay on the spot. We can go out later. Find some women."

Mario couldn't know what a terrible mistake he was making.

Chapter Twenty-Nine

Renzo watched the young woman scan the menu before he walked to her table and smiled.

"May I join you for a moment?" he asked.

"Of course," said Francesca. She smiled.

Renzo sat next to her and introduced himself. Francesca knew instantly that this was Leonardo's brother, they looked so much alike. She noticed the long thin scar across his forehead but thought nothing of it. Francesca looked directly into Renzo's eyes, as was her way.

"There is barely an introduction required," she said. "You look just like your brother."

It was a gorgeous summer day. The weather was balmy and a light breeze off the lake pushed the stale air and automobile fumes away. The sky was bright blue with a few scattered puffed-up clouds. It was a perfect day for lunch *al fresco*.

Renzo jumped at the chance to meet Francesca, the girl who so effortlessly caused such utter confusion and turmoil in the life of his bashful brother. Tomaso's goal that day was to formulate a plan to either assist Leo to get to know the young lady better, or to put his poor suffering brother out of his misery.

Renzo arrived at the Michigan Avenue restaurant at the designated time. Leo had reserved a special table saved for him; one he knew would be close to Francesca.

Francesca arrived, was greeted by the host, and was seated at the proper table. Renzo sat at his table and considered this young woman from a short distance. He thought, *She is stunning. Now I get it.* For a brief moment, he considered going after her for himself but thought better of it.

Francesca made no attempt to enhance her natural beauty. None was needed. She was confident in a quiet way. When she smiled, and she definitely had a special smile for Leo, she illuminated the space around her. *Gorgeous,* Renz thought as he further considered her.

Her smile showed off white teeth and full lips that did not need lipstick. Francesca had the most beautiful, big brown eyes Renzo had ever seen. Her shape was perfect as well, with longish legs and full, but not overflowing, breasts.

Francesca was dressed perfectly in the style of 1927. She wore a two-piece outfit, both of which were form-fitted, but not tight. The top portion was light green and she wore a pleated white skirt. She wore brown shoes with a small heel and a plain felt hat with a silver pin.

The red-faced, grinning Leonardo came out with a glass of water and a menu, placed them in front of Francesca, and muttered, "Good morning, *Signorina.*" He directed a small smile to her, completely ignored the presence of his brother, and quickly walked away.

She smiled at him. "*Grazie*, Nardo." She removed her hat to release her long, curly, dark-brown hair, which she let tumble freely.

"*Signorina* Francesca'" began Renzo. "I am here today to speak for my brother. He is a shy young man and, while he is smart and good, he cannot say to you what is on his mind."

She replied, "Oh, I see. Go on. What is on his mind?"

Renzo continued, "Well, you must see that he turns red every day when you walk in."

She laughed.

"As I said, Leonardo is a good young man. He is smart. He is educated and comes from a proper family—my family—back in Sicily. He restores works of art at the Art Institute. He is the first in our family to complete his education."

Francesca clearly enjoyed the attention from the brother of the man she hoped to get to know better. It showed that her attentions were not lost on Leo, and that there might soon be a way to move forward with him.

"I'm here to represent Leonardo because he wants to see you away from the café and on a personal level."

"Oh, I see," Francesca replied.

She thought for a moment about how to agree that she wanted to get to know Leonardo better as well without appearing to be anxious. She simply looked at Renzo and did not reply.

"*Signorina*, can I ask you a question?"

"Yes, of course," relieved that Renzo was guiding the conversation.

"With all respect, what do you think about Leonardo?"

"What do I think about Leonardo?" she replied. Francesca's cheeks turned pink and she shifted her position in her seat. For the first time, she looked away from Renzo and down at the table. Renzo had received the answer to his question before she spoke a word.

"Leonardo? What do I think about Leonardo?"

"Yes, about Leonardo."

"Well, I think he is a fine young man, like you said. I love his smile. I like that he is shy. I like that he is smart and that he loves art. I like that he is funny."

Funny? Renzo thought. *My brother is actually funny?*

"Miss Francesca, I do not want to take a step that is not welcome or is not appropriate."

"Of course not," she said.

"So, with your consent, I will make the required arrangements for you and my little brother to meet away from the café."

After a moment's pause, she said, "You have my consent to make those arrangements."

In this culture that cherished and protected its young ladies, an arrangement such as this was a serious matter of protocol and propriety. As Renzo had discussed with Nardo, he needed to arrange a middleman to reach out to Francesca's father.

The go-between would explain Leo's heritage, background, employment, family, and homeland to the girl's father and ask permission for the two to spend time together. The person he chose had to be male, must be respected by the community, must know Leonardo personally, and must present his case accurately. If the wrong person was selected, the relationship may not even start.

For the all-important task at hand, and as the brothers had discussed earlier, Renzo approached Father Farrucio. Having known Leonardo and the entire Tomaso family since his return from France, and having a genuine affection for the young man, the priest happily agreed.

Renzo learned that Francesca's parents were Rodolfo and Monaca Bianchi and they lived above their grocery store on Taylor Street. Francesca was one of six children—three boys and three girls. An older sister and an older brother were married and established on their own; the other four lived at home.

The wise and experienced *Signora* Bianchi knocked on the door to the bedroom that Francesca shared with her sister.

She opened the door a bit, stuck her head in, and said, "Talk?"

"Yes, Mama," replied Francesca.

Her mother said, "Francesca, if you want this young man to call on you, your father will meet with his intermediary. If you don't want him to call on you, he will stop it. The choice is yours."

"Oh, I want him to call, Mama. I really like him. He's so smart and funny and handsome and nice and kind. I think I might be in love with him," Francesca said.

Only after this assurance from their daughter that she was, in fact, interested in Leonardo, did her father agree to meet with Father Farrucio.

In the Bianchi residence above the grocery store, Father Edo presented the case of Leonardo Tomaso to Rodolfo Bianchi. His wife, *La Signora* Bianchi, properly stayed in the kitchen to let the men talk, but she listened intently.

Farrucio spoke of the stature of the well-respected Tomaso clan back in Sicily. He told of the lad's original intent to become a priest. He talked of Leo's love of fine art and his excellent job at the Art Institute. The priest said that he saw Leo in church every Sunday and on every Holy Day of Observance.

"Do you hear his confessions?" Rodolfo asked. He looked at the priest hoping for any sort of a reaction when asked indirectly about the sins of the young man.

"Yes, I do," replied the priest. He did not elaborate.

Rodolfo inquired about the age and health of Leo's parents, their village in the old country, why they left, how many siblings, nieces, and nephews, etc.

After two hours, it was agreed that *Signore* and *Signora* Bianchi would receive Leonardo in their home for a formal visit.

"*Grazie, tanto,*" said the priest as he rose to leave. "*Grazie.*"

Leonardo was elated when Father Farrucio told him the good news. The first of the hurdles had been overcome: He was going to meet with Francesca's parents.

"Thank you, Father, Thank you so much!" he said.

The next week, Leonardo dressed in his suit. He wore a tie, shined his shoes, and borrowed a modern hat from Renzo. He shaved especially carefully that morning and put on an appropriate amount of his brother's scented lotion. He walked the mile from his home on Cambridge Street to the Bianchi apartment on Taylor Street.

Rodolfo and Monaca Bianchi received the young man properly. Father Farrucio was already seated in the parlor. Francesca was not allowed to be there and left with her sister. Farrucio stood. "*Signore* and *Signora* Bianchi, this is the young man I have told you about, Leonardo Tomaso," said the priest.

Rodolfo Bianchi extended his hand and looked into Leonardo's eyes. He returned the gaze and shared a solid handshake with his prospective father-in-law. He bowed his head to Mrs. Bianchi.

"*Piacere*," said the Bianchis in unison.

"*Tanto piacere*," replied Nardo.

After coffee and cookies had been served, *La Signora* Bianchi left the room and the interrogation began. More than once, Leonardo felt himself tugging at his shirt collar at the serious questioning of Bianchi.

"Have you ever been involved with another woman?"

"No, never."

"Has any member of your family ever been in jail in Chicago?"

"No."

"In *Sicilia*?"

Leo had to stop and think about Renzo's life in the old country for a moment but then said, "No. Never."

"What do you think of the Mafia?"

"I despise them."

"And your brothers and male cousins?"

"They all hate the Mafia."

"What is your mother's name?"

"Katerina Tomaso, and before she married my father, her name was Balsamo."

"What of her family?"

"They were from Cannita. My grandfather was a butcher." He paused. "They owned the butcher shop."

The questions and answers continued for an hour, which seemed more like twenty-four hours to Leo. Bianchi could see that the bashful young man was hopelessly in love with their daughter. He was finally satisfied that Leonardo came from a proper family and was of an acceptable character to associate with Francesca.

They decided that Leonardo and Father Farrucio should first come to dinner and then, after the Sunday meal, the two young people could spend some time together, briefly, and only with *accompagnatrice*, or chaperones.

The ecstatic Leonardo said loudly, "Grazie! Thank you, thank you, thank you!" he shook the hands of both of Francesca's parents and started for the door.

"Leonardo, don't forget your hat!" called Rodolfo Bianchi.

Leo stepped back from the doorway, accepted the hat from Bianchi and said, "Of course. Thank you so much. Goodbye! *Ciao!*"

After church the following Sunday, Leonardo and Father Farrucio joined Francesca's entire family for dinner. Seated at the table was the married sister of Francesca, Lenora, her husband, Luigi, and their one-year old daughter, Mamie. Also, at the table were Francesca's brother, Dominic, his wife, Lancia, and their three year-old son, Nuncio.

The group was completed by the younger sisters, Maria, Graziella, and, of course, her parents, Rodolfo and Monaca. The family seated at the table or helping in the kitchen was the normal Sunday assembly of the Bianchis in a tradition brought from Ferrara years before.

The two guests, Father Farrucio and Leonardo, made this a special occasion. Leonardo understood he was on display, and he felt the eyes of the family on him throughout the meal, especially the hard look of Francesca's older brother Dominic.

For this special meal, the living room furniture had been pushed to the walls and an enormous table and chairs appeared out of nowhere. *Signora* Bianchi and her daughters had begun preparing the meal the evening before. They resumed chopping and cooking before church the next morning and finished after they returned from Mass.

The first course consisted of *fichi* and *formaggio involtini in prosciutto*, a delicious precursor of the meal to follow. The next course was a hot *tortellini in brodo*. Leo soon learned that he loved the cuisine from the north of Italy as much as that from his homeland.

Signora Bianchi next served large platters of *canelloni al forno al angostura*, which surprised Leo with its delicate flavor and mouth feel. Francesca and her sister Graziella set two deep baking dishes of *lasagna Bolognese*, covered with deeply flavored thick meat sauce popular in their home region.

Finally, the ladies brought platters of *fragole con aceto balsamico e formagio mascarpone* and bowls of *insalata verde con aceto balsamico*. An after-dinner drink of *grappa* followed by hot coffee and *biscotti anice* topped off the perfect meal.

After the clean-up of the dining table and kitchen by the women, Leonardo and Francesca were allowed to walk down Taylor Street to the corner and have Italian iced lemonade together, privately. To ensure the virtue and respect of their daughter, the entire Bianchi family also walked to the corner with Leonardo and Francesca, about twenty feet behind.

Leo didn't mind a bit; neither did Francesca. This was part and parcel of a proper, Old World courtship, and they both respected the tradition. That day, Leonardo and Francesca knew that they had met the person with whom they would spend their lives.

Four Sunday dinners after their first chaperoned walk together, *Signore* Bianchi, having come to a point of trust of the young Leonardo, allowed the young couple to leave the family home together and, for the first time, without *accompagatore*.

It was a blessedly cool evening in late summer. Leonardo arrived at the Bianchi home exactly at six, groomed, and dressed in a neat, brown, three-piece suit and matching tie he had borrowed from Renzo. He sported a stylish bowler hat for the special occasion. Leonardo had walked, as usual, to the Bianchi home.

When he got to their building, he entered the dimly lit hallway. He took two wooden stairs at a time and knocked on the door at the top of the stairway. Francesca opened almost too quickly and smiled that beautiful smile at Nardo. He melted inside as he stepped into the apartment. She looked over her shoulder and then stepped closer to Leo.

She said, "You look so nice, Nardo!"

She slid two fingers of each of her hands under the lapels of his suit jacket and looked him up and down. "So nice!" she said. "Go say hello to my parents so we can leave."

The Bianchi parents were sitting at the kitchen table. *La Signora* smiled at him and said, "Hello, Leonardo. You look so nice today."

"*Gracia, Signora*," Leo said.

He nodded his head at *Signore* Bianchi and said, "Good day, sir."

Francesca's father looked at him and said, "Good evening, Mister Tomaso."

He got right to what was on his mind and continued, "This is a very big day for you, Leonardo. You take care of our daughter with your life. Do you understand me?"

"Yes, sir. I understand."

The father asked, "Where are you going?"

Leo replied, "Francesca asked if we could go to downtown for dinner, and then we'll be coming home."

"Very well. Then you'll be here before nine o'clock, correct?"

"Yes, sir. Correct. Definitely. Without a doubt."

The two left the apartment, Leo in his snappy brown suit and Francesca in a light coat buttoned at the neck and trailing down nearly to her ankles. Soon, they stood together, side by side, alone for the first time. They smiled at each other.

She took his hand in hers, which took his breath away. Thirty minutes later, they were at the busy intersection of State and Madison. To Leonardo's surprise, and to the delight of Francesca, there was a large wooden stage standing in the intersection.

A band played loudly on the platform.

She said, "Leo, that's why I wanted to come here tonight! There's a Charleston contest and I want to dance!"

The shocked Leo said, "I can't dance, Francesca. I don't know how."

"Not you, Nardo! *Me*. I want to dance. You watch me!"

A dozen and a half young men and women were forming a line on the stage facing the crowd.

The young Miss Bianchi unbuttoned her full-length coat and handed it to Nardo. He smiled, once again, marveling at the yet undiscovered layers of this woman. Under her coat, and so her parents wouldn't know, she dressed herself in the flapper style of the day.

She wore a silver, form-fitted dress that exposed her arms and ended at her knees. The dress was decorated with rows of frills and sequins. She wore a fake pearl double necklace that hung down to nearly the hem of her dress and was knotted in the middle. Her brown hair was tucked under the red felt cloche hat she wore. She took a tube of bright red lipstick from her coat pocket and spread it onto her lips. She looked at the smiling and amazed Leonardo.

Francesca stood on her tiptoes and quickly kissed Nardo, leaving both of his lips tinged red and his cheeks rosy. He stood there speechless, dumbfounded, and smiling.

She said, "Here I go!"

Francesca ran up the four stairs onto the stage and got in line. Soon after, the band started playing the most popular dance song of 1927, *The Charleston*. A moment later, the dancers started moving to the music. Soon, the beat and the rhythm spread through the line and all the dancers were moving back and forth, throwing their arms and legs out to the side, then swinging their arms low in front of their legs, then pulling back and repeating the movements.

Francesca grinned and laughed as she danced. It was as if a free spirit had been released from within. Leo was once again amazed at her. He stood and watched with a broad smile that spread across his dimpled cheeks.

Another young man who was watching his date dance on the platform stood next to Leonardo. He said, "Which one is your girl?"

Leo said, "My girl?" He smiled at the idea that Francesca Bianchi was his girl.

The man said, "Yeah, your girl. Which one is your girl?"

Leonardo, his eyes shining, his pulse racing, and his eyes fixed on Francesca said, "My girl? She's the beautiful one."

Chapter Thirty

Mob boss Malo Tancredi said, "That's it for this month, gentle-men, except for one small detail. He signaled with a nod to Gazzo D'Napoli, who sat with Santo and Lupo along the back wall.

Tancredi said, "Bring him in."

The large room had ceiling to floor windows overlooking Taylor Street, three stories below. On the interior wall, opposite the windows, two sets of double French doors lead to a private banquet room. On either end of the rectangular room, eight-foot-high wooden doors allowed workers and guests to enter and leave the meeting room.

A ten-foot-long, polished oak table surrounded by a dozen over-stuffed chairs sat centered in the room. In those fat chairs sat the lieutenants of the Tancredi mob, assembled for their monthly meeting. Positioned at the head of the table was Don Malo Tancredi. His brother and *consigliere,* Renato, was on his right.

On Malo's left, in his usual honored position, sat Chicago Police Precinct Commander Michael Johnson. A mug of beer was on the table in front of the Commander, and he puffed his ever-present black stogie. Promoted long ago from running a shift to Precinct

Commander, Johnson sat next to Tancredi and directly across from Renato.

Police Commander Johnson was a part of the gang's inner circle. From his position of power, Johnson now controlled the police assignments of every cop and every detective working Little Italy. The Don paid Johnson well to provide protection, to lose evidence when needed, to bend police testimony, and to assign his cops to other areas, as requested.

The air in the conference room was heavy with grey-blue smoke floating from the ends of the burning cigars and cigarettes, and there were ten opened and mostly empty bottles of wine and beer on the table.

Underlings and soldiers of the lieutenants and bosses sat in chairs along the back wall and listened. Gazzo stood and walked through the door leading out of the office. He returned a moment later, pushing a wheelchair to which was taped a man with a blood-spotted canvas sack over his head. Every man in the room sat up.

The head cover was removed, and the group saw the broken face of Mario Ventimiglia. His left eye was swollen shut, his nose was smashed against his face, and his lips were cut and swollen. Ventimiglia was taped to the wheelchair at his wrists, elbows and ankles. A rope around his belly held his body tightly to the back of the chair. He was gagged. He had pissed his pants and a large wet circle spread over most of his lap.

Gazzo pushed the wheelchair holding the battered and terrified young man to the table. The bosses looked at the life and death drama unfolding in front of them. Some realized that this was being done for their benefit.

Don Malo Tancredi stood and walked slowly to stand behind Ventimiglia. The crime boss had planned this show well and was dressed for the occasion. He wore a perfectly-tailored dark-green suit, silk shirt, a floral-designed tie, large gold cufflinks engraved with the letter T, and his usual diamond pinky ring.

"You see here a stupid man," he said to the room, gesturing with both hands at Mario.

The men seated around the table paid more attention.

"A dumb shit. A lazy bum. A thief."

He grabbed a handful of Mario's thick hair and pulled his head back. "What this man did was steal from us, gentlemen. From you and from me. Can you believe he has the balls to do that?"

Tancredi sat on the edge of the table. He looked down at Mario and continued, "With balls like you have, I should hire you, not kill you. But how would that look? Not good, right? It would look bad. I have to kill you."

He looked around the table. "Am I right? It would look bad if I let every asshole on the street steal from us, right?" The men around the table nodded and mumbled agreement.

"Commander Johnson, am I right?"

"You are correct, Don Tancredi. Correct you are," said the police commander. "You can't let every asshole on the street steal from you."

Tancredi again looked down at Mario and went on, "I must give you bad news, young man. Bad news. Today is the day that you will die."

Mario struggled and whimpered into the cloth and tape gag.

"The only question now is *how* you will die. I guess I should say how my gorilla of a friend here will kill you," Tancredi said.

He paused to look around the table.

"And how your life will end is your decision."

Malo Tancredi nodded to Gazzo, who withdrew a two-foot-long piece of wire with a small handle on either end from the pocket of his suitcoat and handed it to his boss. He then pulled a pistol from his holster and placed it on the table in front of Ventimiglia.

The men around the table shifted their weights uncomfortably as this violent drama played out. They started to pay more attention. Commander Johnson drank his beer and watched.

"You see, Mister Ventimiglia, your friend Cesare is dead." He laughed. "To think he could cut a hole in the back wall of our warehouse and not be noticed. That's kinda funny, no? But he died bravely. I give him that, for sure. He did NOT give you up. Amazing, but true."

Someone at the table made an unintelligible comment.

"Who gave you up was Jackie over on Madison. Now, how fucking stupid are you to sell my booze to my own brother-in-law? Now, that's stupid."

Tancredi laughed and paused to assess his audience, some of whom chuckled.

"And now you, my young friend, will die tonight. In fact, in about ten minutes, you will be dead."

Mario whimpered and struggled against his bindings.

"Stop struggling. It won't matter. You will die soon, and you will beg me for your death. Yes, you will, my friend."

One of the men at the table moved his chair, and it made a loud scraping sound on the floor.

Tancredi said to his prisoner, "I need you to tell me who the other thief was who stole our liquor. Tell me his name and I'll have my ugly friend here put a bullet in your head, so you can die quickly."

Malo paused to let his words sink in. "Don't tell me his name and I will have my friend here strangle you with this wire."

Malo Tancredi paused. He lifted the garrote off the table and let it dangle in front of Mario's face.

"One way you die quickly and painlessly; the other, the wire, is slow, and I guess maybe pretty bad." He laughed a little.

Tancredi gestured for Gazzo to remove the gag from Mario's mouth.

"And now is the time for you to speak. Who is your thief friend?"

Mario Ventimiglia knew that he had only a few minutes to live. There was no second thought, no deal that could be made to save him. He chose to die painlessly.

"It was Renzo Tomaso," Mario in a raspy voice. "Renzo Tomaso."

"Renzo Tomaso?" Tancredi looked around the group. "Does anyone know where we can find this Renzo Tomaso?"

From the back wall, Santo said, "I know who he is. I know where he lives."

Tancredi said, "Very good. You see, that wasn't so bad. Now I need to know how you two geniuses work. How do you pull off your big caper?" He looked around the table and laughed at his joke.

Mario said, "I pick him up and we go...to your warehouse."

Malo asked, "When does he expect you?"

"Thursday," said Mario.

"What time?"

Mario spoke in barely a whisper, "I pick him up at five in the morning. He waits for me on his front porch."

"All right. You did good, kid. Real good. Now, I'm sorry, but we gotta kill you."

He picked up the garrote with his right hand; the pistol with his left. "Which do you want? You want the gun, right? What's your pleasure?"

"Please, Don Tancredi, don't..."

The Don put up his hand. "Stop. Stop. You are already dead. How many men get to choose the way they die, eh?"

Gazzo kicked the back of the wheelchair. Ventimiglia jumped, but couldn't budge.

"Wire or gun?"

"Gun," came the barely audible whisper.

"You say you want the gun." He pointed his index finger at his own head. He pulled the imaginary trigger and said, "Bang!" and jerked his head to one side.

He smiled. The sadistic side of Tancredi was enjoying the game and wanted to continue the display for the gathered thugs.

"Now, you need to ask me nicely to let you have the bullet. Go ahead. Ask me," Tancredi folded his arms and leaned back against the table.

Ventimiglia trembled with terror, cried, and pissed his pants again. He could barely make a sound. "Please, can I have a bullet?"

Tancredi said, "What? I'm not convinced that's what you want. I need you to beg."

The men in the room, hardened criminals, cringed. Many looked away. Several crossed themselves.

Mario sobbed, soaked now with urine and sweat, and yelled, "Please, Don Tancredi, please let me be shot in the head. Please, Don Malo. Please."

"A wise decision, young man. I will honor your request. Gazzo, give this man what he asked for," said Tancredi. He nodded at D'Napoli.

Gazzo pulled the wheelchair back a few feet and then pushed Mario Ventimiglia out the door. Malo Tancredi walked to the curtained French doors. He swung them open to reveal a massive, twenty-foot-long table, full from one end to the other with food and wine. Scattered around the dining room sat or stood a dozen half-dressed prostitutes.

Tancredi said, "Men, 1927 has been a great year for all of us so far. It's only September. Let's keep it up! Tonight, we play. Tomorrow we work."

Cheers went up from the men around table, including from Commander Michael Johnson.

Chapter Thirty-One

"Look how she eats!" exclaimed an ecstatic Gianna. Weeks had gone by since Rosa's arrival and, while still tiny, the preemie had grown. And she was always smiling.

Nonna said, "She smiles because she's glad to be here."

Since the early morning of Rosa's birth, Gianna and her mother alternated feeding her every four hours around the clock. Gianna was especially thankful on those long days and nights that her mother was there to help with the family and especially with Rosa.

Isabella also helped with the infant's care. She held the delicate baby for hours at a time and only gave her up when it was time for her feeding or for her to be changed. Rosa consumed every drop of milk she was offered.

Eventually, slowly, the women saw the result of their twenty-four-hour-a-fday labor. While lying in the crook of her big sister's arm, Isabella lifted the baby so the entire family could see her. At that moment, Rosa lifted her head for the first time. It was as if she wanted to see her family.

Uncle Leo said, "*Brava*, little one, *brava!*"

Slowly, Rosa's cheeks filled out and she gained weight. Mama was able to nurse the baby girl for the first time. At six months of age, Rosa was the size of a three-month-old. At one year, she was six months in size. On her second birthday, Rosa was an inquisitive, normal-size toddler, eating, walking, and starting to speak.

When Rosa was six months old, Gianna asked Paolo to take a walk with her. The early hot day had transformed into a beautiful evening. A cool breeze off Lake Michigan pushed its way through the buildings and down the city streets, cleaning the air and refreshing all in its path.

"Paolo," she began. "I have something to tell you."

He said, "Is everyone all right?"

She smiled and said, "Yes, everyone is fine. The news is that you're going to be a father again."

Paolo stopped and looked at his wife. She saw the worry in his eyes and heard the unasked question, *Will it happen again? Another early baby?* Paolo saw and lived with the worry and anguish Gianna felt those first months of Rosa's life and didn't want her to go through it again. After a moment, Paolo gained control of the silent turmoil in his mind.

He smiled and said, "*Tesoro*, this is great news. You've made me very happy." He kissed his wife and said, "Can I please have another boy?"

The months rolled by with the family preoccupied with life, school, and work.

When the time came, midwife Anna Moliare returned to the Tomaso apartment. She barreled through the door in her usual fashion and went right to Gianna's side. "Let's have a look," she said as she began the exam.

Anna looked up at Gianna. "We're good here. Let's have a baby."

The delivery was not complicated, and the healthy girl baby was born full term in early 1921. They named her Sofia. Paolo was overjoyed. Luca and Isabella had happily welcomed Rosa and now Sofia into the family. They both helped care for their little sisters.

In February 1922, a year after the birth of Sofia, Mrs. Moliare was summoned again.

Baby Katerina joined the family during the worst snowstorm in two decades. It was a normal birth of their fourth daughter.

Gianna thanked God, Jesus, and the Holy Mother every day for her family. She was grateful for her hard-working husband. Yes, he sometimes drank and talked too much and staggered home from *Bepi's*, but he was a good man, a loving man.

Luca and Isabella were students at the elementary school. Paolo and Gianna would have preferred to send them to *Our Lady of Devine Mercy* for a Catholic education but there was no money for that.

At the time Katerina was born, nine-year-old Luca was in the third grade and spoke nearly perfect English. When the family went out, Luca was the translator if needed.

Isabella had successfully completed kindergarten and was proudly in the first grade. Now that she would have regular school hours, her big brother walked her to school every day, ate lunch with her, defended her, and walked her home every day.

Gia had a houseful. When the two oldest were at school, she and her mother were home with Rosa, Sophia, and Katerina, all born within three years of each other. It was those days when Gianna was more thankful than ever that her mother came to America with them.

Years slipped by unnoticed.

In what seemed an instant, all five Tomaso children were in school, mastering English and bringing language lessons, tales of American history, and arithmetic problems home with them. They did their homework together at the kitchen table.

Luca usually presided over his four sisters, answering questions and making sure they understood their assignments. When Katie started kindergarten, Luca was in the eighth grade. He wore his status ribbons proudly pinned to his shirt. His grades were nearly perfect, and he was a natural born leader who thrived upon responsibility.

When Luca graduated from grammar school, Paolo, Gianna, Isabella, Rosa, Sophia, Katerina, Uncle Renzo, Uncle Leonardo, and *Nonna* Cassio sat in the first row in the school auditorium. Completing the row was Father Farrucio and LaDonna and Emilio Mazzone. Seated In the row directly behind them sat midwife Anna Moliare, her husband Arturo, and their five sons.

They were all there to witness and honor this great and wonderful occasion.

After the ceremony, they went to the Tomaso apartment to celebrate with a dinner of *pasta, ravioli*, chicken, *carciofi, pizza*, and *melanzane.* Gianna made *cannoli* for dessert and splurged to bring home *gelati.*

Isabella, two years behind her brother, loved to learn, made friends easily, and enjoyed school. Rosa, Sophia, and Katie followed the examples set by their older brother and sister. They learned their lessons well and earned a few coins for Gianna doing odd jobs after school and in the summer.

During their summer break, Gianna packed lunches and took the five kids to the beach, to the zoo, or to one of the museums on free admission days. Unless Father Farrucio gave them a ride in his big car, they would take one or two street cars to the area and then walk the rest of the way.

Days spent at the beach were the best for Gianna. She could relax and watch the kids splash and swim in the water of Lake Michigan.

In the ten years since their arrival, life had become better for Gianna. She was more at home in this strange city than ever before and had established a comfortable routine. She enjoyed the little things.

As her children grew, she could see them become Americans. That pleased both her and Paolo. Gia delighted in her family but never grew accustomed to their apartment. She would always miss the farm and her homeland.

To make tenement living a little more tolerable, Gianna gathered assorted pots of varied shapes and sizes and planted flowers of different colors. She kept these plants on shelves Nardo installed for her in the kitchen. He also made her a flower box and anchored it to the outside of their kitchen window. She filled it and nurtured the plants with loving care.

Paolo got up six mornings a week at five o'clock. On most days, he ate breakfast, had coffee, and left carrying a black lunch box. Mama made sure she packed his favorite sausages, bread, cheese, and a piece of fresh fruit.

A happy and contented man, Paolo walked to the streetcar stop on Halsted and rode it to the slaughterhouse. He returned home twelve hours later. Even though he still had the stench of the slaughterhouse in his nose and on his cloths and boots, *i bambini* ran to him for hugs and kisses.

Sunday was the day of the Lord for the Catholic Tomaso household. When each member of the family was properly dressed for church and inspected by Gianna or her mother, they began the walk along Cambridge Street to *Our Lady of Divine Mercy*.

Leading the procession to the ten o'clock Mass was Paolo, Gianna, and *La Nonna*. Five-year-old Katerina walked hand in hand with her parents. Young Luca, fourteen, tall, rail-thin, and growing into a proper young man, wore his best clothes and cleaned and polished shoes. Each of the four girls wore a clean and pressed dress.

The eldest of the girls, Isabella, started every dress, passed it down to Rosa as she grew, who passed it down to Sofia. Each dress eventually made its way down to little Katerina, who proudly wore the garment with just a little tailoring by Mama.

On the walks to church, Isabella, now a lanky twelve-year-old, always walked alongside her brother. Next was Rosa, who was now a normally-sized child, walking with her sister Sofia. The two held hands as they walked.

Bringing up the rear of the column was Leonardo. The kids adored their Uncle Nardo. His job on these Sunday walks to church was to prevent stragglers.

Uncle Renzo attended church only on special occasions, including the Baptism of three of his nieces and the Confirmations and First Holy Communions, plus an occasional funeral Mass for a lost friend or associate.

Along the way to *Our Lady*, they walked past a dozen four-story tenement buildings, just like theirs. On most Sundays, the sidewalk was busy with families going to Mass. They walked past Bepi's Taverna, where some of the men now heading to church had been drinking just a few hours before.

The five Tomaso children were well-mannered and polite, always saying good day, and good afternoon, and thank you in English, as their parents wished. All five Tomaso children were thin but not from lack of food. They each had dark brown-hair; large, dark-brown eyes; and beautiful, olive-toned skin.

After church, family dinner was the highlight of the day. The kids were allowed free time to play outside. The men usually went to the social club to play *bocce* and drink wine. The women prepared the meal.

Every Sunday dinner was important to the family, as it was to many immigrant families. It was a time to relax and regroup from the week that just ended. The Mazzones frequently joined in the cooking and eating of the special meal.

Sugo, left simmering on the stove for hours, filled the apartment with a delicious aroma. Gianna often served a chicken or two, sometimes a goose or a roast. There was always plenty of hot, aromatic, and delicious *pasta* topped with *La Nonna's pomodoro* and sprinkled with grated cheese.

Sometimes, Gianna served *pasta al'amatriciana*, one of her favorite sauces. It was made with *guanciale*, which rendered the most luscious fat and flavor of all. The dish was topped with grated pecorino cheese, made from sheep's milk. She got the four-hundred-year-old recipe from her father who learned it during a trip to Rome.

They often finished the Sunday meal with *dolce*. *Nonna* Cassio's specialties of lemon poppy- seed *biscotti*, anise flavored *pizzelles*, and the fig cookies were delicious and savored.

On special days, Father Edo was at their Sunday table. The kids loved the priest who sometimes picked them up and drove them in his huge green car to one of the city's museums, or maybe even took them to a Cubs or a Sox ball game.

The past years, overall, were wonderful for the Tomaso family. Life seemed nearly perfect, if that was ever possible. They were blessed with food enough to go around. The five children were happy, healthy, and learning American ways.

Paolo had plenty of work, respect, a family and a loving wife. Living arrangements were crowded but served their needs well enough. Paolo and Nardo worked hard, Renzo contributed, and Gianna managed the money. They ate well, paid their rent and bills on time, and were able to save a small amount each month.

The Tomaso apartment had three bedrooms, a large kitchen, and a bathroom. Isabella, Rosa, Sofia, and Katerina shared one bed. Luca slept on the old couch. Uncles Renzo and Leonardo slept in the same bed and shared the room with *Nonna Cassio,* who had a sleeping cot against one wall.

When his sisters were talking or giggling instead of getting to sleep, their older and wiser brother, Luca, would jump up from his sofa, stomp into the girl's room, and say, "Enough! Get to sleep. We have school tomorrow."

Some of the time, the only way Luca could silence the four sisters, especially the little ones, was to climb into bed with them, which he secretly liked doing.

Mama and Papa had their own bed, and it was known by the kids to be a safe harbor for all. On many mornings, one child or the other woke up in the parents' bed. When there was a thunderstorm, all the kids would climb in.

Paolo loved when one or more of his children would sneak into the bed and snuggle with him. He would hold them, smell their skin and hair, and feel their warmth as they slept. As he held one of his sleeping daughters or his son close, he would silently thank God for this child, for all of them, and for Gia. Paolo never knew such love existed, and he carried those special moments with him his entire life.

Life was good, even in this ugly city.

Chapter Thirty-Two

A large, well-buffed black Packard sat idling, a sole occupant behind the steering wheel. The red glow of a cigarette lit his face every time he sucked the hot smoke into his mouth and lungs. He lit one cigarette from the one before and flicked each butt onto the street.

The powerhouse under the hood of the big car pushed large plumes of grey smoke from the tailpipes as the driver watched the building across the street. The car's window was down, and the hot breath of the sole occupant was visible each time he exhaled into the cold, dark morning air.

On the seat next to him sat a loaded Colt .45 caliber revolver. A Remington rifle with a scope rested on the back seat. It was loaded too, just in case.

The pungent smell of city air and urban streets attacked, insulted, and dominated the senses as clouds of stinking, unfiltered coal exhaust drifted steadily down to the streets and cars below. It was the first truly cold Chicago morning in months. Furnaces in the hundreds of tenements, factories, and thousands of homes and businesses were roaring with flames. Chimneys throughout the city belched and passed hot soot and ashes into the air.

From where he was parked, Gazzo could see *Bepi's Taverna* in his left rear-view mirror. It was quiet at this early hour, not that he cared. He would do his job, and no one would say shit to him. Not even the police, who were paid to stay away that morning. He sat and smoked and waited for his prey.

The crime of Renzo Tomaso, the man who would soon walk into his death trap, was a crime of theft and, worse, of disrespect.

To Gazzo D'Napoli, the offense was immaterial. He couldn't have cared less that his intended victim stole whiskey from the warehouse of his boss, Don Malo Tancredi, and sold it for cheap on the street. His orders were all that mattered.

For the job, Gazzo chose two men he knew well: Lupara and Santo. Since their arrival in Chicago, the two had become cold-blooded killers like him. They were reliable and, as Gazzo had witnessed on more than one occasion, capable of incredible and stunning violence.

The three thugs formed a triangle, each one hundred yards from the doorway, the porch and the five concrete stairs from which Tomaso would emerge at any moment. The triangle sealed off any possible means of escape. Efficient. Certain. Deadly.

Gazzo stepped from the Packard and walked slowly across the street to a small, tucked-away recess in the building, where he had positioned his counterpart.

"Lupo! Stay awake! He'll be coming out any minute. Let him get down the stairs to the sidewalk and strike then. Got it? Just walk up and Boom! If he sees you, he'll run across the street and one of us will take him there. *Capice?*"

The reply was a grunted "*Si.*" He held a loaded 12-gauge shotgun under his coat.

Gazzo walked to the other point of the triangle, across the street, where he had positioned his other button man.

"Santo, listen to me. If he runs this way, shoot him in the body. When he falls, walk to him and pop two into his head. Got that?"

"*Si, va bene.* Okay, boss"

"Attention now. *Fare la guardia.*"

Gazzo returned to his position in the triangle and fingered the handle of his well-oiled pistol as it rested in his belt. He leaned back and lit another smoke.

D'Napoli flourished as a Tancredi soldier in this dark and sinister web of violence, deceit, treachery, and murder. He followed orders without question and without fail. He was proud of his reputation: Gazzo D'Napoli never fails.

His love of being a crime family soldier was understandable given his life on the street in *Napoli.* Mob life, bosses, orders, and steady pay got him off the street and gave him a pocket-full of money. His was cruel, dark, and violent work but the Malo Tancredi gang was the only family he had ever known.

The three assassins smoked and stamped their feet to warm them while they waited for their unsuspecting victim to emerge. As the killers waited and watched, they noticed that a light clicked on in the fourth floor of the tenement building. More lights were on in the apartment now, and it looked like the intended target was on schedule and would be coming through the door soon.

Gazzo whistled to his team, and they receded back into the early morning light shadows. Each stared at the door to the building. D'Napoli was well-experienced at this type of job. He planned to get this done and go home. He wanted to pick up that new teenage prostitute he had seen on the street near his apartment. Tancredi told him that he can't beat the whores anymore. *Oh well. It was still good,* he thought, and he could never go against anything Don Malo told him.

Any time now...

That morning, Gianna got up early. She made coffee and hot buns that would soon be slathered with homemade peach marmalade. With frost on the window, Gia dug warm weather clothes out of a large box in a closet near the front door. Weather here, she had learned, was predictably unpredictable.

When she looked outside into the dim morning light, Gianna saw a large black car sitting, idling. *That's odd*, she thought. She had never noticed it on any other morning. *Whoever that is must be waiting to drive someone to work,* she thought.

Paolo was the first of the men out of bed. He hugged and kissed his wife before he took his place at the table. Renzo came out next. Instead of sleeping until late in the morning, as was his preference, his friend Mario was picking him up early again today.

Leonardo was usually the last of the brothers to leave for work, but today was special for him. He would receive a promotion at work that day and would then earn enough money to marry Francesca. He couldn't take any chances on being late. Not today.

Paolo said, "Nardo, this is your big day, and I want you to know how proud I am of you. You've studied and worked hard since we came to America, and you've earned the promotion you're getting. Good job, little brother."

Renzo, who was quietly sipping hot coffee said, "You're doing real good, little brother. Tonight after work you, me, and Mario will go out to celebrate. Don't worry. We'll eat; that's all, and you'll be home in bed by eight."

Leonardo smiled at Renzo and said, "Okay, you got it."

"We're all so happy for you, Leo," said Gianna. "It's all the kids talk about, and they're all so excited about it." She opened the ice box and took out a white carnation. "This is in honor of your big day," she said as she inserted the flower's stem into the buttonhole on Leonardo's suit coat. Gianna hugged her brother in law; he hugged her back.

"Thank you," said Nardo. 'Thank you so much." He smiled and left for work.

Leonardo opened the front door of the tenement and stepped onto the concrete porch. It was dark except for a single bulb burning overhead. An old, gray, tattered baby buggy sat pushed off to one side.

This brisk, cool air was something Nardo loved about Chicago that he could rarely experience back home. He inhaled a deep breath of the cold, refreshing, morning air into his lungs. He loved the crisp feeling and always thought that it made him feel alive.

Seeing him, the killers walked slowly in his direction, concealing their weapons.

Leo pulled a pack of cigarettes from his suit pocket, took one out, and replaced the pack. He put the cigarette to his lips and lit it with a match, which illuminated his face in the dim morning light. He took a deep drag, and exhaled, utterly unsuspecting that he was the prey of murderous hunters.

"It's him," said Santo from across the street.

Lupara was just ten feet away when Tomaso stepped off the porch and down the first couple of stairs. He stood in front of the startled Tomaso said, "Renzo Tomaso" and raised the shotgun.

The shocked Nardo could only mutter a stunned "No, no... Le..." before the twelve-gauge exploded into his chest. The blast from the shotgun lifted him up and backwards through the air. He came down on the porch, flat on his back, a gaping wound pouring blood from his shredded heart and lungs.

Lupo turned and walked back to the Packard, removing the shell casing and putting it in his pocket as he walked. Santo, having not been needed to slay a fleeing Tomaso, quietly turned and walked to the car. Gazzo leaned in to see the dying face of their target. Blood gurgled from Leo's mouth with each shallow, fading breath. D'Napoli had killed enough to know what death looked like.

So that he could claim the killing shot, Gazzo pressed the muzzle of his .45 into the wound of the dying man and fired a single shot, blowing a hole through what remained of Tomaso's chest. The bullet chiseled a chunk out of the concrete stair before it ricocheted away, tearing a gash in Nardo's shoulder.

Gazzo turned and slowly walked to the big car, got in, and drove away with Lupara and Santo. One block from the murder site, Santo said, "Drop me at the corner. I live here."

Within moments of the shooting, lights were turned on throughout several buildings. People opened windows to see what happened, and several came outside.

In the Tomaso kitchen, *Nonna* Cassio dropped three plates when she heard the *Boom!* of the shotgun blast. The two women and two men looked at each other. No one moved. Then, just a moment after the blast, they all heard the sharp, loud *Crack!* from Gazzo's pistol.

Paolo said, "What the hell?!"

He walked to the window with Renzo. They couldn't see anything from their vantage point.

Gianna gasped, "Leonardo just left. No! No! Not Leonardo!"

The two brothers barreled down the four flights of stairs jumping from landing to landing. Renzo burst through the door with Paolo on his heels. They saw the broken body of their younger brother lying there soaked in his own blood.

The only words Renzo could utter were, "Oh God! No! No! No!" as he lay down on the porch next to the dead body of his younger brother.

Paolo stood in stunned silence until the reality of the horror struck him. He dropped to his knees gasping for air and kissing Nardo's dead, bloody hand.

Renzo kept repeating, "Nardo, Nardo not you...They wanted me...not you! It was for me... they want to kill me, not you! I'm sorry. I'm so sorry, Nardo!" The rest of his words were incoherent. Eventually, he just lay there sobbing in his grief.

A crowd of people slowly assembled and surrounded the stairway to the Tomaso tenement in a semi-circle, as if the porch were a stage. The memories of violent killings in the old country were all too fresh in the minds of many of these immigrants. They thought they had escaped this butchery, but the same senseless violence was here too.

Gia said to her mother, "Keep the kids in the apartment!" She ran down the stairs and saw the blood-soaked body of Leonardo on the porch with Paolo and Renzo kneeling by his side.

"Oh, no...not you Nardo...not you...not dead...not dead... not dead!"

She dropped to her knees, kissed the bloody face of her husband, and then knelt to pray by the body of this young man she loved. The white carnation she had given him only a few minutes before was now blood red.

She turned to the neighbors who had gathered and said, "Someone go get Father Farrucio. Hurry!" With that, a man in the crowd turned and sprinted toward the church. "And call a doctor!" she shouted after him.

Renzo, his face soaked with blood, was utterly inconsolable as he cried into the chest of his dead brother. Paolo crossed himself, rocked back and forth, clasped his hands together, and prayed. Gianna knelt next to Leonardo's head and wiped blood off his face with her apron.

As she wept, she said, "You sweet boy. You sweet boy. You are with God now."

Father Farrucio ran from the rectory to the building. He wore his sleeping clothes under a hastily clad jacket. He carried his purple stole. He understood instantly what had happened when he saw the Tomasos crying and praying over the fallen young man.

The priest walked up the stairs to the porch where Leonardo Tomaso lay murdered. The three people were in shock and looked blankly at him, not able to comprehend his presence.

Farrucio kissed and placed the purple stole around his neck and knelt next to the slain Leonardo. He crossed himself and made the sign of the cross on Leonardo's forehead, praying all the while. He anointed the body with holy oil and prayed the Sacrament of Last Rites.

Paolo, Gianna, and Renzo knelt next to Leonardo's body. They crossed themselves and prayed through their tears. One by one, the two dozen men and women who gathered in front of the porch lowered themselves to their knees on the street or sidewalk. Many held burning candles in the early morning light. They were crying at the brutal and tragic waste of human life. Soon, all knelt. All prayed.

Sirens heard in the distance were drawing closer.

Farrucio stood and faced the kneeling group, his hands and vestments red with Leonardo's blood. He blessed the impromptu Mass and led them in prayer. The priest was interrupted when a police car, sirens blaring and lights flashing, screeched to a stop in the middle of the street.

Two burly coppers walked through the crowd of kneeling people up to the stairs to where Leonardo Tomaso lay broken, bloody, and dead.

"Who saw what happened?" one officer asked. He glanced through the crowd and realized—or didn't care—that he was not going to get a reply.

One cop, not knowing the significance of this gathering, said, "All right, the show's over. Break it up and go home. Go on now."

The people who had knelt to pray waited to see if Father Edo would speak to them. No one moved.

An ambulance rolled up. Two white-clad men laid a stretcher on the porch, a few feet from Leonardo's body.

Detective Jimmy O'Shea pulled his Buick up next to the police cruiser and shut it off. He grabbed his note pad and his hat, stepped out of the car and walked over to the crime scene. He saw that the priest from *Our Lady* led thirty or so people, now kneeling in prayer. He walked to the stairs and onto the porch.

A police photographer was taking pictures and each time he snapped a photograph, a flashbulb popped, and the garish scene on the porch was brightly illuminated. The grief-stricken family was asked to step away from the victim so the photographer could do his work. They stayed huddled together.

Jimmy O'Shea used his own shorthand to write notes on his pad: *klld w/shtgn + pstl. Lved in bldg. Lvng fr wrk. Yng Itln male. Wll drssd. 2 men, 1 wmn at scn. Approx. 27 y/o. Kllng Rndm? Mstkn ident? Mob ties?*

The detective took one last look at the victim and then nodded his approval to the ambulance drivers to remove the body. Jimmy checked the porch, the stairs, and the front sidewalk for shell or bullet casing and found none.

He then walked back to his Buick, leaned against the fender, moved his hat to the back of his head, and lit up a Lucky. He sucked the smoke into his lungs as he watched the ambulance drivers do their job. *Why was this young man murdered?* he thought. O'Shea looked up at the porch. His eyes briefly met Paolo's.

One of the brawny ambulance drivers grabbed Leonardo roughly under his armpits. The other grabbed under Nardo's knees. One said, "Got a grip? Okay, lift!" With a grunt from both, they raised the body up and laid him on the stretcher.

The driver spread a white sheet over the body, which immediately turned spotty dark red. They lifted the stretcher, carried it to the open doors of the ambulance, slid it in, and locked the doors.

"You can claim him at the city morgue," the driver said. He got a small note pad and pen from the front of the vehicle and came back to get information.

"What is the name of the deceased?" he asked the three Tomasos. No one answered. Paolo, Renzo, and Gia were too shocked and lost in their grief to comprehend. The ambulance man looked at the group of three immigrants and said loudly and slowly, "What is his name?" Again, there was no answer.

The driver, thinking he was being deliberately ignored became angry and demanded, "Hey! Does this dago have a name?"

Gianna, her clothes saturated with blood, walked down the stairs to the side of the large man. She kept a firm grip on the handrail and took a deep breath to compose herself. Gianna focused her eyes on the white clad man and said clearly and loudly, "His name is Leonardo Tomaso. Leonardo Tomaso."

The driver said, "Okay, was that so hard? This is 1102, right?"

"Yes," she said. "1102. Fourth floor."

Father Farrucio came to Gianna's side and put his arm around her shoulder. He said to the driver, "That's all for now."

The man wrote down the name and address and got in the ambulance passenger seat. It drove away into the cool morning air as the priest, Paolo, Renzo, and Gianna watched, still stunned.

"They came for me, and they killed Nardo," Renzo muttered to himself. He sat on the side of the porch, head in hands, crying and mumbling. Paolo sat next to his brother in silence.

Gianna said quietly, "Father, please have everyone go home now. Have a Mass for Nardo on Sunday. Thank you."

Father Edo hugged her and said, "Of course, of course."

She said to Paolo and Renzo, "Come upstairs when you're ready. I'll go tell the children that their uncle is gone." Gia slowly climbed the stairs, crying softly.

Gianna sat in silence on the edge of her bed for a long moment, stunned. Her tears began slowly, and then it was as if a dam broke, releasing a deep, powerful torrent of sobs that came from deep within her heart. Her uncontrollable, soul-shattering grief overwhelmed her, took control of her, and then subsided.

She washed her face, arms, and hands and changed her bloody clothes. She woke the children and gathered them in the kitchen. She told her son and four daughters that their dear Uncle Leonardo was gone and that he was now in Heaven. The kids, sobbing, hugged their mother as never before, the five of them lost in shock and grief.

Paolo and Renzo stood side by side on the porch in silence for a long while.

An hour later, the body of their younger brother Leonardo, the hard-working, artistic, quiet, young Sicilian immigrant, lay stretched out on a cold metal slab in the Cook County Morgue, his chest blown apart.

Chapter Thirty-Three

Gianna tapped on the front door of the Mazzone apartment. LaDonna opened it.

"Oh, my God, LaDonna. He's dead! Nardo is dead!" Gianna sobbed and fell into the arms of her good friend.

"I know, I know," said LaDonna. "I know, *cara*. Come in. I'm so, so sorry, Gianna. Leonardo was such a good boy."

Gianna cried, "Monsters run the streets here. Who would do such a terrible thing? These *teppesti*, these thugs are as bad here as they are at home. Like a wild animal! They shot him dead like he was a wild animal! They gunned him down!"

"Sit. I'll get you some tea."

"Such a good boy! He was so excited about his promotion today that he left early. Ha! The one day he left early, and it got him killed," she sobbed. "*It got him killed! And to die like that!* Like a mad dog! Shot down!"

"Sit, Gia," said her friend.

"He was going to be a priest back home, did you know?"

"Yes, *cara*. He would have been a fine priest."

"He never should have come to this country. He was too good for America."

LaDonna said, "Yes, you are right. Nardo was too good.... too good."

Through tears, Gianna said, "Nardo loved everyone... and art... and he was getting married soon, did you know?"

"Yes, I knew, I knew." LaDonna brought hot tea. It sat on the table, unnoticed.

Despite the difference in their ages, Gianna Tomaso and LaDonna Mazzone had grown to become close friends. They were, after all, immigrants, countrywomen, and they had lived across the hall from each other for ten years.

LaDonna loved the Tomaso family. She was always close by and an enormous help for each birth. She watched the kids grow and attended every Baptism and most school functions, as well.

The two women met often to have lunch or coffee and to share their thoughts and feelings. LaDonna always had good advice for Gianna about being a woman in a foreign land, and the difficulties involved.

Quietly now, Gianna said in a whisper, "Leo is gone... Leo is gone...oh my God, my God, my God." She put her forearms over her midsection and rocked forward and back, forward and back.

"It's so wrong LaDonna...so wrong...I just want to scream at God about the injustice."

LaDonna said, "I know, *cara*, I know."

"What about my family? What will happen next?"

"Don't even think that, Gianna. Your family will be fine. You'll hold them together. You will, Gianna. You can. Only you."

"I don't know what I can do," replied Gianna. She looked at LaDonna. "I'm not that strong."

The older woman replied, "Stop it! You're not the simple little farm girl that left Sicily ten years ago. You're a much stronger and much smarter woman now."

"No, I know, I know - but this is too much," said Gianna. "Did you see my poor husband today? Too much, LaDonna. It's too much for me."

LaDonna said, "Yes, I saw Paolo today. He is destroyed. Grief is eating him. Anger...he wants revenge, he needs *la vendetta*. Paolo will not be himself for a long time."

Gianna said, "You're right. My husband is gone. His eyes are empty. He loved his brother so much. He feels that he has failed."

Signora Mazzone said, "Paolo has not failed. This is not his fault in any way. You have to make sure he understands that."

Gianna said, "And Renzo might be dead now, too. We don't know where he is. That would make this much worse for Paolo."

LaDonna continued, "Gianna, hear me. It's important."

Gia stopped rocking herself and looked at her friend. "God gave you the strength deep inside to protect your family—what is yours. This is your woman's strength, and it's different from a man's strength. Your strength comes from your heart and from your soul, not from your back and arms."

"I'm not sure I'm that strong," Gianna said.

LaDonna said, "I'm sure you are. I'm absolutely certain. I know you have this strength. I see it in you every day."

"Thank you, my good friend. *Grazie*. It's late. I have to go see that the kids are sleeping."

LaDonna said, "I'll be over in the morning."

The two friends hugged, and Gianna went across the hall to her children. *Maybe*, she thought later. *Hopefully, LaDonna was right. Maybe, because of all I've been through, I am the woman she thinks I am.*

That night, after the kids were asleep and the apartment was quiet, Gianna lay in bed and prayed to the Virgin Mary. Unable to sleep, waiting for her husband to come home, Gianna closed her eyes and as she often did, and thought of her childhood on the farm she loved all those years ago.

How could she know that her father would die just six days after her wedding? Gianna loved her father deeply and often saw him in her dreams. He always comforted her and, all these years after his death, her Papa still made her feel loved and safe.

Gia thought of how their peaceful life was interrupted by the murder of Roberto Tomaso that day at the *festa*. She remembered the ugly and terrible act of revenge by her husband and his brothers.

She still had nightmares from the visit of the two old Mafia bosses and their mounted bodyguards. Gianna remembered the utter terror she felt as the two men confronted her father-in-law on the porch. She learned respect for calm, intelligent reasoning of Tomas Tomaso that day.

Her mind ran though that early morning, years ago now, when they found Renzo beaten nearly to death and dumped in the front yard of the farmhouse. It was she who pushed her mother-in-law aside and stopped the bleeding. She saved Renzo. *Her.*

Her faith and her belief in her God were tested and strengthened with the birth of tiny Rosa. She always felt that her God empowered her to nurse the tiny baby to life when Rosa could have so easily died.

Painfully, she saw the man she loved – the strong, smart *contadino*, the farmer she fell in love with sacrifice and demean himself every day by doing the filthy, backbreaking work necessary to put food on the table and to educate their children.

Earlier that morning, she had sat on the cold concrete porch next to the bloody and murdered body of Leonardo and prayed for his soul while his blood was still wet on her hands.

Lying in her bed that night, Gianna knew that she must be strong for her family. LaDonna was right. She had adapted to this dirty, grey, violent city. Life was hard, and it had made her hard. She was no longer meek or weak; she was strong. If she had to fight to save her husband and fight for the survival of her family, then fight she would.

Gia fell asleep with the rosary beads between her fingers, praying for strength and guidance.

Chapter Thirty-Four

The first rays of early morning light were seeping through her windows when the sleeping Francesca heard Leonardo call her name. She heard, "Francesca! Francesca! It's me, Nardo!"

At the same moment that she heard his voice she saw him. But this was strange; she knew she was asleep. She must be dreaming.

Leonardo was standing far away and looked small. He was surrounded in black. It was as if he was walking on air. There was no floor and no walls; there was just space.

When she saw him, he smiled and walked toward her. He grew larger and larger as he came closer and closer to her.

A smiling Nardo kissed her lightly on the lips and then he was gone.

Francesca fluffed up her pillow, pulled the covers up against the chill in her room. She smiled, thinking of how much she loved Nardo and how happy she was with him in her life.

She went back to sleep.

Chapter Thirty-Five

Later on, the day of the murder, Paolo and Gianna went to the police station to answer questions and to sign the required paperwork. All the questions the police officer asked Paolo were answered by Gianna.

After the police investigator was satisfied, the Tomasos went to the Mazzone Funeral Parlor to arrange the burial. They sat in heavy, overstuffed chairs facing their friend and neighbor Emilio Mazzone, who looked at them from across his desk and through his bifocal eyeglasses.

Mazzone knew Leonardo well and his heart was broken too. With a deep breath, he gathered himself emotionally to do his job.

"*Mi dispiace.* I'm sorry, Paolo, but I have to ask some questions," began Mazzone.

Paolo could not speak. All he could do was motion to Mazzone with his hand to proceed as if to say, *ask the questions you need to ask.*

Mazzone asked, "Where do you want Leonardo interred?"

Paolo looked at Mazzone blankly, lowered his head and said in a voice so low that even Gianna, sitting next to her husband, could barely hear. She put her hand on Paolo's arm.

Gianna said, "You decide, Emilio. We trust you."

The undertaker had to ask about the choice of casket, visitation, and death notices for Leonardo. When she was unsure of what Paolo wanted for his brother, she looked at him. He could only utter a word or two or move his head or his hand slightly.

The arrangements concluded, Gianna opened her purse, took out a small number of bills and extended the cash to Mazzone. The undertaker said, "No, Gianna, no. There is no cost to you."

Gianna, too emotionally drained to disagree, stood and said, "*Grazie* Emilio. Thank you."

Paolo sat still, looking at the floor, not speaking.

Gianna said, "Let's go home, Paolo."

Paolo didn't move or even acknowledge that his wife had spoken.

"Paolo, we have to go home now," she said and squeezed his hand.

Without looking up, Paolo asked, "Is he here?"

"What did you say, Paolo?" asked Gia.

"Is Leonardo here?" Paolo asked.

Mazzone stared at the paper he was preparing on his desk. The undertaker sighed, knowing where this question would likely lead. He raised his head to look at Paolo and removed his glasses.

He said, "Yes, Paolo. He's here. We picked him up already. He's downstairs. We'll take good care of him."

When the undertaker answered Paolo's question, a sound Gianna had never heard before came from her husband. It sounded like a soft moan of terrible grief and a tragic sigh of despair. He seemed to slump and get smaller in his chair.

Paolo said, quietly, "I want to see him."

The undertaker looked hard at Paolo, seeking confirmation that he was aware and in control of his actions. He looked at Gianna. Her face was without expression.

"Are you sure?" asked Mazzone.

Paolo answered, "Yes, I'm sure."

Mazzone looked at Gianna. She nodded her consent. The undertaker said, "Come with me then. And listen to me: there are other bodies in the room."

They padded along silently on thick carpeting and walked along a corridor. At the end of the hallway, Mazzone opened an unlocked door and said, "He's downstairs. Watch your step."

When the three stepped off the bottom stair they walked into the undertaker's work area. Several other corpses were under sheets on metal tables in the large, cool room. Each was waiting their turn with the undertaker.

Paolo saw Leonardo, covered to his neck with a green sheet. He gasped at the sight of his young brother lying there, pale and still. Paolo took a step and staggered to his right. Gianna took hold of one arm, Mazzone of the other. He took two more steps and stopped. He pulled his arm from Mazzone. Gianna put her arm around his waist. Together they took the final few steps to reach the table that held Leonardo's body.

Gianna held Paolo tightly and, when she felt him go weak, she held him tighter. Paolo stood looking down at the torn and broken body of his youngest brother. He could not speak. A minute passed, then two.

Gianna said, "*Tesoro*, enough. We have to go home now."

Her husband did not reply.

Again, slightly more firmly, she said, "Paolo," and then "Paolo."

Her husband looked at her through blank eyes that could not comprehend. Gianna knew her husband's world had been shattered and nothing would make sense to him in this nightmare.

"Let's go home now," she said softly.

Silently, Paolo turned to leave. His wife led him to the stairway and up. Emilio Mazzone followed. The two walked slowly out of the funeral parlor bound together as if one.

That night, Paolo lay awake in bed after a few hours of unnatural, restless sleep. He felt paralyzed, shattered to his deepest core by the sudden, shocking, overwhelming, utterly unbelievable death of his brother. It was as if his world had collapsed onto him. He couldn't move or think. He was drowning in grief and despair, as if he were sinking in quicksand.

Tomaso couldn't breathe. He swung his feet onto the floor and sat on the side of his bed, gasping for air. Gianna heard him from the kitchen and hurried in. She sat next to him.

"Are you okay?" she asked.

"Okay? Am I okay? No, I'm not okay," he said. "My brother is dead! I am not okay!"

The words were surreal, impossible to believe and yet true. He slid to the floor and put his head onto Gianna's lap and said, "I want my brother."

For the next several hours, her husband alternated between gut-wrenching sobs and restless sleep. Gianna had never seen him so humbled and distraught. When Paolo came to the kitchen, he ate a small supper in silence. He drank gin. After a while, he said, "I'm going out".

"Please, please be careful, Paolo." She held him close.

Paolo asked, "Where is Renzo?"

Gianna said, "No one's seen him. He's gone, probably hiding someplace."

Paolo stepped into his wife's arms and said, "Now they'll kill Renzo, too. Both of my brothers, both Leonardo and Renzo. Oh my God, what can I do?"

Gianna said, "It's good to cry, Paolo," as she pulled his face to her shoulder.

Paolo said, "Gia, Nardo is gone! My baby brother! Nardo! The best person I ever knew. I can't bear it."

"God will help you to accept this, Paolo. What is the other choice? To join him?"

Paolo didn't reply.

Gianna said, "Listen to me, Paolo."

Her husband looked at her.

"I will take care of everything. You have only to get your next breath. Just that, nothing more."

Chapter Thirty-Six

Franco and Alessa Zignano draped wide, black banners across the front of *Bepi's Taverna*. They knew the Tomaso family from church and, although Leonardo was not a regular like his brother Paolo, they knew him, too.

The Zignanos echoed the sentiments about Leonardo that they heard spoken throughout the day. "A fine young man," "Smart and kind," "Did you know he was almost engaged?"

By the time that evening rolled around on the day of the murder, *Bepi's* was packed. Bowls of hot *pasta* and *pomodoro* were put out, compliments of Franco and Alessa. Word of the murder had spread through the neighborhood, and to the stores and factories for blocks around.

Workingmen came to drink and to mourn the senseless and brutal murder of one of their own. Some came to grieve, some to swear revenge.

"Who will they kill next?" asked a middle-aged, swarthy man from Calabria. He wore a closely cropped beard and had his hair tied in a bun on the back of his head.

"Another of us killed by these scum and the police won't do a Goddamn thing!" Dino Nicosia, a laborer from the neighborhood, said, "The boy did nothing. Nothing at all, and they gunned him down. No one is safe! I say we find these bastards and kill them ourselves."

Most of the men in the tavern didn't know Leonardo but they knew what violence was. Many thought they left such random terror behind when they immigrated, but this murder was more proof that things were just as bad here.

The men had gathered out of frustration that one countryman could kill another. They were angry there would be no police help; angry that gangsters ran the streets here; angry that they were helpless against such violence.

The customers were workmen all: diggers of ditches and tunnels, movers, haulers, loaders and unloaders, shovelers of everything from shit to coal. As each worker filed through the door, he brought traces of his work.

Each uniform or jacket, every shirt and pair of pants carried the smell of that man's day's labor and reeked of fuel, coal dust, tar or oil. Sledgehammer men from the slaughterhouse on Halsted stank of dried blood. Each pair of boots carried the coal dust, tunnel mud, smashed fish guts, horse manure from that man's labor.

The air in *Bepi's* was bluish grey from the smoke of hundreds of cigarettes, pipes, and cigars. The assault on the senses continued with the smell of filthy sawdust, vomit, and urine from the drunks, the stench of stale beer, and spilled whiskey.

Tonight, it was an outrageous act of evil that brought them together. The cruel murder of Leonardo Tomaso was big news in the hundreds of tenement building with their thousands of occupants.

The unanswered questions in the minds of many were, *Who would bring this violence to their doorstep? Who would be next? Why did this happen?*

The drinkers boasted about how well they knew the victim, even though they mostly only saw the quiet young man walking to and from work and on an occasional Sunday at Mass.

They argued long and hard about who would have tried to have Renzo killed, and why, and how they could have killed the wrong man.

Late that night, the door swung open and into the drinking den walked a grieving and drunken Paolo Tomaso. He was dressed in black and wore a black arm band. The large room became silent, as if all the air had been sucked out. The din of people talking and arguing suddenly stopped. The crowd opened a pathway for Paolo to the bar.

As he slowly passed by them, some offered words of condolence to him, others touched him as he passed; still others crossed themselves. Paolo claimed a vacated spot at the bar and Franco put a drink in front of him. Paolo quickly gulped it down. He gestured for another and raised the new drink into the air.

The barroom was silent until Paolo spoke. "Listen to me!" he began. "Listen to me!" My young brother Leonardo lies dead on a cold slab in this foreign land. His soul is with God. *Vendetta* is for the living, and I vow at this moment that I will find and kill the murdering sons of pigs that took my brother's life.

"Now, my brother Renzo is gone too. Is he in the river or the lake? Is he dead too? These *teppesti*—these thugs, these animals, these pieces of shit, have cut too deep. I curse them! I curse them!" With those words he pulled an old Western style revolver from his belt and raised it into the air.

"I swear on the soul of my dead brother that I will kill these *figli di putane* that murdered him. I vow on the lives of my children. I will hunt these bastards down and slaughter them. I swear to God this *Vendetta*!!"

Every man in the tavern, except for three, cheered. Sitting at a small table in the corner of the tavern sat Gazzo D'Napoli, Lupara, and Santo.

Paolo knew that it was Renzo who was the real target. It was Renzo who was up to no good, as usual. It was the kind and innocent Leonardo who was gunned down while the real target was four flights above. None of that mattered to Paolo. Leonardo was gone and Renzo was in hiding or dead.

The men in the bar drank and argued into the night. Some felt better, some felt stronger as they drank. The three murderers sat and listened to the men talk hatred and revenge. Especially, they listened to Paolo.

The drunken Tomaso ranted on into the night as the bar emptied. "Damn them! Damn them! I'll kill whoever it was myself. They killed my brother! The pieces of shit need to be killed. I can't take it. I have to kill them. They murdered my brother! A family man, just a boy really, not a fucking criminal like these animals. He was getting married soon! They shot him down like a mad dog outside of his home because they thought he was someone else!"

As lights were being turned to their full brightness in the now mostly empty barroom, Paolo stood to leave. He staggered toward the door until he was stopped by Lupara.

"Hey, friend. Why don't you stop shooting off your mouth, eh? Nobody knows who killed your brother, so let me buy you another drink and then I'll walk you home to make sure you don't get shot too."

A drunk and obnoxious Paolo slurred, "No! I'll find out who did this and make them pay. Dead! Dead!"

Franco Zignano took his loaded shotgun from its place behind the bar. He held the gun and watched the situation carefully.

Gazzo D'Napoli stepped in front of Paolo Tomaso, and the two men saw each other for the first time. The scarred, thick, ugly, violent mob enforcer and the slender, gentle farmer-turned-slaughterhouse-laborer glared into each other's eyes.

"Do you know what you're saying?" asked Gazzo, clearly fed up with the threats. "You talk this shit, make these threats. I cannot let you get away with that. You insult and embarrass our employer, and this you cannot do."

"Leave me alone!" replied Paolo. He stared into the eyes of the killer and drunkenly pulled the gun from his waistband.

Gazzo ripped the gun from Paolo's shaky hand and said, "You hold a gun to me? *To me?!* I run this neighborhood and you threaten *me?*" The thug easily broke the pistol in two pieces over his knee and tossed the parts across the barroom.

"*I* killed your fucking brother! It was me, Gazzo, and there's not a Goddamn thing you can do about it. And now I'm going to find that other piece of shit thief coward brother of yours and kill him too."

Paolo was wide eyed, shocked, and terrified but through his emotions, he stared back at the face of evil. He spit in Gazzo's face and said, "I'll kill you; I'll kill you."

Gazzo wiped his face with his hand and said, "You've just signed your own death warrant, peasant. You and your thief brother are dead men!"

Zignano banged the butt of his shotgun on the bar and the men looked at him. Gazzo saw the deadly look in his eye. Franco gestured to the door with his chin and said simply and firmly, "OUT!"

Gazzo smiled at Franco and he, Lupara, and Santo moved slowly toward the exit, all the while looking from Franco to Paolo and back again. They left.

Franco said, "Paolo, come here, my friend."

Paolo staggered back to the bar and put his head down. "It was them; it was them," he said.

Franco offered, "They work for Malo Tancredi, Paolo. Don Malo Tancredi. You know who he is. Let it go. You cannot beat the devil. Be smart. Think of your children and Gianna. Come on, I'll walk you home," he said and went to look outside in all directions from the windows.

He thought that Tancredi's boys would never harm such a good liquor customer as him. Just in case, he carried his loaded double barrel in his right hand as he hooked his left arm around Paolo.

When he got to the door with Paolo, Franco turned to look at Alessa who was standing behind the bar. His wife, as always, saw and heard everything. Franco's eyes met hers. She nodded in agreement and the two left for Paolo's home. The street was deserted.

Ten minutes later, Paolo was propped up against the wall next to the door of their fourth-floor apartment. Franco pounded on the door; Gianna opened.

Franco said, "*Signora*, keep him home. No matter what—do not let him leave."

Gianna nodded her assent.

Franco turned and retreated down the stairs. Before he left, he turned and said, "This could not possibly be more serious, *Signora*. These are bad, bad people, and now they want your husband dead too. Keep him home no matter what."

Gia heard the urgency in Franco's voice and saw it in his eyes. She said, "I will. Thank you. Thank you." Gianna helped Paolo stagger to their bed where he collapsed in a drunken heap. She undressed him and covered him.

The next morning, a sober Paolo sat with his wife at the kitchen table. Word of what had happened at *Bepi's* the night before was already on the street as Gianna learned when she went to the market that morning.

She said, "How could you be so stupid to insult these gangsters? You know how they are. What will we do now? Call the police? Ha! That's a big laugh. It's worse here than at home."

"*Tesoro*, please," replied Paolo. "It'll be fine. I'll think of something."

"Don't *Tesoro* me! They want to kill you!" she said softly so the kids wouldn't hear. "You understand? They want to gun you down like they did Leonardo." She crossed herself. "How could you do that? You insulted them!"

"I was drunk."

"It doesn't matter if you were drunk or not. You know how they are, or did you forget?" she said. "For them, it's all about respect. Control. Fear."

Gianna put a cup of coffee in front of Paolo. She looked at their five kids sitting together in the small parlor. She asked, "What will we do now? Your family, Paolo. Your family cannot survive without you. You can't work; you can't even leave the building."

Paolo sat silently and listened to his terrified wife. There was nothing he could say. There was no answer and no solution.

Gia continued in a whispered voice "I heard what you said... *big mouth! Big man!* You're gonna kill them all!"

"Gianna, please stop."

"Paolo, you're a farmer working in the stockyards, not a fighter or a killer. What were you thinking?"

"Gia, enough. Stop yapping. I'll think of something," he said louder. "And let the kids go out. They're safe. No one will touch them."

With those words, the kids looked up hopefully.

Gianna said, "Alright, your father said you can go out. Be careful. Luca, watch out for your sisters. I mean it! And stay right in front of the building."

The five Tomaso kids scrambled out the door and ran down the stairs.

"Paolo, I'm so scared! What will we do? What can we do?" She sat in his lap, put her arms around his neck, and cried. "We can't lose you."

Paolo sat silent.

"You haven't done anything...just threatened. And you were drunk. Why can't they just forget this happened and let it go?"

Paolo said, "Because they can't forget it, Gia. You know that. They will never let this go."

Chapter Thirty-Seven

Father Edo Farrucio's ten-year-old Pierce-Arrow was parked in the lot behind *Our Lady of Divine Mercy*. The dark green shine of the vehicle was faded now after all those harsh winters. The chrome bumpers and spokes tried to sparkle but showed their years.

Even considering its age, the Pierce-Arrow was still a rich man's car, an expensive vehicle. The priest used the vehicle to do what he called *God's Work* in and around Little Italy since it was given to him by the Archbishop years before.

To Father Edo, God's work meant taking people to and from doctor's and dentist's appointments, to their hospital visits, for delivering groceries to shut-ins, and to handle whatever important errands his parishioners couldn't do themselves.

A big part of God's Work, Farrucio reasoned, was helping to keep the neighborhood kids busy. With that in mind, he would often be seen driving as many kids as would fit into the passenger compartment of the car to the *North Avenue Beach*, to *Lincoln Park Zoo*, or sometimes just around the block a dozen times.

That morning, a young monk in brown flannel robes with his hood up against the morning chill walked across the parking lot of *Our Lady of Divine Mercy Catholic Church*. He walked past the

Pierce-Arrow, got into and started the other church vehicle, a 1920 Studebaker truck, which was a small vehicle used for shopping and light hauling. He drove it to the gate of the parking lot.

Farrucio had entered the parking lot from the other direction. When the young priest saw him, he stopped the truck and pulled his hood back off his head. Father Faruccio was his boss, his mentor, and, he hoped, his friend.

"Father Edo, do you need anything at the pharmacy?" asked the monk.

"No," Faruccio shook his head and smiled. "Thanks for asking."

The priest had a problem inside the rectory that needed his immediate attention: a fugitive was waiting for him.

A few minutes later in his private rooms, the priest sat across from a visibly shaken Renzo Tomaso. A young nun entered the room carrying a large tray of food, which she placed on a table in front of Renzo. In German accented English, she asked, "Father, can I bring you something to eat or maybe some tea?"

"Yes, just tea, please, Sister George," said Faruccio.

Renzo began eating but had little appetite.

"Father, I don't know what to do. They came for me and murdered my brother. Dear God, forgive me! Leonardo is dead because of me! What a gentle boy! You know, I never even saw him angry, not even one time. The bastards, excuse me, Father, killed him."

At that, both men crossed themselves without saying anything.

"And now they're going to kill me too!" wept Renzo. "They will find me and murder me like they did Leonardo because no one will stand up to them. No one! I'm a dead man!"

"Renzo, we'll think of something."

"Father, here I am, hiding, and I can't leave. They're looking for me now. I have to get out of town, but I can't."

Sister George walked in, placed the tea service on the table, turned and walked away. Faruccio said, "Thank you, Sister."

"Father, what should I do? What would you do?"

"Renzo, let's start at the beginning: I've known you since you arrived in Chicago. Admit it—you are a petty criminal."

The comment surprised Renzo.

"Yes, you are a criminal, and everyone knows it. You were a street hustler and thief in Palermo, and a womanizer. I know what they did to you," the priest said, looking at the long scar across Renzo's forehead.

"Yes, it's true, Father."

"And now you're stupid enough to steal from evil, violent men. A Mafia Don, no less: Malo Tancredi."

Renzo looked at the priest in surprise.

"Don't look so shocked, Renzo! Everyone knew it. Your friend Mario kept no secrets. I'm only amazed it took Tancredi so long to find out."

Father Farrucio stood.

"I know your parents are good people. You come from a good family. What happened to you? Do you think you're too good to make an honest dollar? You'd rather steal?"

"I don't know why I'm like this, Father."

"Renzo, I don't like people like you...lazy bums... thieves. Actually, you disgust me."

Renzo hung his head and accepted the verbal lashing.

"Do you not understand that the young people, especially in your family, look up to you and see what you do?"

"I never thought of that."

"No, I'm sure you didn't..."

"I'm sorry, Father."

"Your entire family comes to Mass every Sunday. Sick, rain, snow—every Sunday! You, I only see you in church at Baptisms, First Holy Communions, and funerals."

The priest was trying to get to the spiritual core of this man. Farrucio didn't care that Renzo was deep into fresh pain and lost in grief. He wanted to break him down, and he thought, *Then maybe, just maybe, there could be a chance for him.*

"I'm heartbroken that Leonardo is gone. Such a fine young man! But you know what, Renzo? I'm glad you're here. I'm glad you're here. And I know exactly what you have to do."

"You do? Tell me Father. Anything. Please. Anything," said Tomaso.

"First, you have to get right with God, and by that, I mean Confession. You have to get down on your knees and confess all your sins to God through me now. All of them."

"I will do that, Father."

"Secondly, after you clean your soul, Renzo, you have to pray and ask God to guide you."

"I will, Father. I will."

"Do you believe in God, Renzo? Do you have faith?"

"Yes, I believe" replied Renzo. "But I haven't prayed or confessed in years."

"We'll do it now," said Farrucio. The priest stood and walked to a cabinet to get his purple stole. He kissed the silk stole and draped the holy garment around the back of his neck.

"Begin," Edo said.

Renzo eased himself down to his knees and began his Confession. He started slowly and shyly with, "Forgive me, Father, for I have sinned. It's been twenty-four years since my last confession."

"Continue," said the priest.

An hour later, the Reconciliation was done.

Father Faruccio said, "Renzo, you've done some terrible things, and now your entire family will pay the price for your mistakes forever. That's not fair, but if life was fair, you'd be dead now and Leonardo would still be alive."

Renzo sat and listened to the rebuke.

"You've sinned greatly and frequently, but I believe that you are sorry for the life you led and for the sins you committed," said Farrucio.

"I am sorry, Father. I am."

"I give as your penance the death of your brother Leonardo Tomaso. The grief and the guilt you feel now and will feel the rest of your life is your penance for all that you have confessed to me."

"Yes, Father."

The priest blessed Renzo and pronounced in Latin, "*Et ego te absólvo a peccátis tuis in nómine Patris, et Filii, e et Spíritus Sancti.* I absolve you of your sins, in the name of the Father and of the Son and of the Holy Spirit."

Farrucio thought of his own confusion and suffering and of the relief he felt after being absolved by His Holy Eminence in Rome years ago.

"Now go to bed, Renzo. Pray to God tonight and ask for His guidance. Ask Him what you should do. Pray, Renzo."

"Yes, Father. I will. Thank you."

I have an idea or two myself, thought the holy man.

Not long after Renzo went to bed, Father Farrucio walked to his desk, sat, and opened the deep drawer on his left. From the rear of the compartment, he withdrew a metal box.

The priest released the clasp on the container and took out two small, cloth-wrapped bundles. He opened the smaller of the two packages and removed the French Legion of Merit award and his Congressional Medal of Honor. He set them on his desk side by side.

Farrucio looked at the medals for a long time, while his mind travelled back to that night in France nearly ten years before when he defended the field hospital. Farrucio still wept for the men he killed and prayed for their families, just as he did for the soldiers, doctors, and nurses killed in that terrible early morning attack.

The second cloth-wrapped bundle contained the long, sharp bayonet he used that night in France. The priest unwrapped and placed the weapon in its metal sheath on the desk next to the medals. He withdrew the blade from the scabbard.

He hadn't seen the knife in years, and he marveled at how it gleamed and reflected the lamp's light, as it looked back at him. The priest touched the blade. It had lost some of its sharpness but was still formidable. Edo took a sharpening stone from the bag and slid the blade back and forth against the stone until it was, once again, razor sharp.

After more long moments lost in thought, Father Farrucio re-wrapped the medals and returned them to the drawer. He pushed the knife back in its sheath but did not return it to its place in the desk. He set it, instead, under a small statue of Saint Jude, the saint of desperate and lost causes. He lit a small candle above the killing tool.

Early the next morning, Father Edo, after a night of tossing and turning, awoke to find Renzo sitting at his small breakfast table, waiting.

"There may be a way, Father," said Renzo.

Chapter Thirty-Eight

"Lemme tell you all something and listen good: I don't give a flying fuck if you agree with me or not. This big mouth has to die. Got it?!" Gang boss Malo Tancredi shouted to his crew. Even in his tailored pastel suit, French cuffs and diamond pinky ring, his face pulsated red in anger.

His younger brother, Vincenzo, stopped arguing with his older sibling and boss and said, "Fine, fine. Let's get it done, then."

"Now, you know where this Goddamned loud mouth lives," Malo said, looking at Gazzo. "This Paolo Tomaso."

D'Napoli nodded.

"Wait outside. He'll have to come out sooner or later. Then kill him. I want him *dead*, and I want him killed in daylight so everyone will see it. *Tu capisci*?"

"Yes, sir. I understand," replied the thug. "You want him dead."

Tancredi nearly exploded in anger thinking that Gazzo was being insolent. He pounded the table with his hand and yelled, "That's right. I want him dead; I want him killed in daylight; I want him bloody; I want his dead body lying on the street in front of his building for all to see! Is that fucking clear?"

The men in the room sat in silence.

"I've had my fill of disrespect from these neighborhood people. These are my streets. *Mine!* "Is that clear to everyone?" yelled Malo Tancredi.

Someone said, "Yes, boss."

Tancredi took a breath, exhaled and said quietly, "So, yes, I want this Paolo Tomaso dead." He paused and then continued, "Gazzo, don't go too far. Just the target. No one else. Understand?"

"Yes," said Gazzo.

Tancredi, knowing that Gazzo could easily snap with the slightest provocation said, "Santo. Lupara. You two watch Gazzo. No other civilians are to be hurt. Just Tomaso. You got that?"

"Yes, Boss. We got it."

Tancredi said, "Now all of you get the fuck out of here. Go back to work."

As the heads of a large Chicago gang, Malo Tancredi and his five brothers knew that they could not tolerate the slightest disrespect from within their ranks or from the people on the street.

The members of the gang and the community had to fear the Bosses. Without fear, there would be no respect, no order, and no control. The stature of the gang would be weakened, and profits would go down.

Unless any sign of revolt, however minor it may be, was squelched immediately and decisively, opposing factions could spring up. More killing would follow. Honest cops would bring more heat to the operations, and the newspapers would report all the gory details.

This was a pattern of enforced respect that went back centuries in Sicily. The criminal bosses and their lieutenants and captains understood it well. The disrespectful Paolo Tomaso must die. The killing would be a message, a statement to the immigrant community that they were of absolutely no importance when compared to the interests of the Tancredi gang.

Later that day, Gazzo parked his black Packard directly across from the entrance to the building that housed the Tomasos. He exited the vehicle to position his two thugs.

"Like the Boss said, we wait for him to come out. We kill him on the spot, like we did his brother. Lupo you gun him first; we finish him."

"Yes, boss." came the reply.

Gazzo said, "Santo, go there," as he pointed to a small opening between the buildings.

"Lupo, you go over by the pole," he said, pointing to a wooden telephone pole.

Each man took his position per Gazzo's instructions. Another solider watched the back door and had instructions to kill Tomaso on site.

"Let him get all the way out before you move," said Gazzo.

The three murderers stayed and watched the building throughout the day. At dark, replacements arrived. The next day, Gazzo and his two thugs came back and continued the stakeout.

Word leaked out to the neighborhood that Tancredi ordered the killing of Paolo. Tenement residents saw the squad of killers waiting for its prey and were utterly powerless to prevent the murder.

Police Commander Michael Johnson made certain that his men would not interfere.

Every porch in the neighborhood was clustered with men debating what they could do. The wives went about their day; the children were told to stay indoors or in the alley, not on the street.

Dino Nicosia said it first: "There are more of us than of them by far. We can overrun them, grab their guns, beat them, and send them away."

Someone in the crowd said, "We don't have guns; they do. We can't beat them, Dino."

Nicosia replied, "We can't just stand here and watch this happen. They'll own the streets."

"Listen to me," said an older grey-haired workman from the block. "They already own the streets, the police, and the mayor. They can kill us all and nothing will be done to them."

No one supported Nicosia and his idea died quickly.

Franco Zignano made the journey by trolley car across the city to see Don Ernesto Chiuderre, the *Capo* of one of the other powerful Sicilian mobs in Chicago. That they knew each other from childhood is the only reason Franco was able to gain access to this dark inner sanctum of extortion, murder, pimps, and thieves.

The two men were physical opposites: Franco was short and thick; Don Ernesto was tall and lanky. Franco was clean-shaven except for his mustache; the Don wore a trimmed white beard and a thin moustache. Chiuderre was a handsome man who considered becoming an actor before the path of crime opened for him.

That his childhood friend earned such status in the underworld was no surprise to Zignano. As a boy and as a young man, Chiuderre had always been prone to violence. He was smarter and stronger than most and simply took whatever he wanted by cunning or by force.

Franco entered Don Chiuderre's private chamber and smiled at his old friend. When he stepped closer to where Chiuderre sat, the Don raised his right hand. Franco took his hand and kissed the large ring on his middle finger. Chiuderre said, "Good, Franco, good. Please sit. How is Alessa? The children?"

The two men sat across from each other in the small, quiet room. The floor was partially covered with a thick, oval tapestry. The drapes were closed, and the room was dimly lit by just three small lamps. Zignano had no way to know that light hurt the eyes of his boyhood friend or that the Mafia *Capo* only rarely allowed anyone into his private rooms.

A young man carried a tray holding a small pot of strong, thick coffee and seven *anisette biscotti* into the room, He placed it on the table between the two men. To please his boss, it had to be seven biscuits, not six or eight. Seven was the only acceptable number and the servant never questioned why.

"Would you like anything else, sir?" he said.

"No thank you, Nello," said the Don.

Chiuderre poured *espresso* for his guest and handed the cup to Franco on a small round saucer. The Don offered the plate of biscuits to Franco and said, "Please."

Franco accepted the biscuit. He served himself as well and took a bite from a crunchy biscuit.

After small talk about their home country and old friends, Chiuderre said, "So what brings you here, my old friend? Is it the situation on Cambridge?"

"Yes, it is. You see, Paolo Tomaso," Zignano explained, "is a family man. He works hard. Yes, he drinks too much sometimes and, yes, he sometimes talks too much, but he is a good man."

"Yes, yes," said Chiuderre

"Five kids! Four girls and one boy! *Per piacere*," Franco said as he touched his fingertips of one hand to the other and used his hands to gesture. "Don't let our fellow Sicilian die for a few drunken moments! I beseech you, Don Chiuderre. I beg you to intervene with Don Tancredi."

After an appropriate time to consider the words of his old friend, Don Chiuderre spoke slowly and deliberately. He said, "No, Franco, no. I cannot interfere. This is not my business. It is up to Don Malo, not me. I would not tolerate Tancredi's interference in my matters. I have to extend to him the same courtesy."

"Is there nothing I can do or say to change your mind?" asked Franco.

"No. *Niente.* I'm sorry, my friend. It is final," replied the mob boss. He then ended the meeting by saying, "Thank you for seeing me. It was good to talk about old times. I wish you well."

Franco stood, understanding that the session was over. "I will leave you now, Don Ernesto. I wish you continued health and good fortune."

"Nello! Bring the car around and drive *Signore* Zignano home," the Don ordered.

"Franco, you take care of yourself when this happens. Sometimes it's better to look the other way," said the Don.

Chiuderre liked the idea of the Tancredi family alienating an entire neighborhood with yet another stupid act of violence. He saw it as a possible door opening for his organization to reap profit from yet another fertile neighborhood of the city.

On the ride home, Zignano realized that there would be no help for Paolo from the neighborhood; no help from Renzo; no aide from the police, or from anywhere else. Tancredi would send assassins for Paolo; they would hunt him down or wait him out, no matter how long it took. This was a matter of respect, and respect was a sacred thing.

Paolo Tomaso stood alone.

Two days after the slaying of Leonardo, Paolo got up from bed at the usual time. The kids were still asleep. He felt that he could no longer cower there and do nothing. He had decided to confront Gazzo face-to-face and challenge him. He didn't know what the challenge would be; he just knew he couldn't go on this way.

He and Gianna ate a quiet breakfast together, just the two of them alone at the kitchen table. Gia kept a close eye on her husband, this man she knew and understood so well.

"You know you cannot step out the door," she said.

Paolo just looked at her.

She said, "Paolo, I know you and I can see in your eyes that you want to do something. You know they're waiting just outside to kill you. Where do you think you're going today? And don't lie to me."

Paolo remained silent.

Gianna was visibly upset and stood as she demanded, "I asked where are you going?!"

Still, Paolo refused to answer.

Gianna stepped close to his place at the table and removed the dirty dishes from in front of him. "Do you think you're going to go find those *teppesti*—these animals—and try to make some sense of this?"

Paolo finally replied, "I don't know...but I can't sit and wait."

"I see. You're going to explain to them that they killed the wrong Tomaso? And you think then that they'll leave you alone?"

"Maybe. I don't know," replied Paolo.

"The talk everywhere is how you shamed them, how you threatened them, how you insulted them."

"I know."

"Then you know they must kill you, Paolo. You know how they are."

Paolo did not speak. He stood and put his jacket on and reached for his hat.

Gianna said, "The animals are waiting for you outside. If you step out that front door, you will be slaughtered like your brother, and then what?"

Paolo walked toward the door, holding his hat.

Gianna blocked the door.

"Paolo, we cannot lose you!"

He said quietly, "Move out of my way."

Gia didn't move. Instead, she put her back against the door and made it clear that Paolo would have to move her physically.

"You silenced me ten years ago when you did your terrible *vendetta* for your cousin. I'm not the same farm girl anymore. I will not be shut up again!"

"Gianna, move!" said Paolo.

"These people in America don't want us in their country. There is no help for us. You know that. What would we do without you? We have no money. Five children. We'll be on the street, Paolo. I will not let you leave!"

Paolo stood there waiting for her to finish. Gianna could see a vein throbbing on his forehead. He was determined; so was she.

"Paolo, we need you. I can't lose you. We must stay together to survive, to raise these children. You can't go!"

Paolo put his hat on his head and took a step toward the door. She saw, for the first time, that he had a long pistol stuck in his belt.

"You and your guns! You killed that boy in the mountains for revenge. There would have been more death if your father had not stopped the retaliation. Remember?"

Paolo did not speak.

"You're a farmer, not a killer! Is this the legacy for our children? Why did we come to America if not to get away from those ways? What will you do? Get killed? What's wrong with you, Paolo?"

"I have to do something. I have to try," he said.

Gianna said, "It's no wonder the people here hate us. They think we're all from the gutter. Think of who you are. What would your mother want? Your father? What would Leonardo want?"

"Please Gianna, please. I have no choice."

Gianna said loudly, "No. I won't let you go. Enough of this killing. It stops here! No!"

Rosa and Sofia, in their nightgowns, came out from the bedroom and saw that their mother upset. They walked to her and stood by her side, crying.

Rosa said, "Pa, why is Ma crying? Did you hurt her?"

At that moment, tall, thin, fourteen-year-old Luca came into the room and saw what he thought was a threat to his mother. He said nothing, but stepped between his parents, facing his father, his hands at his sides balled into fists, ready to strike Paolo to protect his mother.

Tomaso took his hat off and knelt on the floor by two of his girls. "No, I would never hurt your mother."

Frustrated and emotionally exhausted, Paolo crossed the room and stood at the kitchen window, silently looking down at the street below. Gianna walked up behind him and put her two hands high up on his back. She said, "Do you see what this has done to us? This is not the life we want; this is not who we are."

Frustration welled up in his eyes. "I don't know what to do," Paolo whispered.

Chapter Thirty-Nine

"Mama, what's happening up there?" asked Isabella.

Gianna felt her pulse quicken and blood rush to her cheeks. She answered "I don't know. We'll see when we get closer."

On that sunny morning, Gianna, twelve-year-old Isabella, and little Katerina were walking home from the market. Gianna and Isabella each carried a paper bag full of groceries. Katie walked alongside her mother, holding her hand.

Gianna felt safe walking with the girls knowing that in the sacred Old-World tradition, they were not to be touched. Since the murder of Leonardo a few days before, Paolo paced and watched the sidewalk thirty feet below anytime a family member left the building. Today was no exception, and he stood at their kitchen window looking down at Cambridge.

Tomaso had seen the shiny black car pull up just fifty yards from their front porch, the same landing where his brother was slaughtered. He saw the rear door of the luxury vehicle open and the bloodied and dead body of a man pushed from the car and onto the curb. He saw the car speed away.

Ten minutes later, he saw a police patrol car pull up, followed by an unmarked police vehicle. The cops spread a white sheet over the body, and a young officer was ordered to stand next the murder victim. A few minutes later, an ambulance arrived. It was then that Paolo saw Gianna, Isabella, and Katerina walking toward the building and the crime scene carrying bags of groceries.

Seeing the police vehicles, a quarter of a block ahead, a terrible sense of dread overwhelmed Gianna, but they could not get home unless they walked past the scene. They continued walking. Isabella couldn't know that her mother grew more fearful with every step, and that her heart pumped harder as they drew closer.

Fifty yards from the front door to their building, they saw a white sheet covering what Gia knew was a dead body. The corpse was lying across the curb, half on the sidewalk and half in the street.

Paolo was all Gianna could think about. *Please, God. Not Paolo under that sheet. Please.*

As they drew closer, they saw that the white sheet was stained dark burgundy with drying blood. A large, red-faced young police officer in a fresh, new uniform stood guard next to the victim. A half dozen more cops milled around smoking and taking up time. Gianna saw that the police didn't care about the victim or who killed him. It was just another of many gang slayings and no big deal to them.

Detective Second Grade Jimmy O'Shea also stood by the sheet-covered body. He had built a reputation as a tough, by-the-book cop who never took a cent from a bootlegger or anyone else. O'Shea walked a large circle around the remains, looking for clues. He questioned spectators, all of whom knew a total of nothing. *No surprise there*, he thought. The detective took notes. He underlined what he thought were the most important words. He wrote on his pad *no bld on grnd, bdy stf. vctm nt mrdrd here, trtrd, dmpd.*

The police photographer took a dozen pictures of the victim. O'Shea leaned back on his Buick and pushed the brown, wide-brimmed fedora hat back up on his short, cropped, auburn hair. He put a Lucky between his lips, dug in his shirt pocket, pulled out a match, and ignited the smoke with a scrape of his thumbnail. He inhaled deeply. Something bothered him about this murder.

He didn't have to read his notes to known that a young Italian man was gunned down just a few days before, not fifty yards away. *What the hell is happening on Cambridge?* he thought. *This was a typical gang hit, but the dumping of the body here was too much to be a coincidence. The two murders had to be somehow related.*

The detective rolled through questions in his mind. *This victim was killed someplace else and his body dumped here. Why? What did he know that was so important to get him beaten, tortured, and murdered? This was no doubt a gang murder and a message—but what was the message? Who sent it and to whom? Something was wrong on Cambridge, but what?*

O'Shea lit up another Lucky and walked back to take another look at the body.

The ambulance men were the same two who took Leonardo to the morgue. The driver looked at Gianna with icy contempt. She remembered how disrespectfully he spoke to her the morning Leonardo was brutally cut down. She glared back at the ambulance man. The driver turned and said to his coworker, "It's them again, Tommy. These fuckin' wops. They just can't stop killin' each other."

Gianna, now terrified, steeled herself. She put her hands on Isabella's shoulders and looked into her eyes. "Isabella, go look under the sheet and see if it's your father." The young girl looked at her mother for a long moment, her saucer-wide eyes filled with tears.

Gia said again, "Go see if that's your father. Go now!"

Seeing that her mother was serious, she nodded and said, "Okay, Ma." She turned and walked slowly to the sheet-covered corpse.

The police officer who was standing next to the body saw her approach. "What do you want, Miss?" he asked in a not unfriendly Irish brogue.

Isabella said, "My mama told me to come see if that's my father under the sheet."

"Your father?"

Isabella nodded.

The young cop hesitated and looked at his fellow officers. They were paying no attention to him and could not have cared less. Detective O'Shea had joined the rest of the cops. The officer said, "Come on, Missy. I'll pull the sheet down for you. But don't you touch anything."

Isabella replied quietly, "I won't."

A few short steps put her standing next to the corpse. Isabella felt as if her heart would pound out of her chest. She looked down at the covered body, trembling and terrified, and pulled a deep breath into her lungs. Her thin body shook from the earthquake happening in her chest as the officer pulled the sheet back to reveal the dead man's face.

It was not her father, not Paolo, but she knew who it was. The left side of the victim's head was gone, and he was covered in dried blood.

"So much blood!" was all she could say. "So much blood!" She turned and ran back to her mother.

"It's not Papa! It's not Papa!" she said. Gianna hugged her young daughter. "I know who it is! It's Uncle Renzo's friend Mario. It's Mario. A part of his head is gone!"

From high above, Paolo saw his family stop to look at the bloodied sheet. He saw his wife talk to his daughter. He saw

Isabella look into her mother's eyes, as if doubting or needing clarification.

Oh my God...Gia thinks it's me under the sheet, he thought. Paolo grappled with the thought of what his daughter must be thinking as he watched her approach the young cop standing by the body. He bolted from the apartment, down the stairs, and ran the fifty yards to his wife's side.

Gianna said, "You're can't be here! You can't be here!"

Paolo hugged Gia and their daughter and said, "I know. Let's go home." He took the two shopping bags. "Come, hurry along, girls."

She took their two daughters by the hand and the four of them hurried to their building. Detective O'Shea, his fedora still propped on the back of his head, walked toward them, his note pad in one hand and his pen in the other. For an instant, Paolo Tomaso and Jimmy O'Shea locked eyes.

Paolo said, "Leave us alone!" as he walked his family to the shelter of their tenement building. O'Shea thought, *I remember him. It was his brother that got killed.* Jimmy nodded his acknowledgement of Paolo's demand and watched the group until they crossed the concrete porch and entered their building. The four went into the building and climbed the stairs to their apartment.

When they entered, Gianna saw that Paolo's face was an ugly red. They both knew that this murder and dumping of the body was a message to him. Isabella ran to her father, who kneeled to embrace his daughter. She threw her arms tightly around Paolo and cried from fear and relief, feeling safe in the arms of her father. He could feel his young daughter tremble.

"You were so brave, little one. So brave!"

Paolo raged inside. Tomaso wanted—needed—revenge. He needed to hurt these people who killed his brother and now terrified his family. Gianna now understood more clearly than ever before that the lives of her children were nightmares because of the animals that ran the streets. She knew, too, that something had to be done.

Gia saw the same look in the eyes of Paolo she saw the night he killed Lurio Scarletto. She said, "We did nothing to deserve this...why won't they leave us alone?"

"They can't," was the reply. "They won't stop until I'm dead."

Chapter Forty

The sun shined brightly onto the tenement streets on another cool, crisp morning. Father Farrucio had been up since dawn, preparing. Cambridge Street, normally full of happy, energetic youngsters even on a chilly day and at this early hour, was deserted. Not one child and not one adult walked in any direction. It was as if the plague was in the air, or wild dogs roamed the street.

It was a day owned by Satan himself.

Gazzo, Lupara, and Santo again formed their murderous triangle. This time, they waited for Paolo to come out of the building. Another of Tancredi's men watched the back door, and they had a man on the roof. All possible means of escape were sealed.

D'Napoli leaned on his car, smoking as usual, with his Colt .45 stuck in his waistband. Santo was in the same recessed area where Gazzo stationed him to wait for Renzo. Lupo leaned against the same pole, smoking a cigarette.

Into this somber setting, rounding the curve in the street from *Our Lady of Divine Mercy* walked Father Farrucio. He carried only his bible as he entered the tenement building next to *Bepi's Taverna*, the farthest on the block from the Tomaso home. Gazzo saw the priest and assumed he was making his rounds, trying to keep the block calm.

Farrucio continued to the next building in the row and the next until he stood in front of the Tomaso's building and just twenty feet from Gazzo.

"Hey Father, come on...Bless me. I've been a bad boy." Gazzo stood looking at the priest. He smiled but even a grin on the ugly, scarred face couldn't help his appearance. His half-ear sat on the side of his wide head and he looked at the priest through his deep-set eyes with overhanging forehead and flat nose.

If the devil had a face, thought the priest.

Father Farrucio walked over to Gazzo. He was not afraid of the sociopath and stared into the dead eyes of the murderer. He raised his right hand and etched the sign of the cross in the air in front of Gazzo. As he did so, he said, "May the devil that spawned you pull you back into the fires of Hell from where he spit you, you piece of crap."

Gazzo coiled at the bold insult and balled his fists. He looked around to see who else heard it. Sancho and Lupara were close by, watching, but not close enough to hear what the priest said. For an instant, the rage that directed his life since childhood nearly took him over. Gazzo didn't care about the rules of the street gangs and mobsters. He could kill a priest, a nun, or even a child. This time, D'Napoli held his rage within. He thought, *Not today, priest, but someday soon, I will kill you.*

As Farrucio turned and walked away, Gazzo spit on the ground and said, "Fuck you, priest."

He looked at his two pals as Edo entered the Tomaso building. *Maybe*, thought Gazzo, *the priest came to give Last Rites to Tomaso.* He could not have suspected that Farrucio was delivering much more than a final blessing.

Standing on the concrete porch, Father Farrucio stared down at a makeshift altar that honored the spot where Leonardo had died. There was a lit candle in a glass encasement. Next to it stood a crucifix held vertically by a wooden stand. A small framed photograph of a handsome, smiling Leonardo stood in front of the cross. The candle, the crucifix, and the picture sat on a black cloth positioned to cover the dried blood of Leonardo, but still much of the red residue was visible. The dark stain had settled into the concrete despite the hard scrubbing and bleaching by the building's women.

He blessed himself and said aloud, "May you rest in eternal peace, Leonardo Tomaso."

Farrucio crossed the porch, opened the door, and entered the building. He trudged up the four flights of stairs and knocked softly on the Tomaso's door. Gianna opened and gasped the word "Father!" as she quickly pulled Farrucio in. Paolo stood there, unshaven and in his undershirt. The two men hugged.

Gia noticed how Father Edo had aged since they met when she went to her first Mass ten years prior. She also thought about how important this man was in her life, and how she loved him. She often recalled the private Baptism of tiny Rosa, who was now nine years old. She knew that day that she loved this man. Since the Baptism, he had grown even closer to the family. The priest now had a receding hairline and his hair was a distinguished-looking salt and pepper. He had the beginning of a double chin, and several creases in his forehead.

Over the years, Father Farrucio had heard the confessions from the Tomaso family. He had baptized their children, gave each of the kids their First Holy Communion, and confirmed them in the faith. He performed Last Rites for Leonardo and presided at his funeral and burial. Edo Farrucio was an important part of Gia's and Paolo's life together and had a huge impact on their family.

Out of breath, Edo panted, "I have a message from Renzo."
Paolo said, "From Renzo? Thank God, he's still alive!"

Father Farrucio prayed with the family. He loved all children, and these five were special to him. Holding back tears, the priest blessed each child with the sign of the cross on their forehead. He hugged and kissed each of them.

Edo offered to hear their confessions, took the purple stole from a pocket, once again kissed it, and draped it around his neck. Gianna confessed first followed by her mother. Each of the children confessed their minor sins to the priest. He thought, *How pure are the hearts and minds of children everywhere.*

As he heard their simple missteps tearfully confessed, the priest remembered roaming the streets of Paris and Rome after the war ended. He adored the simplicity of young ones, but he knew all too well the evil nature of too many men, like the animals waiting downstairs.

While the Tomaso children prayed and confessed their trivial sins, murderers waited downstairs to kill their father. Gazzo wiped his pistol clean and checked the bullets. He took his scoped Remington rifle from the trunk. He put it on the back seat of the Packard, loaded and ready just in case Tomaso got past them and ran.

In a corner of the kitchen, with a dozen potted plants breathing color from the wooden shelves that Nardo had built, Father Farrucio sat facing Paolo to hear his sins. Gia called the children into the living room to give the men privacy. Paolo confessed drunkenness, hatred, and anger. They prayed together; the priest absolved Paolo of his sins.

"Father," asked Paolo. "Why Leonardo? Such a good, good man."

The priest said, "No one can understand why things happen the way they do. You and I know there are evil people in this world who do terrible, brutal things."

Tomaso looked at the priest.

"I'm so sorry that your family became victims of these monsters, but Paolo, you must find the strength to go on. Your children need you. You have no choice but to accept the unacceptable."

"I'm not sure I can."

"It's not a question of *can*. It's a matter of *must*. You can either focus on the blessings in your life, or you can live in bitter anger and hatred. The choice is yours." The priest stood.

Confronted by reality, a sober Paolo knew that the priest was right: He had to accept that his brother Leonardo was dead, and nothing could bring him back.

On the sidewalk below, Lupo raised his shotgun, as if he were shooting it from his hips and said, "Boom, Boom" under his breath. Santo paced impatiently, waiting for the kill time.

With the confessions complete, Edo took a vial of wine from his jacket pocket and opened a packet of wafers. He placed the wine and the wafers on the kitchen table and blessed them as he prepared to deliver the Holy Sacrament of Communion to the family.

The priest gave Communion to the children first, placing the blessed wafers onto the tongues first of little Katerina, and working his way up to Sofia, then Rosa, followed by Isabella and then Luca. Farrucio then placed a wafer onto Gianna's tongue, and finally that of Paolo. The priest made the sign of the cross with his thumb on each forehead, as he softly prayed. He then said the prayer of Communion while the Tomaso family sat silently, listening to the Latin words.

As the priest said prayers and blessings in Latin, Gazzo lit another smoke and paced the street below. He thought that he may have to go in and pull Tomaso out by his neck and throw him down the stairs just to get this done.

Only after the confessions and Communion did the priest feel that he had brought the family to the invisible line between this world and the next. Farrucio would do anything in his power, including sacrifice his own life, to protect this family, but he had to be ready for any and all possibilities. Father Edo Farrucio had prepared each of the Tomasos to enter Heaven.

The priest said, "Let's say the Lord's Prayer. Luca, you lead us, please." The boy confidently recited the prayer along with his four younger sisters, his mother, father, grandmother, and his priest.

As he stood at the door to leave, Father Farrucio said, "God will be with you all today. Do not be afraid." The Tomasos looked at the priest.

He said, "Now let's do what we have to do."

Chapter Forty-One

"O'Shea, you're working in Uptown today, all day. Get going up there right after the meeting," said the duty sergeant when he gave out the daily work assignments at the morning cop meeting.

"Uptown?" O'Shea asked, "Why Uptown, Sarge?"

"Don't know why, but you're in Uptown."

Uptown? O'Shea thought. *Why the hell would I be working in Uptown? I've been working Little Italy every day for ten years.*

"Detective O'Shea," said the sergeant, a little louder this time. "You got it?"

"Sarge, you sure you mean me?" asked O'Shea.

"Yeah, I mean you. Orders straight from Commander Johnson. Stay away from Little Italy today. Go straight to Uptown. You got it?"

"Yeah, Sarge. I got it."

As Detective O'Shea climbed into his car, he again wondered why Johnson was sending him to the Uptown neighborhood and ordered him to stay away from Little Italy. His silent detective alarm sounded loudly. *What the hell was happening on Cambridge Street?* He felt it the other day when he saw the murdered kid in the street. *Something's going on over there.* Jimmy went through the million-to-one odds in his mind again.

First, the Tomaso guy was shot-gunned on his porch. A few days later, an Italian kid with his head half blown off was dumped on the street next to the building where the first murder happened. Now, his commander had Sarge tell him to stay out of Little Italy. Why?

O'Shea pointed his car north from the Maxwell Street station, toward Uptown. He figured he would drive through Little Italy and along Cambridge Street on the way.

Father Edo Farrucio left the Tomaso's building under the hateful gaze of Gazzo D'Napoli and began his walk back to *Our Lady of Divine Mercy*. As he walked past *Bepi's Taverna*, he saw inside that another of Tancredi's goons was blocking anyone from entering or leaving the bar. Edo thought that cutting off the supply of liquor for the day may be a good thing, even if it was done by Tancredi.

After the priest was out of sight, Gazzo leaned against his car and yawned. He was bored, hungry, and wanted this to be over. He walked to the opposite side of his car and urinated on the sidewalk. *It shouldn't be much longer now*, he thought.

D'Napoli looked up when he saw and heard a group of thirty or so men led by Dino Nicosia across the street and walking toward them. The mob of angry immigrants carried clubs, bats, and shovels. Their intent was clearly to remove the threat of these thugs from their streets once and for all.

In their minds, they wondered, *Who would be next? A son? A brother or a cousin?* The men planned to take this to the end and to send a message to the Tancredi brothers: *Leave us alone. Things are different now.*

Gazzo stood erect and watched the mob approach. He shouted to his men, "Santo! Lupara! Look at this!" Each of the two instantly became alert. The three killers drew their weapons, intending to stand their ground. They would fight and kill as many as necessary. Gazzo thought, *If they want a fight, they will all die.*

From the window of *Bepi's Taverna*, a half a block away, Franco and Alessa saw what was happening. Alessa walked up quietly behind the goon who was sent to secure the bar. She struck the back of his head with an echoing blow from a heavy cast iron skillet. It made an ugly sound as she opened an eight-inch gash on the back of his skull. The man crumbled to the floor, knocking over a table and two chairs as he fell.

Franco looked at his wife, stunned and speechless, his mouth wide open. Alessa said, "Get out there and tell those fools to go home. Hurry, before someone gets hurt!"

She walked behind the bar and got the loaded shotgun and returned to where the thug lay bleeding and unconscious on the floor. She pulled up a chair and sat with the twelve gauge across her lap, watching the unconscious, bleeding man. She looked at her husband who had not moved and ordered, "Go!"

Franco ran out the front door and toward the crowd of angry men. He still had a white towel tucked into this belt, a pencil behind one ear and his sleeves rolled up, as usual. He knew the gangsters would not and could not be intimidated, and that the angry mob was facing three heavily armed and police-protected, professional murderers. These good men were neighbors and friends, and he knew them and their wives and children. He cared about them all.

"Stop!" the bar owner yelled as he ran to face the mob. "Stop! Nicosia! All of you, stop! What do you think you're doing? How many of you will die before you understand that you cannot beat these men this way? They are animals."

The mob leader yelled back, "Then we have to be animals to stop them!"

Zignano went on, "They will kill you all! When you lie dead in the street, they'll go have coffee without a second thought."

Nicosia yelled back, "This has to stop!"

Franco walked closer to the mob. "Who will feed your children after they kill you? Who will keep them warm and off the street?"

"The police won't help us; the city doesn't care. We have to protect our own," said Nicosia.

Ignoring what he said, Zignano looked at Dino Nicosia. "Who dies here today? You?" He looked at one man who was holding a shovel. "What are you going to do with that? Dig your own grave? I don't know the answer, but I know that you men dying here won't change anything."

The mob didn't move.

Franco yelled, "Use your brains, men! Go home!"

"The answer is that we stand and fight," Nicosia said. "We're not going anywhere."

The tavern owner tried again loudly, "You'll all get killed. Go home!"

A few of the men walked away but most stayed, determined to bring this to an end and take back their streets. Nicosia said, "Old man, we're going to end this here and now. If what happened to Tomaso was okay, we'd have all stayed in Italy."

Exactly one hour after Farrucio's departure from the Tomaso residence, fourteen-year-old Luca stepped out onto the front porch of the building. The appearance of the young man caused Gazzo, Lupara, and Santo to take their focus from the mob and fix their attention on the building. Luca looked at the mob and at Franco Zignano trying to stand them down. He then looked intently toward *Our Lady* as if for a sign. He went back inside.

Gazzo said to his team, "He'll be coming out soon. The boss wants this to be seen by everyone, so just shoot him on the spot. I'm hungry; let's get this over with."

Soon after Farrucio's return to the church, the young monk, huddled deep in his heavy brown robes against the chilly morning air, started the old black truck used to run church errands.

It turned over with a clunk, clunk, clunk, and began to run. He steered the small truck out of the lot. The old Studebaker chugged and rambled away, rounded the curve, drove past *Bepi's* and past the row of tenements. The small truck approached the Tomaso building.

As Franco continued to try to disperse the mob, many of them looked up at the old truck. It was odd. The Studebaker was a normal thing to see and hear on Cambridge on any other day—but today was not a normal day.

The driver saw the mob of men and saw Zignano in front of them. They all watched the old vehicle advance. No one moved. Once again, Luca stepped onto the porch and looked down the street. He saw the truck approaching, as did D'Napoli.

Gazzo said, *"Attenzione*, you two. Tomaso might make a run for it."

He looked in his backseat to make sure his rifle was handy just in case he needed to make a long shot. When Gazzo saw that the truck was being driven by the monk, he focused back on the mob. *Bring it on,* he thought. *Just try it.* He would not hesitate to kill as many as need be. He'd kill all of them if they pushed him.

The old black truck drove slowly up to the curb in front of the Tomaso building, just twenty feet from where Luca was standing on the porch. The vehicle didn't stop but rolled slowly by. The monk driving the vehicle passed between Gazzo, who was behind him, leaning on his car smoking and the building's porch, where Luca stood looking at him.

The driver looked directly at Luca, with Gazzo seeing just his back, and the other two goons out of the line of vision. The monk pulled his hood back just enough to reveal his face. It was not the monk. It was Renzo Tomaso. When he was certain that Luca saw him, Renzo pulled the hood back, so it again covered most of his face. He continued to drive slowly away until the small truck slipped through cross traffic at the intersection, disappeared across the next street and went out of sight.

In the church parking lot, the big Pierce-Arrow sat idling with Father Farrucio behind the wheel and the young monk beside him. The priest was looking at his pocket watch. He knew he had to wait exactly fifteen minutes after the Studebaker left before he could proceed.

The plan was for Farrucio to proceed from the church parking lot to the Tomaso building only if he did not hear a car horn signaling him to abort the plan. At the exact right moment, the priest, having not heard a signal to stop, began his slow drive following the route taken by the Studebaker exactly fifteen minutes before.

Once again, Luca stepped out the front door to the hateful stare of Gazzo and his men. The killers wanted an end to this game. They had better things to do, and to complicate matters, the mob across the street had begun to hurl rocks along with threats and curses at the mobsters.

A black Chicago police car approached. The driver was a uniformed officer. Seated next to him was the red-faced Commander Michael Johnson, chewing an ever-present cigar. The cops saw the three heavily armed men and the mob carrying bats and shovels across the street. The driver said, "Commander, would you look at this? We got some real Old-World shit going on down here."

Johnson and his driver got out and walked past Gazzo to confront the angry men. As they approached them, a half dozen bottles, and a dozen bricks were hurled from the back of the mob. They crashed to the ground at the cops' feet. Men in the crowd yelled obscenities and threats.

Commander Johnson drew his sidearm and looked hard at the group. The men in the mob took a few steps toward him. He gave them a hard look, thought better of it, and holstered his pistol. The two cops walked back to the squad car.

Johnson yelled at Gazzo, "Get this done! *Capice*? Finish it! You got a fuckin' mob here, now! I don't care if you have to go up there and drag him out! Get it done!"

Gazzo grunted and straightened up.

Commander Johnson said to his driver, "Let's go."

The police commander said, "Fuckin' wops. I wish they'd all kill each other."

They drove away.

The mob was getting closer and louder.

Gazzo opened the trunk of the Packard. He handed a *bandolero* of shotgun shells to Lupo, who hung it over his neck and shoulder. D'Napoli gave Santo a Thompson sub machine gun. The thug saw that it was loaded and cocked it.

Fourteen-year-old Luca stepped out onto the porch. He glared at the man who killed his uncle and was there now to murder his father.

The mob got louder and hurled more loud insults at the mobsters. More bricks and bottles flew, some nearly hitting the thugs. Santo stepped toward the mob and fired a burst from the machine gun into the air. The bricks and bottles stopped.

Chapter Forty-Two

Exactly fifteen minutes after the little truck pulled out of the parking lot, Father Farrucio wheeled the big, green Pierce-Arrow out onto the street. He drove slowly along Cambridge. When Luca, still standing on the porch, saw the big car pass *Bepi's* and drive toward their building, he ducked back inside. Once again, the three thugs shot to attention.

"He might run for it now, boys. Don't let him get to the priest's car," said Gazzo as he set his hand on the Colt in his waistband. "Grab him or drop him right here. I don't care either way."

The priest drove to a spot in front of the concrete stairway that led to the door to the Tomaso's building. The vehicle was separated from the stairway by a six-foot-wide concrete sidewalk. Farrucio stopped, put the car in neutral and set the parking brake. The plan was about to unfold. Farrucio was determined but afraid for what could happen next.

The front door to the tenement building swung open and Luca stepped out. His father, Paolo, the target of the murderers, was close behind him. Paolo's two hands were on Luca's shoulders as they slowly advanced.

Gazzo yelled, "It's him! It's him!"

The head of every man in the mob and that of Franco Zignano turned to look at the porch.

The slow-thinking Gazzo suddenly understood what was happening. This was a plan to get Paolo out of the building. The first step was the visit of the priest to lay it all out to the family. The driving by of the old black truck was a signal. And now, the last step was the arrival of the Pierce-Arrow to snatch Paolo from his grip.

"Shit! Shit! Shit!" was all the furious, hulking, and now impotent monster could say.

Luca and his father took another step through the doorway. Seven-year-old Sofia had her hand firmly attached to her father's belt on the right side. Rosa was holding on to the belt on Paolo's left side. Another step through the door revealed the oldest daughter, Isabella, walking with her two hands attached to her father's belt from behind. Five-year-old Katerina sat, smiling in her innocence, on her father's shoulders.

Gazzo raised his revolver halfway but had no target. Santo and Lupo hurried over, but they, too, realized they had no one to shoot. Paolo was completely protected in the circle of his children. Gazzo was fuming, as he ran towards the priest, the family, and back at his own men, waving his Colt in the air and swearing loudly.

Not accepting that he had been outsmarted, Gazzo raised his pistol, held it in two hands and aimed it at Paolo's head. The line of fire from the pistol to Paolo's head was just above Luca's head. Katie was sitting on her Pa's shoulders. A bullet would almost certainly kill a child, but Gazzo didn't care.

Luca looked at the barrel of the gun and stared defiantly into Gazzo's evil eyes. The boy did not flinch or hesitate.

The group kept moving forward, step by step.

Santo yelled, "Gazzo! You'll hit one of the kids! Stop!"

Gazzo did not lower the pistol. He couldn't hear Santo and could not control his actions; he was enraged; his face was nearly purple; the veins on his neck and head pounded visibly.

"Stop it, Gazzo!" Santo yelled louder this time and put his hand on D'Napoli's forearm. "Stop!"

D'Napoli turned his head away from the Tomasos and looked blankly at Santo. In his rage, he slammed the butt of his pistol into Santo's head. The man staggered back, and then caught his balance. Trying to stop what would certainly be a disaster for them all, Santo again yelled, "Gazzo, stop! We'll follow them and get him later. Not now."

D'Napoli was running back and forth, punching the car, and cursing at the top of his lungs. He had never been made to look so incompetent. Rage pushed lines of saliva through his lips as he rampaged. He thought for an instant about shooting out the tires of the green car but realized that would make him look even stupider. He finally realized that Santo was right: They would follow the green car, ram it, and grab Tomaso.

The tight circle of children continued to form a protective shield around their father as they advanced across the sidewalk. Father Farrucio, sweating and nervous, held the door open as Paolo and the kids loaded in. He closed the door behind them.

After they were safely in the big car, Farrucio motioned with his hand to Gianna and her mother. The women were standing on the porch, next to the picture of Leonardo and the burning candle, watching and praying. Both *Nonna* and Gia carried two stuffed carpet bags.

Luca jumped from the car, crossed the sidewalk, and grabbed one satchel from each of the women. Farrucio took the other two carpet bags and escorted the women down the five stairs. They put the bags in the trunk of the car. *Nonna* Stella got in.

Gianna straightened her black, hand-sewn dress and patted her tied-down hair as she stood next to the car. She looked in to reassure herself that her family was safe, smiled at the kids and turned to face the hulking, fuming, drooling Gazzo.

Gianna Tomaso walked up close to the murderer. She stared upwards into the black, dead eyes of the man who murdered her brother-in-law and was there now to kill her husband. Gazzo stared down and cursed her, his spit splashing into her face, his beady eyes glaring at her from under his thick forehead.

"This does not end here," he growled. "You think you're free from me, but you are not. Now, I will kill all of you! You will never escape me."

Gianna stood on the tips of her toes and slapped Gazzo D'Napoli with all her strength, full and hard, on the side of his scarred face. Her rage-driven blow landed with a sharp *whack!* Gazzo's shoulders straightened, and he raised his hands as if he were going to strike her. Gianna did not move or flinch; she defied him. His two men watched for his next move. The raging monster stood immobilized by the little woman.

Gia glared at him and said, "*Disgraziato!*"

In the back seat, Isabella said, "Oh no...did you see what Mama just did?"

The priest crossed himself.

Gianna again straightened her dress and patted her hair. She walked to the car. The door was held open by a worried-looking Farrucio who said with a slight bowing of his head, "*Signora.*"

After Gianna climbed in, Farrucio jumped into the driver's seat, released the parking brake, engaged the gear of the big green roadster, and pulled forward twenty feet. He then turned the steering wheel far to the right, shifted to reverse and floored the gas pedal.

The big car lurched backward in a ninety-degree curve and slammed into Gazzo's shiny Packard at the front wheel. The impact knocked the wheel completely off its mount and bent the axle. Father Edo mumbled to himself, "God's work. God's work."

The priest pulled the vehicle forward, shifted back into reverse, and again slammed the gas pedal to the floor. The car jumped backward and again slammed into the Packard, this time cracking the rear axle and bending the frame. Father Edo shifted gears and drove his passengers away, following the same path as the Studebaker just twenty minutes before.

Katerina looked out of the back window at the men holding guns and standing speechless in the middle of the street. She smiled the smile of sweet, pure innocence at the would-be slaughterers of her father and waved until her mother pulled her down. "Katerina!" said Gianna.

Gazzo stood with his gun in his hand, his arm dangling at his side. He glared pure evil and hatred at the back of the green car. He was powerless. At that moment, his brutal and ugly mind didn't have the capacity to reason or to think. He acted out of rage and fury, much the way he had lived his life.

The escaping Pierce-Arrow headed south on Cambridge but was forced to stop by heavy cross traffic at the first intersection. It was impossible to move forward. They sat.

D'Napoli, the sociopath, needed to hurt and wanted to kill these people; the priest, children, the wife—and he did not care how Malo Tancredi would react. He saw that the fleeing green car was blocked and sat motionless.

The mob stood motionless and speechless.

Gazzo saw his opportunity, got a steady grip on his Colt .45, and took careful aim. He squeezed the trigger twice. The loud *bang! bang!* of the controlled explosion pulled the heads of the men in the mob to attention. None of them were courageous enough to walk into gun fire. They watched.

The bullets scorched their way forward at an invisible speed. The slugs struck the rear window casement, just above the glass and the heads of the Tomasos. Gianna and *Nonna* heard the bullets striking the roof of the car and pulled the kids down. They protected the children with their bodies.

Gazzo gripped his pistol tightly with two hands and aimed carefully at the back of Farrucio's head.

Again, Santo yelled, "Gazzo! Stop! You'll shoot a kid and the boss will have us all killed! What are you doing? Let them go! We'll get him later!"

Gazzo couldn't hear. His body and his actions were controlled by the fury that had dominated his life since he was a boy fighting for his existence on the streets of Naples. The sociopath fired two more rounds. The priest heard the slugs explode from the gun barrel and felt the bullets scream past his right ear, missing by just millimeters. They made two perfect round holes in the windshield.

Farrucio pushed the gas pedal. The big car squealed and fishtailed as it jumped twenty feet into the cross street before it was forced to stop by another line of trucks, who all laid on their horns. The Pierce-Arrow was again frozen in place and unable to move forward or to either side. It could only back up, toward the shooter.

Gazzo's violent, sick mind was focused on killing, and he pulled the rifle from the backseat of the damaged Packard. Peering through the scope, he aimed carefully and deliberately once again at Father Edo's head. Gazzo had his target in the crosshairs of the scope.

At that moment, Santo again tried to stop Gazzo. He blocked his line of fire. "You cannot shoot them! Tancredi will kill us all! Let them go!"

Detective Jimmy O'Shea turned the wheel on his big Buick and headed along Cambridge Street. Up ahead, he saw a crowd of several dozen men. In front of them stood Franco Zignano, the bar owner. He saw ahead what he knew to be the green church car stuck in traffic. The cop heard two gunshots. He drove faster. He heard two more pistol shots, and this time, he saw the back window of the green car shatter. The car swerved, accelerated, and stopped.

O'Shea drove to the spot where he saw smoke from a pistol and slammed on his brakes. He jumped from his car and drew his service revolver. He walked closer and saw a man he had arrested more than once, Gazzo D'Napoli, aiming a rifle at the departing car. O'Shea heard Santo yell at Gazzo, "Stop! You'll hit a kid. Malo will kill us!"

The detective saw Gazzo lower his rifle, flip it around, and slam the butt of the long gun against Santo's forehead, who went down to one knee, dazed. Santo put his hand on his forehead as blood gushed through his fingers.

Gazzo once again took careful aim with the rifle. He centered the scope's crosshairs on the back of the head of Farrucio. He said, "Goodbye, priest."

From twenty feet away, O'Shea drew his service revolver and yelled loudly, "Chicago police. That's enough, you! Basta!" He took Polly from her holster on his hip. He stood there with a pistol in each hand.

The traffic jam let up, and Farrucio slammed the gas pedal to the floor. With a screech of burning tires, the car lurched forward and flew through the intersection on its run to safety.

The detective pointed one pistol at Santo, one at Gazzo. "That's enough! Lower your weapons now!"

Gazzo looked at the cop. A smile broke his ugly face.

Lupara, a hundred or so yards behind O'Shea, walked in the direction of the detective, shotgun in hand.

Santo, blood dripping into his eyes, struggled to his feet and started to raise his pistol toward the detective. O'Shea ordered, "Drop it, shithead!"

Santo continued to direct the barrel of his pistol toward the detective.

O'Shea shot Santo twice with the gun in his left hand, both bullets striking the thug in the center of his chest, blowing him backward off his feet. The bullets passed through the man and emerged from his back, leaving an eight-inch round, gaping, bloody wound. Santo was dead before he hit the ground.

As the detective turned his vision back toward Gazzo, the thug pointed his rifle at the cop. He pulled the trigger. There was no loud *crack!* of a bullet being fired; just the dull thud of a misfire. Gazzo fired again, and again nothing happened except a clunk of a firing pin hitting a dead bullet.

"Shit! Goddamn it!" D'Napoli cursed. He dropped the rifle and pulled his Colt from his belt. He fired two rounds at Jimmy. The first round from the big pistol struck O'Shea in the lower right abdomen. He winced and doubled over but remained standing. The second round missed him.

Instinctively and immediately, O'Shea fired Polly three times. Twice, bullets struck Gazzo. The first entered his belly and exited his back. The second stuck him in the left side of his chest and lodged in his lung. Detective O'Shea thought Gazzo was finished and stopped firing.

Lupara was now standing just twenty feet behind O'Shea.

The powerful Gazzo again fired the Colt. The bullet struck O'Shea in his left shoulder. The cop kept his feet under him and fired both his service revolver and Polly together at Gazzo until both clicked empty.

One of the bullets entered Gazzo's head through his right eye and slammed against the back of his cranium. The hot slug circled around the interior of his skull a half dozen times and liquefied his brain before it exited his left temple.

Gazzo stood, dead on his feet, and looked at Jimmy as if he wanted to say something. His brain was already mush, and he looked at the cop who shot him through non-seeing eyes. D'Napoli dropped to his knees and a reflex in his body forced a sick grin onto his ape-like face. The bloody, empty eye socket glared at Jimmy. With his knees on the pavement, Gazzo's body bent at his waistline and slowly tipped backward until the back of his head met the hard surface.

Standing now just a few feet behind O'Shea, Lupara leveled his twelve-gauge shotgun at the detective and pulled both triggers at the same time, releasing the red-hot shot.

The explosion struck Jimmy in his lower back. The impact of the blast blew him forward and shattered his spinal cord and pelvis. It forced his intestines out through his belly and cut him nearly in half. Jimmy O'Shea lay dead between the crimson corpses of Santo and Gazzo. He still clung to his two pistols, one in each hand, like a wild-west gunslinger.

Lupara, his shotgun now empty, turned to walk away. He removed the spent casings from his shotgun and took two fresh shells from a large pocket on his coat. He began to reload the gun. As he crossed the street and got to the edge of the mob, Dino Nicosia, without saying a word, stepped out of the crowd and swung his baseball bat at him. The hickory column of wood struck Lupara just under his nose. The impact drove the cartilage up into his brain and lifted him off his feet. He landed flat on his back, spread-eagled in the middle of the street.

The men in the mob who had absorbed and swallowed years of bitter frustration and anger, stomped and beat the body of

Lupara into a heap of bloody pulp and broken bones. Many spit on the smashed corpse.

When it was done, the mob drifted away. Some went home; some went to *Bepi's Taverna* to drink away the day's events.

The thug stationed in the tavern got to his feet and was escorted to the door at the end of a shotgun held by Alessa. He ran, looking over his shoulder.

A police cruiser and an ambulance arrived. The detective asked the appropriate questions and got no answers, as expected. He left to file his report. The police photographer took a dozen pictures of the three bodies in the position they fell. The corpse of Jimmy O'Shea lay almost touching that of Gazzo D'Napoli. Santo was a few feet away. Lupo, or the thick, crimson muck that what was left of him, lay in a red puddle across the street.

The ambulance drivers heaved the four dead bodies into the backs of their rigs and headed to the Cook County Morgue with their bloody cargo. A fire truck hosed the blood away.

Soon after the city vehicles departed, parents and children began to appear on the sidewalks. As the day went on, more adults, both men and women, emerged from their tenement homes and grouped up in pockets along Cambridge Street to talk about what happened. Soccer balls and softballs appeared. Games began. A girl of twelve squatted to draw chalk hopscotch lines on the sidewalk for her and her friends. Flirting and kid-life began again.

Alessa smiled at Franco and joined him outside of *Bepi's* to take a deep breath of fresh, cool air. The breeze off the lake had picked up again. They looked hard down the street at the Tomaso building. Without saying a word, Franco put his arm around his wife.

As word of the escape - of victory over evil - spread, the street once again became its normal sea of organized chaos. The shouts of the boys and the screams of the girls brought a smile to the faces of parents.

The Zignanos saw Sister George and three other nuns walking past the tavern. "Good morning, Sisters," Franco said loudly and with a smile. She was a beauty, if a nun.

"*Guten Morgan, Herr* Zignano," came the smiling reply, as the women continued their walk.

They had been instructed to pack the contents of the Tomaso apartment and give everything to the poor. The four nuns walked through the throng of happy, busy, young people.

A fruit vendor rolled his cart along the sidewalk. He shouted, "Strawberries! Strawberries!"

This was a day no one on Cambridge Street would ever forget.

Chapter Forty-Three

Farrucio said, "It can't be far now." He looked for the mailbox with a bandana tied to it. The green car, with its rear window shot out and two bullet holes in the windshield, was now covered in a coating of reddish-brown dust. As it motored down narrow, dirt roads, it passed one farmhouse after another. The group had nearly arrived at their destination.

Only the priest knew where they were going. They had driven for several hours, the last ten miles over rough, dusty, rutted roads. Farm fields, stripped now of their summer products, formed a many miles-long corridor.

The serious Luca was worried and kept looking in all directions. The girls enjoyed the adventure. When they got too noisy, Gianna would silence them with a touch and a *Shhh*. Along the way, Gianna handed each child and adult a piece of fruit or a sandwich she packed for the trip.

Paolo and Farrucio were quiet, each reflecting on their escape and on their all having survived the ordeal.

All silently thanked God for protecting them.

After an hour or so in the car, Gianna, who had held her family together by sheer will-power and prayer, felt herself crying. She reached for a handkerchief and dabbed away tears. She must be strong, she knew, for the children and for her husband.

Nonna Cassio saw her daughter's tear-filled eyes and placed her hand on top of Gianna's. *"Forza,"* she said as she patted Gianna's hand, and then in English: "Strong."

Gianna Tomaso felt like crying because of seeing her children, in their innocence, walk into the eyes of the devil. She was nearly overcome with emotion and relief at how young Luca stared into the eyes of a monster and faced it down. She thought, *My boy became a man today.*

She nearly cried from the memory of when her daughters formed a circle around their father and protected him from certain death. *What strong women they will be*, she thought.

Paolo had chosen her and their family over retribution, over more violence and more killing. She had never been prouder of him than at that moment on the porch when he put his faith in his God and his family.

She cried from the relief of knowing they were all well and that they had survived. Her tears somehow eased the tension she felt throughout her body. Her contemplation was broken by Isabella. "Mama," she said, "You slapped that big, ugly man really hard." Gianna smiled, and Paolo laughed a little. The comment eased the tension of the terrifying event, just a bit.

After driving the dried out, narrow road for several more miles, Farrucio spotted a red cloth tied to a dilapidated and leaning-over, rusted mailbox. He said, "There it is! We're here, kids!"

He turned the car onto the beginning of a driveway and drove toward a large, old farmhouse. The weatherworn boards had faded years ago. A bunkhouse for farmhands from days gone by was just behind the dilapidate barn. It had once been dark red but now, after standing up to so many winters, it was a faded shade of itself. The farmhouse sat across the yard, overlooking the two farm buildings.

As they slowly drove toward the farmhouse, they saw the old Studebaker sitting off to the side. The priest pulled into the yard and shut the engine off. Edo stepped out first, followed by Paolo from the front passenger side. Luca emerged from the back seat, followed quickly by Isabella, Katie, Rosa, and Sophia, who jumped from the four doors. Gianna and her mother got out last.

Renzo saw the car pull in and ran from the farmhouse to greet his family. He was overjoyed to see them. "Thank God, you made it; you made it," were all the words Renzo could get out through his tears.

He first hugged Paolo, followed by Gianna and Luca. He then dropped to his knees and hugged and kissed each of the girls. His nieces hugged their Uncle Renzo. Paolo asked, "Renz, what is this place? Whose farm is it?"

Renzo replied "It belongs to a friend of mine and Mario's. We needed a safe place, right? Me and Mario rented it for, you know, business. Just in case, you know. It's ours now."

"So, this is where you've been going," said Paolo.

Renzo said, "Yep. This is where. So, brother, you do remember how to farm, don't you? How to grow vegetables and fruit? Fatten hogs?"

Renzo then turned his attention to Father Farrucio. "Without you, Father...nothing. Thank you," he said as he embraced the priest.

Farrucio held the humbled man in his arms and whispered in his ear. "Your prayers were answered. I was but an instrument. God blessed you. And don't forget that it was your idea."

After the greetings and tears passed, the kids scattered to look around. Paolo and Renzo went to look at the fields. Farrucio pulled the old work truck into the barn and then drove the green car in, right behind it. Gia and her mother left the group to look at the house. As they drew closer, Gianna said, "Oh, my Lord!" and to her mother, "Mama, look at this."

Along one side of the farmhouse stood an outdoor grilling and eating area. It was fifteen feet long and ten feet wide. The area obviously hadn't been used in years but was still intact. To cook and serve her family their first meal in their new home outside in the fresh air seemed like a dream come true, especially given the events and terror of the past week and of that morning. *Yes*, she thought, *al fresco would be a good way to start this new life.*

The outdoor kitchen area was dusty and a little overgrown, but not dirty. There was an eight-foot-long table made from hand-hewn boards and sawed-off timbers for legs. Benches made of the same rough-cut wood spanned the length of the tables and similar-looking chairs sat at both ends of the table. There were no walls, just a roof and ten bark-covered vertical beams holding it. A large, rock firepit stood at one end of the roof-covered area. The cooking surface was two feet above the ground and the chimney portion went up ten feet, just past the roof.

"This is amazing," said a smiling Gia.

The cooking pit and the chimney were made from rocks taken from a local creek bed. The stones, from the ground to the top, had been concreted in place many years ago. Steel grates, used for grilling and cooking by past occupants, still spanned the large cooking pit. They were dirty and rusty, but the women knew they would be perfectly usable when cleaned.

There was a cut tree branch two inches in diameter and six feet above the ground, spanning the two uprights closest to the grill. Hooks attached to this connecting piece of timber were there to hang the freshly killed chickens, rabbits, or quail.

Isabella, Sophia, and Rosa cleaned the eating and cooking area. They dumped buckets of fresh, cold water from the well onto the tables and benches. They swept away the years of dried leaves that accumulated, as well as the spider and cobwebs. Little Katie wandered and helped as she pleased, or not.

Paolo, Renzo, Luca, and Father Edo walked to the garden on the other side of the farmhouse where they saw a treasure trove of early autumn vegetables growing wild and waiting to be picked. Before long, the men had gathered a bushel of ripe tomatoes, zucchini, red peppers, some large basil plants, and several heads of lettuce. They walked to the woods and carried back armloads of dried wood for the cooking fire. Wild prairie chickens roamed freely and with lighting quick reflexes, young Luca caught three of them. He found nests containing a dozen eggs.

Gia went into the house and was amazed to see that it was clean and organized. She chuckled and shook her head that Renzo had this secret get-away and that he was a good housekeeper.

In the kitchen, Gianna found a bag of flour, drying bunches of garlic, and other herbs, spices and even some dried yeast. She found a block of aged Parmesan cheese, which she grated to be sprinkled on top of the *pasta alla pomodoro* she would be serving soon.

Isabella and her mother washed plates, bowls, glasses, and silverware in the sink. Next, Gianna prepared and kneaded bread dough, covered it, and put it in a warm place to rise. She skillfully blended the flour and eggs and rolled out a couple of pounds of fresh, wide-noodle pasta.

Soon, the outdoor kitchen was cleaned and ready. The men were back with their harvest. *Nonna* Cassio gutted and plucked the chickens which Luca hung on the hooks provided.

When the grates were cleaned and the wood in the fire pit was hot enough, Gianna put a pot over the burning wood. She added olive oil, chopped garlic, cleaned tomatoes, and fresh basil from the garden. For good measure, she added some salt, pepper, and a little sugar. She stirred the mixture, brought it to a boil, then moved it to a spot where it would simmer.

The cleaned chickens were seasoned and put opposite the sauce pot on a section of the grill where they would roast to perfection.

The aromas were heavenly, and the family sat back to review the day and to relax a bit. Even with the loss of Leonardo a week before, they began to smile, just a little. Renzo appeared with a gallon jug of homemade red table wine. Soon, they all assembled.

Paolo sat at the head of the table. He still didn't say much, but just marveled about what this family had been through and survived. Mostly, he thought about how happy they were to be together. He was in awe of his family and what they accomplished.

On his right, and still standing to cook and serve, was Gianna. *Nonna* Cassio stood at the cooking grill guarding the *pomodoro* and the chicken. She also kept a close eye on the pot of boiling salted water where Gianna would soon drop the fresh *pasta.*

Gia called the kids in from their explorations and ushered then into the farmhouse. She had them wash up and go outside to sit at the table, so they could enjoy their first meal in their new home. The four girls sat together on one side of the table. They giggled about the ugly ogre that Mama slapped, the drive, and the farm.

Luca sat proudly, knowing that he had that day helped to protect his family. Renzo sat at the opposite end of the table. He was solemn but smiled and clearly enjoyed everyone and the surprise feast.

Two of the freshly baked loaves of bread were cut open length-wise down the middle and laid open-side up on a cutting board. Gianna drizzled olive oil on both halves the length of the loaf, sprinkled the bread with freshly grated cheese, and topped it with just a pinch of ground pepper. The split loaf was then cut into ten small pieces and distributed to each family member. A large bowl of salad was placed on the table when Gia noticed that Father Farrucio was not there to bless the meal, and that little Katie was missing, too.

When the table was being set, Farrucio slipped away and went to the car he had moved into the barn. He walked to the back of the vehicle and opened the trunk. The priest turned and went back to the open doors of the barn. He looked long and hard at the surrounding area for dust clouds of any approaching cars or trucks. Satisfied that they were not followed and were safe, he walked back to the open trunk. Edo put his hand into his black jacket and withdrew the twelve-inch knife he had brought back from the war. He buried the knife under the trunk's floor mat and said out loud, "Thank you, My Lord."

At that moment, he heard the voice of little Katerina from the barn door. "Hey," she hollered at him. "C'mon Father. Let's eat!"

"Okay, okay, Katie, let's go," he said.

The priest closed the trunk, turned and walked to the child. He smiled at her and extended his open hand. She clasped his hand, and the two walked from the barn to join the family at the table. Gianna heard their laughter and looked up.

She saw the priest and her daughter walking toward the family, hand in hand and smiling.

Epilogue

"Please hurry, driver. We need to get to the hospital in time. It's my mother."

Katerina Tomaso Wright and her granddaughter Katie had arrived at O'Hare Airport and grabbed the first cab in line. The cabbie drove them to the hospital as quickly as the dense Chicago traffic would allow. He pulled up to the hospital doors and stopped hard.

Katerina handed the man a fifty-dollar bill and said, "Keep it...we gotta go."

Gianna's youngest daughter, now a grandmother herself, prayed that she would get there in time to see her mother one last time and to say goodbye.

She and fifteen-year-old Katie, arms linked, rushed into the enormous hospital and to the elevator. They got off at their floor and hurried down the corridor. Katerina knew she was nearing the room when she saw her sisters, Sofia, Isabella, and Rosa standing in the hallway, along with three of their adult children and a dozen grandkids. She hugged and kissed them all.

Katerina gave a special greeting to Isabella's twin grandsons. "You boys look just like your Uncle Luca," she said.

"How's Mama?" she asked Isabella.

"We're near the end," was all that was said.

Katerina and her granddaughter entered the room. Gianna smiled at them. She looked so small, so white and so wrinkled, but still had that certain twinkle in her eyes when she looked at her family.

"Ciao, Bella," she said and smiled.

"Ciao, Mama. I'm here. I brought Katie to see you, too."

"She's beautiful...just like her mother. *Bella facia.*"

Katerina was relieved that they got there before the end, even though with not much time to spare. She sat with Sophia, Rosa, and Isabella on either side of the bed to be as close as possible to their dying mother. Their husbands gathered around with their grown children and grandchildren, four of Gianna's great grandchildren among them.

They had come to see the woman they all called Mama one last time.

The name tag worn by the duty nurse that night said, "Maggie." She had been in and out of the room repeatedly during the afternoon and evening. As the hour advanced, she stayed closer.

"It won't be long," she said to Isabella's husband. He nodded.

A little later, Maggie saw Katerina walking past the nurse's station. The nurse looked at her and said, "I've been here for thirty years, and I've never seen a bigger turn out. You've got a great family. I hope you appreciate what you've got."

"We do, we know it, thank you."

Maggie sipped her coffee and said to her, "So, four girls?"

"Yeah, four girls," Katerina stopped and replied, not wanting to talk about Luca.

"Is your father still alive?" asked the nurse.

"No, he's gone," said Rosa.

"I'm sorry to hear that," said Maggie. Curious about the family, she asked "What did he do for a living?"

"When they first came to the U.S. from Sicily, he worked at the slaughterhouse on Halsted. He had the worst job there but stayed for years to feed the family."

"Oh, wow," said Maggie.

"We left Chicago for a long time... lived on farm in Michigan for almost ten years. We were tenant farmers, you know. My Dad and my Uncle Renzo farmed the land. They were farmers back in Sicily. My father loved it."

Maggie asked, "It sounds so nice. Why'd you all come back?"

Katerina said, "Oh, a lot of reasons. My older sisters didn't want to live on the farm anymore, and then the owner sold it, so we couldn't stay anyway."

She remembered the reason they left Chicago and that ugly brute of a man who was outside their building on the morning they fled. Katerina didn't want to go into detail about the Tancredi gang, how they murdered her Uncle Leonardo and ordered her father killed.

She knew that Malo Tancredi and two of his brothers had been killed by an opposing gang a few years later and that the remaining brothers returned to Sicily, but she didn't want to talk about it.

Katie simply said, "And things changed in the city, so we came back. Pa had the idea of bringing fresh fruit and vegetables back from Michigan and selling it to grocery stores and fruit carts. It worked great and in two years, my parents opened a store of their own."

"No kidding," said the nurse.

"Yeah, he was a good man. A good father. I miss him."

"What happened to him? I mean, how did he die?"

"Pa finished work one day—the man worked until he was eighty years old—then had dinner and went to bed as usual. In the middle of the night, he woke my mother and said, "My chest hurts." Ma put her arms around him, and he died. Just like that. It broke my heart. All of our hearts."

"I know, honey. I know," Maggie said. "Is your uncle still on the go?"

"No," Kati replied. "Renzo passed years ago, too. It was a hunting accident. My mom is the last of her generation."

"It's a tough thing to lose a parent."

"Yeah, it's a hard thing. Thank you, Maggie."

Gianna dozed, and as she did, her dreamlike memory traveled through the many years of her long life. She saw the beautiful landscapes of Sicily and the farm she loved. She remembered seeing Paolo for the first time in church. She now saw him, in her dream state, riding up to her home on that big black horse she loved to ride.

Her mind wandered back to their beautiful wedding day, when Leonardo led Dante under the archway of flowers with her sitting on the horse's broad back. She remembered how happy she was that day, surrounded by family and friends and marrying the man she loved.

Gia remembered the big table in the Tomaso farmhouse and how they used to sit, eat, talk, laugh, and enjoy every meal. She thought of Tomas and Katerina Tomaso and how much she loved them both.

Gianna felt as if she were floating through her dreams.

She remembered the little faces of newborn Luca and Isabella, and how much she adored them. Life was good and she worked hard at caring for her babies and her garden on the farm.

In her mind, Gia saw the arrival of the family in Chicago, and their shock at the ugliness of the cold, unwelcoming city.

She saw the smiling and warm face of her good friend LaDonna Mazzone and remembered how she helped her make sense of it all during those first scary years and when Leonardo was murdered.

Gianna recalled the birth of tiny Rosa and how hard she worked and prayed for the life of her baby girl. She remembered Father Edo and his insistence upon the Baptism of new-born Rosa. How she loved him!

Father Edo Farrucio had lived eighty-seven years. More than 2,000 people came from all over the country to attend his funeral. It was one of the largest in the history of the city.

Her sleeping body recoiled, and a tear formed in her eye as she saw the tragedy that took Leonardo away from them. She saw his gentle eyes and his beautiful smile. Katerina saw a tear form and slide down her mother's cheek. She touched it with a tissue and thought, *I wonder what Mamas dreaming that brought a tear?*

Gianna saw the Michigan farm. She loved living there. Some of the best years of her life were on the farm, watching her family blossom.

In her dreamy state, she looked up and saw the kids and Renzo standing next to her hospital bed. It was the day they escaped the monsters on Cambridge and arrived at the farm. They were so young then, and her mind now saw them as they were that day. They were so beautiful, smiling and happy.

How I love to see things grow, thought the old woman.

Gia awoke a bit when a young, blond haired priest entered the room. He had heard Gianna's confession and performed Last Rites the day before. He was there now to help in her transition to her next life.

The holy man draped Gianna's rosary, the one given to her so many years ago by her mother-in-law, now almost white, around her hands, and laid her hands on her chest. He made the sign of the cross on her forehead and said a prayer for her in Latin.

"Thank you, Edo," Gia said ever so softly.

The priest smiled and took a chair in the corner to wait and to be with the family.

Katie sat sideways on the hospital bed holding her mother's hand. Isabella sat across from her, holding her mother's other hand, lost in her thoughts and memories. Rosa and Sophia sat next to their sisters at the center of the bed. All were watching their mother's last moments of life.

Gianna, frail and ancient now, looked at her daughters sitting on her bed, all softly crying. The men and the younger people in the room were crying as well. She smiled at her daughters.

Gianna said, "You are all here...my girls...all grown... imagine that."

"Thank you, Mama. Thank you for what you and Pa did for us," said Isabella.

"Thank you, Mama," whispered Katerina. She kissed her mother's hand.

She leaned forward to hear her mother whisper. "My family, my family. *Ti amo.*"

Life was fading from her old body. She would soon be free from pain and illness. Her eyes were barely open, her heartbeat slowing; her breaths were farther and farther apart.

Oh, my God, Gianna thought. *I see the colors from the baptism. The colors! How beautiful!* The gold, pink, and red blended together, but somehow there were shimmers of silver and what looked like ripples of a light blue. They were warm, inviting, and comforting. Peaceful.

The soft and somehow vivid colors filled the room and, even as the last bit of life was slipping from her body, she knew they were just for her. Only she could see them and feel them. *How amazing*, she thought.

She slept again and saw Luca. *How handsome he looks*, she thought. When Luca was killed in the war, she felt that she would die, too.

The citation that accompanied Luca's Silver Star read: *"During fierce fighting at Troina, Sicily, 8 August 1943, Captain Luca Tomaso led his squad against a well-defended enemy pillbox installation that had been raining machine gun fire onto the American position.*

Captain Tomaso saw three of his men killed and ordered the rest of his squad to dig in. After nightfall, Tomaso belly-crawled a quarter mile up the hill under enemy fire. He used two hand grenades to destroy the pillbox before he was shot and wounded. He struggled to get back to his squad.

Immediately upon his reuniting with his men, enemy soldiers stormed the American's foxhole. Captain Tomaso—although seriously wounded and facing certain death—used more hand grenades, a machine gun, and finally his service pistol to kill or wound fourteen of the enemy attackers, forcing the rest of them to retreat. Captain Luca Tomaso died of wounds received."

Gianna and Paolo did not need the citation to know that Luca had died bravely; they knew their son. For all those decades since she received word of Luca's death, Gianna kept an altar at home in their living room. A framed picture of Captain Luca Tomaso, in the uniform he was so proud to wear, stood in the center.

Draped from the top of the picture frame was the Silver Star his commanding officer awarded to him posthumously, presented to her and Paolo. Close by was Luca's childhood rosary, given to him by Father Edo at his First Holy Communion. Gianna kept a candle burning for her son. She never let it go out.

Paolo wept for his dead son and grieved his death until the day he died.

Strange how things happen. Luca died in Sicily fighting to free Italy. He was an American.

Gia slept for a while.

When she opened her eyes, Paolo was standing at the foot of her bed. *Imagine that*, she thought.

A smiling young Paolo stood there in his shiny, black, knee-high boots, black slacks, a dark red shirt, and his black *coppola*. He looked exactly as he did the first day he came to call on her so many years ago.

"Paolo, my love. I've been waiting for you," Gia said so quietly that there was no sound.

She smiled.

Her daughters wondered what brought that beautiful smile to her face that one last time.

Paolo extended his hand to her as she rose to join him.

Made in the USA
Monee, IL
18 November 2020

48366245R00203